A DIFFERENT SUN

A
DIFFERENT
SUN

A Novel of Africa

ELAINE NEIL ORR

BERKLEY BOOKS, NEW YORK

THE BERKLEY PUBLISHING GROUP
Published by the Penguin Group
Penguin Group (USA) Inc.
375 Hudson Street, New York, New York 10014, USA

USA / Canada / UK / Australia / New Zealand / India / South Africa / China

Penguin Books Ltd., Registered Offices: 80 Strand, London WC2R 0RL, England
For more information about the Penguin Group, visit penguin.com.

This book is an original publication of The Berkley Publishing Group.

Library of Congress Cataloging-in-Publication Data

Orr, Elaine Neil.
A different sun : a novel of Africa / Elaine Neil Orr.—Berkley trade pbk. ed.
p.   cm.
"An original publication"—T.p. verso.
ISBN 978-0-425-26130-9
1. Young women—Georgia—Fiction.   2. Plantation life—Georgia—Fiction.
3. Missionaries' spouses—Fiction.   4. Missionaries—Nigeria—Fiction.
5. Americans—Nigeria—Fiction.   6. Self-realization—Fiction.
7. Nigeria—Social life and customs—Fiction.   I. Title.
PS3615.R58843D54 2013
813'.6—dc22
2012030108

PUBLISHING HISTORY
Berkley trade paperback edition / April 2013

PRINTED IN THE UNITED STATES OF AMERICA

10 9 8 7 6 5 4 3 2 1

Interior text design by Tiffany Estreicher.

For the dearest—
My husband, Anderson Orr
Our children, Joel and Dominique
My mother, Anne Thomas Neil
Becky Neil Albritton, sister
And to the memory of my peerless father, Lloyd Houston Neil

It is more difficult to love than to die.

—BEN OKRI

You just can't fly on off and leave a body.

—TONI MORRISON

My heart is up to something that is alarming the
rest of my body, in fact. I must go pray.

—MARILYNNE ROBINSON

ACKNOWLEDGMENTS

The world has its stories and will yield them to a seeker.

Thank you to anyone who ever told me to pick up a pencil and write.

Thank you to Lloyd and Anne Neil, my dear father and mother, for their unceasing love.

Thank you to Andy Orr, who listened as this story unfolded, who talked me through rough periods in the writing, and who gave me scenes out of his own imagination.

Thank you to Joel Orr for his love and support.

If ever a novel was the product of a multitude of teachers and friends, this is it. Of course, any errors of history or geography are mine. I plead artistic license for making the Oba River larger than it ever was and for placing blue pools on Ogbomoso hills. Maybe they are there to the beholding eye.

I owe a world of thanks to Sena Jeter Naslund and Angela Davis-Gardner: To Sena, who first recognized that I might be a writer and who believed in Emma's story from my first groping sentences. To Angela, who invited me into her writing group and responded with grace and encouragement to this novel's rough beginnings. Thanks to all of the writers in that group, including the matchless Lou Rosser, for reading early chapters, listening to broad swaths as I read aloud, and encouraging me always. Thanks also to Angela for introducing me to my amazing agent, Joelle Delbourgo, who waited six years for this book and then sold it in three weeks. And to my extraordinary editor, Natalee Rosenstein, who knew she wanted this story and found the title, who told me with the skill of a surgeon the three areas that still needed work and sent me back into the woods to do the work! I am also deeply grateful to Leslie Gelbman, publisher and president of Berkley Books, for an enthusiasm that ran as deep as Natalee's and the energy that powered our course.

A large *e se*, or thank you, to Yomi Durotoyo, who planted the seed for the plot and served as my Yoruba guru throughout the writing of this book.

Thank you to Joel McRay, Greene County (Georgia) historian, for pointing me in the direction of the houses and places and people who mattered for this story. Thanks to Carolyn Reynolds Parker for inviting me into her house and showing me a particular writing box. Thanks to Mamie L. Hillman of Greensboro, Georgia, for the loan of important books without which I could not have written this one.

Thank you to Burster Iyere for assisting me on research trips to Nigeria, for seeing to my accommodations, for making important connections, and for offering his friendship. Thank you to His Royal Highness, the Soun of Ogbomoso, for inviting me to attend a Friday meeting with his chiefs, and to his fourth wife, Ronke Oyewumi, for dancing with me and inviting me into the palace receiving rooms where I viewed a number of crowns and some elephant tusks. Thanks to Lawrence Alawonde and James Oladayo Ojeniran for driving me about in Nigeria, for picking me up in Lagos and returning me there all in one piece. Thank you to Elizabeth Adetutu, librarian at the Nigerian Baptist Seminary, Ogbomoso, for help in retrieving historical papers. Thanks to John Olasunmibo for catering for me in Ogbomoso. Thank you to Pastor Adedokun for his friendship and prayers. Thanks to Amos Adeniji for restoring me to old friends. Thanks to David and Esther Adeniran for hospitality and friendship.

I am extremely grateful for fellowships from the Virginia Center for the Creative Arts for a number of residencies without which this novel never would have been written. I started there. Thanks to Hambidge Center for the Creative Arts and Sciences for residencies at the beginning and the end. And thanks to the Writers' Colony at Dairy Hollow for five important summer weeks. Thanks to the Wake County Arts Council for a fellowship at an important moment.

A huge thanks to Peggy Payne, Marjorie Braman, and Susan Ketchin for brilliant guidance at just the right time.

My deep gratitude goes to Tony Harrison, my department chair, for supporting my work. Thanks to my college dean, Jeffrey Braden, for rewarding my research efforts and to the College of Humanities and Social Sciences, North Carolina State University, for several summer research grants. Thank you to my students at NC State. No one ever gave a person better reason to keep growing and learning and feeling hopeful than a class full of good students.

For reading the entire novel at one point or another and offering valuable insight, thanks to Sena Naslund, Angela Davis-Gardner, Nell Joslin, Wayne Caldwell, Phil Deaver, Linda Holley, and Jill McCorkle.

Thank you to the community of writers in the brief-residency MFA in Writing Program at Spalding University for practicing the generous notion that a rising tide lifts all boats.

Thank you to Wilton Barnhardt for an early conversation that helped me understand the structure of the novel and to Julie Brickman for early instruction on point of view that saved me months of floundering and for offering her theory of the historical novel as a mediation between past and present. Thanks to Nick Halpern, who suggested early on that I had it in me to write a novel about a person of faith.

Thanks to the cheering section: Richard Goodman, Becky Neil Albritton, Jon Low, Jon Thompson, Nancy Olson, Kim Church, Jeanette Stokes, Robert Doty, and Nina Sichel.

Thanks to Louis Urrea and Margo Rabb, Bread Loaf gurus, and to all the writers in our Bread Loaf group.

I am grateful for a number of private and improvisational residencies. Thanks to Gita Larsen, who first invited me to join her at John Foster's cabin in Black Mountain, North Carolina; and thanks to John, who invited me back five more times so that I could write. Thanks again to Gita for accompanying me on a trip to Greensboro, Georgia. Thanks to Preston

Browning and Wellspring House in Ashfield, Massachusetts; to Jeanette Stokes and Pelican House retreats on Emerald Isle; and to Susan Watson and her family and Abba's House. Many thanks to Carrie Knowles for wonderful writing space at Free Range Studio.

I am indebted to Edie Jeter, archivist at the International Mission Board, Richmond, Virginia; to the Mission Board for access to files; and to Vicky Black and Barbara Koontz, for aid in accessing photographs. Thanks to Edgar Burkes for early conversation via e-mail when I was just beginning. Thanks to Anne Charles-Craft for her hospitality in Richmond.

Many thanks to Charlie Farrington, Mary Kohn, and Jason McLarty for assistance in researching Antebellum African-American English of the American South.

Thanks to Jim Crisp for conversation about Texas in the period significant to my novel and to Don and Patsy Meier for reading a chapter that dealt in medical matters. Thanks to Peter Gilliland for sharing his maps of nineteenth-century Yorubaland and old Ijaye, and for conversations about history and geography. Thank you to Toyin Falola for sending me to J.D.Y. Peel's *Religious Encounter and the Making of the Yoruba,* a source that profoundly influenced my thinking. Thanks to Robin Morris for tutoring me on the mechanics of the percussion cap rifle.

For last minute proofreading assitance I am forever indebted to Ryland Swain and Tasha Pippin.

Thank you to everyone at Berkley Books for producing and shepherding the beautiful material artifact of this book, and especially to Robin Barletta, for day-to-day interactions.

I sing praise to my muses, among them: Nathaniel Hawthorne, Henry James, Henry David Thoreau, Virginia Woolf, William Faulkner, Tillie Olsen, Nadine Gordimer, Flannery O'Connor, Toni Morrison, Ben Okri, Michael Ondaatje, Cormac McCarthy, Marilynne Robinson, and Charles Frazier.

Part One

THE BENT
WORLD

Greensboro, Georgia

1840

I N GRAY MORNING light, Emma Davis stood before the old slave's garden at the back of his cabin, looking upon the precise rows of cabbage planted for fall. The gentleman she called Uncle Eli had taught her to count by fours and she was quick to note he had four rows, sixteen cabbages apiece. "That will be sixty-four," she whispered. When she looked up, the sky had emerged pale blue, still too early, she knew, to impose herself on the old man. Emma felt a sense of guarded expectancy, enough life behind her to know hope could lead to disappointment. She was not that old. Eight years today.

Uncle Eli's cabin stood thirty paces from her own family home, a nice big house on a corner lot, creamy white, two-storied, with stairs leading up to a broad back porch. It was built in 1832, the year Emma was born, and always she thought the house was for her. By now she knew everything it had to offer, from the bedrooms upstairs on either side of the hallway—she and Catherine each had her own—to the stairway with the landing and the picture of the wild turkey, to the downstairs hall with the parlor and the sewing room on the right and the dining room and the breakfast room with the butler's pantry on the left. Papa's library opened at the very end of the hall.

A ruffle of wind came up the hill from the creek and Emma hugged her chest. She hopscotched to the center of her backyard and turned in a circle. Now she smelled biscuits and cast her eyes toward the kitchen where Uncle Eli's daughter, Mittie Ann, was making breakfast. The windows of the small building glowed as the woodstove inside it burned, and Emma knew that when Mittie Ann opened the oven, little sparks would fly. She let her feet follow the dirt path between the kitchen and back stairs. A low stone wall ran along the perimeter of the house for flower beds, and rather than step up and into the house, Emma launched herself onto this elevated path, taking it all along the side of the house parallel with the street and to the front yard, watching her feet, her arms extended straight out at her sides. In a moment, she caught sight of her mother moving across the grass with her red scissors and a flat basket. Emma stepped down, her arms still out.

"Good morning, missy. You're mighty early. Are you warm enough?" Mama said. "Come. I'm making a nice chrysanthemum bouquet for you."

The house faced to the southeast and the sun struck here first, just as now. Emma leaned over the blooms, catching their sharp, oily scent as her mother cut the stems long, each one curved in its cutting, and laid them in the basket. They would go in the tall crystal vase at the center of the dining table.

"Quick to put them in water," Mama said, placing a hand at Emma's neck. Then she was gone, the rustle of her dress behind her.

Emma looked down the road toward the center of town two blocks away. In winter, she could see the courthouse but the September leaves were still full, just beginning to color. Half aware she was taking the full circuit of her home, she meandered into the side yard, a corridor deep shaded by pines, floored in pine straw, almost dark at this early hour. Midway in her passage she came upon a long light-colored feather—an owl's, she considered—stuck at an angle into the straw.

She bent to take it like the gift she wanted. *I can make a writing pen*, she thought and slipped it into her pocket just as Mittie Ann called for breakfast. Emma skipped around to the back steps, galloped up the stairs and into the house.

"You seem in a hurry," Papa said. "Give us a kiss."

A ceremony had occurred in the breakfast room when Papa brought in a new clock and placed it on the slate mantel. "Repeating brass, eight days, clock, manufactured by Davis and Barber, Greensboro, Georgia," he read from the bottom, "warranted if well used." Emma's family was not related to the Davises of Davis and Barber, but she felt proud anyway. Her father taught her to say "warranted if well used." When she performed for him, it didn't matter that Catherine was the pretty one. Papa would tell Mama things Emma liked to hear. "She drums her fingers because she has places to go," he would tease. "Just watch when I teach her to ride."

Here came Catherine, late as usual, and they could start. The biscuit shaped like a heart was for Emma. "Thank you," she said when Mittie Ann laid it on her plate.

And then it was fully day, breakfast over, and Emma could go, as she did most every day, to call on Uncle Eli. This habit came out of her life—Catherine several years older, Mittie Ann and her husband Carl, who lived with Uncle Eli, occupied with work, task by task, day by day. "The old African," as Emma's mother called him, was favored because he was an artisan. His carpentry, carried out in the yard, allowed him sitting time; his age gained him some leisure. Emma found him a good talker. Her mother said his English was better than most because he had been for several years the companion of a well-to-do white boy in Savannah. Uncle Eli called Emma his white bird, meaning, she knew, he had chosen her as special. It was the first reason she loved him. That and the way he threw his feet out when he walked, as if clearing a path.

"One tomato two tomato three tomato four," she said, winding her steps across the same yard she had traveled at daybreak, scratching at her neck where her hair was rolled up.

The old man was settled on his bench at the stoop of his back porch, his hands busy inside a basket. But he was looking away out into the distance where the morning sun lit the hill. She stood a moment, twisting her hair roll so it began to come down.

"Morning, Miss Emma. What you bringing?" he said.

"This," she said, pulling the feather from her pocket, running her fingers against the grain. She sat next to him on the bench. She had bitten her cheek at the breakfast table and if she pressed her tongue to the sore place, she could still taste blood. After a while, she leaned right over the basket where Uncle Eli was occupied. It smelled like a cow yard. Maybe there were dried eyeballs in there. She began to see: old corncobs and something that was innards or roots, snatches of dogwood with berries. He bundled his collection this way and that until at last he took a bit of twine from his hat brim and tied it all up. "What is it?" she said, a prick in her palms.

He didn't answer.

"It's a star," she said.

"Not a star," he said.

"What's it for?"

"You still have that feather?"

"You see I do."

He stuck the silky frond into his arrangement like a last stem into a nosegay. "Keep out bad spirits," he said, his eyes opening so she could see into them. They were like a dark space in the woods.

A rush of fear came up from Emma's stomach. "Don't scare me," she said, feeling everything go slant. When she stood she fell straight over from her leg falling asleep. She waited there on the ground, smelling the earth, seeing his broad feet. Uncle Eli pulled her up and dusted her skirt. He pressed her head between his hands.

"You gonna be all right," he said.

Something steadied in her, as if her bones were now solid and she were real.

"I have to go," she said, "for my lessons."

"I'll be seeing you," Uncle Eli said.

Emma slipped into the library. Papa's large desk sat before a window and on it a brightly colored globe. She had a habit of spinning the globe to see where her finger would land. Mostly it landed in blue Africa, where the pyramids were. She loved the shape of the continent and how mysterious it seemed.

Right now she was a little sorry she had given up the owl feather. She peered back into the hall for a sign of her sister or anyone, but the house was quiet. It took no time to unstop Papa's inkwell, press her frilled sleeve back to her elbow, dip the pen, and drag the bright nib up the pale underside of her arm, leaving a brilliant black trail and sending a wave along her skin all the way to her chest. She blew quickly to dry it, replaced the pen, and stoppered the well. Emma caught a reflection of herself in a glassed picture on the wall. Then she looked at her arm, determined it dry, and pulled the sleeve down. In this cocoon of her self, she opened the text she was supposed to read, *The Girl's Own Book*, a gray volume all about correctness of principle. After a bit, she pulled out her Greek mythology. It was better, offering the story of Romulus and Remus, which made the whole world alive. Finally, she dipped into *Cousin Lucy among the Mountains*. Emma could tell it was not a very good story. It was too unlikely. She itched for her own paper.

THEN FALL CAME. Emma was in the backyard playing marbles. She looked up to see a girl from her father's plantation. Emma knew little about the farm three miles out of town and the forty slaves who worked it. She was familiar only with Carl because he lived in her yard and this one girl who came to the house on errands, riding in the back of a wagon when someone came into town. She might carry a basket of blackberries or deliver news that a baby had died.

"Watch," Emma said, as the girl stood close. "Watch how I do it."

"What your name?" the girl said.

"Emma. You call me Miss Emma."

"What it mean?"

A tightness gathered in Emma's stomach. "It doesn't mean anything. It's my name." But the girl pointed with her cinnamon fingers to the sky.

"My name Hannah. Mean Jesus loves me," she said.

Just then the back door opened and Papa came heavy down the stairs.

"What you doing here, girl?" He was talking to Hannah, who was now looking at her toes in the dirt. Emma watched her father. His hands rested on his belt. He was close enough to reach out and touch the other girl's head. Why didn't Hannah speak up?

"I was showing her marbles," Emma said in a rush. But her father kept looking at Hannah and Hannah at the ground. What if he hit her? Emma felt wild, as if a frightening world lurked nearby that might open to things she didn't want to know.

"How old are you?" her father said.

"I'm nine year old." Hannah swayed in her hips.

"Almost like me," Emma said, trying to reach the girl and her papa, trying to stay clear of that other, scary world.

"Old enough to be in the field with your mama," her father said, ignoring Emma. "Next time you tell your folks to send a younger child. Now you go on."

Right then Emma knew there was something wrong with the way they lived: Hannah with the creamy skin whose name meant Jesus loved her wore only a shift you could see through while Emma was layered in more clothes than she cared for. The wrongness was so bad she wanted to pinch someone.

"Go on," her father said, and Hannah turned, her dress slipping down one shoulder. Something fell away. Emma wanted to cry, not weep, but cry, like the Bible says: someone crying in the wilderness. Instead, with the heel of her boot, she stomped the shooter marble into the sandy yard and then the others. "I don't care about marbles," she muttered under her breath.

The next morning when Papa came into the library, Emma was in her place, a seat at the round table in the center of the room. "I want some paper," she said.

"You use your slate for arithmetic," he said.

"I want to draw and write," she said.

"I don't know as girls write," he said. "Let's hear your multiplication tables in elevens and twelves."

Emma rolled it out. She loved her father.

"That's my girl," Papa said. "Come with me now. I need to talk with Mr. George at the bank. Get your gloves." At the front door, Emma claimed his hand. To a point, he seemed to know her worth, and beyond that, what he could not fathom, was a fault in her or a fault in him. She was not sure which.

EMMA STUDIED THE print in her dress. Papa had said he would not come to the revival. Now she pressed closer to Mama. The coal stove against the wall was not enough to warm her. Something shook in the preacher's voice although the voice was smooth. She looked up at him and felt a power coming at her. It licked her feet and rose all through her into her neck where it seemed to wait for her to remember taking up her father's pen without permission, envying Catherine, letting Hannah walk away, all her other wrongs. When the man called for them to come, to confess Jesus as Lord and Savior, she almost stumbled in her hurry, pulling her mother, or was her mother pulling her, and Catherine. They knelt and he blessed them and a hundred more, so many that the walls of the church seemed to bend out, blessed them in the light of their sin.

After the revival, Mama doubled up on the "extras" for the slave quarters: scraps of cloth for quilting, pots of molasses, and old blankets cut into pieces for newborns. She sent money to a Reverend Humphrey Posey in north Georgia, who had built an Indian church. She held devotionals for the household in the sewing room on Sunday afternoons. Uncle Eli and Mittie Ann and Carl professed Jesus as Lord. But not Papa.

Emma found it harder and harder to escape that sense of foreboding, that dark other world she had first sensed when Hannah's dress slipped off her shoulder. Papa's not being saved made it like a shadow in the house, like the black line she had drawn on her skin, there even when it was washed off.

December came wet and unseasonably warm, causing hay to rot in the barns. Emma sensed an ill mood in her father. On Christmas Eve, she and Catherine were to recite "Nativity," but as Emma entered the dining room, her mother instructed her directly to take a seat.

"Let us say grace," she said.

Emma prayed for clear skies and cold, only briefly pondering letter paper and a box of pencils. "Amen," she said, opening her napkin. Mama rang the bell and Mittie Ann came in to serve. Emma forgot about the bad weather and kept her eye on the wishbone. Papa began to talk.

"It's happened," he said.

"What's that, Charles?"

Emma sat up, alert to Mama using Papa's first name.

"Our friend Mr. Joel Early is going through with it."

Her mother said nothing. Mittie Ann was holding the chicken platter and didn't move.

"He's freeing his slaves, giving every last one a hundred dollars in silver, and sending them back to Africa."

Emma thought her mother's lips trembled. "Mr. Early was always odd," she said, "from the first day I knew him. Girls, look you don't dip your sleeve into the gravy boat."

"He's arranged passage from Norfolk," Papa went on. "Even giving them a new set of clothes." Her father dug into the rice as if it needed discipline. The platter of chicken hadn't moved, and Mittie Ann, who should be moving it, was standing like a stone.

Mr. Early was wealthier than Emma's father. He owned a new coach driven by a fine-looking Negro in a red vest. Suddenly she imagined the Negro gone, Mr. Early's coach flailing downhill, the horse wild, the whole world coming apart.

"Let Early go with them; I hope they all drown," Papa said, pounding his fist on the table.

No one looked at anyone.

"Let us keep our own dignity," Mama said finally. "Pass the chicken, Mittie Ann. It's getting cold."

"You wouldn't want to go to Africa, would you, girl?" Papa said, looking at the colored woman.

"No sir," Mittie Ann said.

Emma wished the woman had said it stronger, to make her believe. When the chicken finally arrived, she took a wing and left the wishbone, though she could imagine that tender white meat between her teeth, the coat of flour fried to a sweet crisp. In her mind floated lines from the poem she and Catherine did not recite.

But peaceful was the night
When the Prince of light
His reign of peace upon the earth began.

. . .

THROUGH THE WINTER, Uncle Eli kept a small charcoal fire on his back porch. Why he sat there and not in his house where he had a sturdy fireplace, Emma had stopped considering. He had all sorts of greetings when she visited: *good morning, good afternoon, I'm seeing you after a long time, have a nice sleep.* And odd sayings that Emma thought of as small animals because they seemed to stir and move. Like *close the light* instead of *snuff the candle.* The old man cooked sweet potatoes in the ash. She would sit on the ground with him, though he always spread a sack for her. "Don't want missus vexing," he would say.

They could spend long periods not speaking. The fire was like another person. Emma pulled herself close. She took her gloves off and held her hands to the warm glow.

Sometimes Uncle Eli hummed in an off-key way that seemed oddly to put things right. "Now you remember," he would say, "four holes in your button, four eyes in the dogwood bloom."

"Yes," she would say, this the best prayer.

While it was yet winter, Carl went away and Mittie Ann made lots of noise as she worked in the house. Emma could hear her from the library in the mornings. "What *kind* of people?" she said over and again. Emma thought it had to do with *her* people, not Mittie Ann's.

"Why did Carl have to leave if they're married?" Emma said.

"Your father hired him out to Mr. Franklin," Mama said. "But she can visit him one night a month."

All Emma knew of Mr. Franklin was that her father said he did the land a disservice by owning it. Now Carl was off somewhere with that man. Emma felt sorry for Mittie Ann. One day she offered to help in the kitchen. She thought her offer would be welcome. Uncle Eli always enjoyed her help.

"You want to help me?" Mittie Ann said.

"Yes," Emma said.

The woman laughed. "Pray your father sell us all to Mr. Early."

The next morning Emma woke shivering, the fire not remade in her room. She put on her new Christmas boots and skipped in the upstairs hall. No one came to stop her. She found Catherine in the breakfast room, hunched over her grits. "I'm wearing my new boots," Emma said.

"You ninny," Catherine said.

"Where's Mama?" Emma ran her hand across the tabletop. Now she could hear voices.

She found her mother on the back porch, only her hair was not put up in its becoming way. Mr. Franklin was in the yard. He had Mittie Ann by the arm. Emma didn't like the man's way and looked sideways at the ferns. They were limp from the frost, dark and matted.

The man was talking. "Like I said, she was over my place last night, keeping my man up when he need to be sleeping. Your husband, Mr. Davis, hired that nigger out to me. This girl's slated to come the fourth Sunday of the month. But she keeps insistin' he's her husband and it's no harm her comin' late to bring his food." He stopped to scratch his head. "Way I see it, he's not her husband when he's working my farm. You keep her on your place. She got no business on mine. I'd whip her. Otherwise, she'll be back just like a dog."

"You can stop right there, Mr. Franklin," Mama said.

"What's wrong, Mama?"

"Go inside, young lady." Emma didn't move. She looked at Mittie Ann, who was missing her scarf so her face looked naked. And Mr. Franklin who didn't even own a proper horse, there with his old rifle.

"I hate you," she said under her breath.

A wind came late morning and snow fell sideways.

Mittie Ann served the midday meal, her face still seeming naked even though she had her scarf back on. Papa sat at the table in hard silence; Mama excused herself early and Catherine after her. Mittie Ann came for the dishes.

"Mr. Davis," she said, her eyes cast down, "my father at the back door, calling for you."

Emma jumped up to answer, but Papa told her to sit down. He laid his napkin aside. Emma slipped out behind him.

"What is it?" he said out the door.

Emma watched Mittie Ann press her back against the cupboard.

"Whatever it is, I'll take it."

The old man's voice seemed to come through a tunnel. Mittie Ann's head fell forward.

"She shouldn't have run off. She knew," Papa said.

"She all I've got," Uncle Eli said.

"You know what happens when a man has a reputation for weakness? I'll have my niggers dancing up and down all over the county." Emma wished her papa wouldn't talk like Mr. Franklin.

"Won't do no good to hurt her; she'll still go. Do me, she won't run again."

"I'll think on it. Haven't you got some work this afternoon?"

"Yes sir. I'm finishing those table legs missus wants."

"You work on them in the carriage house."

"Yes sir."

The door sounded terrible in its closing, like a heavy lock falling into place.

Papa looked at Mittie Ann pressed against the cupboard. *Just try to do good*, Emma wanted to say to him, *just try*. But she could not.

"Find Catherine and finish your lessons in the library," Papa said. "I believe you were delayed this morning."

Emma left the room but tarried in the hallway, her back against the wall like Mittie Ann's had been against the cupboard. She splayed her arms and legs out in the posture of a star. Then she curved to enclose herself, turning full around until her forehead rested against the cool plaster. She heard her father's voice.

"You tell Uncle Eli to report to the overseer in the morning. He wants to take it for you, I guess that's his business. I hate to have it done. Ought to shame you"—Emma felt a wand of guilt wend through her—"that you've brought this on us. Don't disappoint me again."

"Yes, master."

Emma fled to the library. Catherine sat near the window, facing out, no book, her hands in her lap. There was no fire in the library either. The snow had turned to rain.

Emma walked to the bookcase. She heard Catherine leave the room, and her tears fell and she wiped her face with the skirt of her dress. The spines of the books were all alike in the dim light, and she ran her hand across them. At the window she began to imagine a picture she would draw of Mittie Ann. She would start with her head-dress, impossibly large. As the drawing progressed, Mittie Ann would come into possession of a broom that had a likeness to a rifle. As if she had drawn herself into the trance, Emma left the library for her bedroom. The first thing her eyes lit upon was her bureau. She opened the top drawer and removed handkerchiefs, gloves, and collars, leaving only the smell of wood. Then she closed the drawer.

UNCLE ELI WAS gone until summer, and when he came back his hair was almost white and he walked with a limp, no more throwing out his feet like clearing a path. Yet he held his head up. That at least was still true to him.

Her parents' bedroom door was closed. "It's terrible." Her mother's voice. Nothing from her father.

Emma sat on her back steps.

One afternoon Uncle Eli came out. He did not look in her direction. Another time she ventured to his garden and saw him sitting on his porch. He moved his whole face to look at her, but his eyes seemed to say, *Stop. Stop right there.* A new girl was in the house now and Mittie Ann worked outdoors, tending chickens, even washing out the carriage house. A circus was coming to town, and Emma kept her mind on it. The broadside in the storefronts showed an elephant standing on its back legs and a man in front of the great animal looking perfectly in control. Emma traced the images with her finger and went to bed at night thinking about the circus world, where men balanced upside down on poles and women rode standing on horses.

The day of the circus she found a place at the bottom of the hill where Main Street marked the boundary of her family's property. Maybe the elephant was from Africa. Neighbors were lined up across the street. A friend waved at Emma.

"Come," she said.

"No," Emma said.

The girl shrugged.

Finally a band showed up with drums and brass horns, along with a clown and a funny monkey on a leash. At last Emma saw the elephant and when she did, she felt sure it would burst from the parade and charge her. If only there were a tree she could climb. She should run, but her terror was too great. The elephant's ears flapped forward. *I am a white bird: fly*, she thought.

Someone laid a hand on her shoulder. She knew it was Uncle Eli and she leaned back into him, pulling his arm around her shoulder, closing her eyes in the curtain of his sleeve. His chest rose and fell and they waited together until the circus sounds had passed.

"I was afraid," Emma said.

"You shaking," he said.

They turned together and in the turning she looked down to be careful where she placed her boot and her gaze rested on his left foot. At first she mistrusted her sight.

"Let's go on up to the house," he said.

She was not mistaken. His three small toes were missing, clean off, like cut with scissors. Emma felt her mouth open, but she could not speak and she remembered that time—it seemed long ago—when she had fallen and studied his feet on the ground. The old man advanced several steps. She put her head down and pressed forward. When she caught up with him, she held his hand like she did her papa's. They got as far as his bench before she began to sob.

"Does it hurt?" she said finally.

"I expect," he said.

"Why?" she said.

"Overseer say whippin' wasn't enough."

"Enough for what?"

"To make an impression."

The word sounded like something that bears down and changes you forever.

"It's good you cry," Uncle Eli said.

As her sobs subsided, Emma thought she could hear her own heart beat. The taste of salt was on her lips. A red cardinal stretched its wings in a nearby dogwood. "What birds live in Africa?" she said, her eyes on the red bird.

"All kinds," Uncle Eli said. "Owl, sparrow, bush fowl, firebird, hawk, pigeon, wading bird, white egret—all kinds."

"I NEED SOME extras," Emma said to her mother.

"What for?"

"I need some old boots, some of Papa's. I need them for Uncle Eli."

Her mother pinched her lips.

Emma spent the afternoon collecting everything she could find. Half-used bits of soap, stockings from the mending pile, tag ends of thread, hardened circlets of candle tallow, and finally a new jar of fig preserves. She went to her mother with her collection.

"These are extras," she said, talking as if her mama were a person who might not remember her own mind. "I need the boots." She was surprised that her mother had found a pair. She left her filled basket on the old man's front porch, not going around back. Emma's effort yielded her a sense of relief and even pride. She had done something loving. But in the heat of the day, the good feeling evaporated. Only insects sounded. It was as if the whole world had become the shadow, though the sun exposed every surface of the outside world. For the first time, Emma wondered if her parents were real enough. It seemed she knew more than they. More even than her mother, who had prayed so fervently. How far did her prayers go? Not far enough. Emma would have to pray for them. But what would she say?

That night she could not sleep for fear she would die and go to hell.

In the morning she thought if she could write a prayer, she might know what to say and save herself. In her searching for extras, she had found a discarded envelope.

In the library she took up her father's pen for the second time. Beginning was hard and she gave up on a beginning. *Forgive my papa*, she wrote. *Forgive me. Watch out for Uncle Eli.* She hid the envelope in the Greek mythology and pressed the book even with the spines of all the other books on the library shelf.

Two days later Carl was back, but there was no happiness. It was as if someone had broken the necks of all the flowers in Georgia.

Sunday after dinner, while her parents were still in the parlor and Catherine had gone to visit friends, Emma followed the path down to the creek, still in her best dress. She took her slippers off and waded in up to her calves, careless of her skirts. Dragonflies hovered over the water. After some moments, it occurred to her she wished to scoop the mud at her feet. She did, and then she wiped her hands on her skirts. The feeling this brought was akin to freedom. She bent over again and brought up more of the silty creek bottom. This time she wiped her hands across her bodice. The wetness seeped through to her chest and refreshed her. She thought to press her sleeves back beyond her elbows. Again, she bent to retrieve the wet silt and now she smeared it up and down her arms. A kind of glory stirred in her center. In a single movement, she curved into herself, came down to sitting, and spread her whole body back into the water, her fingertips beneath her, her head half submerged. The sky above was a map without mark.

A bird flew by and she sat up. Once more she reached for the silty bottom and repainted her arms.

In the field heading home, she kept to the shady edge, biding her time. She came around a tree and right there was Uncle Eli, squatted on his heels.

"Just this minute was a copperhead where you standing," he said. She pulled at her muddied skirt and stepped sideways.

"Gone now," he said.

He had a piece of wood in his hands. He was always carving— rabbits, deer, even turtles. "You trying to get yourself in trouble?" he said.

"What are you making?" she said.

"You watch," he said. He breathed onto the wood, and then he rubbed it with a wad of leaves. He smoothed it against his trousers, a kind of cluck and sigh and then the dull *whap* as he struck the wood against his palm and turned it.

"Why do you breathe on it?" she said.

"Put me into it," he said.

"Can I see?" she said, squatting. He pressed it into her hand. Then the wedge seemed full of heat. She ran its smooth sides against her face, to put herself in it too and for a moment, Emma saw that Uncle Eli was a buffalo, like the one in her animal picture book, dense and dark, his eyes all-seeing.

"Now you dream on going home," he said, his voice woolly and his hand on her head.

Emma saw no need to dream where she already was; she dreamed of some other place, like Africa. As she closed her eyes, everything went blue.

THE ONLY PENALTY for the dress was that Emma had to wash it. She did so in the yard. She thought her papa seemed sorry.

The next day she asked again for paper. Two weeks later she came into the library to find a brown package tied with twine and beside it a new pen and a pot of ink. Emma felt she was being guided by Jesus or fixing to marry. She sat down and opened the package. The paper was cool in her hand and smelled like the clean underside of a pillow. She opened the ink pot and dipped her pen to write the sentences she had already imagined. *My name is Emma Davis. I will soon be nine years old. Today I have determined to make an account of myself. I already know a great deal and have seen many things. There is a gentleman in my yard who came from Africa.*

She heard someone in the hallway and covered her writing with a blotter. A few minutes later, she carried the page upstairs and opened her bureau drawer. "This is mine," she whispered, looking into the frame of air. She placed the page facedown, the smooth creamy side up.

2

Calling

M OST GIRLS ENDED their studies when they turned twelve. Catherine had, giving her attention to social rounds. At thirteen, Emma read Latin and French in the library every morning, writing out words she found particularly useful or lovely: *numen, meminisse, sesquialter.* She also made it her business to read the farmer's almanac and when she came across them, a set of pamphlets urging crop rotation "that rich Georgia soil not be laid to ruin like that of North Carolina." In her mind, Emma had ascended to a place of significance in the family. She was the smarter daughter and the chosen one. It was she, not Catherine, her father took to Savannah to meet an important businessman. Papa allowed her to hold his gold watch, attached to her wrist by a silk ribbon, all through the journey. Furthermore, she felt a difference within her, born of that awareness of a second world close by, like a beast against the door. In this way, it seemed God had set her apart toward some important purpose. She persuaded her father to let her ride in a proper saddle and gained a fuller view of the plantation and the people who worked it. No longer were they the quiet group in their modest clothes gathered to receive Christmas "extras." These were folks who worked hard in the field, beginning in the morning at a pace they could keep to from sunup to sundown. One day she saw a little fellow completely naked, carrying a hoe as large as he was.

She felt stabbed in the heart. It was cotton that brought in the money. But growing and picking it was the hardest labor. "Your land is going to get tired if you don't diversify," she said to her papa, not daring to argue on behalf of the people.

"What do you propose?" he said, appearing both humored and perplexed.

MITTIE ANN WAS back in the house, and it fell to her to assist Emma with her new corset. Sometimes she took hold of Emma's elbows and tugged at them as if to wake her. Emma knew the woman held her accountable. She must try to make amends. "Wouldn't it be good if Papa grew less cotton and we started a horse farm?" she said.

"How's that?" Mittie Ann said.

"The work would be lighter."

"Not lighter, just less of it. Master gonna sell some of us."

"What do you mean?"

"Your papa figure the cost of every slave, believe you me. He got less work, gonna sell some folks off, including children. My Carl a strong man; might sell him first."

"What can I do then?"

"Think of something else."

"Like what?"

"Put in peanuts or soybean, corn. Don't turn to tobacco. It nearly as bad as cotton."

Emma blinked.

"You surprise I know so much. Who you think knows?" Mittie Ann said, straightening Emma's sleeves with a good jerk, then leaning to retrieve the slop jar.

"Leave that be," Emma said. "I'll do it."

Later in the day she chanced to look out a window to see Mittie Ann and Carl sitting on low stools in front of the cabin. She had him holding his hands in front of him while she respooled her yarn around them. Likely, she had pulled one garment out in order to knit another. Carl leaned toward Mittie Ann and whispered something, his hand on her shoulder. They laughed softly. It was troubling and mysterious to see them in such a state of ease and happiness.

Emma's father agreed to putting forty acres in corn. On a late July afternoon, their crop coming in, father and daughter rode together to the mill. Two hours later, Emma left before her papa, discouraged. The black men looked ragged as ever. Two boys not eight years old were employed in conveying sacks of ground meal. Their eyes spoke such sorrow, Emma wondered what they had seen. She raced the horse back home by way of the old road. Her bodice and under-clothes were soaked when she left the horse with Carl. Upstairs, she lay down on the bed in the hallway. A breeze came through, and she pulled a shawl over her shoulders. She dozed and woke again, feeling worse, a dull kind of weight in her abdomen. *I rode too hard*, she told herself, and turned over. In her dream, her father was walking down a long path away from her. Once or twice, he turned to look back. The day was fading. She called to him but he didn't hear, and her legs were too heavy to bear her forward.

When she woke, Emma could see through the large window at the end of the hall the pine spires bent by wind. A girl came to fill the tub. "I want Mittie Ann," Emma said. When she got down to her drawers, they were stained a dark red like rust, though there was one bright spot, pink-red as a camellia.

"I'm calling your mama," Mittie Ann said.

"I want you to help me," Emma said.

"Help yourself," Mittie Ann said, more brazen than ever. So Emma did her own bathing and washed her hair.

"I'll brush it out," Mittie Ann said.

Emma tried to work up her courage. *It wasn't my fault about your father*, she wanted to explain, but she could not say it because it would be a lie. It was her fault, her family's fault, and she could not soften it.

WITH WOMANHOOD UPON her, Emma turned for a season to her sister and mother. Maybe she could be like other girls after all. She spent more time on her piano and sewing.

"See, Emma," Catherine said, showing her how to adorn her hair more becomingly. "You can be quite lovely." Such a gentle sentence; Emma thought she had never loved her sister more. After a ladies' tea at Aunt Lou's, her mother said something just as kind. "You stand so well, Emma. I've never seen a young woman with a more graceful carriage." She felt lifted up.

They rode home in the buggy, singing in rounds. Nearing the house, Emma spotted Uncle Eli at the edge of the yard. He seemed to be waiting for them. As soon as she could, she headed out to see him.

"Where you been?" he said.

"To tea."

"What happen there?"

"Why, we talked," she said.

"What about your book?" he said.

"What do you mean?"

"Your own work." He tapped his head with his fingertips as if to indicate her mind. She brooded as he pulled sweet potatoes from the ash.

On an evening of a day so hot even Georgia rhododendron wilted, Emma overheard her parents in the sewing room.

"She spends too much time reading. She hasn't got your beauty to count on." Her father's voice. It was hard to say if she loved him more or less for hearing it. But she felt a gulf open between them, canyon deep and sheer as rock.

In the dining room, she bent to look into the mirror of the sideboard. She began by focusing on her long forehead, moist from the heat. She turned her face to the side to study one angle. Slowly she turned to the other side, avoiding her own eyes. At last she faced forward, beholding an oval face and a receding chin. A sound of china cups rang from the butler's pantry. Regardless of what Catherine and her mother said, Emma was plain and she would never become prettier. Her eyes might have saved her if her hair were darker and if she had longer lashes.

At the dinner table she told her parents she had decided to go away to school; she said it like picking fruit hanging low from a tree. They looked at one another. Her father cleared his throat. Her mother said, "You seem very sure."

"I'll go to Georgia Female College in Madison. It's only ten miles away."

"You can't be a common schoolteacher," her father said.

Emma decided to pursue exactly what her father said she must not. Mittie Ann helped her pack, and once, for a moment, out of the corner of her eye, as the woman was laying out her gloves, Emma saw her pat them. *She's in favor,* she thought, *even if she doesn't forgive me.*

Uncle Eli was standing on his porch when she went to say goodbye, a cloth hat on his head.

"I'll write to you," she said. "I have all my papers in a basket, my book as you say." She smiled.

"I finna see you anyway," he said. "I been watching you all this time."

THE FIRST YEAR was disappointing. Lessons went toward the color of fabric for lining one's bonnets and where to turn one's eyes in the company of young men one might wish to marry. The answers were pink and downward. The second year, Emma studied the New Testament with Rev. Miles. "What does Jesus mean?" he said. "Blessed are the merciful."

None of the other girls answered.

"He must mean, those who are kind to others will find God's favor," Emma said.

"Do you believe good works will bring you favor with God?" Rev. Miles said.

"I don't know," she said. "Surely God wishes us to be kind."

"Look up *mercy* in your dictionary," he said.

"Charity," Emma said, seized with the answer. "Charity is love. Blessed are those who love."

"Amen," Rev. Miles said.

Emma felt a thrill. One other girl gave her competition in the classroom, but Emma thought she was edging her out.

She almost liked Rev. Miles. In the evenings, with a bit of imaginative flourish, Emma was sure she liked him. But in the day, the fantasy was punctured. His hands were shapely but not strong. His chest dipped a little beneath his coat. She was sorry because she believed their minds might agree. Emma was even sorrier when Catherine's engagement was announced and she had to anticipate going home for the ceremony without a beau. She longed for a companion, someone who would be a confidant. In the middle of the night, she walked out along the flagstones in the courtyard, seeking Jesus. *Be merciful to me*, she prayed.

In the last year of her studies, Emma attended a lecture on Ann Judson. Ann and her husband, Adoniram, had left Massachusetts to be missionaries to Burma. But Mr. Judson was taken prisoner and set in shackles for months because of war with England. It had fallen to Mrs. Judson to walk from palace to prison among the Burmese, ministering to her husband and petitioning for his release. Emma thought of Ann Judson's booted feet finding purchase on the Burmese hills.

She could imagine the missionary's gloved hands patting the heads of youngsters. She could even see her standing in front of a lifted gun, looking straight into the eyes of a would-be assassin. Emma saw herself in Burma, only her unremarkable features had become defined.

Later that night, Isaiah 6:8 came to her as a proclamation. She was lighting a candle in her room when the verse blazed before her:

Then I heard the voice of the Lord saying, Whom shall I send? And who will go for us? And I said, Here am I. Send me.

3

A House Waiting

EMMA MEANT TO write at length about her sense of calling, but an emotional breathlessness overtook her. Recording a promise to God seemed very grave. She imagined a path of stone. At last, she wrote a few sentences. *As far back as I can remember, I have felt something amiss, whether in myself or in the world. I am no more perfect today than I was yesterday. But as God calls, I follow.*

In May 1849, she found herself packing for home. She was seventeen years old. Soon she would discern her next step. But the return was harder than she had expected. The porch behind Uncle Eli's cabin still held his baskets, but now they sat unattended. Emma had a sudden vision of that long-ago morning, her father answering the door to Uncle Eli. The old man's words, "I'll take it." The white panels in the dining room felt icy to her touch. At church one Sunday she heard of a mission with the Cherokee in Arkansas. She approached Rev. Howell to ask if she might begin a Sunday school for the colored children. "I need practice," she said. She would call it the Pilgrims School.

The first Sunday, she found the children already in attendance, sitting so close on the single bench that she thought they might all fall if someone sneezed. No one would even look at her. *What a poor vessel I am*, she thought. The following Sunday, she found a broken chalkboard and a mite of chalk left in the room. She picked it up auto-matically. *J-E-S-U-S*, she wrote, *L-O-V-E-S*. She was about to write *Y-O-U*, when she chanced to glance at her pupils. They were gazing at the slate with great hunger. In an instant she remembered that Geor-gia law prohibited Negroes from knowing their letters. Her brain struggled against her dilemma. Hot as it was, she felt chilled. She laid the slate in her lap. "You," she said. "You."

That evening, her only beau called, a freckled second cousin. Emma tried to entertain him with poetry, but he had no capacity for hearing it. In moments of great guilt, she wondered if she was meant to stay here in Greensboro, to suffer for her family, to take on humil-ity. Humility, perhaps, but not abasement. She dismissed the beau.

Before supper one evening, she sat in a window alcove, finishing a bit of smocking.

Her father passed by. "I haven't seen Tommy of late," he said.

"I'm not courting him," she said.

"You're wasting your time with those pickaninnies," he said. "I don't know a man around here who wants as a wife a teacher of coloreds."

"I enjoy teaching them," she said, making a knot. "Our slaves might at least look forward to heaven if we instructed them in scrip-ture." She broke the thread with her teeth. At the dinner table, her mother spoke of Catherine, who was expecting a second child. Emma felt the walls of the room closing in. "I hope to be a missionary," she said. It seemed the muscles tightened in her father's face, and she was glad of it. "I can at least teach children to read and write."

"Well I'll be," he said, like a man who has been told there is no more use for cotton. "I thought you'd take over from me and your mama if marriage doesn't suit you. Everything we have is yours." He rubbed his hands up and down his whiskers. She watched the roll of his midsection rise and fall with his breath. Fleetingly she caught an image of her hair fading through the years as she slipped her feet night after night under the sheets of her girlhood bed.

"No," she said, and had the presence of mind to add, "How can I accept any more from you?" She leaned into the dense element of her rebellion and felt lighter for it.

She went regularly to her bureau drawer to read her girlhood thoughts. "I'm studying myself," she said one night when it dawned on her what she was doing.

One evening she sat in the library, several sheets of paper stacked in front of her, candles lit, casting pools of light. Her needle was prepared with heavy thread. With a ruler, she had drawn a line down the middle of the top page. She pressed the needle through the stack at the very center. It seemed she might be piercing her skin. Dimly she desired this press against her own skin. She worked from the center out in both directions. When she was finished, she would fold the sewn pages together. In just this way she made her first journal.

She wrote bits of self-instruction. *Jesus was thirty before he began his ministry.* She wrote wonderments. *For some reason, an old slave knows more about me than I do myself. His name is Eli. I have always been drawn to him.* She recorded her longing. *If only someone might join me.* One night she filled an entire page with one repeated question. *What am I to do?* Her bureau drawer became a library of herself.

Still weeks passed and months and no definite plan revealed itself; she was not drawn to the Cherokee in Arkansas. Two Septembers came and went and Emma turned twenty. On her birthday, she called on Uncle Eli. A look of knowing came across his face as she approached.

"It's the white bird what come to visit," he said. "How your book coming?"

"I'm not getting anywhere," she said.

"Why you put mud on your dress that day?"

"I can't remember."

"Yes you can."

About the time robins were flocking to dogwood trees for red berries, Rev. Howell announced that the first Baptist missionary to Africa would visit their congregation in November. This news was conveyed at the end of the Sunday morning service. Emma had heard of Rev. Henry Bowman and even read his reports in the Baptist paper. But she had not quite believed in him as someone who could show up in her yard. The news of his near visit put a storm in her brain. It was so loud, she almost missed the missionary's letter as Rev. Howell read from it. She caught the tag end —*When I look round on these thousands of people ever ready to listen to the gospel, who can wonder if I should think that neither tribulation nor distress, nor persecution, nor famine, must be allowed to lead one away from this work of the Master who has said: "Go and lo I am with you!"*

Africa. That bright blue mass on her father's globe. She could almost taste it, like the sea, and Emma surged in her conviction. Yes. Rev. Bowman could tell her all about it. Perhaps a single woman could volunteer. If the church sent female missionaries to Arkansas, why not Africa? What if she traveled as Rev. Bowman's secretary?

She was angry and then amused to hear her friends talk after the service. Sarah Martin declared that all the folks who had accompanied Rev. Bowman on his first tour had died or gone blind. Ruth Ferguson reported that her parents were doubtful about whether niggers went to heaven. Rebecca McAlister went on to no end about how she would like to marry the missionary and go overseas.

"He was a Texas Ranger!" she said, "I've heard he came back to Georgia looking for a bride."

The comment caught Emma off guard and she nearly dropped her Testament.

Rebecca was just beginning the social rounds, and Emma knew she spent an hour each night wrapping her hair in paper and two hours in the morning arranging it. She could hardly control her glee, imagining this vain girl in Africa.

The night the missionary was to preach, Emma wore an austere gray wool. At the last minute, she set a silver pin at her throat, and avoided her mother in the sewing room, who complained earlier of a headache and expressed misgivings about Emma's going back out in the cold. She arrived early on the pretense of setting out hymnals and was finishing her task when she heard the church door open. In the vestibule, she found a man shaking out his frock coat. Apparently he had forgotten his hat, as his hair was damp. In a moment, he pulled a white handkerchief from his pocket and wiped the floor where it had been wetted. Then he stood and looked at her, and Emma thought for a moment of an angel, though the gentleman in front of her looked nothing like one. His hair and complexion were dark, but he seemed somehow otherworldly. Then she saw it was the missionary's eyes. They were blue and in the queerest way appeared to move independently of one another, as if he weren't quite in agreement with himself or with the world. She was so captured by his intensity that she couldn't speak. When she started to curtsy, the man seemed to think she was falling and held his hands out. "Careful," he said, his voice a golden glow pouring through her. Right then Rev. Howell bustled in. Other members of the congregation pressed around, and Emma found her seat in the sanctuary.

All through Rev. Bowman's preaching, he held out his handsome hands. "Won't you help me carry the message to those lost souls that Jesus is the stalwart night watchman, ever ready to show them the path from darkness to light?" he said. A series of tiny fires seemed ignited in Emma's chest. When she thought the reverend's eyes lingered on her, she wrenched her handkerchief into a tight ball. Then she saw the missionary looking at old Mrs. Thornton in the same way, and Rebecca McAlister too, who was looking up at him with a smile on her face. *I will study him*, Emma thought to herself, *just like anything else*. She could not deny his eyes. His lips were almost too pretty. But his nose flared toward the nostrils, and his firm jawline conveyed a power that spoke to her depths. The hollow of his tanned cheek was like a moment of sadness in the late afternoon. When he sat down at the end of his preaching he looked like someone who has failed at his endeavor; yet when they stood to sing a final hymn, she could hear his voice above the rest. She was overtaken. Here was a true man, like no other she had known, intelligent and handsome, compassionate and brave.

Emma was not surprised to see Rebecca making conversation with the missionary during the reception. She glanced once more at Henry Bowman, bitterness in her throat. But his eyes *were* fixed on her, over Rebecca's head. Emma started across the room, the same feeling in her legs she had as a child in a foot race. "I am Emma Davis. We met before the service. I believe you have touched us all," she said.

Rebecca stepped back and Emma pulled her skirts around to face Rev. Bowman.

"You, Miss Davis, at least seemed to be listening," he said. Her heart expanded. He had set her apart from the rest.

"How could anyone not be touched by the plight of people in such faraway lands who have never heard of our Savior?" Standing next to the missionary, Emma saw they were the same height. Now that his hair had dried, it would not stay set but curled about his ears and the back of his neck, making him look young. Yet he appeared suddenly gloomy, facing in another direction, and she wondered how to take her leave.

"Of course, many are interested only in their own welfare," Rev. Bowman said, still looking off.

Emma was at a loss. It seemed premature to ask whether a woman might go to Africa, to ask after her own interest. Yet she could not let go of the conversation. "I will pray for your mission in Africa. I feel so for the children." She raised a hand to her face and covered her chin, suddenly self-conscious.

"Have you ever considered the mission field?" he said, looking back rather abruptly, his eyes again seeming at odds with each other. But then they softened as he looked on her. His lips parted as if he were pondering something.

"I have been called to some service," she said, her eyes moving to his jaw, the beginning of his neck. What would it be like to touch him there?

"I spent years running from God," he said. "The price was steep."

He seemed to have embarrassed himself with this confession because he turned sharply and left her standing alone. She turned just as quickly, hoping to give the impression that the end to the conversation had been mutually struck. *I didn't do anything so terrible*, she thought to herself. But she felt ashamed and naïve that she had indulged a romantic inclination.

At home, her mother was waiting for her upstairs. "Well? Did you meet the missionary?"

"I greeted him. We all did."

"And that's all?"

"That's all."

Her mother touched her cheek, and Emma wished for all the world to tell her everything. In her bedroom, she was stunned by her grief over a man she had known to think of for only two weeks. She slipped her praying hands between her legs and rocked in sorrow.

The next day, Emma came late to breakfast. A dullness seemed to cloak her, a feeling of dejection she had not known before. She drank tea and did not write or tend to her regular duties. Late in the day, a boy called at the back door, his skin dark to a mirroring. He carried a letter from Rev. Bowman addressed to Emma. *This must be how African children look*, Emma thought, her hands shaking as she pulled at the envelope. The reverend asked if he might call two days hence. As a pilaster against hope and disappointment, Emma kept focused on the child long after he had left. After all, Henry Bowman might wish only for her to create a church circle to raise funds for his cause. It was an agonizing thought.

At dinner, she sensed her parents' skepticism when she mentioned the letter. "I wonder what it pays a man to be a missionary," her father said, and then they ate for some minutes in silence. Her mother recommended that Emma serve pound cake to her guest. "I've heard that travelers from such ill countries come home gaunt," she said.

Early the following morning, Emma saddled the new mare. It seemed like an eternity until the next day and she was too nervous to sit still. She carried her journal in a leather pouch hanging by the saddle horn. With the winter sun breaking through the trees, she cut down the hill, took the back way behind the neighbors' houses, and let the horse find its crossing at the creek. A pair of mallards turned slow circles in a cove, the male showing his bright green head. Up the hill on the other side, she intercepted the road leading to the sawmill one way and the granary the other. She passed a teamster hauling wood, but the mare acted nicely. A cardinal winged by, red against the evergreens. She followed a path that ran to an old pottery works, now closed. But she felt oddly separate from the scene. The mare had slowed to a walk; it wandered into a field and grazed. She pulled her journal out to reread a recent entry: *What do I believe? The purpose of life is to manifest God's love.* She had skipped a line and then: *What does God require?* Beneath this she had drawn a hard line before penning: *Preach the gospel to the poor, set at liberty them that are bruised.* Emma touched her face. It was an enigmatic verse. She closed the book and returned it to the pouch, pulled the reins to the right, turning in a circle, and surveyed the land of Georgia. The slopes of the hills were like the fine curves of the animal's back that carried her.

As she brought her horse up to the front of the house, she saw Rev.

Bowman on the porch. Her mother was framed by the doorway as if perhaps she were barring the entrance. Her visitor came into the yard to help her dismount.

"I thought you said tomorrow," she said, hoping her exercise would account for the flush in her face. She kicked her left foot free of the stirrup iron, and as she pushed back from the horse, he caught her right at the waist.

"Excuse me, I thought you might fall again," he said. "Well, you didn't fall—the other night, I mean. Or now."

Emma wondered if her mother had observed the minister's quickness with his hands, but when she read his eyes she did not care. They told her he had not come to speak of women's circles. "I haven't fallen since I was eight," she said, feeling her power.

"No, I suspect not, the way you ride, Miss Davis," he said.

Emma unhitched her pouch from the saddle horn, and her journal slipped to the ground.

The reverend retrieved her book and dusted it off. "Do you write as well as you manage that horse?"

"Why shouldn't I ride so?" She hoped her eyes flashed.

"There's no biblical injunction I know against it," he said.

"Good," she said. "I don't know how well I write. It's for myself."

"I'm early," he said, as if she had not observed the same already. Neither of them could quite get the conversation moving. But he pushed ahead, determined. "I have to leave tomorrow for Richmond. I wanted to see you."

"Won't you invite your guest into the parlor?" her mother called from the porch.

Emma looked from Rev. Bowman to the house. "Yes, but I expect we may enjoy a stroll first. We'll walk down to the creek and back." She had noticed a small nick in her caller's left ear, and it stirred her immensely to think of him as strong and vulnerable.

"You have an independent streak," he said.

"Yes," she said.

A few minutes later, Rev. Bowman held a branch of the chinaberry tree and they bent together to pass beneath it. He pressed a hand to his abdomen. Their eyes met.

"My liver and spleen were first attacked by the ague in Texas. It may be that the African malaria has worsened my case. Occasionally the organs act up."

"I'm so sorry," she said. "How horrible it must have been to suffer far from home."

"Yes. In fact, it was sometimes horrible. But I have survived."

"Yes," she said. She felt she was already seeing into him, and this was in his favor.

"I mean to do better when I return. A more deliberate work schedule."

He had regained his posture and looked perfectly stable, even robust. He seemed the very essence of a man.

"In any case," he went on, "my difficulties deepen my commitment, not the other way around. Africa must not be lost." He paused as if to weigh the effect of his last sentence. He took his hat off and stroked his hair and returned his hat.

Emma was dazzled. "No, Africa must not be lost," she said, thinking how this man must not be lost, how she would lay claim to that nick on his ear, how his brilliance would deepen her.

"A bullet from a messmate's fire," he said, a half grin. "An inch or two to the right and it would have hit a jugular."

Theirs was a fine long walk, their strides well matched.

Rev. Bowman wrote weekly. Letters came from Atlanta, Richmond, Washington, even New York. Emma and her correspondent tackled all manner of things. He asked if she had studied languages, and she was happy to report that she had. He had trained himself as a linguist and was working on a vocabulary of the African language native to the area of his mission, Yoruba. He described a land unequaled in all the globe, full of creeks, open woodland, deep forest. "Great granite boulders appear out of nowhere and sit in solitude on the plains like prophets in the desert," he wrote. "Yet fear of slavery still grips the land, though the trade has been outlawed."

Emma awaited each letter in a storm of anticipation, and when it arrived she pressed the pages against her face.

"What of their religion?" she ventured in her next letter, happy to be his pupil.

"They are monotheistic," Rev. Bowman answered. "It's all the spirits that get in their way. These *orishas* must be appeased every time the people turn around. There's one in the tree and another at the crossroads and another at the creek. The poor folks spend half their lives making sacrifices to them, or to their dead ancestors."

Ten days passed without an epistle. Emma's hands felt cold when the next one arrived. "I'm closing in on forty years of age," her suitor wrote. "I believe you are yet to turn twenty-one." She considered her next letter carefully. "Age is a matter of mind and heart, don't you think? Some people are old when they are born, others are young all their lives. I am glad I shall continue to hear from you, as you promised." In the next letter he said nothing of age. "My mission is in Ijaye," he wrote, "pronounced *Ee-jie-ee*, all syllables equally stressed. The town is thirty thousand strong."

She sounded the town's name and it sounded like a song. Emma had never corresponded with a man whose mind ran so deep or who expected hers to be as agile as his. Certainly she had never known such heat emanating from paper. Twice her mother made allusion to Rev. Bowman's age, and her father asked again how a missionary sets his store against the future, but their concerns only increased the reverend's power. She did wonder about falling ill. Once she was playing Bach's Prelude in C Major when a sudden sense of loss came to her, and she paused, listening for the sound an illness would make in Africa. It would not be Bach. For the rest of the afternoon, she swung between fright and self-chastisement.

After the evening meal, she wandered into the yard. Uncle Eli was in his usual spot. His eyesight was failing and he didn't whittle much anymore. She felt sad that she had not spent more time with him in his old age.

She drew off her gloves and touched his shoulder. "How are you, Uncle Eli?"

"Me, I'm doing fine," he said. "Have a seat."

She did.

"How you been?" he said.

"My folks are a little worried about me," she said. "What if I told you I might travel to Africa, as a missionary, as a missionary's wife?"

"I already heard. Mittie Ann tell me." He rocked a little. "See," he said, "that what I mean. You remember that day you wade in the creek in that nice dress? You was getting ready then."

She thought he might be making up things.

Somehow it didn't matter.

Two days later, Henry Bowman sent a note from town, and in an hour he was at her door. The afternoon was warm and they sat on the front porch. Mittie Ann served fresh apple cider. After all of the conversation in letters, Emma felt curiously shy and she thought her suitor did as well as they cradled their cups, looking out over the street. At last, he reached for her hand, and in a moment, he pulled her with him to standing, turning her as a gentleman would a lady in a dance step. He looked nobler than she remembered. "I'm not effusive," he said. "You'll find that out if you say yes. I'd like you to marry me."

Emma looked at his hands, not his eyes.

"I told you about the African fever when we first met. I'm telling you now—I was out of my head for a spell." He dusted his hat. "Does that frighten you?"

"Yes. A little," she said, looking at his chest now.

"I mean to live frugally," he said.

She wanted to back up the conversation, to ask a bit more about the fever.

"There's one more thing I must tell." He paused and took a deep breath, letting it out like a whistle. "I was a wicked young man on the Texas prairie. Do you understand what I mean?"

She took this to mean more than killing Mexicans; he meant he had known women. The confession rushed through her and she quivered. In a gauzy way, she knew his early waywardness was part of his power; it was almost thrilling, certainly dangerous to think about. Being courted by such a man put Emma in a new relation to herself. She was now attractive. And wasn't the man before her like the apostle Paul, a wicked man who had seen the light?

Emma looked down the road she had been studying for two decades, feeling deeply drawn. She pinched one of the big curls on the side of her head, making sure it was tight. This was the time to ask about the illness.

"Fair enough. I'll understand if you decline me," Rev. Bowman said.

"I haven't declined you," she said, looking back at him, raising her shoulders.

A neighbor's wagon came up the road. *This is what is happening*, she thought; *this is where I am going. What puny faith if I would not die for it or care for a man who has already risked his life for the gospel.*

"Yes," she said, like jumping from a cliff. She would do something to make the world better. And in the mix she would live largely and passionately with this man.

"Good," he said. The wagon passed.

Emma was hushed by what had just happened. Her eyes misted. What a great mystery, that God might be at work redeeming the world through her. Henry pressed a finger on the soft place at her neck. Then he put his whole hand up under her chin and held it. She felt his other hand at her waist, pressing, and she surged forward until he kissed her. She thought she was conquered, and her will trembled in her.

Now he studied her hand as he talked. "There's a house waiting," he said. "I made it myself: six rooms with verandas all around." Already she was in a different country. They left the parlor for another walk in the orchard—the minister without his frock coat—and when Emma saw the way his trousers fell across his backside, she knew what is meant by desire.

· 4 ·

Signs of Grace

Henry's route from Greensboro, Georgia, to the Foreign
Mission Board headquarters in Richmond should have taken
him from Augusta through Columbia, South Carolina, and on to
Raleigh, North Carolina, and to the village of Wake Forest, where he
would visit the brethren at the Baptist college. But he had an invitation from Rev. Elias Dodson in the town of Hillsborough, North
Carolina, west of Raleigh, to come and preach on a Sunday. The fellow
was a strong supporter of missions. But what most attracted Henry
was that Dodson had bought the old Hillsborough courthouse and
rolled it intact to a location where he pleased to set it out for his congregation. Thrift and innovation appealed mightily to Henry. Maybe
he could persuade the man to join him in West Africa.

He preached on Sunday, and though Dodson had no inclination
for Africa, the congregation raised two hundred dollars. A snow came
in the night, and by the second day the accumulation was too great
for travel. The hotel proprietor surmised Henry's need for a greatcoat
and lent him one. Midday, Henry set out for a view of the Eno River,
two biscuits in his pocket. The water looked smudged and the current
slow, but he was attracted to it anyway, following an indention alongshore where he might make progress. At last he came to an enclave of
rock jutting into the water. He found his way easily to the largest

among them, flat and commodious enough for his picnic. It was always better to sit looking upstream, and this he did.

A dimple in the water made him think of Emma Davis and her funny hairdo—the big coils rolled into buns on each side of her head. He lingered on her neat virgin's chest and the nice fan of her behind. She might be a room where his masculine heart could rest; it had not found a home in twenty-three years, not since his mother died when he was fifteen. One day she was peeling figs; the next she was ill. A week later, she was spitting blood; it was tuberculosis. She lost so much weight she looked older than his great-aunt. Then one morning she was dead. His father waded into grief like a man walking into the sea to find a ring dropped from a boat, with no hope whatsoever. Henry did not know how his mother had come to be his hearth. What he did know was weightlessness. Now he was not required Sundays to put on shoes and walk two miles to church. No one sewed on his buttons, and his shirts levitated in air, with no hand to moor them. At fifteen, there was no limit to his heart; it roamed out way beyond the land. In the spring, walking behind the mule, he spotted a bone turned up by the blade. His mother's deadness hit him. He left the mule and in the hayloft rolled and wept until he fell asleep. For weeks he hardly ate, but no one paid any mind and he took his belt in. The paroxysm of grief returned every few days as he felt again that absolute absence and wept until he exhausted himself.

After a while, he thought he would make a religion against God since his mother had loved God and look what had happened. He dedicated himself by stealing whiskey. Once he put his middle finger into a vise until it bled under the nail. He practiced striking lucifers and holding them as long as he could. By midsummer he thought he was well steeled.

One day he noticed a girl at the dry goods store. He knew her from before, at the county school, but he had paid her no mind. Now her chest was high under a tight-fitting frock. Janie became the vessel for his grief, and even then he knew it. In the evenings, after the farm work, Henry and his father shared a cold supper. His pa lit a candle and stared into it for an hour before he went upstairs. Henry must bed down the horses, and he did so carelessly. Janie would slip into the barn, wearing the dress and a black ribbon around her neck. The ribbon was slender and smooth, unlike anything else in his life.

"Do you like it?" she said.

"Yes," he said.

"Then do something," she said.

Once he did not wait for the loft but pulled her down in the stall with the mare, and when he moved from Janie and looked up, he was spooked by the horse looking at him. He laughed in fright, the sound thin in his ears. What if she made a baby? "Now tidy up," he said, "and vamoose." He picked up the ribbon he had untied and threw it at her. Her eyes were puzzled and he grabbed her by the wrists. "I said for you to go." She had been able to sneak out because her folks were poor and cleaned the dry goods store at night; she was their only child. It wasn't long before Henry heard she was marrying an old fellow whose first wife had died in childbirth. A deep remorse crept into him at his ruination of the girl. To fight it off he stole a bowie knife from a neighbor, putting himself beyond redemption.

The sound of a red-bellied woodpecker pulled Henry back to the present and the Eno River. The bird's staccato echoed about the woods until finally he saw it, working away on the main stem of an old dogwood. He welcomed the interruption and pulled out the biscuits. The sun emerged and the rock warmed. This was mighty slow water. Henry felt a moment's disorientation. Had he gauged the current right? He studied the surface again before he bit into the first biscuit. He ate slowly, until the woodpecker flew and then he rolled a cigarette, lighting it with a flint and steel. A deep inhale and his mind followed the woodpecker. Birds had their nests. But as a boy he had lost any comfort at home. His mother dead and his father a ghost, he signed on with a group of volunteers fighting Cherokee resistant to the Removal Act.

One night, his unit circled a village. Henry carried only the knife; it wasn't much a matter to him if he died. An Indian boy surprised him, jumping out from behind a tree. Being killed was all right, but Henry hadn't meant to be taken advantage of. Lucky for him, the boy was overexcited and missed with the hatchet. The two came into a hold. Henry was larger but couldn't get the better of the boy, who was all greased up. They tangled until Henry thought he would fail. At last they rolled into a gully. They lay for a moment in tight embrace until a cry broke over their heads. Henry looked up to see a woman struggling against a man of his company. The way the boy responded, Henry thought she might be his mother. It was just what he needed; the boy relaxed his grip and Henry brought his knee up fast, ramming it into his stomach. The fellow's head swung up. Henry threw his arm around his neck, finding it slender as a girl's. He was furious that a youngster had given him so much trouble. And then the child spat in his face. "God damn it. What'd you do that for?" Henry said. "I might have left you." He ran the boy through with the knife.

It was easier the next time.

In towns he always found a girl. They seemed to think he was prettier than they were. He began to see in the mirror what they saw: a head of dark, wavy hair, prominent eyebrows he learned to tighten, sharp features, blue eyes, and broad lips. His body was lean and well proportioned. Regardless, he woke every morning with a sense of foreboding, as if he had left a child in a field at night. After a while, Henry became accustomed to a clench at his center so that he noticed it only when it wasn't there. As a boy he had read one book he cared about and that was *Robinson Crusoe*. Occasionally he considered it was only travel he wanted, not fighting. But the weightlessness of his heart drove him every day and he threw in with the others, battling like a wizard. On one occasion he and a fellow volunteer found them-

selves against a rocky cliff, hemmed in by Indians. Their only escape
lay in running the gauntlet. Henry struck out through a shower of
bullets, emerging untouched. His companion was less lucky. Henry
got promoted.

His cigarette done, Henry looked once more at the Eno. Snow
melted from the trees and fell in large clumps to the water but not
onto Henry's sunny rock. He took the coat off and made a pallet and
lay on his back with his eyes closed. He considered the valleys between
Emma's fingers. The smell of a close-by fire wafted in his direction.

When he was twenty-three Henry left Georgia for Texas, intending
to join the cavalry. The war with Mexico was over, but there were
skirmishes aplenty along the boundary. One night he camped with an
odd band, including a dwarf in a blue cape who distinguished himself
by pulling out a gold-edged volume to read. But a drunken wayfarer
snatched it up and threw it into the fire. Henry pulled it out. The book
was Mungo Park's *Travels in the Interior Districts of Africa*. Henry paid
the dwarf and carried the book into Texas, reading into the night.
What a world! Larger than Crusoe's island, a place of glorious kingdoms. The book increased Henry's wanderlust, but how would he veer
from Texas to Africa? When Henry got to Falls County, he signed on
with the Texas cavalry. He was a genius at survival. Soon he was a
lieutenant, in charge of a company of soldiers who were not geniuses
at survival and had no trouble dying. Over and over he vowed to quit,
but he saw no easy way. He became a Ranger. When gangrene set in
on one of his men, Henry had to saw the leg off. It was time to stop.
He was twenty-six years old.

"You're a fine soldier," the corporal said, reluctant to accept his
resignation.

"No such thing," Henry said. After three years in Texas, he left off
his commission and traded in his land grant for a wallet of money he
sewed into the pocket of some tattered trousers no one would bother
to steal.

Heading in the general direction of Georgia, he spent his first night camped alone. The second night he traded cleaning a stable for a room at a crossroads. His horse needed shoeing and he spent two more nights doing repairs to the stable as credit against the cost. The leaves of the Spanish oaks were turning red. By the third night he had earned enough for supper at the bar. There was a woman behind the counter with her face cast down. "What have you got to eat?" he said. When she looked up, he saw she had a widow's peak.

"Steak and tortillas," she said. "The steak is good."

"All right, I'll have some," he said.

She served him and waited. He thought she wanted to see from his face that her word was true. He ate deliberately and treated the food with respect. She took his plate and he came back the next night. "My name is Laurie," she said.

The next day he rode out to a river and did some fishing and filleted the fish and fried them with cornmeal. "Why are you still here; why don't you move on?" he said to himself.

The next night when he went to the bar he saw the black chips in the blue of her irises.

They met the following day, riding to a place where trees leaned over the water. They swam in their underclothes. "*Dame un beso*," she said, "give me a kiss," and she pulled him close. Later, she led him to her place. It seemed to have been bored out of the ground after the hotel was built. He followed her down a set of steps to a room divided by a curtain. As they entered, another woman left. A girl slept on the only bed. Her hair was like something cut out of a night with rain and he knew right away she was part Mexican. They met so for weeks while the daughter slept. Henry worked at the stable and put away spending money. He never asked about the girl.

One night Laurie wasn't at the bar. When Henry asked for her, the men laughed, as if he were a boy. He walked out. *So I will leave now*, he thought. Then he heard her pleading. At the back of the hotel, a

Mexican careened on a horse, the daughter hauled into him. Laurie had caught the reins and leaned against them like someone might a sail on a tilting craft. The horse fretted and pulled, and Henry started toward them, but the Mexican pulled out his pistol; he had another one still holstered. Henry stood motionless and Laurie watched him, then let her arms go limp, releasing the horse before sinking to the ground. The other woman came out of the house and pulled Laurie in to her. Henry did not mean to fight another Mexican, though he regretted it for his own sake, and for hers. He turned away, Laurie's cry behind him.

He rode out at daybreak, making it clear into Alabama before he stopped to sleep. When he did sleep, he dreamed of the Indian boy. The child was beautiful—his locks long and dark, and he was speared in the side. The following morning Henry mused on the dream. The boy was meant as Jesus. He had helped crucify him.

Drink and women and even killing were so much scrollwork on the frame of a painting compared to the central subject, Henry's cardinal sin, ignoring his Redeemer. In the quiet of the countryside, he led the horse and moved slowly. At moments, he was filled with remorse so great his heart felt like a millstone, and he stopped to sit in the road and cry, his face to the ground. He shivered in the heat. Then he sweated something terrible. "God forgive me," he cried. "Give me another chance." When the chill returned, he wrapped himself in a blanket to ride. It seemed logical he would be ill—sickened with his own sinning.

Late in the day, he came upon an abandoned house. There were some gnarly apples in the fenced-in yard and a well. He watered the horse and left him to graze. Then he sat on the porch, gnawed on his last bit of jerky, and ate the fruit. Before sundown, he made his pallet on the porch and sank into sleep. He woke sick to his stomach and heaved until there was nothing left. He felt his side sore and thought it was his spleen. *I need water*, he considered, and reached for the can-

teen, but he had not refilled it. He tried to stand but fell into the yard.
He turned on his back, rested his hand on his sore abdomen, and slept
again. A cramp in his leg woke him. Both legs seized up, the pain like
daggers to his calves. He tried again to stand but could not. He cried
out in every foul phrase he knew, rocking in agony until finally he
called, "God help me." In a moment the pain subsided. He slept
through the day and night. Early in the morning, a sweet wind blew
through. Henry looked up to see a fellow sitting on the porch. He
wore overalls and a straw hat.

"I knew you would wake before long," the man said. "You might
could use some water."

Henry saw his canteen beside him. He picked it up to find it full.
He drank eagerly.

"Figured you might want something besides apples to eat. I brought
fish," the fellow said. He started toward Henry, carrying a small basket. "Take it easy, not too much at a time."

Henry opened the basket to find fried fish, still warm.

"You fix this for me?" he said.

"Well, I fixed it. Always carry dinner."

"Won't you need it?"

"Not like you do."

"I thank you," Henry said, shaking the man's hand. The hand was
large and Henry expected it to be rough, but the palm was tender as
a baby's bottom in heaven.

"You'll be fine now. Try not to ride yourself to death, or your
horse," the man said.

Henry watched him walk off until there was nothing left to see. He
ate half of the fish and lay back down.

He spent a week at the abandoned house. Rabbits were plentiful.
He recalled Bible verses his mother had taught him. *For God so loved
the world He gave His only begotten son.* The man who had brought the
fish never showed again, and Henry began to believe he had been

visited by an angel of the Lord. The more he thought on it, the greater his joy. God in heaven loved him and longed for his soul.

Henry's ideas of Jesus came clean and fast. The Savior had found a field of labor among the least of these. He taught in the countryside and healed the sick wherever he found them. He stood against the high priests who sought only to expand their own power. Henry's complaint against God had been His demand. Give all you have, even your mother. Now Henry wished to give up everything, especially his guilt, and keep only God.

When he passed into Georgia he traded in his horse, using money from his stable work to purchase a better one. But he kept the rifle, a Yager. A muzzle-loaded, smooth-bore long gun, it carried a ball and two buckshot and it was heavy. If he used it again, it would be to shoot himself if he were fixing to die anyway in some lonely place where God would forgive him for not letting the bears or mountain lions eat him before he was dead.

His eyes still closed, Henry felt along the river rock out of habit. But of course he didn't have his firearm on the Eno River. He was having a good rest on the sunny shale. When he checked his midsection, he could tell his organs were behaving better. With that reassurance, he let himself enjoy the sun a little longer.

Henry had feared what he might find at his father's farm, but the man had set himself straight, hiring a young free Negro to work and take part of the yield. "You'll stay with me," his pa said, patting him on the back. "I knew you'd be home. If you don't favor your mother. All the good looks was on her side."

Henry was a little sorry his father didn't need his help more. "If I won't discommode you," he said, "I'll stay."

"You're joshing me," his father said. "What a way of speech you always had."

Henry cleared his throat. "I'm through fighting. If I can find a way, I'm going to preach. I guess I got some religion from Mama too."

"Like I said, you're from your mother. If it hadn't been for that tuberculosis." The old man seemed graveled and Henry thought he might choke up, but his keen blue eyes shone content. "I'm proud of you, then," he said.

Henry was offered a nearby church, but by the fourth Sunday he could feel the women pulling at him. He meant to live without a woman, without a wife, hoping such penance would relieve the guilt. "I'm going to do some circuit preaching," he told his father. "There's many a person moving into Georgia that hasn't got the gospel."

"I wouldn't stop God, no sir," his pa said.

Henry preached so for five years, into north Florida. The clutching in his stomach was gone, but another feeling took its place, something below his breastbone. It made him think of a throng of birds caught in a domed ceiling trying to break through to light. He took it as a sign of spiritual limitation and began studying all the theology he could find, the history of religion, and the early American preachers. Jonathan Edwards was ruthless; Winthrop too benign. He found his best direction in John Wesley, with a little bit of Calvin thrown in. Though firmly based in scripture, Wesley never divorced faith from reason and he believed in personal experience, salvation by grace. But Calvin kept you on your toes. God couldn't be taken for granted.

Henry aligned himself with the Baptists because it was his mother's church. When the debate over ministers owning slaves came up, he argued against it on the principle that ministers must live simple lives common to the lowly in their flock. At an associational meeting in Decatur, he heard there was going to be a split in the denomination. The new Southern Baptists wanted to send missionaries to Africa. The dark continent fairly glittered in the light of south Georgia, where more than once, revival meetings broke up into calls for whiskey. Henry was the first to volunteer, putting his cavalry money into the mission. He left the smooth-bore Yager with his pa and purchased a fifty-caliber percussion cap rifle. Trimmer than the Yager, with brass pipes and furniture, steel lock and hammer, and a rifled barrel, the percussion offered greater accuracy than the Yager. There was, in the country to which he would travel, the same sort of fighting over territory he had seen in Texas. He meant to be protected. Wild game was abundant and the firearm could bring down an antelope or stop a lion. At least he hoped it could.

In 1850, he had gone to Africa. But in his three-year tour he had greatly desired a wife. There was the practical side; he needed a nurse for those times he was ill. Furthermore, he was sometimes attracted to an African woman and felt he might—in a rash moment—give in. Spiritually he needed a companion. Perhaps his penance was over.

The evening he found Emma in the vestibule of her church, he looked with new admiration on the Lord's capacity for humor. She was a tall girl of ordinary looks but with a swayback that suggested motion even when she stood still. It was clear she was waiting for him and just as clear that she was going somewhere regardless of who took her. Cleave, he thought, and meant it both ways, but it was not a sin because he intended to marry her.

The sun slipped behind the bare trees around the Eno. Henry sat up and as he did, a blue heron lifted and flew across the river. Its wingspan was astonishing and he felt a thrill of communion with the magnificent animal. The bird resettled itself. From across the way, it turned its head to look at him. After a bit it went back to its activity, collapsing its long body, pulling in its neck so that the head was just over the current. Occasionally it cocked its head sideways, listening rather than looking for fish. And then like a snake the long yellow beak struck water. How various were the wonders of God, that an animal of such size could be so agile. Just so was it with Henry—a body of contradictions, a man of great sin chosen to carry the love of Jesus. He pulled on the borrowed coat and headed back to the hotel.

The next day, Henry was on his way to Richmond. He spent a week in the company of his fellows at the mission board. They expressed pleasure with his progress: the fledgling church in Ijaye, the house building, Henry's articles on the African country. Still it burned him how men of God were keeping on with their slaves and luxurious houses. Yet what was he to do? He needed their support. People died by the thousands every day who had never heard the gospel. These men couldn't *feel* it as he did. He left them more determined than ever.

He spent Christmas with a minister in Petersburg and from there picked his way south into the New Year, 1853, stopping where he might to preach and raise money. He wrote to Emma. *I am comfortably set in Ijaye.* A year, he thought, long enough for her to become acclimated. *A British missionary has his own mission in the town, a Rev. Moore, a mighty fine neighbor.* Meanwhile, he would explore a more northern location. It was his dream—reaching the interior, converting the Mohamedan. A sudden worry crept up and tapped against his brain. What if his sweetheart was less flexible than he thought? He believed he had taken her measure. But wouldn't most women want a home, and hadn't he implied as much? She might want to sew curtains, that sort of thing. He penned his next sentence as delicately as he could. *I must consider how the Mohamedan mind can be brought to Jesus. It is my greatest desire to travel to their district, farther north.*

Yet another delicate subject needed explaining. *Spirits are a necessary part of mission life in the tropics,* he wrote, *as medicine, to calm the system and fight the malaria. It's better than quinine.* Through their correspondence, Henry grew fond of Emma's mind, and when finally he saw her again, he was fond of the whole of her. Nothing in her physical appearance had changed, but he believed she cherished him. And because no other woman had shown such care for his ideas, he felt the proudness of a young man, not a near-forty-year-old.

In the Davis parlor he asked for Emma's hand. Her parents seemed a bit shrunken, as if slipping into oblivion, and Henry felt his advantage. Later, he joined Mr. Davis in the family library. The man was dusting a frame above his desk. Henry thought he was meant to take an interest. "Miss Davis's college diploma," he said after reading the print.

"Yes," Mr. Davis said. "I should have seen her ambition."

Henry made no response. Mr. Davis folded his handkerchief and offered him a seat.

"You're a talented man," Mr. Davis said. "You've soldiered and traveled in places most Georgia men have not. Emma tells me you're self-taught but know more than any professor." The man studied his fingernails. "Your father is a farmer, if I'm not mistaken."

Henry thought of his papa's few acres, dull beside this man's plantation. He resented Mr. Davis for drawing comparisons that went against him and felt a tremble in his left hand. How had this thing turned so quickly? Mr. Davis must have observed his consternation because he took a deep breath and now he looked not at all like the shrunken man in the parlor. His vest expanded and Henry heard the rich leather breathe.

"I was wondering," Mr. Davis went on. "How many bales of cotton you think a man could make off an acre of Greensboro land?"

"I have no idea," Henry said. "I've not been studying cotton."

Mr. Davis pulled on his mustache. "That's too bad," he said. "I had planned to give you fifty acres as a wedding gift." He got up and stood at the window. "Thought to plant it for you while you're traveling. And put the money up toward future need."

"I have at present no way to pay for beginning the administration of such lands," Henry said, feeling his indignation stiffen him up.

"I'm talking about a gift," Mr. Davis said.

"It would be a great distraction to you," Henry said.

Mr. Davis sat back down. Henry could have sworn it was for the effect of the vest. He knew this sort of man, had met him many a time.

"I have plenty of Negroes," Mr. Davis said, and then he added, with the drama of a practiced line: "Don't tell me you're for setting niggers free just because you preach to them."

The man was baiting him. "I'm not telling you anything about your livelihood."

"I'd like to know how you're going to care for my daughter."

"I can teach and I can preach and I'll be productive for as long as the good Lord wills."

"Small harvest comes that way," Mr. Davis said. "But I won't press lands on one who'll do nothing but fallow them for jackrabbits and mountain lions."

"No sir, I reckon you won't." For a moment Henry wondered if Emma had been in on the design. Perhaps he had been reckless, not giving the man time to explain. He reprimanded himself for acting on impulse. Well, it was too late now.

"Good day," he said, setting his hat on his head and walking out of the room.

"Well?" Emma said when he met her on the porch.

"Your father offered land and labor to work it in our absence—to see to your security—but I wouldn't take it. He had already agreed to the marriage because it was your wish." Emma's face seemed to drain of color and he thought, *Well, there she goes, like a little goat; I'll have to restart this business of courtship.* But she latched on to his lapels.

"You were right, of course," she said. "We will wait on the Lord."

"The way is open, then," he said. "As I see it, you choose a date."

"I'm happier," she said, her eyes thoroughly charming.

"Happier than what?"

"Than I ever was before."

Something in him turned clean over. He loved her. She would be enough to wrestle with and she would keep him alive.

A Seal Is Set

Emma held Henry's gift in her lap.

"Open it," he said. "I made it from a mahogany packing box. It's larger than most and a little heavy, but you'll be glad for the accommodation later. Anyway, you'll have a boy to tote it."

The rectangular writing box stretched across her lap and beyond on either side. Eighteen inches wide, she surmised, maybe ten inches front to back, seven inches deep. The wood was dark brown, the shiny lacquer bringing out the natural grain in ribbons of gold, one section of grain rounding like currents in a stream.

"A man in Richmond gave me the inset handles."

The top sat flush to the sides. Emma slid her hands up and down over the perfect handles.

"The latch came from my host in Petersburg," Henry said. "This way you don't have to keep up with a key. Just push the little swing arm to the right to open it."

Emma brushed the latch with her thumb and ran her fingers over the brass corners.

Henry had worked a slender groove half an inch from the lid's perimeter. Emma sent her index finger along its circuit. "How did you do this?" she said.

"A V gouge," Henry said. "A man in Petersburg lent me his tools. I spent more time sharpening than carving. Mahogany is dense."

"No. I mean how did you do all of it?"

"I guess I've fiddled with making things most of my life," Henry said. "I had some time on my hands over Christmas. Open it."

The hinges moved like silk and held the lid propped. Etched into the lid's interior so she might read it upon opening, *In my heart a seal is set.* A verse from Percy Shelley she had written to him in their weeks of correspondence.

"I saw your journal the first day I called—figured you ought to have a writing box," he said. "Do you like it?"

A brush of memory. His hands at her waist. The hand-sewn diary falling to the ground. Then a vision of her bureau drawer lifting of its own accord, lost for a moment in a swirl of winter leaves, settling now in her lap. Henry had seen into her heart.

"You'll have a great deal to record in Africa," he said.

"It's the nicest thing anyone has ever done for me, Mr. Bowman," Emma said, awed by this mystery.

"Now look here. I'd like you to call me Henry when it's just the two of us," he said, the hint of a smile in his lips.

Wouldn't he kiss her?

"I put steel screws in the interior to strengthen the joints," Henry said. "Here's the writing surface covered in baize to be good and sturdy." He was serious again. "When you unfold it, you have your desk." She wanted to touch him. But she opened and closed the box. "I've already got most of what you need—ink, quills, nibs, paper. I found the diary in Washington at a stationers' shop," he said. The book was bound in red leather. The firm cover and thin pages gave her a feeling of great tenderness and security.

Finally Henry showed her the secret drawer by lifting the pen-and-ink holder and pressing a latch. "For your most private thoughts," he said.

Currents flowed through her like the brown waves in the wood. She closed the box, hushed. She slid her palm across the top. "What is

this?" she said. In the center was a single scallop, worked out like the
perimeter groove but deeper.

"The sway of your back," Henry said.

EMMA COULD NOT sleep. "What is it?" she said to herself after hours
of restless tossing. The moon threw sheets of light into the room. As
she sat up, she had a sense of her bed as a small boat at sea.

For her March wedding, Emma wore a blue silk dress with a white
rush at the neck. She imagined she might look pretty coming down
the family staircase and was disappointed when Henry averted his eyes
as she entered the parlor. But when she reached him, he put his hand
to her elbow and held it like an exquisite object coming down on a
current. They stood so close her bouquet was crushed, and the scent
of evergreens and camellias filled Emma's senses. She had invited the
Pilgrims School, though the children remained outside in the yard.
After the ceremony, she greeted them, giving each a flower. One of the
older Negro girls pushed a tag of bark into her hand. *JESUS*, it read,
the letters made with a charcoal shard. It tore at Emma's heart. What
of these children right here in Georgia? Didn't they need her? Was she
running away? She felt dizzy and closed her eyes. *One two three four
remember.* When she looked out again, the girl was gone.

Indoors, Emma sought Henry and found him standing before a
display of boxed gifts in the hallway. He was rapping them with his
knuckles as he might a watermelon.

"A silver tea set," Aunt Lou said, her voice as large as her satin-
banded dress.

"It's not something I would think of," Henry said.

"You'll take it for your wife."

"We hope to," Emma said in a rush, fearful Henry might say something about the extravagance of silver in Africa. "But we can only
carry so much."

"Of course we'll take it—for Mrs. Bowman," Henry said, a sly glance at Emma.

"Good," Aunt Lou finished. "It won't break."

Emma felt someone's eyes upon her. Mittie Ann stood at the door to the butler's pantry. She looked stately in her brown empire dress. "My father's expecting you to come by," she said. "He has something." The woman started out and Emma followed.

At the cabin door, Emma waited for her eyes to adjust and took in the smell of camphor and ash. In a moment she saw Uncle Eli sitting in bed, looking toward the window that offered a view of the garden. Several of his bundles—what she had taken long ago for stars but were to him warnings against evil—still hung from the ceiling. She chose her steps so as not to bump her head against one of them.

"I feel you a-comin'," the old man said when she moved around where he could see her.

"Good afternoon, Uncle Eli."

He gestured with his chin toward a rocking chair. She preferred to stand because of her skirts, but she sat anyway. The old man's white hair was huge, as if he had decided against ever cutting it again. It ranged and peaked, the liveliest part of him.

"Been some while," he said, "since you call on this old friend."

She knew how she had recently avoided him. She was going to Africa. He was taken from there against his will. He would die here. She felt her pity roused for him. She was even bitterly sorry. Yet this was her wedding day. She should not be asked to feel sorrow like this. "I've been busy preparing for my journey. You'll remember to pray to Jesus, for his mercy, and pray for me and my husband going into your homeland."

"I don't forget to pray," he said. "I pray all the time."

She had a sudden urge to ask what he remembered. "What's your favorite memory, Uncle Eli?"

"You mean my country?"

"Yes."

"A big yard where I run around with my brothers and sisters, my mother there cooking. Oh, we had a good time."

She sat and brooded. Uncle Eli's hands rested on top of the quilt tucked snugly around his legs. She looked toward Mittie Ann, but the woman was a silhouette against the light of the door frame.

"Is there something I can do?" Emma said.

"You might could get me a glass of water," Uncle Eli said. "Some cooling on the porch." She left the cabin and found the clay pot and a ladle and poured water into a cup and brought it back. When she returned he had a burlap package tied with twine on his lap. She handed him the drink. "That's good water," he said.

"I'm glad," she said, thinking how stuffy the room was.

"You remember now, don't you?" he said.

"Yes," she said, remembering much but not sure of what he meant. Then she thought of his toes, something she would never forget. Uncle Eli turned and gazed on her, his eyes, she knew, hardly seeing, yet mysteriously knowing.

"I teached you how to look," Uncle Eli said, tapping his head. He turned back to the window, the parcel still resting in his lap. She brooded more, her eyes cast on the quilt until she made out the faded blue pattern, something like petals in a square.

"I wish I could take you," she said finally.

He didn't look at her this time.

"My legs tire," he said. She thought again of the wound to his foot and the crime of it. It was too confusing, all this harrowing up. She must get back to Henry. No one knew where she was. Soon she would be perspiring through her dress.

"I made something for you," he said. He held the parcel out and she took it, the stays of her corset pressing against her flesh as she leaned forward.

"Let me open it," she said, an urgency now in her fingers. But she couldn't unknot the twine, and Mittie Ann helped her. *She must wonder if I'll be able to take care of myself,* Emma thought, feeling childish. Uncle Eli was looking out the window again.

"Some travel is one way to go and some travel is another," he said. He did seem to ramble now. She pulled against the burlap. Finally she clasped the gift, one of his carvings. At first she wasn't sure what to do with it. The item was long and thin, tapering to a point, one side straight as a ruler, the other slightly arched. The broad end was whittled into the likeness of a man's head and on top of that, the figure of a bird. She held it like you might a cross, the wood gleaming yellow. "It's lovely," Emma said. She perceived how she might understand it. "It's the bird; it's you with the bird; it must be you and me." She felt a flood of release. He was offering her an emblem of their friendship, a portrait. As she turned the carving in her hands, she saw it might work as a letter opener; surely that was his intention. "I love it," she said. "How did you make it shine so?"

"It's the leaf I take to rub it," he said. "You remember. Now you carry that with you. It wants a place to lie."

"Yes, I promise." She was still feeling a great relief.

"That's good. When you get there, you look for a place. I know you will. You teachable. Now Mittie Ann, she teachable too. But I knowed she couldn't go. You could go. Remember now. Don't forget, you won't get lost."

Emma's eyes rested on the quilt again. Something floated up. Her anxious night, her bed like an unmoored boat. She had been afraid. But here the old man reassured her. She *was* capable of Africa. She just had to remember her conviction.

"I'm back to the house," Mittie Ann said all at once, and Emma heard the door of the cabin close and the woman's one step from the porch onto the ground.

"I'm ready now," Uncle Eli said.

"Yes, I'm ready," Emma said. That was what he meant: *You're* ready. "But I'll miss the garden terribly. I'll make one in Africa."

"You take that with you," Uncle Eli said, pointing to the letter opener, his eyes now closed. "You find the right place."

"Yes," she said, her eyes tearing. "I have to go." She leaned over and kissed his cheek. He found her hand, even with his eyes closed, and pressed it to his lips. Then he released her.

On the way out, she forgot and her head hit one of the old bundles; dried berries rained on her shoulders. She nearly tripped in her hurry to get back into the house, going straight for her husband, who stood by the fireplace smoking. "Look," she said, handing the object to him.

"What's this?" Henry said, rubbing it like a gold piece to check its worth. "It looks almost African."

"But he's *from* Africa."

"What do you mean?"

"The old slave, Uncle Eli, he came on a ship, directly. He's the one who made it."

"Well, I like it better than the silver tea set. Don't mislay it."

That was it. Uncle Eli told her to lay it in a good place. She slipped the gift right into the writing box Henry had made. The old man only wanted to be remembered.

First nights for a couple are powerfully inscriptive. Henry and Emma would spend theirs in a cottage loaned by a friend in Madison. As Henry was checking on the horses, Emma slipped out of her crinoline petticoat and climbed into bed still fully clothed. She didn't even take her boots off. She hoped it wouldn't happen. Now that the time had arrived, it seemed preposterous, unimaginable that such an arrangement could be made between her body and her husband's. She had thought Henry's experience might diminish her alarm, but she found it did not. Throughout the courtship, she had been filled with ideas of heaven, the thrill of Henry's letters, delightful kisses that made her spin for days in her own sheath of energy. Not this, which would surely make her pass out.

She tried to breathe evenly when Henry approached and leaned over, whispering into her ear, "Where are my Emma's toes?"

Clumsily, he felt about the bed for her feet, acting the part of a blind man until she started to giggle. "Here they are, you silly," she said, and produced her boots from under the covers. With great seriousness, Henry began to unlace, hook by hook. On each foot's release, he leaned over and kissed her still-shrouded toes. Slowly he walked his fingers up her legs, spider fashion, until he came to the pink garters at her knees.

"Emma toes," he spoke as he untied each garter and pulled down the white stockings she herself had decorated with her new initials. His mastery was magnificent. How much he knew. Exactly how to unbutton, unhook, untie every article of clothing. He folded each article as he took it off, shoulder to shoulder, hip to hip, anklet to waist. She watched his serious face until she thought her body would break open. But he took his time. And as each part of her emerged into the pale candlelight, he named it "Emma toes," touching softly with his fingertips. At last he had her very place, and she found that some miracle had occurred as they pulled together, almost like riding a horse. They were both together—the horse and the rider—all the way across the plain, to a great flowing river and then a waterfall.

It was unseasonably warm the morning they took the train out of Atlanta, and Henry joked about how Africa had come to meet them. Emma was happy in a new spring dress with only a shawl and delighted in Henry's company. What her husband did in the day was as exquisite as what he did at night. In the dining car, he decided on rack of lamb, for example. He looked to their things. In their compartment, he dipped his pen in the inkwell and with greatest care set nib to white paper. He rolled a cigarette with the deliberation with which one would seal a love note. She liked the smell of the smoke. Even the odd way Henry held his teacup—with thumb and middle finger—

seemed worldly rather than rude. Sometimes he seemed to study the newspaper overlong and forget her, and once he left and was gone for more than an hour. In his absence, she opened the writing box, the lovely lid propped. Uncle Eli's letter opener greeted her eye, and she felt a fondness envelop her. She laid her hand against her New Testament. Then she unwrapped the only personal item she had brought from her bedroom, a clear glass prism she had selected in a Savannah store on a trip with her father. It sat on a short square base that fit within the palm of her hand and then tapered like a six-sided pyramid. She had been immediately enamored when her father held it in the store window, showing her how it cast a rainbow. She rewrapped it and brought out the red journal to make a note. *The landscape changes before my eyes. Pines taller than ours in Georgia, then hills, then a river far below us. What will the world of Africa show me?* When Henry returned, she thought he had alcohol on his breath. "For a headache," he explained. She observed the back of her husband's neck. Loving a man was like finding a forgotten book of the gospel: luminescence and dark mystery. Throughout it all, the sound of the train on the track brought foundation to her skimming heart.

In Boston all of the houses were tall and smashed together like books on a shelf. The horses seemed to prance higher as if they had nowhere to go but up. Hooves on cobblestones replaced the sound of the train. Emma felt she could lean into the city's rumbling and it would catch her, everything so odd and regular. But she felt perfectly comfortable. Her husband looked out for her. They dressed for their photograph.

"Imagine yourself a tree on a still day," the photographer said. Emma held herself tight, but still it seemed that something inside her clambered and sang. God and Henry were very close in her mind on that morning in Boston.

On earth as it is in heaven . . . remember.

Part Two

CHILDREN
OF GOD

· 6 ·

Arrival

. . . I long felt the want of something fulfilling, something to give my life purpose as God willed. I know now more than ever that in going to Africa, I shall find what I seek. It seems to me I have embarked upon the road to eternal life.

—EMMA TO HER MOTHER, ABOARD SHIP, 1853

THE *NIAGARA* SET sail for Liverpool, and right away Emma learned how little she knew of ships. The second night she was seasick. A few days later, she smelled fire and ran from their room, but the flames were already extinguished. An overeager subcook had fired the stove too high. The watery deep sent shivers up her spine. "What time I am afraid, I will trust in thee," she whispered, walking on deck, forcing herself to face the sea. Henry, on the other hand, appeared completely at ease, conversing with the captain about weather and masts, passionate about movement.

England was a wearying, cold place, and she was glad when they could leave on the steamer. She was not seasick this time, even in a squall when they had to take their dinner sitting on the floor. Later on deck she saw her first Africans, or she supposed they were her first Africans, for they were not slaves but sailors, three of them, all at ease and confident among their mates. One day she saw a woman so well outfitted she looked as if a small empire were required to set her up. She had enough cloth on her head to make three girls' smocks. On her body she wore a loose green bodice; her wrapped skirt corresponded in a green-and-white print, and about her she pulled a yellow shawl. To this arrangement was added sandals of dyed leather. Emma pressed her skirts; her dress seemed a little bland by comparison.

"Surely," she said to Henry in the dining room, "she must be a princess."

"More likely she's kept by a European. It's a disgrace," he said.

Emma was doubtful. She could not imagine the woman being lorded over. Henry ate hastily and stood before she was finished. It put a first dent in her image of his fitness as a husband.

One day in mid-April warm winds came up from the south, smelling almost green with land, and Henry, eager for Africa, talked nonstop about the mission. "You'll be called *oyinbo* for 'white person,'" he said, "but it's not to be taken unkindly." They practiced conversations in the Yoruba language. He told her the history of the area where they would live, how the northern Fulani tribes had first conquered the Hausa and then swept southward, destroying the old kingdom of Oyo, getting as far as Ilorin, bringing Mohamedanism with them. But they had been stopped at Ogbomoso, a town he had once visited. Emma saw great brown men on steeds, carrying furling flags, but was challenged to remember which kingdom was which. "Imagine," he said, "a line of mission stations, going into the interior to central Africa." He ran his fingers up and down her sleeved arm as he said this, gazing out at sea.

EMMA WOKE WITH a sense of being alone. She felt along the bed. In a moment she lit a candle. Where was Henry? She became agitated. By the time he returned, she was distraught.

"Where were you?" she said, hitting at his chest with her fists.

"What is it?" he said. "Are you unwell?"

"You left."

"I only took a stroll. Why are you crying?"

He pulled her to him, but she pushed him away.

"Has someone alarmed you?" he said.

She collapsed onto the bed, shaking. How could she begin? At last she thought she could compose herself, and she sat up, wiping her face. "You know I am sincere," she started, "about our work." She stopped, overcome by her own pity. Then she felt another surge of desperation. "We can't be always moving," she said, turning her face to him, pleading and angry, "up and down the country. You must stay with me!"

"My dear girl," he said, sitting beside her, pulling her close. "We'll be fine. I'm here. You'll see the house. Remember, I told you of Rev. Moore. We have enough white people for a village."

It was a silly, ridiculous thing for him to say, and her heart turned at his effort for her. She even laughed in a sad way.

They lay together again.

In the morning, Henry woke her, bringing coffee. "I've saved some good news."

Emma thought he looked more stalwart than ever.

"The Smithsonian has agreed to publish the Yoruba vocabulary I've been at work on, as soon as I finish the manuscript. They want a basic grammar with it—idioms," he said.

Emma forgot all about her doubt, her husband's leaving in the night, talk of moving to the interior. He was so brilliant and true, she could serve him as a handmaiden if he asked her.

The port at Bathurst was deep, allowing the ship to dock close in. Henry went ashore to purchase rope. Emma waited on deck. It was becoming quite clear to her that she did not like this being alone when he was the only person in the world she knew. What if something happened and he never returned? She imagined all sorts of disaster: Someone had lured him into an alley to take his money; he had fallen and hit his head and lay wounded, unable even to send for help. At last she spotted him on the wharf, and all night she clung to him. The next day he was sick with dysentery. Her fear of losing him the day before made her oddly happy to nurse him. A small dosing of laudanum improved the dysentery, but Henry was weakened and one night she woke to find him shaking so with chill she feared he would fall out of bed. African fever, the captain told her. "Do you mean malaria?" she said.

"Something like that," he said.

She treated her husband as the captain instructed: extra blankets for the shivers and cool baths for the fever that followed. She fed him sugar water. The pattern of chills and fever repeated itself three times, and only on the fourth day would Henry agree to a little quinine from his medicine kit. He gagged on the bitter drug. "It's worse than the malaria," he said, gulping water furiously. But it seemed to turn the illness. In her journal she recorded the first sickness: *cold, heat, cold, heat, X 4. Very depleting of husband and myself in worrying over him.* She meant it as a helpful note, but when she returned the journal to her writing box she felt a little sorry that it had been necessary to fill the beautiful pages with a portrait of Henry in weakness.

Once well, he was twice impatient with her. She attributed his state to the illness and forgave his diminished gallantry. She considered adding another note to her journal, about the effect of illness on the spirit. But then Henry was so considerate in their intimacy.

At last they arrived at Accra. After breakfast Emma discovered a fullness in her throat. Her brain seemed dull and she thought she should return to their room and find a less constricting dress. She sank into bed and fell asleep. When she woke, she was chilled to the bone. "It's my turn to nurse you," Henry said, but six blankets could not warm her. Finally she slept again only to wake with her head afire. The illness was like an animal in the room that she watched from a perch outside her body. In the morning she lay absolutely still, her eyes following an oblong of light from the portal as it moved across the wall, turning from white to pink. When the light was gone, she could still see it with her eyes closed. Her whole preoccupation was holding the light against the animal. On and off she slept. When the fever broke, she was drenched in sweat; the tangled mass of her hair took hours to comb. They weighed anchor in Lagos on May 1, but Henry and Emma remained on board two days due to the roughness of the sea. They witnessed an unloading of coffins. "What are those for?" Emma said.

"British officers bring them on assignment," Henry said.

Emma was too weak to experience dread. If she had to endure the African fever too many times, she might rather die. Early the next day, she and Henry were lowered into a canoe that took them to a lardman barque waiting in the shallows. Emma observed the long belt of green along shore, huge crashing breakers on a short steep beach. She held Henry's arm with both hands. "I'm going to close my eyes," she said. *God be with us*, she prayed in her heart.

"You'll miss your entrance to Africa," he said.

"I've already seen it," she said.

Heading into a Lagos crowd was different from viewing the Bathurst market from deck. Everyone shouting and calling *oyinbo*, white man. Children running like low-flying agile birds. Men along the street taking advantage of their arrival as a good time to rest, watching and pointing and carrying on with each other. A thick smell of fish and smoke. This was a different sun. It scattered color and rearranged it. Blue under the curves of coconut palms. White on the ground. Red shadow where the gullies ran. The sky green. Emma raised a hand to shelter her eyes. A boy pushed a toddler into their path. When she reached for him, the poor child wept as if he had been left in a lion's den. Everyone laughed. Emma held on to Henry.

"There's Daniel now," he said. They were to stay at the guesthouse of the Anglican mission—also known as the Christian Missionary Society. Henry had told her of the native British agent who would come to greet them and look to their loads. As Henry conferred with him, Emma noticed several women headed their way, all with trays on their heads and most of them only half dressed. The bottom half was dressed, the upper half full open to the sun. She knew to expect it; Henry had told her. But to see them coming was an altogether different matter. Emma felt herself utterly naked and ashamed.

"Mah," one woman said. "Please, buy." A fly landed on the woman's chest.

"Not now," Henry said to the seller.

The woman clucked. "Please mah, buy," she said, lowering her tray, displaying the contents. Emma recognized nothing.

"She knows English," Emma said, trying hard not to look at the woman's chest.

"Enough to bargain," Henry said.

Daniel intervened, dusting the women away, and by pulling her hat close around her face, Emma was able to walk the three necessary blocks to the guesthouse without seeing much.

"A bath," Emma said when the British woman asked what she could get for her. Shown to their room, Emma saw that their bed frame was set in tins of water. This was against ants, Henry told her. She wondered if it might be against scorpions too. This nearness of danger brought her personal effects leaping to mind. "My writing box!" she said. "We didn't leave that to the agent, did we?"

"He carried it on his head, coming with us, didn't you see?"

"Please go get it," she said, trembling.

At dinner they learned that their Ijaye associate, Rev. Moore— the man who, with Henry and Emma, would be enough for a white village—had gone to England to see to a deceased uncle's estate. "He expects to be back in three months' time," their hostess reported. Emma was disheartened.

When they took their first walk down a Lagos street a few days later, she found her new world more harmonious than what she had experienced on their initial landing. Because the British women strolled along these lanes, she was not such a spectacle. The native yards were neatly swept, every one of them boasting lovely shade trees; however, the doors to the houses were so low that Emma could not imagine getting her skirts through. Then suddenly, she heard a rallying cry and from every corner women emerged with baskets on their heads and babies on their backs, several of the women uncovered in the manner of the ones who had so distressed her. Her hands flew to her bodice, the sense of harmony extinguished.

"They're going to collect fish for the evening meal," Henry said.

"If you don't mind, let's turn back," Emma said, her eyes stinging. How would she ever become accustomed to such immodesty?

She sought the high veranda of the mission guesthouse and had a good cry, but it left her dull, not restored. Out in the harbor she saw a ship. They might still escape. No. Henry would not leave. She was wretched. He should have prepared her better. It was late afternoon when he came to call her.

"Your hair has fallen," he said, giving her shoulder a squeeze. Then he squatted in front of her. "It's time for tea."

"Oh," she said. "Oh!" Her torment came back full force.

"What is it?"

"Those women," she said.

"What?"

"They're uncovered." Her voice rose. "It's shameful. I can't bear it. Think of me!"

He lifted a fallen braid. "Pin this up," he said, "and listen."

She looked into his face, browner now from the days on deck.

"They are children of God. The custom here is different. We must love their souls."

He stood and pulled her up and into him and she pressed her damp eyes against his shoulder. "I am not much help to you," she said.

"You are perfect," he said.

The next afternoon, Henry returned from town in good humor. "I have our carriers," he said. "They wanted to rob me, but I've got them down to a reasonable price."

It would be hard to rob a man in this country, Emma thought. The currency was strings of cowry shells, forty to a string, and bunched together into what was called a head. It took two thousand shells to make a dollar. A robber would need swift oxen to make away with such money.

Taking their leave on a Monday morning, Emma gazed on the comfortable accommodations of their British hosts, with their French moderator lamps and wool rugs and lace doilies. "Do be careful, dear," one of the women said to her in an aside; "the swamps are full of boa constrictors and crocodiles."

Henry estimated a full week's journey to the house in Ijaye. Emma insisted that her writing box should be covered in burlap and carried in front where she could keep an eye on it. The man who picked it up placed on top of the packaged box a large fan of palm leaf to shield him from the sun. Other carriers assisted one another in heaving loads onto their heads, and off they went. Emma was carried in a chair for some way and then they took to canoes. Once out of the low country, Henry planned to purchase a horse. The early rainy season was under-way and the increase of water swelled the vaporous lagoons. Emma dreaded to think what slimy things were in them. At one stop she watched a huge horrible insect emerge from a rotting log. Finally they reached a place with firm shore. Emma needed to relieve herself. "Where must I go?" she whispered to Henry.

"I'll take you," he said.

"I don't believe I can," she said, but she followed him down a path where he whacked down some underbrush with a cutlass and then stood with his back to her to protect her privacy.

Henry rolled a cigarette and they started again. Under the midday sun, Emma sweated until her clothes clung to her cruelly and she itched something fierce. She wore a hat with netting over her face and tucked into her collar—to keep out insects—and now she ripped it off.

At first the food seemed palatable—beans and rice. But after three days, Emma could hardly stomach it. She longed for fried chicken, lima beans, a biscuit, a mere carrot. Rather than enjoy a wholesome meal, she must watch the carriers dig into their dinner with their hands, talking with their mouths full, licking their fingers.

As they progressed, she became a great oddity. Rather than *oyinbo*, one frightened woman called her *"Eemaw!"* Monster! before running for cover, quick as a fox. Emma had thought Africans might find her attractive. It was a great disappointment to learn they found her appearance disagreeable. She retrieved the netted hat and put it back on.

All of the people everywhere were as loud as could be. No one talked but he must throw his arms up and down, side to side, and move his head as if always agreeing with himself. Emma continued to be surprised by the people's clothing. The men wore yards of cloth for parading about town in their *agbadas*, or gowns, while the women's outfits were hardly existent.

"I cannot," she said one night, undressing by candlelight in what was to pass as their night's chamber—a mud room, eight feet square, stifling hot, the roof so low she must stoop. Her petticoat was brown from trailing in the mud. When she took off her gloves, she found her wrists were dark with dirt. Her malodor was frightful. As she poured water into a bucket, something fell to the ground and scooted out the low door. She screamed, her heart hammering. Surely Henry would hear her. When he did not come, she had no choice but to pray. "Dear God, forgive me. I will fail. It is too much. If something lands in my hair, I will die. You must shield me." Her misery was severe. She thought of her mother; her own white, plump bed at home—all she had left without a second thought, in order to sit in this hovel scared to death of whatever lizard or bug might crawl up her leg. After the merest bath, she slipped an undergarment over her head to serve as a gown. In her dreary state, she opened her writing box and pulled out Uncle Eli's carving, so beautifully smooth and clean. She clung to it lying on the pallet, meaning to wait for Henry. A moment and she slept.

In the morning, Henry attended to a man whose foot had developed a sore. Emma had time to pull out the lap desk and her journal. She wrote down everything. *I had thought in marriage to be less alone but closeness makes distance more acute. The people are friendly but I find no point of contact. Keeping clean will take all of my strength. Henry teaches me that the emblem of peace is the palm tree.*

At last they reached farm lands in the rolling plains. These seemed broader than any fields Emma had ever seen, and in the wooded glades, the variety of greens emerging with the rain was so dazzling she thought there could not be enough words for such color. She felt her first happiness in the country. Here were acacia trees like gazelles springing into air. When she saw the women bearing yams and other fruits out of the farms, she observed how their posture was akin to colored women back home carrying melons on their heads. She felt a delight of recognition and pulled off the netted hat. "I'm not wearing this," she said to no one in particular. Emma had discovered that the mosquitoes hardly bothered her anyway though they gave Henry fits. It was only at night when they buzzed around her head that she hated them.

She was grateful for deep woods where the forest canopy seemed half a mile tall and knit tight as a cathedral ceiling, and in the middle of the day the light was blue and the temperatures lower. Unlike oaks and maples, whose upper roots spread along the ground, the great African hardwoods were anchored with natural buttresses as tall as Emma was. Once in the bush an elephant came out and stood in the way. *This is a real elephant*, Emma thought, *not a circus one*, and rather than panic, she admired it. Some of the carriers wanted Henry to shoot. *No*, Emma thought, *not this glorious being with its great animate ears and swinging trunk.* She was immensely relieved when Henry said no. They hadn't time for slaughtering, and besides his rifle wouldn't take it down; the elephant would run after being wounded or charge and it would need lots of spearing. There seemed a general disappointment before the elephant crashed off.

They came to a village on a river where the huts were built on stilts. To this point, all of the towns had been alike, one after the other, full of windowless mud houses, open markets, potteries and clothmaking out of doors, shrine houses for the *orishas* or community gods, lots and lots of drumming, and the air lavender with smoke from cooking fires. The fires produced a smell Emma had already come to enjoy, sweet and peppery. Here at the river village, they must, as always, ask permission to enter. An old chief came out, a string of women and girls behind him. It seemed a lot of daughters for one man. When things were settled, Emma asked about them.

"They are his wives," Henry said.

"His wives?" Emma said. "They look like schoolgirls and he looks a hundred."

She glanced toward the courtyard, where a number of the girls were eating around a common pot. She couldn't tell that they were suffering, but it seemed an awful plight to be married off to a voracious old chief. They wore light wraps, their hair cut close.

"Do you think I might speak to them?" she said.

"By all means," Henry said.

Emma made her way over to them. They watched with interest, but when she came close, several ran off. A brave young wife offered her space on a mat and Emma took a seat, grateful she had already decided against her stiff petticoats. She said "Good evening" in Yoruba and was met with much glee in this salutation. Emma wished she knew a Yoruba song, but she didn't. So it was *Four and twenty blackbirds, baked in a pie. When the pie was opened, the birds began to sing; wasn't that a dainty dish, to set before a king?* The girls began to clap and required her to sing the rhyme several more times. Then they insisted she take her gloves off. They took turns trying them on and examined her hands. "Well, I'm charmed," Emma said, and she was. She liked their spunk. Maybe that old chief had not ruined them entirely. The wife who offered Emma a place on her mat slipped a pair of milky beads over Emma's neck and would not let her return them when Emma stood to leave.

One night between villages, the carriers had to build up a booth of grass for them to sleep under, and Henry preached in Yoruba and English, to include her, Emma supposed.

"Think of your love for your children. This is how God loves you, only ten thousand times more and still some. Leave off your idols. Through Jesus you will arrive at your Father, the one true God. The only gift you need give is yourself," he said.

Her husband seemed to find such opportunity for witness in the wild interior of Africa more than sufficient payment for all of their sweat. But in a moment, preaching had to be put off, for a violent storm came up, shaking the territory with thunder.

"My things!" Emma called.

The gullies on either side of the road were soon converted to creeks as Emma sat atop a crate holding her writing box. She was frightened near to death, the huge treetops pitching, branches creaking, the deluge turning everything gray.

"I've seen worse," Henry said.

"Well I haven't," she said.

Visitors

B<small>Y LATE</small> M<small>AY</small>, Emma was settled in Ijaye in the house that Henry had built on a gentle incline of land. By Georgia standards, it was a fine cabin. Here it seemed a castle. Though constructed of mud and plaster, the work was finely done, the walls deep and smooth. There were six rooms in the rectangular home, three across the front for their use, one opening on the side yard for guests, and two across the back for servants, though, at present, they had only one servant, a man, their cook, named Duro. After days of sleeping in dark huts, Emma gloried in the windows, which looked out on a fair-sized yard before one's eyes came to rest on a town lane. A veranda, called by Henry "the piazza," ran the entire perimeter of the house and the rooms opened onto it, though Henry's and Emma's rooms could also be passed through from one to the other on the interior. The thatched roof jutted far out over the piazza, providing deep shade. In the back were the kitchen and garden area where Henry had established a lemon tree, a batch of mint, a stand of banana trees, and a row of tobacco. *Clever man*, Emma thought. The privy occupied one corner at the very back of the property. At present the stable stood empty, as they had not, after all, purchased a horse. Catercorner to the house in the front stood Henry's chapel. Their compound was enclosed by a low wall on one side and a hedgerow on the other, the space close to an acre and a half. They were located near a good-sized stream. Half a mile in the other direction was the center of town and the king's compound. The lane in front of their house was always busy, especially in early morning and at dusk with farmers going out, market women coming in, children doing as they wished, and even cattle, goats, and pigs—some attended and some not.

Emma set about at once to create a home. She did not believe that a mud floor could be clean and asked Henry if they might purchase native matting to act as rugs.

"It will mean more work," he said, "taking mats out to air and sweeping beneath."

"I prefer it," she said.

Henry agreed, and Emma was pleased with her first decorative touch. Later she would add a tapestry or picture to the walls. Henry had shown her that by boiling nails, he could hammer them into the plaster easy as butter. But at present she had no artwork. Some sort of curtain she would have. She asked Henry to put a bamboo rod over the front window. "I'll simply drape one of my shawls across the upper beam," she said, "until I have time for sewing." Henry seemed to find her efforts surprising, and she thought he must long have desired a feminine touch. There was little furniture except a wardrobe Henry had purchased from a British missionary, wooden packing boxes now turned to side tables, a dining table and chairs, some locally made benches, their long trunk fashioned with a wooden pocket for stowing the rifle, one stuffed chair, a bed, and an extra mattress. Emma gave her writing box pride of place on a bench next to the good chair in the sitting room. Here she would make her devotional, compose letters home, and keep her journal. Whole books might spiral out of her.

The neighbors' goats tended to cluster on the piazza, liking the nice shade. She shooed them off, but they always came back. Shooing off the large brown lizards that congregated on the outer walls was nigh impossible. They only moved a few inches higher into the cool shade. Henry was right about her "rugs." Because the yard was dirt, dust inevitably sifted into the house, and she must shake them out almost daily. In lighter moods, she enjoyed the industry, but in darker ones, she imagined nothing could stay clean in Africa.

They were in the heart of Yoruba land, a walled town of thousands overseen by a warrior king named Kunrumi who had once planned his own son's execution on suspicion of his being a traitor. This gentleman kept a large fighting force of men. It seemed discordant to Emma's pastoral view that it should be so, and she was often spooked by the drums at night. Then she clung to Henry. At least the town had seen *oyinbos*, her husband, of course, and Rev. Moore. Still, people stood on the lane and watched and pointed and commented as she moved in the yard. Any little thing she did could create uproarious laughter. In the evening as the townspeople went home, they called to Emma in gentler voices, wishing her "good evening." During that brief twilight, the palm tree forest on a distant hill was clothed in mist, and the sweet smell of fires filled the air.

Soon enough some of Moore's schoolchildren gathered with Emma in the mornings, including two older boys well versed in English. They differed from many youngsters in that they wore some clothing at least, all but the youngest, who had only beads around their necks or waists. Emma had never seen bolder children, and that they were black made it all the more amazing to her. They smiled broadly and waved to say hello, not good-bye, their hands fully extended. They felt free to touch her any way they pleased, to pick at the fabric of her dress and discuss it with one another, and to ask for anything they wanted. She found deep pleasure in their company. To the question, "Who made the bird?" they answered, "God made the bird." To the question, "Who is Jesus?" they had all kinds of answers, including "your husband," "my uncle," "the *alufa*"—or Yoruba priest—and "my friend."

In the afternoons, women from Henry's congregation brought pine-apples to the house before the evening service. The fruit was exquisite, running with juice when cut, and so pungent, Emma thought it must be God's apple. The women bowed almost to the ground in their greeting, and Emma found herself doing a little curtsy and with everyone she went through all the litany: How is your husband, how are your children, how is your house, *titi lailai*, forever and ever. When they sang in the yard, the women crooked their elbows, made little fists, and swayed their arms side to side. They tended to bend at their hips so their backside stuck out a bit, and they observed the movement of their feet with great dedication. It was all so liquid and natural and lovely except it lasted indefinitely. There was no such thing as stanzas. Everything, Emma could see, took longer in this world. She looked forward to a time—surely soon—when people would stop their constant coming and going and gawking.

One morning Emma and Henry called at the king's palace and were received by the elder wife. She insisted on showing them a number of carvings made from elephants' tusks ornamenting a large room, some mounted on wooden boxes, others stretched out like canoes against the wall. Emma counted two dozen pairs. The wife went to prepare a native refreshment while her guests were left to gaze on the ivory. The room was hot and Emma moved to the door, heavily carved in what appeared to be scenes of village life and hunting. The whole composition was edged in birds.

"What do those mean?" she said.

Henry came to take a look.

"As I understand it, they represent *iya*, mothers whose protection the king must have if he is to rule," he said.

"They're quite innocent-looking to have such power," she said. "They're shaped like a thrasher. Well, with a shorter tail."

"They're happy right now," Henry said, smiling. "They can turn into powerful night birds, witches, who go on the prowl, punishing anyone who steps out of line. I hope you don't turn into one."

"Why are women always the witches?" she said, not sharing his humor.

"Oh, it's not so bad," he said. "The Yoruba associate women's child-bearing with great mystery, something like metamorphosis. Then they make it into magic. If women can produce children, why not turn into birds? Even the men are dedicated to a fertility goddess. Simple ignorance."

Emma was not accustomed to casual speech about the private capacities of a woman's body, and her cheeks burned. By the time they met Kunrumi, she was feeling deflated. Next to the tusks, the warrior seemed small, wearing a rather insignificant robe. But his eyes were bright and she could see he had brains.

When they arrived home, Emma remembered Duro had the evening off. "I need to rest," she said, and soon she was asleep on the bed. She slept into evening and woke to find Henry had made dinner like a picnic, mats spread before the tin lantern in the parlor. It was much more pleasant than real camping, Emma thought. After clearing the dishes, Henry reclined, lantern light spilling around him. Soon he was snoring. Emma gathered her writing box. She was alert from her rest and it seemed a good time to make a record in her diary. *I wonder what it is like to grow up in this country, to become a woman here. It seems so far from me. The king's wife, for example. Did she wish for her life? Does she enjoy it?* Emma glanced at Henry, one arm thrown over his head, the other resting on his abdomen, rising and falling with his breath. It was so perplexing, these many wives with one husband. Emma wanted to write about *that*, but she closed the journal.

In a while, she threw a light shawl across Henry's shoulders and found her way to bed, but she lay awake and felt herself still moving. The images and smells of the past weeks, walking and canoeing, the constant noise and talk, the unpacking and greeting, the white birds turning to ravens, ran through her in waves. In her mind she walked through all the rooms of her Georgia home and counted everything she remembered. Once she woke in the night to think on Uncle Eli's old arrangements hung from his ceiling. They must have been his private magic, like the king's birds, but she could not hold it against him. If anything, she was happy with herself, as if she had been tasked with solving a great puzzle and had found one piece that fit.

It was dawning on Emma that she found Yoruba men more approachable than the women. The men knew some English and dressed reasonably and had things to talk about. Daily she overheard them with Henry discussing theology, the town's history, the trade routes. A great deal of labor devolved upon the women, who took care of babies as they sold their goods and had already been out that morning to the farm, harvesting before they came into town carrying enormous loads on their heads, loads that seemed more likely for a horse. Then they were grinding corn in their great pestles. They cooked even in the market, making up things to sell. And yet they must return home to cook for their husbands. Surely, Emma thought, she must turn her heart in sympathy toward them as she had the girl-wife who gave her the milky beads. Emma made a note in the red journal. *I must reach the women and not only the children, for in every way, the mothers make the children.* She pulled out a hair comb and used it to scratch her scalp. It was a good commitment, but she knew her heart wasn't yet in it.

A month after their arrival, there was no letup in the press of people. Morning to night, folks showed up to watch most anything they did. At mealtime, children's faces filled the windows. One afternoon Emma looked out to see a group of all sorts, young and old, men and women, pointing to her unmentionables on the line. She bolted out the door, down the step, and right into their midst.

"Why are you here?" she said. "This is my own yard. You must leave. Go. Go." She tried to shoo them, but they barely parted. A young man made a comment and the whole group laughed. She recognized no one. A woman ran her hand up and down Emma's corset. She might as well have raised her private garments on a flagpole. She swatted at the woman's hand and hit it lightly. Everything stopped. The woman looked first at her hand, and then she looked at Emma and then at her companions as if she had just been spat upon. The fun was over.

"Ah, ah," an older man said and shook his head.

It was all wrong. They had intruded upon her and now they acted as if she were the criminal.

"Mama," Emma said in the African way, hoping to make amends with the woman. But the lady was leaving, her face set.

Henry came into the house that evening, his face grim. "The news in town," he said, "is the *oyinbo* woman strikes like a cat. Would you like to tell me what happened, Mrs. Bowman?"

Emma stiffened at the formal address. She relayed the story, the intrusion upon her things, her dismay, the slight reprimand. "Just the slightest touch," she said, "like a feather." Henry continued to look at her, his eyes going a little funny. "I've had just about enough of being a circus attraction," she continued, dismayed at his look. "Must they forever be gaping at me? Would you stop them if they came into the house and ran through the wardrobe?"

"Has anyone come into the house and run through the wardrobe?"

"No," she said.

"Has anyone hit you?"

"No," she said.

"You know what will be next?" he said. "They'll make you into a witch. It's a very fine line you walk. We're already thought by many to be unnatural."

"Henry," she said, pleading, a great longing in her for him to understand. She began to cry but he seemed only sterner, as if she were waging unfair battle.

"This is a black world. You are the visitor. Do you understand? You are in their yard."

"Yes. We are guests. Well, I don't go gawking at my guests day and night as they do." She wiped her tears. "Moreover, dear husband, you don't have such things as I have to hang on the line, to dry properly, as you say." Her voice rose. She flung her hands out. "As you say over and over: 'Emma, be certain your clothes are fully dry. You'll be ill if they aren't.' You!" She stopped for a moment. "You insisted I hang my private things in the backyard. In case you did not learn it in your cavalry or your first mission or wherever else you've been, a woman must have some privacy."

His shoulders sank a little and she thought she had gotten through. Indeed, she felt triumphant with her speech.

"Wife," he said, "you must learn to distinguish between genuine harm and your perception of it. You have not been wronged. Your pride is wounded. The only healing for it is humility. Go to the woman you struck and apologize."

"I won't."

"You will."

She felt for a moment that indeed this man was larger than her father, and something trembled in her for what it might mean. Alone later, she lifted the prism from the shelf where she had set it and touched its cool planes to her cheek. In the morning, she and Duro sought the woman's house to apologize. The burden of waiting was worse than the trial. But the lady had gone to her farm and would not be back for days, so Emma had humiliation and the trial still before her.

Fewer people stopped by. Emma spent more time with her cook. His build was average, his head so fine and neat from the back you would mistake him for a younger man. But his face showed maturity, creases across the forehead, a few gray hairs at his temple, and one front tooth missing. His hands were his best feature, well proportioned with neat nails. He was delicate in his work. Emma loved the smell of frying cassava flour, or *gari*, that he prepared for himself. She was grateful he did not seem to bear her a grudge for hitting the woman. Perhaps he felt they were now equals, and she didn't mind sitting at the outdoor kitchen with him, making hoecakes. Henry had told her the cook had lost three wives to illness. His numerous children were grown and living in the village with his mother, where they kept up the family farm.

"I wish I had an orange," she said one afternoon, sitting with him. The next morning, Duro was gone out and he did not return until afternoon. He was holding a single green orange.

"The only one I can find mah," he said.

"Thank you," she said, deeply touched.

Henry came in as Emma was taking down her hair, her bodice already loose at the neck. He put his hands on the curve of her hips. "I was too hard on you," he said. "I only wish for us to do well."

"I used to dream about your hand on the letters you wrote to me."

"Let me trace a word here."

In her heart, even in the intimate act, Emma knew she *would* seek to love as Jesus loved, whose clothes were stripped from him and who wore a crown of thorns and was whipped and cursed and spat upon and nailed to a cross and yet he blessed them.

Days later she went to market with Duro, and when she returned she saw Henry erecting a bamboo-and-thatch enclosure in the yard. It was a private drying line for her private things. She said nothing and neither did he, but her heart was full as a river in rains. She took up her writing box and made a record in her journal: *a trial survived; happiness returns.* Placing the red book back in the box, she saw Uncle Eli's letter opener. *I wonder how he fares*, she thought, and then closed the lid because she did not wish to disturb her happiness.

.   .   .

AFTER IT HAPPENED, Emma made a careful record in her journal.

I sketch this incident for its illumination of native custom and my own learning:

"She is here mah, the woman you are calling on." That was Duro, our cook.

I hardly recognized the woman I had so lightly tapped. She wore a fine dress of blue fabric and an ivory-colored headdress fringed in cowries.

I must have said something under my breath. "Lands sakes!" I invited her in.

"Ko si nkan kan," she said, meaning "You are welcome."

"E se," I said, meaning "Thank you," but taken aback. Would not I be the one welcoming her?

She gave me her name, Tela. I had not remembered her being so robust and then I saw it was the large headdress she was wearing. Her skin was a smooth brown, her eyes bright, and her smile revealed the most beautiful teeth.

I hurried my apology in my best Yoruba. "I'm sorry I hurt you." I asked Duro to be certain she understood. "Tell her I beg she not be angry," I said.

Tela proceeded to gather my hands and shake them gently, waving them as she talked at some length. According to Duro, the proclamation all came down to "It is fine."

"Joko," I said to her, "Have a seat." I instructed Duro to bring punch. We sat for some while looking through the front window, she reaching out at intervals to claim my hand again. As a parting gift, I gave Tela a small collapsible fan. Watching as she walked off, I saw she had already put it to use.

She won me over and I thought it would take God's doing to turn my heart toward the women. How strange a world I have entered.

On days when Emma did not have time to make a record in the journal, she nevertheless opened the writing box and drew in its scent of oil and lemon. The organization of the box, with a place for everything, the cool serenity of the glazed ink pot: These were elements mysterious and comprehensible, a reassurance of her being, like a prayer. And then she closed the lid and carried the box back to its resting place.

ONE MORNING IN June, Emma took up scissors to cut fabric for a new dress and experienced a rush of nausea. Not again, she thought, remembering her illness at sea. She was queasy all morning but with neither chills nor fever. Still she lay down and closed her eyes. Over and again, the thin pink light cast on the ship's wall came to mind, and she thought she would be very sick if she kept returning to it. There was drumming and she focused on that.

"Don't you know?" Henry said, finding her in bed.

"Know what?"

"A child."

She looked hard out the window beyond him. True, her last bleeding had been a trickle. She had attributed the small show to strain. But then, musing back through May to April, she felt with a certainty her husband was right. She was aghast. Certainly, she had meant to do something first, establish herself in her work. It seemed a betrayal of her body to be so vulnerable. Emma believed she was ready to enter the African world fully. Why, she might eat with her bare hands, as Henry did, rolling *fufu* balls to dip into soup. Her idea of her stately self was suddenly replaced with Catherine's navel stuck out in the last month before birth.

"The child is only the briefest mite," Henry said, sitting beside her. "Hardly two months. You'll be over the sickness soon." His eyes shone with something she had never seen before.

"I hadn't known," she said. "Had you?"

"I suspected," he said, "but was afraid to hope. I never thought"—his voice gave, and he waited for his composure—"to be a father," he finished.

She pulled herself up and leaned into his chest, claiming his shirt around her face as she breathed him in.

"I might die," she said, suddenly pushing away from him, searching his face.

"You won't die," he said, smoothing her hair. Then he made her a plate of hominy and sat in bed with her as she ate.

The rains continued with the early pregnancy, thunder sounding in the distance, then a broad fan of wind, clouds gathering in huge gray billows, the sound of the deluge coming over the hills, and then in an instant it hit like a waterfall, rain descending in curtains, the sound now a solid roar. Emma was ill with the fever once and knew that Henry feared losing the baby, but she came through and set about letting her dresses out. Two weeks later, Henry took a bad cold. It went into fever so that he pitched in the bed and had to call Duro to hold him. Henry complained of his spleen, what he called his "old ailment," and took tinctures of laudanum to calm his system. "It's the damp oppressive weather," he said, explaining why the illness was worse than on ship. "It's more than just malaria." When he could sit for a stretch in bed, he worked on his sermons and wrote letters. Emma considered a letter to her family, but there were too many demands, and she feared telling them about a child she might lose before its birth. Then Henry was well enough to recommence preaching in the yard. He called it *declaiming*. Emma thanked God that they took turns in illness so one could tend the other, and she prayed Henry would be well when her time came.

She loved to hear her husband preach. He looked so fine in his trousers and white shirt, the sleeves turned up, his Bible open. *Jesus tells us there are two commandments: Love God and love one another.* Of course, no Yoruba disagreed with this, as they all believed in God and they all loved their brothers. *But mind you*, Henry continued, *loving one another includes your enemy.* This was where the declaiming came in. For loving an enemy was not so natural a concept. The more the men contested the point with him, the more fervently Henry argued the other side. *We must slay our enemy*, he would say finally, *but only with the sword of the Spirit which is Love.* Victory was his, for the men loved more than anything a good turn of phrase.

As weeks passed and her new shape emerged, folks exclaimed their greeting to Emma. "Ah, Mama," they said, "we salute you." She thought perhaps it was better to be with child in Africa than in Georgia. There was a greatness in it. Then she wished mightily for her mother and sister, Catherine. How dear it would be to share tea, to talk, to plan the infant's clothes. In the cooler month of August, she calculated she was midway and selected two dresses to enlarge with extra fabric at the seams.

Emma walked into the bedroom just in time to see a large snake wending its way across the bed. In an instant, she fled, calling the cook.

Moments later the dead cobra was laid out on the veranda, the gunmetal gray body eight feet if it was an inch. "Thank you, Duro," she said, still shaking, examining the snake's slick head neatly chopped from the body, the body smashed in places where Duro had hit it with a stick. "What would I do without you?"

"A spitting snake," Duro said, "hitting the eye."

"You must be able to protect yourself," Henry said when he saw it. It seemed he meant against more than snakes, though she couldn't imagine anything worse. "We'll go shooting. I should have taught you before." He seemed humbled. With Duro's help, he spent the rest of the day searching out any break in the house by which the serpent might have entered. Emma didn't believe she would ever sleep again and insisted Henry investigate every inch of the room for several nights before she would enter.

They went out on a Friday, the two older boys from her school and Duro, and, of course, a crowd of neighbors, including Tela and two of her women friends, Henry bearing the rifle, though many offered to lend him a hand. Emma thought it might be good for the women to see how she could try something that only men were thought to do. Native melons were set all in a row on a stretch of abandoned wall. Henry demonstrated first. He missed the first pawpaw but ripped the second. There was huge clapping from the crowd, and a few more folks arrived for the show.

"Now I'll teach you to load," Henry said.

"I'm nervous," she whispered, "with all these people."

"Pay attention to me," her husband said. "Take those gloves off." He had the rifle, barrel up, and handed it to her. "You can rest the stock on the ground. Keep your face clear of the muzzle."

She took the barrel in her fist.

"Take the powder horn," he said. "When you push the measure, it releases just the right amount."

This precision of instruments Emma found rather delightful.

"Now," Henry said, taking the horn from her, "the patch. It's already greased. Ram it in with the tamper. It holds the powder in place. Are you listening?"

"Yes," she said, looking up into his eyes.

"If you're in a great hurry, you don't have to use the patch. It's an extra step. But it keeps the barrel clean and you always pack it in if you're going to travel with your weapon loaded."

"Yes," she said, breaking from his eyes, looking at the barrel in her fist, taking up the patch, and running it in.

"Now," he said, "you're ready for the ball. It fits snug and you have to ram it."

She took the ball from his palm. Emma thought she would soon manage this quite well.

"Last is the cap," Henry said. "You want to station the firearm on this hip like so, to hold it steady."

She did.

"Pull back the hammer with your thumb. The cap fits right here over the nipple."

Emma stared hard at the rifle. Henry had used that word but not like this. She let out a deep breath. Then she did just as he had demonstrated.

"You can lay the hammer down easy and travel with a rifle that way," Henry said, "or keep it in the house, just so. Then you're ready. But if you drop your firearm, it's liable to go off."

Emma held the rifle alternately with one hand, then the other, drying her damp palms against her skirt.

"I'm ready," she said.

"Yes," Henry said. "Now raise the rifle and place the butt plate against your shoulder; lean your head in."

Emma gazed at Henry. He moved around behind her and encircled her arms with his, pressing her head gently with his own.

"Now close one eye and use that bead at the end of the barrel to sight your target. Never pull back the hammer until you're ready to shoot. Then pull the trigger."

He stepped away from her.

Emma could have sworn she saw the side of the pawpaw fly before she heard the rifle's report. The women brought their skirts to their mouths to hold a laugh, and the boys and men clapped and cried out. Emma's ears buzzed.

"Oh," she said. "Henry! Mr. Bowman!" Her hands thrummed; the vibration went all through her. She was thrilled with her success. "Let me try again," she said.

This time she managed the steps with no assistance. The people's talk was no matter. She was completely absorbed.

"Here I go," she announced.

But she missed the second melon.

"Never mind," she said. "I want to try again." She didn't look at Henry but proceeded to load again. She had not experienced such physical capacity since Georgia. Her third and fourth shots found their mark. She meant to continue, but she caught Henry's eye. An odd half smile crossed his face, his brows were furrowed, and he had one hand over his midsection.

"Are you all right?" she rushed, a sudden wild thought that she had shot him.

"Not as right as you," he said.

"You take another turn, husband," she said, feeling an enormous joy in their rightness together.

The boys set up more melons, taking time to stuff blown bits into their mouths. Tela took Emma's hand and held it with both of hers and swung it as if half the gain was hers. Henry found a greater distance this time, missing the first shot and then hitting three melons in a row. The assembly was enjoying itself now. A man broke a kola nut and shared it around with the men. Emma thought Henry hesitated when she reached again for the rifle. But she wanted more practice. She made the first, missed twice, and made the last.

"I do feel we did well," she said on the walk home.

"It's the first shot you need to make," Henry said, and she saw he was unhappy with how he'd done.

At dinner, he ate little.

"Are you feeling ill?" she said.

"I hope not," he said.

The following day Henry seemed withdrawn but took his usual walk into town to preach morning and afternoon. Two Mohamedan men escorted him home, and Emma thought this would enliven him. They were his greatest challenge and his greatest desire, and for three reasons she could tell. One, they were almost impossible to persuade on religious matters, and Henry loved debate. Two, he believed they worked on the minds of the heathen kings, persuading them against Christian missionaries. Unless some Mohamedans were converted, the road north would never open. Finally, she believed he thought of them as the Egyptians, a mysterious race of Africans, and he desired some knowledge from them. But Henry did not mention the men at supper. Emma hated to think her husband might be unhappy over her good show with the firearm, but she could find no other cause. Best to maintain her own equilibrium.

Monday morning she took up copying some of the vocabulary words he had asked her to inscribe into clean manuscript. This work went well, and that afternoon she met her students as usual, along with Tela, who always claimed Emma's hands and seemed to bring a different child each time. For the first time, Emma pulled out the Yoruba book of ABC, which included brief teachings on the gospel. She had feared everyone would grab for it, but one of the boys took control, making everyone line up by height, and then she gave each a chance to hold the book, down to a toddler who could barely stand. Emma forgot all about Henry and served her young guests a pan of corn bread. She hugged each one before sending them home.

In the evening she spoke freely about the school. Henry listened and then clasped his hands together, turning them out as a man will do to crack his knuckles. He stroked his chin, pulled out his handkerchief, and wiped his forehead. Then he ran his fingers through his hair.

"My word, Henry," she finally said. "What is it? You've been sour for days now. Nothing pleases you."

He said nothing, and they sat in tight silence. The baby moved. Here was a great miracle, but Henry was so engaged in wounded pride he would rob them of joy. Hadn't he required her to give up pride? Did not the same apply to husbands?

"You're sour because I did well with the rifle," she said finally. "I thought you liked my capacities. Why are you against them now?"

His lips seemed thin and when he opened his mouth, it was with a click, as if he had been forced. She expected a remark against her infemininity. He would quote Paul on women submitting themselves to their husbands. At the moment, Paul did not inspire her.

"We're short on funds," he said at last. His whole body seemed to constrict. For the first time, she thought he looked his age.

"What do you mean?" she said. She knew their supply of packaged goods was late; they had received letters but once. Still Henry had shared their accounts in Lagos, only three months back. They had enough to get them through the year and into January. A full third of their loads coming off ship had been cowries traded for in Accra, enough African money to last a good while. In addition, hadn't Henry told her he had personal money in European coinage? She had trusted him to keep the large view while she tended her corner of the budget. A splintering fright filled her heart, and she wanted it to go away immediately. "How are we short?" she said when Henry didn't speak. "We've followed our plan."

"There have been expenses. It seemed best not to worry you—with the baby. But if you're going to feed the multitude, you may as well know."

How smallish of him! Feeding the multitude. "I can't imagine a pan of corn bread has put us back," she said.

"I thought you wanted to know," he said.

"Yes, but putting it on me for giving crumbs to children."

"Every bit counts," he said.

"Perhaps you could enlighten me to the additional expenses," she said. The room was hot, and she got up to push the shutters open.

"You'll be sick with the evening damp," he said, and got up just as quickly to close them.

"You've worried me plenty enough now," she said, careless in her language.

"For one thing, I paid a man to clear the field and prepare the shooting lesson."

"Oh, Henry, that can't have cost more than two strings. Certainly our personal account has not been expended." She said this more as a question than a declarative.

"If you don't want to hear, I don't know why you asked. Perhaps when you've cooled down," he said. "I'm going out to smoke."

As soon as he left, Emma took up her sewing. She should have been in charge of their funds. She knew how to keep books! After a while, she pulled out the diary, making a record she hoped someone might read: *feelings deeply wounded.* But as she closed the box, light struck the scallop on the lid; she remembered how in making the gift, Henry had seen into her heart. She considered going to him on the veranda. But he would not yield, not this soon. She must learn to see into *his* heart. She pulled the journal back out and blackened the line she had written. She prayed. "Let me grow in light and grace. Make me a solace to my husband. Bring us into your perfect harmony." She snuffed the light, then lay with her hands crossed over her chest, listening to the drums, feeling the rise and fall of her breath.

· 8 ·

The Wasp

Henry made a selection of Yoruba words to send to the Smithsonian, along with a proposal for the grammar section of the book. He sealed the package before beginning a letter to the general secretary of the mission board.

Sept. 12, 1853

Dear Brother Taylor,

Greetings again from Ijaye in Yoruba land. We are in the rains here. It's a fine thing on a Sunday morning to gather in the chapel as the clouds open and the people's voices rise in thanksgiving. I wish there were a way I could capture the sound so that you might hear it.

The work progresses well. I preach at least twice a day. People gather in droves, in my own yard and in town. There has been no recent fighting in the country to distract their attention. As I speak of Jesus, I see the spark of the gospel in many a face.

We have been back in this country for nearly five months and we have received only one packet of letters. You can imagine how hard this is on my wife. I have made do on a single payment in addition to what we brought with us. If we do not receive something soon, we will

be down to cassava flour. The trip upcountry cost double what I
imagined. On the chance that my earlier letter did not make
Richmond, I enclose again an itemized account.

Since I last wrote, I have been fighting illness, on one occasion
shaking so violently my wife and cook must hold me. The fever
inevitably deranges my spleen and liver. I might welcome such
tribulation as a lesson in discipleship, but it is too much for a
woman to bear.

Isn't there another man who can come help us? My heart bleeds for
the multitude of this country who have yet to hear the gospel. Two is
better than one, and a threefold cord is not easily broken. If any
brethren in Georgia . . .

Henry paused. He recalled that poor man in Texas, the one whose
leg he sawed off. The whole panorama of Indian slaughter, fighting
Mexicans. Women whose names he never bothered to know. His sin-
ful years plagued him like the devil.

Emma entered the house. He slid the paper under his blotter. She
went out again, but he left the letter where it was. Maybe he wished
she had been less handy with the rifle. But that outing was the least
of his concerns. Nor was it finances that worried him most, though he
had calculated too close to his costs as a single man. Rather it was his
health. Just after the wedding, his nerves seemed to worsen. He'd had
to slip away and take care of himself on the train, drinking a whiskey.
He hadn't thought how much he would feel the responsibility of a
wife. Perhaps he had been too quick in turning down Emma's father's
offer of land—it appalled him to think she might consider him a
blunderer. Then the sickness on ship and his spleen acting just as before. As glad as he was to think on a child, Emma's condition brought
an extra burden. It was a frightful lot: a wife with child in Africa, in a
town far from the next station, and he her doctor.

If he were sick again, the waking nightmares might return. What would his wife think, seeing him in such a state? It was one thing to contemplate in a Georgia garden a husband out of his head, quite another to confront his craze in an African town, far from family and friends.

In a thatch enclosure at the back of the kitchen, he washed in cold water. Midway through his toilet, he checked the area of his spleen. It protruded slightly, but it wasn't worse. Henry had enough medical training to be haunted by bulges. He was likewise troubled by breaks and erosions in the skin. This fear he transferred to cracks at the bottoms of houses, fissures in the earth, interstices anywhere indicating a breakdown. One of his toenails had developed a fungus, making it thick and yellowed on one side. He tried to keep it filed and neat and yet, viewed in a certain light and from the right angle, he could see into the nail as into a small catacomb.

Back at his desk, he felt more confident for the cleansing and finished the letter to Taylor. Henry turned his wedding band. He considered that his progress with Emma had been good; she was adaptable, if occasionally smug. For a moment he let himself remember her at night, the pale crescent of her collarbone, her arms winged back against the sheets. This point of charity helped him feel his mastery more keenly. Their time in bed was more than good; it was sublime, and the understanding that God had allowed him such a gift after his early sinning rekindled his conviction.

A map of the African country lay to his right, and he pulled it to the fore of the desk. With Lagos now under British rule, the mission could assume a permanent office in the port city. The next station would be Abeokuta, where the Anglican mission was strong. It was a great town to be sure, almost glorious, nestled in rocky cliffs, rising and falling in stony waves. A green missionary could stay there, maintaining a church and serving as a relay station for those farther inland. Next was Ijaye, his present residence. If only another man could be sent. After Ijaye came Ogbomoso; he had scouted the town on his last tour. The altitude was higher, the land drier. It was a perfect location for his next move, and the king was eager for a white man. Henry kept his pencil aloft, taking care not to damage the map. After Ogbomoso came Ilorin, a true Mohamedan town. The first time he had seen the turbaned men in flowing robes mounted on their gaily caparisoned steeds, his heart had run with the eagerness of love. Not as one loved women but as one loved the greatness of the earth. The men seemed purely themselves like the horses they rode. If only he could reach them.

Something in Henry pressed forward, as if motion itself might yield the miracle of contentment he had sought as far back as he could remember.

A wasp came into the room, and Henry watched its lazy spin. It had been building a nest for two weeks but accomplished little. Emma had asked why he allowed the thing. "I want to see how long it takes," he said. He was beginning to believe the wasp might never finish. Amazing how even the insects slowed in the heat. "You carry on," he said to it. "Let me see what you've done by tomorrow." Henry touched up his hair in the manner he liked and found his hat. Rev. Moore was due to return any day. The fellow was a bit odd, a confirmed bachelor, his station a mile's distance from Henry's house, uphill, through town, and down the other side. He might as well walk over and see if Moore's servant had the house in order.

The man had arrived the evening before. "Why didn't you send someone to alert me?" Henry said.

"No need. I was just getting ready to walk in your direction," Moore said.

There was no mail from home, only a note from David and Anna Hathaway, Anglican missionaries in Ibadan, another large town in the region. Moore had stayed with them on his way up. Twice before, Anna had sent gifts to Emma by carrier. There were newspapers from England, but neither payment nor supplies from the board in Richmond.

Henry started home, feeling more tender toward his wife. He
wished he had a letter for her.

The fellow nearly ran into him. "*Wahala*," he cried, "trouble—at
the town gate."

From twenty yards back, Henry could see how oddly the body lay.
Closer by, he recognized the young man who had asked for baptism
some weeks ago. A medallion of blood pooled at his head. His confed-
erates quickly related the story. A hunt. The lad was on the lookout in
a tree; a branch snapped and he had fallen, hitting his head on a rock.
The mother was sent for. Henry knelt beside him. "Can you hear me?"
Henry said.

"Yes, master." The fellow's mouth smelled like broken twigs.

"Do you believe that Jesus is the true Lord, the Son of God, the
only Redeemer, who died to save you and rose on the third day?"

"Yes sah." Barely a whisper.

Henry ordered someone to find water.

"By the grace of God you are saved," he said to the young man with
the broken head.

The hunter seized, then relaxed.

"Because you desire it, I will baptize you," Henry said, his hands
on the fellow's still heart. An African lament began, the down tempo
of men, the high trills of women. The young man's eyes never opened,
so there was no need to close them. When a woman brought water,
Henry poured it on the lad's forehead and kissed him.

The incident troubled Henry, and he spent the afternoon outside
the town, walking through farms and saluting the folks he found
along his path. He came upon a baobab grove of three trees, decorated
with magic trifles and a diviner "on seat" in a little mud house for
anyone who came by needing his fortune told. In the shadow of the
trees, Henry told himself that the death of a Christian believer was
cause for celebration, but still he trembled, thinking on the young
man's broken head. Finally he shook himself up. "What a fool I have

been," he muttered, "fretting on matters small as grocery money when men are dying about me." Thinking so, he experienced that strange excitement that came with fighting, desire and fear together. Back at the house, he added a *p.s.* in his letter to Taylor: *Wife with child.* A reliable man would carry it to Abeokuta; the letter would be in Lagos in five days and might arrive in Richmond by the end of the month. After sealing the envelope, he examined the wasp's nest. "Not one bit of progress," he said aloud. The experiment was over. He took a stick and knocked it down.

Midafternoon, Henry talked with two of his churchmen about dividing the town into sections for preaching. Privately, he considered his wife, how through preoccupation with her he had let himself weaken. He embellished this train of thought. Emma was overindulged. He had become distracted by baser whims. They must resubmit themselves to their calling, and being husband and minister, he must lead. This thought once gained shone clear as a glorious rainbow.

After supper, he offered Emma the newspapers and the letter from the Hathaways. When it seemed she might speak, he moved ahead of her, reporting the young man's death. Even then, he did not allow himself to show feeling and made little room for her to express sympathy. His voice carried forward like a locomotive at set speed.

"I have let myself tarry like that wasp," he said. "Our true home is not this house but the church, and our task is to build up the kingdom. We will spend more time in prayer. In the afternoons when it is too hot for you to be out-of-doors, you will copy words into the manuscript for the vocabulary. With concerted effort, we might send the whole off before the baby arrives."

Emma looked at him with large eyes, her hand on her belly. He remembered she had already been doing the copying. How could he have forgotten? Well, she could do more.

"Do you understand me," he said.

"Yes," she said.

He thought he had gained enough ground and patted her hand. "Invite Moore to dinner."

"Yes," she said.

Henry kept to himself in the bed. The next morning he was up before daybreak, took a cold breakfast alone, and when Duro arrived, left word for Emma that he would not be home for dinner. He preached all through the town, finally arriving at the night market, where he ended with the parable of the talents and the servant who buried his when he might have invested for God. Duro was waiting on the piazza with a lantern, a shower of light escaping the tin globe. "Thank you," Henry said. "You may go to bed." The man said nothing, but turned, and Henry thought: *He's hers now.*

He kept this pace for two weeks. He was grateful Moore was back. The British missionary dined with them regularly. Henry introduced topics to draw Emma to converse with the reverend and let his mind dwell on his own work. His stamina was good, and the crowds he drew were lively. He was sure his health was improving. Wouldn't it be so, God rewarding him for the renewal of his commitment? Their little chapel swelled to overflowing, crippled men coming in to sit on mats, just as in the New Testament. Emma led the choir, and he thought she seemed content enough, expecting the baby. The rest of the congregation joined in on the chorus, with all sorts of improvisation. Women in the front began to dance, their arm bracelets adding to the general pitch of music. Even some birds flew in and circled around. Henry thought he had gotten the balance of things in goodly order.

Many Things in Her Heart

*One of the mysteries of the spiritual life is how we learn the depth of
an experience only as it befalls us. I am confident enough now that
I may write to share the news. I will bear a child. Four months hence.
But what I refer to above is this. I had little awareness of what you
felt when you were the same and now that I wish for your counsel,
I find myself far from your side.*

—EMMA TO CATHERINE, IJAYE, 1853

EMMA DISCOVERED LINES on her skin. The dry season had come, a silent stalker, and little by little green grasses browned, lower branches in palms grayed like tree moss in South Carolina, and dust rose in the streets. Henry had turned to eating African foods, cassava and native sauce and *akara*, the Yoruba bean cakes. It might have been a kindness, Emma considered, letting her enjoy corn pudding and biscuits—if only he didn't lean so over the bowl in sopping up the soup. He withheld himself. Her feelings were hurt, and out of that hurt she made a tighter circle with her baby. Yet it was still fine to see her husband so diligent and commanding. His speech was far more elegant than his African eating habits, and she enjoyed the attention he drew in the town. She had longed for guidance, and Henry was offering it. But then she remembered how he blamed her for their pinched finances. She read her Bible and tried to pray. The hedgerow around the compound gave small yellow trumpet flowers, and she collected these in a vase. Then she would see some ignoble thing in the town—someone flogging a child in public—and it would set her back. Another turn of her mind and she would consider how adult Negroes were beaten in her own country. Had she thought it would be easy to follow Christ in any land? Many came to church but there were no converts, even after all of Henry's time here. In the afternoon—her schoolchildren and Tela gone for hours, Duro not back from market, and Henry not expected for hours—Emma doubted she could endure another five minutes. In such a dolorous mood, she had no power to write, nor pull out her sewing, nor even to worry about snakes. Her abdomen was large with the baby.

She was grateful for Rev. Moore. What an uncomplicated man he was next to her husband. After a while, she confided in him.

"My husband is powerfully devoted to preaching, several times a day," she said.

"You think perhaps overly so," he said.

"A body needs time for restoration," she said.

"Are you worried about him?"

"Why do you ask?" she said.

"He was quite ill before. I'm sure he's told you."

"Why, of course. Rev. Bowman told me everything before we married. He was completely candid." Emma remembered how she had wanted to ask Henry more when he proposed. But now she felt defensive on his behalf. "God uses us—imperfect vessels though we are. With Him all things are possible."

"Of course," Rev. Moore said.

They sat silent, Emma watching a bird with tail feathers a foot long perched on a swaying stalk outside the window. "Henry's commitment is so great," she said, her hands on her belly.

"Rev. Bowman is a driven man."

"That's a way to put it," she said, sighing deeply, letting go of her reserve. "I fear he forgets his basic needs. He's lost weight. He seems hardly to sleep."

"Ah," Moore said, looking into her. "You're lonely."

She smiled. "Of course I'm lonely. But soon I'll have the baby and plenty enough to keep me busy."

"What's your guess, a girl or a boy?"

"Oh, a boy certainly, for my husband."

She meant for herself: a boy to love.

One late afternoon, after a visit with Moore and alone in the house, Emma saw that Henry had Uncle Eli's carving and was using it as a rule for lining paper. It pleased her, and she almost believed she could hear the old man's voice: *I taught you how to see. Remember.* An illumination shone in her mind: Uncle Eli had spent his life far from the aid of family, far from home. Surely she could endure.

By November, the grass was so brittle it broke beneath Emma's feet like the carcasses of bugs. Lizards clustered as high as possible on the outer walls of the house. The heat was fierce. Her belly sat ponderous on her lap and she developed a skin rash. Henry slept on the piazza while Emma stretched herself across the bed, lying on her back. Occasionally she woke to Henry slapping at a mosquito, and she turned over. In the morning she sat up thinking of muslin. She made a simple light dress and was much relieved by its airiness. *I suppose if the disciples had been women, we might have heard more about ordinary life*, she wrote in her journal. *Such as how to keep cool and refreshed in travel and free of illness.* Well, she thought, women would have talked about having babies, or how not to. But that wasn't something to write.

Then Henry took sick again. Emma was sure it was from sleeping in the open. She knew the illness now, and it was a bad case: vomiting, chills, heat, and fever. Moore insisted on helping her. "Look at your condition. You must not be alone." He moved into the guest room. They treated Henry with laudanum and wine mixed with quinine, though Henry fought the quinine. When the fever broke, Emma took broth to his bedside.

"Henry," she said.

"Why have you painted your face?" he said, gazing at her.

"I have not," she said, touching her cheek with her free hand.

"Something is wrong," he said. "I don't like it."

"Henry, what do you mean?" She tried to smile.

"The colors," he said.

She set the bowl aside. "I will send Rev. Moore to help you," she said.

Midway down the hall, she heard her own thin wail. A sob tore out behind it. And another. She could not stop, even when Moore caught her up. "He's seeing things," she managed finally. "Oh my Lord."

"Here, here," Moore said. "I'll take care of him."

Emma counted up to one hundred and back, over and over.

Poor Duro, she thought, observing the cook in the doorway as she and Moore shared an evening meal. *He's worried about us, and for himself.* An intense sympathy stirred within her.

"You may rest for the night," she said. *O daa ro.*

"Yes mah. Good night mah."

She and Moore retired to the parlor. She took the chair next to her writing box. Soon she was running her finger along the groove, then resting her hand on the scallop.

"Emma," he said after a bit, "this thing with Henry."

"Yes?" Her finger again ran along the groove.

"We pray for the best."

"Yes, we pray for the best." She opened the box, turning her face from Moore. *In my heart a seal . . .*

"However."

What an unpleasant word.

"It sometimes happens with the malaria," he continued, "that a person can be momentarily broken by it, someone who has seemed perfectly stable before. The spleen condition seems to come with it but does not appear to be its cause."

Emma closed the box.

"You may be comforted," Moore said.

I am not comforted, Emma thought.

"To know I've seen others in this state. Most come back to themselves. Even this evening Henry is much improved. Try to keep him on the quinine."

"I do. He spits it out," she said.

Unable to sleep, Emma sat in the rocking chair Moore had lent her. "We live in God," she whispered over and over, in time with her rocking and the drums far in the distance.

In her journal, Emma sought to make sense of the African illness: *Fever returned. My dear husband suffers much with his spleen even when the illness retreats. Nervousness a contributing factor? And what of me? Will I lose myself? What of the baby?* Her hand shook and she had to stop. When her courage returned, she took some pages and recreated the calendar of their illnesses, beginning with Henry at Bathurst. It seemed evident that her sickness followed the weather, but with Henry, the causes were harder to track. The dry season was not a time to take ill, at least not until December when the harmattan came—that season when sands from the Sahara blew south and evenings could cool of a sudden and bring on a chill. She recollected Henry's activities. If she pressed her evidence, she thought she would find a code. At Bathurst, he had stayed late on shore and been overly stimulated for several days. This time, he had begun his schedule of preaching before dawn and into the night. At times his pace seemed frantic. In his illness, he resisted the bitter quinine and took laudanum or whiskey instead. Then at times the derangement. She kept this evidence beneath her journal in the writing box.

"You mustn't worry so much," Henry said the evening Moore left, declaring his fellow minister sufficiently well. "I always come out. It's only I'm too ambitious, pressing my will onto God's." She was not in full agreement, and he must have sensed it. "I'm only sorry for your sake," he said.

"If something happened to you, husband, I would die," she said. She lay down next to him, her back to his chest, her head on his arm. His other arm she pulled over her. "Sing," she said. He hummed a tune without words, the vibration of his chest a language of this country and themselves in it.

THE HEAT WAS like an iron. Emma's students' legs turned ashen with dust. A report came through the town that slave traders had attacked a neighboring town, taking several children. Drums sounded night and day. Henry walked about town and returned to report that the gates were fortified with soldiers. Herders brought their animals inside the city walls, and there was braying and bellowing all around. Henry seemed enlivened by the commotion. Emma napped in the day and woke to the dry rustle of wind through banana leaves.

Days she thought she would die if she did not have a letter from home. Someone out there thinking of her. She must receive that voice of assurance. She must. Or how would she know she existed? She tried to think on Mary, who pondered many things in her heart and who must have feared greatly, not for what she knew but for what she did not know, who must have felt at times she would collapse in on herself. When Henry looked more robust, she began to believe again in his strength and their power to endure. A woman wants fortitude in a man and will hold much evidence at bay to believe in him.

In anticipation of Christmas, Duro cut green branches from young trees near the creek and made a bouquet. Emma created white flowers from scraps of paper and hung them with thread from the ceiling. She meant them as snowflakes. But Christmas preparations were delayed. The baby came early instead. When Emma first saw the child, she looked at the loud pink thing and wondered whose it was.

"Your daughter," Henry said, who had delivered the infant, with Tela's help. The woman was beside Emma, patting her arm. "*E ku ise o* mah," she said. "Good work."

"Thank you," Emma said, looking at her friend, whose face now seemed always to have been in her memory.

After two days, Emma and Henry agreed to name the child Sarah: woman of beauty, admired even by God, and given an angel as protection. Such a tiny thing she was! Tela brought a small *shekere*, a beaded gourd, to serve as a rattle while Moore made a gift of a dainty silver cup. The church folks created a celebration in the yard, clapping and singing. The house filled with the sweet smell of roasting corn. Emma knew they would have preferred a boy, but any child at all must have been a great improvement over what they had known formerly, a minister without so much as a wife. Now Emma was an *iya*, a mother. In bed, using the lap desk, she wrote to her family in Georgia, and in the writing she was already anticipating a time when they would go home on leave and she would show off her African daughter.

· 10 ·

The Finest Head

I N THE COOL harmattan mornings, Henry wanted his wife. She said
she wasn't ready. "It's perfectly safe," he said.

"That's not how I mean it."

A few nights later he sought her in bed. He felt her arm stiffen,
and then she seemed to relax. Returning to his wife, he felt more
ownership of the child and that seemed a good outcome of their intimacy. Then he felt remorse, reflecting on his stinginess when he was
angry. What made him so desperate that he would punish Emma by
withdrawing from her? He gathered leaves from the lemon tree and
made her a sachet. He took Sarah for brief jaunts about the compound
as his wife dozed on the piazza. Henry understood now why Africans
so cherished their children. *No single man should come here*, he wrote
in a letter to the board on New Year's Day, 1854. *A missionary cannot
understand the culture without his own offspring. Children are the un-
derpinning of everything.* He looked to every detail of the little girl's
existence. "She does have the finest head I ever saw," he said to Emma.
"But she needs a new bonnet."

"I just finished sewing the one she's wearing," his wife said.

"But it's tight. It might limit her brain." He thought Emma looked
at him a little wearily. "I'll find a native woman to make one," he said.

Soon, Sarah was wearing a Yoruba blue bonnet with a long brim to shade her eyes. Emma found it amusing, and Henry thought whatever hurt she had felt about their physical relations had been resolved. Their little family was the greatest sweetness he had ever known. Looking into the infant's eyes, he renewed his vow to care for himself.

He got an idea to tear open a haversack and have it resewn so he could carry the child papoose fashion, only forward-turned against his chest so that Sarah could look out into the world. With an umbrella, he bore her around town. He began to imagine a contraption for carrying her on the horse. In the evenings, he spoke Yoruba to her, holding up objects in the lantern light and naming them: *osan* for orange, *iwe* for book.

They slept with the baby between them. For a while Henry forgot to preach; then he reproached himself. Look at what he had been given. One night he woke nervous and brittle. When the Sabbath came and he preached again, there was release, and he rested better.

Thrown Off by a Storm

A N UNSEASONABLE RAIN interrupted Emma's school one February morning, the children running out to bathe themselves. She gave up trying to gather them back to the piazza, relieved Tela of Sarah, and sent everyone home. Two weeks later, Sarah was fussy at midday. By dinner, she seemed in a chill. In the night, she developed a fever. Emma and Henry made a pallet on the dining table, wrapped the little girl in wet cloth, and kept vigil. Henry sang, *Hush, little baby, don't say a word, Papa's going to buy you a mockingbird.* His fine, melodious voice.

After the fever broke, they took turns holding Sarah and they prayed without ceasing. Finally, the child looked at Emma and held her gaze. "One two three four remember," she said, and kissed the infant's nose. In her journal, Emma wrote, *Let me remember my Creator with praise.*

At ten weeks, Sarah grasped and shook her African rattle in spasms of delight, sometimes hitting her own forehead. She squealed with happiness more than she cried. One Saturday Emma dressed the baby in a blue frock with white smocking and presented her to Henry, and they all together went into town under the umbrella. Several men wanted him to stop and drink palm wine, but happily for Emma, he declined.

"She'll have the smell of Yoruba land in her brain like we know pine sap," Henry said.

They returned home to find Duro roasting two *aparo*, a local game bird, for their dinner. *He must be grateful too*, Emma thought, *that we are all well.*

Later Emma believed her daughter might have started coughing Sunday, but they were greatly pressed with their congregation and a thanksgiving for the early rains. So it was only when Sarah stopped nursing on Monday that she noticed something wrong. The child's breathing became almost a drowning. By Tuesday, her stools were watery. The child was too small a thing for the tinctures they had. Moore suggested a remedy of honey with three drops of whiskey to help her breathing. Henry packed Emma's engorged breasts with green banana leaves and she held Sarah in the curve of her lap, her chest throbbing. She thought of the woman of Canaan who begged Jesus for help with a sick daughter. *Give us crumbs*, she prayed. The next morning, the dysentery stopped and Sarah searched Emma's chest. After the feeding, Emma lay her daughter in the cradle, going to attend her toilet. When she came back, she noticed the baby's dark hair across her cheek. She thought to brush it aside but stopped, holding her arms straight before her like a person beginning a dive.

"No," she said, severely. "You come back." She said it again, her taut arms beginning to tremble. "Now you come back." She pulled her hands in and squeezed them tight, not yet touching Sarah, whose lips were losing their color. "You come." Emma's knees went weak, and she had to think hard to keep from falling. "Come." She released her hands and lifted the baby. Sarah's head fell back strangely before Emma caught and straightened it. She trembled, lifting and jostling the infant. "Now you come back," she whispered.

She did not call Henry but sat and rocked Sarah. The muscle of her heart grew sore like her breasts, and then it became so heavy and large it seemed an independent thing, a rare and growing organism that would break her rib cage.

Within an hour of Henry's finding her so, women of the town arrived. They swept Emma's arms with their hands. "*E pele o*," they said over and over, sorry. It seemed they carried a general grief for all women, and their collective presence gave Emma a distance from her pain. She forgot about Henry as various women took her hands, caressing them. Baskets of food mounted at the door; gifts were laid in her lap. At some point Emma knew Henry must be preparing the baby for burial. She stood and oranges scattered across the floor.

"I'm so sorry," Henry said. Emma clutched his coat and they held each other. He had Sarah in a white dress.

"Why?" Emma said.

"You did nothing wrong," he said.

Emma felt her shoulders lift and fall, but she could not cry. When she pushed away from him at last, Henry's eyes had that funny look.

"What?" she said.

"It's my fault," he said.

"No. No. It's no one's fault. We must comfort one another," she said.

"I should have learned more about treating a child," he said.

"We have been with her together. You cannot blame yourself."

"I'm so sorry," he said again.

Perhaps, Emma imagined, if they never moved, if they only stood just so, holding each other, they might all three of them turn to stone and she would never have to feel again. But then a terrible thought obliterated everything. "She wasn't baptized," she cried, feeling her voice red in her throat. She pushed away from Henry and pounded her fists against his shoulders. "She wasn't baptized!"

He forced her arms down and pulled her back to him. "Shh," he said, "she's an angel now."

Emma felt herself turn liquid with terrible relief. "Are you sure?" she said.

"Yes. Her heart was in yours and yours is in God." He held her close, and she felt how bony his chest was. "I'll go to the man who carves veranda posts for the king," he said into her hair.

As Emma waited, women came and lay down in the yard and turned themselves in the dirt until their blue cloth shone copper. They cried with the high sharp sounds that birds might make if thrown off course by a storm. The yeasty smell of *gari* cooking on a nearby fire filled the air, and Emma thought that Africans knew better than anyone how to weep with those who weep. She wished she could lie with the women and roll in the dirt.

Henry came home with a small box, like a cabinet, adorned on the lid with a bas-relief of doves. Rev. Moore was with him. He had only just come back to town and heard the news. Emma felt strangely aloof seeing the small coffin and receiving her neighbor. Even when Sarah was composed in the interior, Emma thought she was more doll than daughter.

They buried Sarah in the chapel yard, making her the first occupant of the cemetery. Henry made the homily. *We do not grieve as those who have no hope, and yet we cannot help but grieve.*

Two days later Emma returned to her students. She knew they knew. Like their mothers, they caressed her arms and hands and even her cheeks, and finally she cried. She cried for four weeks. She believed she would die from her grief. Rev. Moore was less of a solace than she might have hoped, not that he didn't try. But Emma was no longer interested in books or music or having tea. When she and her husband held each other, it seemed they were lost people. Her only relief came in the mornings, sitting with Duro in the kitchen before full light as he prepared breakfast. Neither he nor she spoke, but Emma found his actions whole and rounded, the sounds and smells of cooking comforting. She thought of how Uncle Eli and Mittie Ann had discovered moments of life within their control as a way to bear their losses. Mittie Ann respooling her yarn. Uncle Eli's small carvings— they were his own, not made for any reason but to bring him ease. She carried the letter opener in her pocket for several days. In her journal, she made a brief record: *Our dearest earthly possession has taken flight. Sadness in the house.*

A month later, Emma believed she was strong enough to pack up the baby things. She stooped to place them in the bottom drawer of the wardrobe. But when she closed the drawer and looked up, the room and the world beyond the window made no sense to her. All was phantom. Her skin crawled. She lay back on the floor and rocked. *My God, my God, why hast Thou forsaken me?* "How have I sinned?" she cried. And in her innermost heart she wondered if there was a God.

"I'm sending you to visit the Hathaways in Ibadan," Henry insisted. "Moore is going down." Whether the journey was difficult or easy, Emma could hardly have said, but she knew it was a relief to her that the couple's marriage—lovely as it was—did not include children. From the Hathaways' front porch, Emma pondered the African women passing by. It might be that most of them had lost a child. But did they feel it as terribly as she did? Then she remembered how the women of Ijaye had mourned with her and was ashamed for her calculation. One night, Emma woke in a fright. She had dreamed of Sarah, but the baby was a growing girl. They were together at the stream down from the house in Ijaye. They were waiting for Henry— only Henry wasn't going to come. Everything was confused. Sarah held the silver cup from Moore and she kept filling it and letting the water go. A man appeared. He picked up Sarah and carried her away. Emma wakened herself with her own scream. Anna came running, and Emma told her the dream. "What do you suppose it means?"

"I don't know," she said.

"It was just as if she was stolen," Emma said.

In the morning she dressed and ate breakfast, then lay on a divan on the Hathaways' porch. Her heart was an open wound, her legs like lead.

Several days later Emma woke to the smell. Sweet and woodsy. By midday, they could see the haze on the horizon.

"Firing the land," Rev. Hathaway said. "The end of the dry season and there's little left to eat. The blaze drives out small animals. Boys and men with hunting sticks range around, waiting for supper to emerge. It's quite clever, really. Clears the farm of overgrowth. In a few weeks, they'll till the soil."

Sure enough, a few hours later small bands of hunters appeared along the road, nearly every one with some catch or other. Even birds, whose wings had been singed by the billowing blaze so that when they flew, they carried the fire until they fell into the arms of their captors.

There was something like a carnival about it, the way the men came in with their minor yet vital success: a cane-rat, a hare. The panorama, the little homecomings Emma imagined as the men met their wives with a gift of meat —it sent her heart toward Henry. She was ready to go home.

12

So Curious

Dear Mother,

This letter will go nowhere but into the fire, you having left this world twenty-six years ago—though it is but a twinkling of an eye in heaven. I wonder less now that you left us so early, remembering all the infants you buried. I do not believe I was much of a comfort to you.

My wife and I have lost our firstborn at three months. She was to me already a complete being—so curious, watching everything, quite amiable. I would never have believed I could love so deeply and for no cause except the child existed.

Emma finds the loss almost unbearable, and watching her grief, I am shattered. I sent her to stay with friends for a week in the hope that a change in atmosphere might improve her spirits. Now it's myself I worry about. I had thought in her absence to dispel the sadness by preaching, meeting up with the men in town. I have tried. But I seem more ghost than man. I have the heart for nothing. When I think on the child, my head turns cold as ice. I consider my own sinfulness. My abdomen seems torn with knives.

Why was the child given to us and taken so quickly away? God does not act spitefully but with purpose. Ever and again I seek to understand my fundamental flaw. Is it lust? Have I wanted too much? Do I strike out prematurely or not quickly enough in seeking to do God's will? The blame cannot lie with my wife, who is sterling to a fault, if that is possible. It must lie in me. I hope it is not a sin for me to ask you to pray for me in heaven.

> *In eternal love, your son*
> *Henry*

13

Where Are You?

BEGINNING WITH LATE-APRIL rains, Emma and Henry were ill on and off, Henry most severely. His fevers pitched him higher and lower than hers did. After such a bout, he was moody and sorrowful, and Emma wondered if he dwelled too much on Sarah. Certainly she wondered at the multiple names associated with her husband's condition and the lack of remedy. Sometimes it was called jungle fever, other times swamp fever, other times malaria; then it was the old ailment—his spleen and liver; then he blamed his errant personality, his unwillingness to submit to God. The pages she devoted to Henry's illness read like a hospital log.

Thursday: Henry hot with fever, refuses food

Friday: Fever abated; complains of aches in his joints

Saturday: Poor husband plunged back into illness, much trouble with his spleen. I took a short walk. Saw a ritual slaughter of a chicken, blood doused upon a stone. Walked farther until I came upon girls washing at the stream. Their friendliness refreshed me.

Emma wondered about the laudanum. "It seems to squander your thought more than it helps in recovery," she said one evening.

Henry raged. "Don't I know how I am lessened by these eternal afflictions?" Though they had been preparing for bed, he lit the lamp and declared his intention to work on the vocabulary. "Does anyone know the value of what I do?" She heard him moving papers around in the next room, a chair pulled out, a book slammed. "Heaven help me!"

Emma trembled that he should go on so when more than anything they needed to care for one another. Just over a year ago, she was anticipating her marriage.

A moment later and Henry was back, his face hollowed in the meager light. "What is this?" he said, grasping a sheaf of papers and shaking them toward her.

"What?" she said.

"This?" He shook them again.

Some pages of his vocabulary work appeared eaten by white ants.

"That cook of yours," he said. "He sits doing nothing half the day. He ought to have been looking into the house, tidying up. He would have discovered the problem before it went so far."

"Duro has plenty to do; we never hired him to clean," she said, near weeping that they had lapsed into agonized quarreling.

"You might have looked to it. I built this house and no one can keep it? Why not leave honey for the ants?"

Henry went over it again in the morning with Duro until Emma thought the man would walk off.

"Are you preaching today or are you ill?" she said when he came indoors.

"It's the house," he said. "I built too fine a house. I suppose I deserve to be robbed by ants. The Africans will always see us as aliens." He drew himself up, and she saw how lost his body was in his clothes.

It was useless to talk with him. He seemed deeply engaged somewhere else, in a world beyond her. That evening he remained in the parlor while she prepared for bed. She heard him speak aloud but to no one in particular. "No one knows where the stone fell, and I fear that I shall never find it." Had he fallen asleep and dreamed? Was it Sarah he meant?

She found him by the lamp, his eyes open but blank. "Where are you, Henry?" she said. He seemed to look through her. She took his hands and placed them on her face and finally he said, "Emma."

The next week she thought he was better until she found him in the storage room with his shirt off and a horsewhip. She stared at him. Neither moved. For some reason she thought of her father and how perhaps he had been right to be against her marriage, but then she considered: *So be it, but I did marry this man and I will not let this happen.*

"You," she said, "listen to me." She lifted her arm in a way of expressing her being.

His eyes were on her, but she was unsure if she had affected him one way or the other.

"How else," he said, "am I to pull out of this nervousness? I'll go mad."

"Now we are together," she said. "You put that down unless you would whip me. This is not God's will." She had to say the sentences one more time, and he released the whip. She took a step toward him and waited until he held out his hand. She took him to bed and held him through the night, and the incident was not spoken of. She looked for the whip in the storage room but could not find it. She wondered if Duro had put it away, knowing.

A few days later, walking on a lane, Emma saw an old man stand and turn to face her, and for all the world he looked like Uncle Eli. She started toward him but he moved away, seeming to vanish into the blue hovering smoke of the market.

She recalled her last time with the old man, his hands on the frayed quilt. The thought she wanted to remember was so close. She shook her head to one side as one does when water has stopped an ear. But no memory come to her, and she walked on home with the sense of a treasure lost though she could not even remember the treasure.

Part Three

ACROSS THE
OBA RIVER

· 14 ·

Guide

*I have learned to think thus: If an evening turns to day, a dry season
comes to rain, and an injury brings pardon, surely I can turn—for the
earth and the heaven have turned me in the night—and take the light
of God's word and walk out again into the day—light into light—and
give myself to the thing I came for, even as less and less I know exactly
what that is. It may be that we follow God only by losing our way.*

—EMMA'S JOURNAL, IJAYE, AUGUST 1854

A ROOSTER CROWED. Emma turned her face, seeking the early light
of her bedroom window, but the wall was dark. She turned the
other way. Of course. Now she remembered. She and Henry had spent
the night with Rev. Moore. After a year in Ijaye and the loss of Sarah,
they were moving to a new mission, farther north, in Ogbomoso. A
week ago, Moore had invited them to stay with him as they packed.
Three days ago, she and Duro had disassembled the kitchen. Yesterday, Henry had covered the mattresses with ticking. There was little
left at the house but their books and Henry's papers, and Emma would
take care of those today.

Henry's side of the bed was cool, and she comprehended that he had
likely been up for hours. The murmur of farmers heading to their fields
entered her consciousness. Would a change in climate relieve her husband's distress? Rev. Moore thought so. She was conflicted. Here she
knew the turns in the stream, had memorized the stones around Hen-

ry's garden, the beautiful lemon tree. And the house Henry had told her of in his proposal had cradled her during those months of grief. And then Tela and her schoolchildren and Rev. Moore were her constant support. Would letters from home ever reach such a faraway place? She feared moving to a town that had never housed white people. Surely chances for misunderstanding would be greater. Who would stand by them? And what of the route there? She imagined highway robbers.

But most of all, there was Sarah, whose grave she visited, imagining her an angel who might counsel and comfort. She would have to leave her.

Still, the unfolding of events seemed divinely ordained. A load of supplies with letters and money had finally arrived. The day it came, Henry entered the parlor, looking more vigorous than Emma had seen him in a long time. It was as though he had touched the bottom of a deep lake and, rushing up for air, had broken the surface with new life. An additional missionary was finally on his way and could replace them here. The fellow had already departed Richmond. "We can move forward," Henry said. His blue eyes shone in their mysterious way but with an original beauty. "We should go for your sake," he said, "a new beginning, a place less sorrowful."

That afternoon, Emma had meditated in the chapel, a stray chicken her only companion. *If we stay in Ijaye,* she reasoned, *the rounds of illness will likely continue. We will be forced to return to Georgia, our daughter sacrificed for nothing. I did not come here to give up.*

She found Duro at the kitchen fire. "If we move to Ogbomoso, will you come with us?" she said.

"Ah," he said.

"Is it too far from your family?"

"It is not too far," he said.

"I would be happy if you would come," she said.

"I will come," he said.

In the parlor, Emma's fingers found their place on the lid of her writing box and she began playing the piano, the keys and notes in her head. Brahms. Light enough for a child, deep enough for a forest, tidal enough for her longing.

"I agree," she told Henry that night. "Duro will come with us."

In their bed, Henry ran his fingers along her lips. "*O-bow-mow-shaw*," he said, emphasizing every syllable the same, and he kissed her and poured the word into her mouth.

After their time together, they talked into the night. "We should aim for August, the little dry season. Four or five days by caravan," Henry said. "There's money for a horse and a hammock. I want you to hire a handmaid. You're going to need someone living in a native house while I build. You can teach her. It will be a comfort to you."

Emma had inquired about one of Moore's former pupils, a girl named Abike, and made arrangements with the mother. "*O ti nri nkan osu*," the mother volunteered, which Emma took to mean "she has begun to see the monthly thing." Emma had not chanced the petite girl's age, but now guessed she might be fifteen, and just as well that she was initiated into young adulthood. One less hurdle. If anything, Emma might need to sew some bloomers for her and offer batches of old cloth.

Everything had come together except that Henry still needed Kunrumi's permission to travel. It was one of the odd customs of the territory. The king must invite the *oyinbo* to come, and he must allow him to leave. Moreover, he must provide guards. It was bad policy, or perhaps a show of weakness, to have a white man leave your town and be attacked on the road. That must be where Henry was this morning, pressing the king for a departure date.

Moore's guest room was now a pink glow. Emma rested her hands in the concave of her abdomen, between her hip bones. In a moment, she stood to dress. Most days she wore a cotton chemise, a single petticoat, and a corset she had made comfortable by relaxing the laces. Over this she slipped a white blouse and dark skirt. She took some time putting up her hair. When she was finished, she lingered for a moment on her image in the mirror. She touched two fingers to her tongue, wet them, pulled wisps of hair down around her neck and across her forehead, and put on her hat. Suddenly she was quite hungry. Moore might serve marmalade for breakfast.

Their friend sat under a tree at a table set with a white cloth and china. "The king has finally come through with the escort," Moore said as he rose to greet her. "Rev. Bowman has gone looking for more porters."

Before long, Henry came riding in on a sorrel horse, a little shabby-looking, but the animal picked his feet up nicely. "Why look at you," Emma said.

Henry dismounted and tied the horse.

"Haven't we got a guava for him?" Emma said. "What's his name?"

"Caesar," Henry said.

"Maybe he'll grow into some greatness," Emma said, caressing Caesar's forehead.

"Were you successful?" Moore said.

"Kunrumi must have gone back and forth ten times on whether we should leave this week or next," he said. "He did offer four guards on horseback. What a fellow." He turned to Emma, his face bright. "A man has applied to be our guide. He heard news of our travel in the market. I'll bring him by the house to meet you. He might stay on with us in Ogbomoso."

Only a table and two chairs were left in the parlor, and the floors echoed as Emma walked across them in her packing. Her two older schoolboys came by and watched from the window, their arms latched up over their heads. They had the aspect of youngsters who have known disappointment. "Another teacher is coming," she said. Their arms fell from their heads and she saw their limbs so long and young, and she thought she would cry. She took in a deep breath and walked onto the piazza.

"Mah," one of them said, "I am sad."

"I am sad too," she said. They laid their hands gently in the crook of her elbows, and she returned the gesture. Later, she did cry. *Everywhere I go I leave children*, she thought. Then she coaxed herself. "I must remember the whole world is God's. He can see what I cannot. My portion is to follow, even without understanding." She shook her head to stop her tears and returned to sorting Henry's notes. Just then her husband appeared at the front door, bringing someone behind him. She pressed at her eyes, to be sure they were dry. The fellow with Henry wore a camel-colored tunic over knee-length pants and had a chewing stick perched at his ear like a pencil. Fresh green leaves sprouted from one end and set against his brown skin provided him a gay and superior look. He was taller than Henry and Emma had to look up to meet his face. She had an immediate sense of force.

"Mrs. Bowman, meet Jacob Ladejo. He wishes to be our guide on the caravan," Henry said. Then he turned to the man beside him, "Jacob, Mrs. Bowman."

"You are welcome," Emma said in Yoruba. She was well enough advanced in the language now to sustain basic conversation with anyone who was accustomed to *oyinbos*.

"Thank you mah," Jacob said in English.

"Where do you prefer to sit," Henry said to the man, "on an English seat or an African one?" He pointed to a mat.

"I know both, captain," Jacob said, and this seemed a joke to Henry and he laughed. They took English chairs, Jacob adjusting his frame to the contours of the seat just as a gentleman in Greensboro might, but wearing leather sandals and still with the green bough on his ear. There was an energy in the room now and as she returned to her work, Emma hoped it was her husband who had ushered it in. From where she stood, she could get an angle on the man. She meant to estimate his age, though it was always difficult to figure an African.

He's not over thirty, she imagined, observing the smooth plane of his forehead. Then seeing how animated his brows were, she lowered her guess to twenty-two. He had not smiled, but still she thought he had a smiling face. It was the direct angle from his chin to his cheekbones. By the time she had finished packing the second box, she had settled at twenty-four and felt she might have gained some mastery over him.

All at once Henry seemed to miss her. "I thought you were joining us," he said.

"I was given to understand differently," she said, meaning to observe the lack of seating.

"Take my chair," he said. Emma obliged, only to find a dangerous propinquity between Jacob's legs and her skirt.

"Jacob was schooled in Sierra Leone," Henry said, his voice echoing in her mind. Emma drew her eyes up from her skirts toward her husband. He seemed enamored with this fellow.

"Several years back he was sold to Portuguese traders headed for Brazil, but the ship was intercepted by a British squadron and he was released in the colony."

Emma's forehead tightened. There was already so much for her to think of.

"Wife?" Henry said.

"You spoke so quickly," she said.

"Our man, here," Henry said. "He was captured, sold in the slave trade as a lad, swapped about these parts until he was put on a boat for Brazil."

Emma felt a shiver. She looked back to Jacob. He didn't *look* like a slave, but let her say something appropriate. "We praise God you were released," she uttered in his direction, her eyes lingering a moment on his nose. It broadened as he breathed, and she imagined he was less couth than she had first thought.

"I was stolen out of my village. Some passersby. For a time, maybe some months, I was traded in the area of Ibadan, from one family to another." He drew lines in the air, to indicate the movement. "You know Ibadan?"

"Yes, certainly," Henry said.

Emma thought of her friends the Hathaways. It was hard to imagine children traded in the shadow of their church. A thought came to her from her own backyard. Perhaps Mittie Ann and Carl had avoided having children because they might be sold. Clouds gathered in her mind. That dream she had of Sarah snatched away. Out of the corner of her eye she saw a stray termite making its stunned and crooked way at her feet, no doubt shaken from Henry's papers as she packed. She placed her boot squarely on it until she thought she heard the faint crunch.

"Were you ill-treated then?" she heard Henry whisper.

"Of course," Jacob said, and his head went back, as if to save himself from a hit. "Iron," he said, "even for children." Emma's eyes rested on the contours of the man's neck. "The British schooled me for four years," he continued. "When I was baptized, I became Jacob."

"It's a strong name," Henry said.

This turn in the story offered Emma some ballast. "You write in English?" she said.

"Yes mah," Jacob said.

"But why leave Sierra Leone?"

Jacob did seem to smile, that odd Yoruba smile of sadness. "Ah mah," he said. "I came looking for my family. But they were all dead in the war. My entire village, everything sacked."

The way he said "sacked" was so physical, Emma felt the hit in her stomach.

"Excuse me," she said. "I need some water."

When she reentered the parlor, Henry was arranging Jacob's fee. "I'll pay you three heads of cowries for the journey; that's fifteen dollars," he said, "though I'm still surprised you'd rather travel with us than apply to Rev. Moore for work. You know the British better."

"I prefer you Americans," Jacob said.

"Why is that?" Henry said.

Jacob waved his hand. "The British, the Portuguese. All of them remind me of slavery. Americans have fought for freedom, no?"

His voice carried the most bewildering tone—old and full of hope. It perplexed Emma as much as did Jacob's idea that her countrymen had fought for freedom for someone like him.

"So we're agreed," Henry said. And when Emma did not immediately reply—"Wife?"

"Yes," she said.

The two men shook hands like partners.

15

Like a Calabash

JACOB LIFTED THE edge of his shirt and wiped his face. The meeting had gone well. Pastor called him "our man." But the interview had also been a trial, especially with the woman. Was it necessary to go into his capture? Bats came into his head.

Ah. That day from boyhood. At first, he had thought it might be some spirit festival he had fallen into—the way he tripped and was pulled into the air, as if a great bird had captured him. The world went upside down, all the trees coming out of the sky instead of up from the ground. His head spun and he screamed. Those ugly men shouting in rude tongues. Only when they lowered the net could he perceive how he had been upside down. He saw other young boys. It must be an initiation. He had heard that it could happen this way. Boys set upon by elders who would take them out of the village for a set of trials. But none of the men was familiar. Unless they were wearing masks. If so, they were not like the masks he knew before. These were too real, like men's faces pressed into themselves. The spears they carried spit fire. One fire reached for a child when he ran. It pinned him in the air and then he fell into a tiny heap, like old cloth thrown to the rubbish.

He had fallen into a very bad world. For several days he believed he might wake. He ate and moved only to save himself abuse by the spirit men. When he was transferred in one village, he found another boy who had a proper tongue. That was how he learned it was not a dream or a spirit bush.

"This man has taken you," the boy said. "Now you are his, like a goat. You must do as he commands or he will flog you."

But how could Jacob follow commands when no one had a proper tongue?

His heart broke like a calabash.

When he was saved by the British and taken to Sierra Leone, he followed every instruction he could understand, fearful of the men without skin. But no one struck him. He was given clothes and placed in a room with boxes for sitting until he began to hear the language. He took it in quickly. In the afternoon he worked with the other boys on a farm. The land was very like his country. There was no guard. In any case, where would he go? Every seventh day, he and the other children, with the white people, entered a larger room with a long golden rod crossed by a shorter rod. Here also, he tried to follow. When he was in the school for two years and comprehended Galatians chapter three, verse twenty-eight, he declared himself a Christian. *There is neither Jew nor Gentile, neither slave nor free.* In Jesus Christ he could never be a slave again.

If his family had survived, or any part of his village remained, he would not be looking for an *oyinbo* father. But it was not the case. Instead he had discovered an American missionary who had been witness to the signing of a treaty between Lagos and England that ended the slave trade. He was on the edge of a new world with this man, Rev. Bowman, and the peculiar wife, who spoke as if she did not know how to bring English to an African ear. But something in her reminded him of a deer, a *duiker*, and he thought she might be better than most *oyinbo* women.

Let Jesus make a new house for him in Ogbomoso.

16

The Hammock

THE DAY THEY were to leave, clouds hung low and full. The church had insisted on a send-off. They brought gifts. Emma's was an ivory bracelet she would never wear because it fell off her arm. She thought this item might suggest she should plump up. Henry's gift was a lavish Yoruba *agbada*. On the spot, he pulled the robe over his American clothes and everyone cheered. Women followed Emma out of the yard, petting her arms. She gave Tela a china teacup to remember her by, and the woman wept more largely than her mother had when she left Georgia. Tela insisted Emma take her blue shoulder cloth.

"I pray mah, I pray," Tela said, her hands still clasping Emma's.

Emma's students stood in a cluster, and she thought her heart would fail her.

"Please mah." It was Jacob in front of her, demanding attention. "It is time."

Emma pressed a wide-brimmed hat on her head and prepared to enter the hammock, an African version of the carriage, but motored by men rather than wheels and a horse. An awning was stretched on a rectangular frame, including flaps that could be let down on either side to offer shade, and from the frame hung a canvas seat outfitted with arms and a footrest. A smaller version of Emma's seat, one facing hers, had been added for Abike, the new handmaid, who was already seated. The porters, she saw, were prepared with ample crowns of cloth to diffuse the weight of the wooden beams on their heads. Still, she worried it would be too heavy for them.

"Enter mah," Jacob said.

She did as she was told, and Jacob left for the front of the caravan. The Yoruba men's talk was polite as roses as they adjusted the hammock.

"Bring it forward small-small."

"Thank you for helping me."

"You have done well."

They were up and off. Emma saw Henry ahead, riding his new mount, with the king's four guards also on horseback. Just then, she heard a clap of thunder and the sky opened. In her last glimpse of her women friends, they were running for cover. Emma tried to get a count. It seemed there were about fifty in their company: twenty-odd porters conveying their loads, Duro and Abike, who now looked rather morose, and Jacob, as well as a number of traders, men and women, who had annexed themselves to the caravan, hoping to avoid taxes charged along the way.

She sat back and focused on the girl in front of her. She had an oval head and her cheekbones were visible when she smiled. Her chin was short but ended smoothly under her full lower lip. And her eyes seemed almost round in a lovely way that made them look diamond shaped. Her eyebrows, arched in the middle, contributed to this effect. She had smallish ears delicately set with tiny gold earrings. And yet she had visible muscles in her upper arms, lapping one upon the other like brown waves. Suddenly the girl began to moan; then she wept.

"Here now," Emma said. "You're afraid."

The girl's shoulders rose and fell in terrible regularity, and at last she raised an arm as if she would wipe her face with the back of her hand.

"No," Emma said, "wait!" She shook Tela's blue cloth to its capacity and began a full sweep of Abike's face. "Now blow," she said. "That's better." Emma had worked with Abike only twice, one afternoon packing kitchen items and another organizing her personal effects. The girl knew English, but it wasn't yet clear how amenable she would be to more instruction. She seemed to have a habit of closing her face. *Either she's stubborn or she's smart*, Emma thought; *however it may be, she's now in my care.* In a compartment of her mind, she knew she was glad for the girl's company.

The rain let up to a drizzle and their throng of travelers looked, to Emma, quite lovely in the mist as they traveled on a tolerable road through areas of farm and open field. Far ahead was Henry on Caesar. At one point, Jacob came back to check the progress. He had some sort of musical instrument strung around his neck and shoulder. It fit snugly against his back and looked from a distance like a tortoise shell. Curiosity rose in Emma like a candle flame.

When it seemed an hour had passed, she began to feel overlooked. They entered a deep wood, the rain intensified again, and Henry was lost from her vision.

It was a great relief from the fretting—against which she had foresworn—when she caught sight of a boy, the only child she'd seen in their company. She tried to keep him in view, but he slipped in and out among the crowd. Each disappearance made her nervous. He was a small, lovely life and she meant to know him. At one point, she caught herself counting, *One two three four remember five six seven eight remember.*

Occasionally when the caravan came to a clearing they would be offered a patch of sky—she would relax and tell herself all was well—

but then they must plunge back into the gloom. Oddly enough, Abike began to relax and appeared in charge of herself. She settled into talking with the porters and keeping herself amused. Emma felt truly deserted. *I must think on where we are going,* she considered, *and not descend into self-pity.* She closed her eyes, hoping to fetch some thought that would inspire her. In a moment, she felt a tug on her arm. The hammock stopped. Here was a woman from the caravan holding out a leaf of fried plantain.

"For me?" Emma said. She turned to the porter. "Am I to pay her?"

"No mah. She is giving it to you so you will not weary."

"Thank you," Emma said. *"E se."* The woman tipped her head.

As the caravan plodded along and Emma nibbled the plantain, sharing with Abike, an idea wove itself into her mind. She would begin a women's class in Ogbomoso, but rather than having it on the mission compound, she would travel into the town and find the women where they were. She would be less constricted, her life active and full; she would know things firsthand. Throughout her pondering, Emma kept her eyes on the boy, and it was clear from the way he sought to emulate Jacob that he was with the guide. Instinctively, she reached for Abike's hand and found it small and warm.

ON THE NIGHT of the second day, they came to an *aroje,* or caravanserai, at the side of a river. The people seemed familiar with Englishmen because they saluted Emma and Henry, but only a few stopped to study them. With the children, it was different. They were curious, slipping up to touch Emma's skirts. She accommodated and even coaxed them a little, walking about more than she had need of. She was waiting for just the moment when she would amaze them by throwing out a slew of Yoruba sentences. The oldest boy eventually got so bold he touched her hand. "What is your name?" she said. "Shouldn't you be at the farm? Won't your father flog you?"

She got just what she hoped for. The children put their hands to their mouths and then swept down, headfirst from the waist in a pendulum movement. They were instantly garrulous. Why were her feet black when her face was white? "Those are boots," she said, and showed them. Could they touch her hair? "Yes." Where were her children? She felt a chill at her heart. What would she say? She put her hands on her hips and sighed so deeply the expended breath raised the hair on her forehead. "My children are in front of me," she said at last. The youngsters looked at her with great seriousness. "I am going to find them." One girl told her she must hurry since her children might be hungry. Several offered to help her look. None appeared disbelieving. Emma crossed her arms over her chest, holding in a surfeit of feeling.

She and Henry were to camp in a hunter's house. The hunter himself was apparently out in search of leopards. One lone pelt hung from the wall. While Henry built a fire, Emma found a native broom to poke at the thatch, encouraging the spiders to flee. She was glad for this bit of housekeeping, which brought her together with her husband. Across the road, the women from the caravan were making fires and fetching water, the men making themselves comfortable.

"I'll never understand why the men of this country sit around while the women labor," she said, coming outside to shake her broom. She caught sight of Jacob. He had behaved responsibly on the road, but now he sat like the other men, swatting at insects and throwing groundnuts into his mouth. In a moment, he reached around and pulled his turtle-banjo into a position to play it. The little boy sat next to him, swinging his arms as a few brief notes vibrated in the air. "Who is that child traveling with us?" Emma said. "He can't be six years old."

"Some relation of Jacob's," Henry said.

Emma became dimly aware of how she had linked the child with Sarah. "Is it safe for him—being on a caravan?"

"Certainly. You know how strong these children are, once they survive their second year."

By the time they had eaten, Henry was complaining of aches and pains.

"Let's go to bed," Emma said. By lamplight, they pulled off their outer garments. "How did this happen?" she said, catching sight of Henry's bruised leg.

"The road was trenched in spots. Caesar had some difficulty. Once or twice, he sent me against a stump," Henry said.

Emma pulled in close to her husband, her head in the crook of his shoulder. As she closed her eyes, she fancied him in his youth, coming home from a scuffle, a fall, his mother finding the bruise, tending it, in a world before she was born.

17

The Oba River

THE NEXT MORNING the Oba River ran green and swollen from rain. Emma had never been good at calculating distance, but she decided it must be forty yards across. The so-called rafts they were to use were actually contrived from the large flat ends of two gourds, cut and cemented to forge round devices the size of a bedside rug. They would have to enter the river and cling to them to cross. The man who would serve as her ferrier assured her there were no crocodiles to be found in these parts. Emma hadn't thought to worry about anything but drowning before he brought up the possibility of being eaten.

"Yes," she said in her Yoruba. "The crocodile isn't here." *That's settled*, she thought, but the ferryman had more to say. According to his witness, red birds enter the river where they turn into red fish and frighten away the reptiles.

"Only our savior, Jesus Christ, can deliver us from pestilence, *ipalara*," she said, her eyes fixed on the vines that hung from the opposite trees, making shapes like huge grottos. "We should pray to him for safety rather than trust in red birds." Had she been right about the distance? She didn't want to think about depths.

"Yes mah," the man said, and it occurred to Emma that he might mistake her prayer for a plea to the water *orisha*.

"Jesus is Lord," she said firmly.

"Jesus. I know Jesus," he assured her, appearing to find no conflict between the risen Savior and his story of the crocodile.

Henry was down the riverbank, sorting the last batch of loads. Every mattress, box, locker, pot, and piece of paper would cross on the round rafts, even their wardrobe. Emma tried to imagine the contents of her mother's parlor balanced on a gourd. The image was preposterous. Yet Emma's whole aim was to put her life in God's hands, to straighten all that bentness in Georgia, to make straight a pathway. This morning their path lay on the other side of the river. "Very well, then." Emma lowered her head. "Let us pray." A wand of hair fell from her bun and she tucked it up as she began. "Merciful Jesus, center us in your grace, guide our passage, protect us from all harm, that we may serve thee, to the glory of God."

Just as the man was intoning a long *Amen*, Henry came up.

"Are you ready, Mrs. Bowman?" he said in his whimsical, formal way.

"Yes. Certainly. We have prayed, Rev. Bowman." How grateful she was for her husband, who had chosen her, saved her from a life of boredom and terror in Greensboro, where not even her mother understood her longing. He guided her into the shallows. The ferryman was waiting, very serious now. Settling into the river opposite him, Emma saw that her dress would rise like a lotus blossom. "Help me," she said, and Henry patted it down. Then she clasped the man's shoulders so their arms were locked across the raft; he gave a push, they left the shore, and she let out a cry. Just then, she felt a splash and saw Jacob leaping into the current, as if she had commanded him. He was swimming with one arm and with the other holding Henry's rifle above his head, pointed toward heaven. *What a crusader*, she thought. Just as quick came the thought that the man was awfully strong. Then came Henry, swimming beside her. His face crested the water as he threw both arms ahead and lifted his breast, and she remembered the first time she saw him, coming into church out of the rain, his hair damp. Just then the raft carrying her writing box appeared in jeopardy of capsizing. She lunged toward it and her head went under water. In that eerie half second she apprehended the movement of some large white apparition. Just as the ferryman caught her up, she knew it was her pantalets. Thank goodness the raft had righted itself. They were safe. Sputtering but relieved, Emma looked about to see the whole party crossing. There was Caesar, looking nobler than he had on land as he plowed through the current, and Abike trying to climb her fer- rier like a ladder. Just then she perceived the river's bottom beneath her feet. They were across.

Henry wrestled the rifle from Jacob.

"You might have lost it in the river."

"No sah. I swim very well, as you have seen," Jacob said.

"Still, you had no authority. There might have been an accident."

"No accident at all." The small lad came up to stand beside Jacob. Emma observed his large brown eyes and the string of blue beads around his waist, a nod to some native deity.

"You don't take the point. You aren't to go off without my lead," Henry said.

Jacob gazed into the distance.

"Yes sah," he said. Emma could not extrapolate the guide's feeling out of his tone, but he seemed to know what it meant to come up against a white man who would not listen to reason.

"We may already have ruined Africa," Henry muttered to no one especially. "What has taken hold here except guns and rum?"

She watched Jacob's shoulders droop as he went to oversee the re- maining loads, the little boy half skipping behind him, holding on to Jacob's shorts. She wished she could explain to their escort about Henry, the great responsibility he felt.

"You ought to change out of those wet clothes," Henry said.

She motioned to Abike and the girl came along, a roll of grass matting on her head, though she took her time.

God help me. God help my husband. Give him grace, Emma prayed in her heart.

At last they were ready to recommence. Emma caught sight of the little boy. He had been given her writing box to carry, and one of her baskets, and rather than walking with Jacob, he seemed relegated to walking with some of the women behind the hammock. Emma tried to speak against the arrangement, but the porters were engaged in lifting the hammock, calling back and forth, and no one heard her.

A swarm of sand flies came up. Oh, they were terrible. Smaller than a flea. Thousands of them. One of the plagues must have been sand flies. They could cover your neck with a thousand tiny bites and they itched like the devil. They seemed to prefer her to Abike. She waved and battled against them furiously. When they at last let up, Emma dozed. She woke to the sensation of cooler air. They were passing through a clear bright brook, not even a foot deep.

"Abike, how did you like the river?" she said, glancing at the girl, feeling playful.

"No mah," Abike said, deadly serious. "If you cross that river again, please mah, I go wait for you."

"You will wait for me on the other side?" Emma said, enjoying the conversation.

"Yes mah."

"And how long will you wait?"

"Until you return."

"That might be a long time."

"God is great," Abike concluded, and then as a final thought, she added, "In the river, your pant it goes flum flum," moving her brown muscular arms to show the swaying of Emma's undergarments in the water.

Well, Emma considered silently. *She was looking at me just as I am watching her.*

"Do you know the little boy's name?" she said.

"Wole," the girl said.

They left the forest and now the country seemed to stretch out before them like a world that had been born to a past world, the hills so gentle and clear before Emma's eyes that she longed for every one of them as a place she would live. The flower-green of the higher elevation and the dark luster-green of palms near the creeks made a great crumpled tapestry like a huge rug of God that had been thrown down for him to step upon. She knew there was some verse of scripture that should be coming to mind. *Oh well, never mind, I'll remember later*, she thought. *All happiness in Africa is of this sort*, she considered, *sudden and unplanned as a storm*. She would write that later in her journal. That and the river crossing.

Just then the porters halted. Food sellers were clustered beneath a stand of scrub trees.

"We won't take long for our meal," Henry said. Emma left the hammock and started toward the vendors. A display of pineapples standing in rows on brightly woven mats made her think of a fall festival. She was hoping the women would not run off or the children scatter at seeing her when she heard Jacob calling for Wole. When she heard the boy's name called a second time, the image of the child's thin ankles and her writing box passed through Emma's mind, getting confused with the bargain she was trying to strike.

"I won't give more than three letters for this fruit," she announced to the seller before she heard the third call. Emma turned to look at their entourage. She only needed to see the boy and the box. There was Henry. "What is it? Has the boy gotten lost?" she said.

"He appears to be missing," he said.

A haunting cool came into the region just below Emma's heart. She tried to remember which woman had been walking with Wole, but she had no clear image, except that he was carrying her writing box. Uncle Eli's letter opener! Henry's eyes had their mismatched look, almost as wild and unsteady as the day of the horsewhip when he looked, for a moment, mad. Jacob ran down the path they had just come, already disappearing into the trees.

18

Lost

WOLE WOLE WOLE. Henry was reminded of a cry he sometimes heard as a young man when Indian women collected their dead. It had thrilled him in a terrible way, going to his loins. Now an acidic taste came into his mouth, watching two of the porters take off after Jacob. He took a last draw on the cigarette, leaned over, mashed the end of it with the tip of his boot, examined the butt to be certain it was out, returned it to a leather pouch, and pressed the pouch into his pocket. Here was Emma.

"You haven't paid for the pineapple," he said. "The woman behind you is upset."

His wife turned around and gave the pineapple to the woman, who flogged her with some discourse.

"How could he be missing?" she said.

Henry didn't know. Kidnapping was less common than it had been even five years back. Still, someone might have followed them from the river and snatched the child. "I'm going after them," he said. He called to one of the porters. "Get that chair unhitched from the hammock. Set it under a tree." He put his hands to her shoulders. "We won't be gone long. I'll take two of the king's guards and leave two here. Duro is with you." It must be muffled thunder he heard in the distance.

"I need the boy," she said, "the scallop."

It took him a moment to understand. He glanced up at the company. Men swatted at flies, and he thought how lazy they were. Then his thinking turned like a switchback in a road. *It's your own fault. You should have put the boy on the horse. Now you're going to squander half a day at least in searching. And how will you feel if the child is lost? Your wife will not easily forget.* Henry's failures shuddered through him: his misspent youth, his lack of converts, Sarah's death.

Emma pressed her temples. He guided her to her seat.

"I will find him," he said.

The boy was too young to be traveling with them. But Jacob had shown up with the lad, describing him as orphaned and a relation, a cousin, but here more like a brother; what was he to do? Henry ran his fingers through his hair and touched the nicked lobe of his ear. When would God figure he was paid up? He looked at Emma, her skin dark in the shade so she looked almost Spanish. Calling the guards to follow, he mounted Caesar and started down the path, the frothed mud glistening like a multitude of mirrors now the sun was out.

From a quarter mile's distance Henry saw Jacob sitting in full sun at the broad landing of the river's edge, his head in his hands. He could make out the porters squatted in the shade. The horse neighed and Jacob jumped up.

"Any sign?" Henry said, dismounting.

Jacob pulled Emma's letter opener out of his pocket.

"I only found this carving, midway on the road." The man stood with a hand on his hip, pained-looking and hunched, so you would have thought a horse had kicked him.

"That was in my wife's box. Well done. The child can't have gotten far." Henry was gladdened by the object that had followed them from home. But the moment it was in his hand, he knew it might signify the worst: The boy had fallen back and someone had grabbed him. The box had seemed worth taking but not an ordinary African carving.

Jacob turned in a circle. Surely the man was remembering how he was seized as a boy. It made Henry dead cold. He pulled the rifle from the scabbard.

"Have you talked to the ferrymen there?"

"They have seen nothing. Nothing."

"We'll look about." Henry motioned to the others. "A boy doesn't just disappear," he said, knowing the lie of it. But looking into Jacob's eyes, he saw a sorrow so dangerous he believed he would sooner have a dagger in his chest than bear with the man if the child didn't show. He wandered to the edge of the landing, feeling almost sick, rested the rifle butt on the ground, and braced himself against a tree, his back to them. The impotence of the carving angered him and he started to toss it into the bush, but a sharp pain filled his side. *Good God*, he said to himself, feeling for his liver and spleen. Henry thought he had a fair knowledge of demons: clawing fingers, spiked heads, razor-sharp tails, hairy arses. There was no armor against them. He slipped the letter opener into an inner pocket of his coat. As he turned back around, he saw the depression in the grass; it hadn't been visible from where he had stood before. But it was clear as day to him now, twenty yards from the river's edge, such a path as could be made by dragging a canoe. "Ho. Jacob. Men," he said. As soon as he pointed, Jacob took off.

The others held back. "Don't tell me about ghosts," he said. "If it's an ambush, better hold together than stand apart." He raised the rifle and they all took off at a trot down the ribbon of earth. They came out to a creek. The swerve of the water had created a sand bar and just there, Henry discovered Emma's basket. A damp dress lay gently on the grass, one of her caps set at the neck. He had the queerest feeling, as if perhaps she had been subject to rapture and left her gown behind.

For a moment he saw her naked, ascending into the clouds, her white legs, that secret place of hers sewn up into holiness. Jacob knelt before the dress.

"What are you doing? Be up!" Henry swatted his hat at the back of the man's head. He felt a skirmish in his chest as if his heart were running away, and he wondered if he was shaking. "Look around, men," he commanded the others. "What do you think we're here for?"

Farther up the sand bar, one of the guards found the writing box and the canvas that had covered it. How queer, Henry thought, squatting, setting the rifle down. The box was open, and in it was Emma's red diary. Beside the box were arranged a pot of ink, four quill pens, and the prism. Another object was more difficult to discern. It appeared like a large mound of pounded yam laid on a green leaf. The entire panorama had the peculiar charm of a set of instruments set out for display in a classroom when the docent has not yet learned their true meaning and they take on, therefore, a splendid individual quality. The boy was not immediately visible, though his footprints were all about.

Henry tried to take in the scene. Suddenly it hit him that he had left Emma alone with their cook and a nursemaid and two guards. Could someone have taken the boy to lure him away from her? What sort of ritual was this? He imagined a galloping lot of masquerades—men in masks—circling his wife. Suddenly the very earth shook. He reached for the rifle. But it was Jacob on his knees, pounding the ground with his fists. "Wole!" he demanded. "Wole!"

Then it seemed to Henry a slender brown tree stepped from the shade and became the boy. Jacob rushed to him, raising his arms, threatening, forgetful of his good English, "Ah, ah, I go flog you now. Look dis trouble!"

Henry slapped his hands against his thighs to cover the shaking. "God help my disbelief," he whispered. He pushed Jacob aside, but studiously, as he might a limb that seemed very like a snake. "The boy is frightened out of his wits," he said.

It took some time for Jacob to coax the story from Wole, who told it in spurts of crying and talking. He had had difficulty keeping up after the crossing and in passing over a stump he lost his load into the mud, the box slipping out of its covering and popping open. He was afraid the white *iya* would be angry, so he went back to the river to wash her goods. Then he was frightened of the river and found the creek instead. He had laid everything out to dry before he realized he was now too far behind to catch the caravan.

The child's story was told as much by pointing and rubbing and even hitting his legs as by narrating.

Henry set Wole on the horse, but within the first quarter mile the child was falling asleep. So Jacob carried him in his arms. Henry carried the writing box, as well restored as possible, while one of the porters balanced the basket with Emma's damp clothing on his head. The other porter and the guards had nothing to haul. When they reached that part of the path where Wole had fallen and Jacob had discovered the letter opener, the man stopped. "Master, Jesus has saved us," he said.

The sun was now directly overhead. Henry lifted his canteen from the saddle, took a drink, and handed the refreshment around. The others poured the liquid into their hands to partake, and one chose to splash his face. When they glimpsed the caravan, Henry pressed forward, looking for his wife.

19

The Door of Her Heart

"THEY'RE BACK. THEY'RE here. Abike! Duro! Oh heaven be praised," Emma said, relief pouring through her. She stood, and her dress caught in a fold of the chair. "Oh, look here." She fumbled with the cloth. Exasperated, she stood, trailing the chair until it shook loose. She ran toward Henry, and her hat flew off.

The boy was all in one piece, his feet tilted, toes in, nestled in Jacob's arms. At her voice, he opened his eyes but closed them again and seemed to wrench himself away from her. She felt a stab of unbelonging. But here was Henry with her writing box. He wiped his face with the sleeve of his shirt.

"Has something gotten into your eyes?" she said, squinting at him.

"I'm happy to see you," he said, and she thought it was the tenderest thing she had ever heard.

"I'm so glad you're back," she said, feeling like a girl again. "But what has happened?"

"The boy took a spill in the mud. He was worried about displeasing you. Took everything back to the river to wash. He had the sense not to wash your journal. The box is in good shape." Henry tapped it. "Though he did rinse out some pages—a letter you had started perhaps; you'll have to recommence." Her husband smiled. "The boy smashed them into a mound to dry."

Emma recalled her worry about her husband's illness, the pages she had recorded. A sense of foreboding passed over her like a dark cloud. But then she trained her eyes on Jacob as he made his way toward the group. A woman in an orange wrap came out, hips swinging, to take in the boy. There was Abike, standing with her arms relaxed at her sides, looking as if something had just been achieved in her favor. The dark cloud moved away. Emma pulled herself back to Henry. Her record of his bouts, her almost mathematical figurings. Gone now; perhaps a blessing. She sighed deeply, letting her breath out through her mouth.

"Watch there," Henry said, pointing to a mud puddle. He followed Jacob, and she clipped after them.

The heat had caught up with them and Henry recommended they rest. Emma took the red journal, blew away bits of sand, and paged through. She looked over where Wole was sleeping and pressed her book against her chest. In a moment, she set the journal on her knee and took up her pen. *Grace seldom comes when we demand it but rather appears unexpected. Will I ever learn?* She was suddenly very tired and leaned her head back against the chair. In her dream, she was trying to catch pages of her writing in a stream, but they disintegrated and fell through her fingers as if her hands were a sieve, and the black words she had written washed away independent of the paper and the fish ate them like crickets.

In the afternoon, a wind came through, and the air turned light and clear. Great flocks of green parrots appeared, their throaty songs coming from every direction. As the caravan lumbered along, a batch would rise in a swarm from the choke of trees and dart down the path in front of them, only to settle again. Emma had the writing box in her lap and she kept patting it, as one would a child one wished to keep in slumber. As they gained the top of a hill, their eyes were greeted by an expanse of undulating prairie, scattered with groves, and bound in the distance by blue hills.

In their tent that evening, Emma slipped out of her dress, took her hair down, set aside her pins, and lay in her underclothes. She could still smell her husband's tobacco and hear him greeting someone occasionally. She cupped her breasts in her hands. When she heard Henry stir up the fire, she knew she would be falling asleep alone.

Oh God in heaven—she began her prayer—*Maker of heaven and earth, of the stars in all their glory and the small yellow flower of the field, look upon Your servant.* She had in mind her husband first, sitting outside there in his breeches and suspenders with his shirt collar open. Then she thought of herself in the tent in her underdress. *Let it be with us as You see fit and if it pleases You, make straight our path in this wilderness, bring some dwelling comfort into our hearts, keep us steady and joined in love.* She remembered something Henry had once said— "Love is the source of all true happiness"—and she was impatient in her prayer, for he showed it so fitfully. Returning with the boy he had been so kind; now she was alone. She prayed again. *Give me new fervor for Your work, let me not be troubled by my own heart but be moved for these thousands of Your lost children who are orphaned in this country without the true Savior.* She called to mind the picture of Jesus in her Greensboro church, the one in which he was adorned with dark locks about his head and his eyes were filled with longing and he held out his hand to her. *Love me yet, dear Father in heaven, as I learn to love those you have sent me to love.* Wole had already slipped through the door of her heart. Abike was at the threshold. Jacob was too large for such passage.

THE LIGHT WAS pink as they lumbered out of the woods and came to a crossroads. A right turn brought them into view of cleared fields and farms. The land sloped, and Emma thought she could tell where the brooks ran. She sat forward. A number of walkers seemed to join them, women bearing loads of wood. It was Sunday afternoon and she was reminded that these were heathen who had no idea of the Sabbath. She pulled a shawl around her head, hoping not to be observed. Suddenly the carriers hoisted her upward.

"Please mah, we have arrived," one of them said. The movement gave her stomach a turn.

"Is it Ogbomoso?"

The man laughed. "Yes mah."

They rounded a copse and she could see the town itself, pitched upon the hills and hemmed by a mighty-looking wall. Two pillars announced the town gates. Narrowing her eyelids, she spotted Henry, his white linen shirt shining in the odd light so that it looked golden. He would see to the tariffs and send word ahead to the king. Now they stopped. The porters were talking to one another in Yoruba, too fast for her to understand, though she imagined they were anxious for rest and eating and no doubt dipping into the palm wine. The wait was tedious. She counted to four hundred.

"Lands sakes," she said. Her legs ached from sitting so long, but she could not dismount. Henry had cautioned her about a likely commotion over the arrival of the first white woman. Sure enough, when she let her shawl slip, a passing woman glanced once, bent her knees, cried out, and scooted forward. Soon she would be telling a hundred others.

"Don't worry mah, that woman is ignorant," one of the porters said. He spoke like a man who has sailed the world. Emma turned around.

"Thank you," she said. Facing forward again, she caught Abike staring at her.

"Are you frightened?" she said.

"Yes mah."

"Don't be afraid. We'll soon have a place for the night."

"The others," Abike said. "They will leave us."

"The others?"

"Yes mah."

Perhaps the girl was afraid of being left alone with her, without the women of the caravan. "I see," she said. "But we'll have Duro and Jacob and the boy."

This assurance seemed to ease the girl. "Yes mah," she said.

Emma looked up, and here came a crowd. "Goodness," she said. "Can't we move forward? Porter. Can't we move forward?"

Suddenly she imagined the hammock toppling. Her neck would break. The porters started up just as she was resigning herself to martyrdom. They swept across a good-sized moat and through the gate before she had a chance to locate Henry. Smoke wafted into her nostrils. Women sat at low tables with items for sale. Down an alley, boys tossed something back and forth. Three large birds took flight from a tree. A stout man with a walking stick stepped out of the crowd.

"*Oyinbo de,*" he said. "The white man is come."

There were whoops of disbelief. One woman leaned over and pounded her skirt. Mothers collected children and deposited them at house fronts. Boys trotted beside Emma's hammock. But a few adults called, "*Alafia,*" peace. Emma felt oddly as if she were coming home. She took the shawl from her head and waved. "*Alafia,*" she said. The women's cloth was blue and more blue, from the indigo pots. It seemed they traversed several miles getting to the center of town. At last Emma heard Jacob calling her porters, and they pushed through the crowd to the front of the caravan where she saw Henry, standing by the horse. Here was an archway and a gate and it seemed to Emma they had happened upon something close to civilization.

"This must be the palace," she said to Abike. But the girl's face was in shadow and she said nothing. A horn sounded and four men materialized, taking positions like posts in a palisade. Then Emma saw the king advancing, taking his time, pushing his legs out—like Uncle Eli! He was piled up in white cloth, his hands hidden somewhere in the folds. Henry came to help her disembark, but just as she reached out to him, he lost his footing. He lurched before recovering himself, so she stepped down alone and then wove her hand through his arm, to steady them both.

There were the usual, everlasting salutations. Seated inside the king's compound, they were offered drinks. A kola nut ceremony began—always for men only. Emma let her eyes wander.

"Emma," Henry said.

"Yes," she said. "Oh!" The king was offering her the first bite. The bitter taste filled her mouth and shot backward into her throat. It was proper to chew so she tried, though she felt her neck muscles straining with the effort. When the king looked away, she swallowed and continued an imitation of chewing. Henry produced his flask and offered it to the king. A communion, she thought, with a kind of hilarity. The flask was actually meant for her, and fortunately the king had the good sense to pass it along. She took a large swallow of whiskey, never more glad for it. Henry held the kola nut and sank his white teeth into it.

Emma tried to follow the conversation, but there was yet much commotion, everyone straining to get a glimpse of them.

Finally they could take their leave. Outside the king's grounds, their group was waiting, the traders and Kunrumi's guards having gone their own direction for the night.

"I take our accommodation to be half a mile's distance," Henry said, "still well within the city walls. Do you want to ride?"

"I'll walk," Emma said. Off they went, following the king's men: Henry leading the horse, she walking beside, Abike, Duro, Jacob and Wole, the porters with the empty hammock, and a band of onlookers following. Drums started up somewhere.

"We've been given an entire compound," Henry said; he appeared all proud and happy now. "The place belongs to the king's brother, but the man's gone off to the ancestral home for some months with his wives. From what I can make out, there's a creek close by."

"Ah," she said.

"The king is called the *Baale* here, *baa-lay*," he said.

"*Baa-lay*," she practiced.

They found the place by last light. Jacob directed traffic for placing the furnishings. Wole walked about importantly, giving little pushes to unloaded objects, as if he were taking ownership of them. Henry and Jacob settled up with the porters, and finally only Emma's carriers were left. She had kept back extra cowry strings for each and handed these around, looking fiercely in Henry's direction, lest he say anything.

"Thank you. I will pray for you," she said. The men were formal and grave, and Emma was sorry to see them go. Her heart seemed full of love, and she thought her prayer of the night before was being answered.

"Are you coming?" Henry said, holding out a lantern.

What Emma took to be the front door to the house turned into a dusky, narrow passageway, about ten feet long. So it was one of those houses with rooms that faced inward, opening onto a courtyard. The center was rectangular, with a view of the sky, and the moon was up. Half an hour later, she and Henry were sitting on a mattress on the piazza, drinking tea while Duro boiled eggs.

"So, Mrs. Bowman, we have set up housekeeping in Ogbomoso," her husband said. Duro brought the eggs and Henry began to peel them and then they prayed. She swallowed a bite, taking sips of hot tea. When she leaned back onto the mattress and closed her eyes, she felt herself falling, as if through clouds, layer after layer. At some point she imagined she heard Henry ask if she wished the mattress to be moved into a room. She turned on her side. A soft wind whisked her cheek and dimly she knew he had billowed a sheet over her.

The next morning, she woke before daybreak. Henry slept, his snore mild, like a young boy learning to whistle. She pulled on her housedress, borrowed his boots, slid her feet across the dirt yard, and headed toward the passageway, darker than night. She pressed her fingers against the wall to guide herself. In an American house, she would have been coming down a hallway to the front door. There was something like a Dutch door here, and she pushed open the bottom. She stepped into the outer compound and pinned up stray locks of hair. A fire shone to her left. She headed toward it and might have tripped over Duro's legs, but he spoke.

"Good morning mah. *E kaaro*." He had the kettle on the coals for coffee. He stood.

"I want to look about," she said.

The dark seemed to settle enough for her to see that the kitchen was right there, a three-walled room with a single table. "We'll need another table," she said.

"Yes mah."

"Thank you for coming with us, Duro."

"Yes mah." He tipped his head. "You are welcome." He said it in English, and she reflected briefly on how much she had depended on him when she first arrived in Ijaye and could speak with almost no one.

Another degree of light and she cut straight across the yard until she reached a low wall, the perimeter of the property. She hadn't put on her corset, and she felt the air through her housedress swathing her chest. This and the sweet communion of her feet in Henry's boots and she felt a thrill of holiness. "I'll be," she whispered.

She kept to the wall, making the rectangular circuit of the compound. At one turn she looked back to see that the house she had slept in rested a little uphill. A knot of trees were clarified in the early sun. Roosters had been crowing since she woke, but now they ceased and a bird's melody filled the air. She wondered if Henry would wake and find his boots missing. The earth continued its downward slope as she walked along so that she came to an African meeting room made of bamboo poles and a thatched roof. A few wooden benches. Such "rooms" appeared in every village, in every family compound.

They might seat twenty. Some such Africa rooms had roofs made of climbing vine, and in the right season they blossomed with flowers. This one, she mused, would do temporarily for a schoolhouse and church. Just then someone from the street called out good morning, and Emma nearly collided with a small edifice. "The shrine house," she said, speaking low, and then remembering the coffee, she veered toward the kitchen. The sun broke just as she was about to enter the passageway, illuminating a room she had missed before. Unlike the others, it opened to the outer yard. She felt an urge to take a peek, but Duro had poured the coffee into a bowl and it was hot against her hands.

Henry sat on the mattress, his back against the wall, his hair tousled and full.

"My wife," he said as she approached with the coffee. "Someone has taken off with my boots."

"They found their way onto my feet," she said.

"What happy boots," he said.

She handed him the coffee, sat herself on a corner of the mattress, and pulled them off.

"Move closer," he said.

She did, her legs and skirt stretched out in front of her. He took a drink and offered her a sip, and they drank it back and forth. When it was finished, he set the bowl aside and placed a hand on her lap.

"We should pray," she said. "I felt happy looking at the place."

"Why don't you recite a psalm," he said.

She felt herself aflutter.

"Go on," he said.

"Be merciful unto me, O God, be merciful unto me," she said. She stopped and he joined her, and then their voice was one. "For my soul trusteth in Thee. Yea, in the shadow of Thy wings will I make my refuge. Though my soul is among lions, my heart is fixed on Thee."

Emma sensed Henry leaning toward her. His fingers ran under

her hair where it had fallen. He lifted a curl and kissed her neck, coffee on his warm breath.

After breakfast, Henry and Jacob went out in search of the creek. They were back in no time with four buckets of water.

"The stream is just down the hill," Henry said. "Local folks call it the Laka River, but in the dry season, you'll be able to cross on planks."

The morning was taken up in inspecting and sweeping out rooms. This task was relatively simple, as the regular inhabitants had stowed in the rafters what items they had left behind. Emma rinsed some undergarments, along with Tela's shoulder cloth that had served for Abike's handkerchief. The cloth was a lovely blue print, a blocked pattern. It seemed she had studied it before. But no time now to ponder. It would go into the trunk for showing later, in America. She would never wear it.

Emma and Abike sat under the odan tree and unpacked the crockery. "How are you feeling?" Emma said.

"Fine mah," she said.

"Your mother loves you. She wants you to have a good life," Emma said.

"I miss her too much," Abike said.

Emma moved to sit beside her. "I'm sorry," she said. "I know how you feel."

They were saved from weeping by Duro, who came through the passageway with a pan of water.

"We must wash the walls and smooth with cow dung," he said.

"Oh," Emma said. She put a finger to her pursed lips. "What if we only wash them down?"

"It's not so good," Duro said.

"But we won't be lodging here that long," Emma said, hoping her answer would satisfy.

None of the rooms had a window, of course, only low doors opening onto the courtyard. But there was one room with two doors, an inner and an outer, the outer leading directly to the kitchen, and the doors to this room were almost as tall as Emma. Light shone in from both directions, providing a flow of air and illumination throughout the day. "This will be our parlor," she told the cook.

She was happy with the deep cool piazza and the odan tree in the courtyard. Its large, glossy leaves—larger and brighter than a magnolia's—would offer shade for outdoor dining, sewing, writing, and visiting. All in all, she thought the *Baa-lay* must be an unusually humane African. She felt solid at that moment, for she could easily see herself out with the women, a ministering angel, a white bird.

"What do you think we should do with the boy?" Henry said.

Emma wasn't aware that they had come to a firm decision on whether Jacob would stay, though she had more or less promised Abike his presence and Wole's in the household. "What are your intentions with Jacob?" she said.

"He and I spoke on the way," he said, "after the fracas at the river."

"Over the rifle," she said.

"Yes," Henry said. "I'd still like to keep him. I told him as much. As an assistant. He'll be more than a servant. He can read and translate. Help with the house building."

"Can we afford to pay a second person?" Emma had no intention of giving up Duro.

"He's agreed to a reasonable salary. He wants the boy educated."

"Oh," Emma said, entirely pleased, as if an unexpected gift had been presented to her.

Henry and Jacob conferred at the entrance to the passageway.

"The child is welcome to stay with us," she overheard Henry say. "He will be a pupil in my wife's school. What do you say?"

She heard nothing back and looked up. This was part Jacob's proposal, after all. Why did he hesitate?

"Let me look at the boy before I make an answer," Jacob said.

Off he went, and Henry sat down with her. Directly the man returned. "It is good," he said. "Your offer is favorable to him. We can agree."

"You and the boy agree?" Henry said, half chuckling.

"Yes. God agrees," Jacob said, resolute.

They both seemed pleased as they went to set the stable straight.

Her writing box glowed in the dispersed light; sometimes Emma could almost catch her face in the wood's finish. She picked it up; was it lighter with the record of illness gone? *You are stronger*, she thought to herself. At her seat, she pulled out the lap desk. Good as new. She opened the nib compartment, the writing tips bright as jewelry. A few grains of sand were still caught in the brass hinges; she wetted her handkerchief with spit and wiped at them, inhaling the familiar smell of her best thing. Her testament, so used it fell open in places. She pulled out Uncle Eli's carving and polished it too. Again she felt the slight nudge of emotion—of being at home, of herself, that holiness in her body she had felt this morning. How surprising that she should feel so content in this native compound! However briefly, she must make some record. *Our first morning in Ogbomoso*, she wrote. *Mild and clear. We came forward in faith.* A morning dove lit on the piazza. *Already I find God's gifts.* The dove's mate flew in and settled and the two walked back and forth. Emma mused on their sleeping arrangements. Jacob and Wole had taken up the room that opened out to the compound. She would ask the cook to choose a room across the courtyard, and Abike would sleep in the room next to hers and Henry's. It would be hard for the girl, being alone, as she was doubtless accustomed to sleeping with family, but Emma could see no other option. She settled the conundrum by thinking how she would offer the girl the second mattress. She looked up to see Wole standing in the doorway of the sitting room, watching her.

"There you are," she said, hoping he could understand her Yoruba. "You are going to stay with us." The boy glided toward her but held his body sideways, as if he might need to disappear. "Soft," she said, setting aside journal and pen. Suddenly the boy was next to her. "Is there something you want?" she said.

"Oracle," he said, pointing at her writing box. He meant, she knew, a priest's receptacle, for holding charms and reading destinies. She would correct him later.

"You want to draw?" she said, making a motion with her hand. He nodded his head up and down once. "You'll need pencil and paper," she said, finding a slip of blotting paper, a nub of pencil. She turned the paper over to show he could use the back.

He took the items and walked away quickly, his figure erect.

"Huh," she said.

Two days later, Emma was back under the odan tree, her box open, the red journal on her lap desk. She looked down at her note. *Husband complained of spleen yesterday. Reports better today.* She frowned. She hadn't meant to fill her journal with their health records. But it wouldn't do to tear the page. Henry came through the passageway, and she closed the book. "What did you and Jacob find in town?" she said.

"Oh, the usual. Some weavers. Indigo pots. A blacksmithers. Most folks live by farming. Less of a military presence than Ijaye"—he wiped his brow with the back of his hand—"unless you count some of the women in the market. They're serious as Hannibal." He grinned in his funny way, as if he wished not to show feeling but the feeling overwhelmed him. "I sat with an old blind man. Said he couldn't imagine a white man before he heard me speak but now he can see me."

"How amazing," she said.

"I ran into some folks who remember me from the exploratory trip on my first tour. My first thought is a trade school. Teach a craft. The church will grow with the school."

"You ought to rest," Emma said.

Henry took a seat on the piazza and pulled off his boots. Then he stretched out, his arms up and his hands cupped to make a pillow for his head. Emma's eyes, half opened, watched the sparkle of light through the leaves. She rested her head against the canvas chair and fell asleep.

A sudden commotion woke her. Two men were releasing chickens into the courtyard. "From the Baale," one of them said. Ten hens, one cock. Emma watched a young woman with a basket on her head step around them and come toward her. She bent her knees in the ritual sign of respect, then lifted the basket straight up before bringing it to the ground. She pulled out two heads of cowries.

"The Baale must mean to win you over," Henry said, adjusting his hat, his feet still bare. "The gift is clearly for you." Emma checked her hair, stood, and smoothed her skirts.

Chickens were everywhere. The rooster strutted before perching on the chair Emma had just vacated.

"My," Emma said, and then remembered herself. "Please," she said, nodding to the girl and the two young men, "give my deepest thanks to the Baale."

"We'll build a coop," Henry said as the gift-bearers departed. "Looking after the chickens will be a good task for Wole."

"You're right," Emma said.

"Of course I am," Henry said, his hand on her shoulder.

Sunday, a week after their arrival, they held their first services in the Africa room, just the household. In a little bit, a good group had gathered at the wall. When Henry called to them, a few shook their heads and passed on, but a half dozen came in and took a seat. Henry offered a lovely devotional on the lilies of the field, how they toil not, neither do they sow, yet Solomon in all his glory was not arrayed like one of these. His message for Africa: You are already fully loved. Emma ruminated. In her experience, it seemed the children already knew this.

Monday morning Emma was still in bed, considering her plan to go out among the women, when she heard Henry coming in a hurry.

"Word of a rogue elephant in the area," he said. "The king has given the townsmen permission to hunt. A man with a rifle is expected to join in."

Her husband was at the wardrobe, slipping on a jacket, checking the pockets, taking inventory of what he needed. "My saddlebag," he said to himself.

She sat up. Her husband no doubt believed the townspeople would be helped by his leadership. She thought it likely they knew how to hunt elephants, being longer acquainted with the animal than Henry was. But there was no use arguing. Henry turned to her. "I might be out for the day."

"Of course," she said. *Kiss me*, she thought. *And is Jacob going?* But Henry had left.

She felt listless. At last she chose a lavender-waisted dress with pink smocking. She fingered her lace collars. *I ought to give one to Abike*, she thought.

Henry returned at dusk. Emma was sitting under the odan tree.

"How are you?" he said.

"I haven't felt well."

"You don't look ill," he said. He put his palm to her forehead and she smelled his male smell, of salt and tobacco and almost like a memory, a whiff of alcohol. Because of the elephant hunt, she felt a thrill of danger, imagining the drink as a feature of his manhood, for once not seizing on his nerves or potential bad judgment.

"What about the elephant?" she said.

"No luck. Though there's no doubt he was here. Dung big as a native basket."

"But why do you say *he*?"

"Because the animal was alone. Females travel together with their young."

"How strange that I forgot," she said. Henry's presence made her wonder vaguely if she might be expecting a child. Not yet, she thought. It was too soon. She wasn't ready.

"I'll wash up," he said.

Emma didn't like her husband's absence, but she liked the confidence a hunt brought into him. *Thank You,* she prayed in her interior heart. *Keep us well in Thee.*

20

Imperative

Henry called on the Baale. It was only reasonable to do so after the generous gifts. Such gestures were always meant to be answered. He carried with him a small clasp knife to leave in return. He had another. Indeed, he had invested mission board money in several of these to offer as signs of friendship.

The gatekeeper saluted him. Henry surveyed the Baale's compound, large enough for hosting festivals. He was led into the king's palace, which was built like the house he and Emma were occupying but was twice as big, the piazza deep and commodious. Everything was brown but the trees. The Baale sat on the piazza, communing, it appeared, with his chiefs.

Henry knew the order of things: the king in charge, a chief for each borough of the town. Then there were the priests, who might be more powerful than the chiefs. It all depended. Every town was different, and Henry had yet to figure the politics of Ogbomoso. The Baale stood to greet him, and Henry was introduced around. Still seated, the men leaned forward from the waist as their names and positions were announced, and Henry did the same in turn. He felt happy for being among men. The Baale, he knew, was a pagan, but he wondered if the man dressed in white might be Mohamedan. A boy came offering punch, and Henry had an opportunity to present the knife.

"Crafted in my home territory," he said, delivering it into the king's large palm.

The man turned it over but couldn't figure it out.

"Let me show you." Henry demonstrated how the blade could be brought out.

"Ah," the Baale said, his eyebrows raised. "It is good. It is very good."

As Henry was leaving, the fellow expressed happiness over his presence in the town and emphasized how he must stay for a long time. On the trek upcountry, Henry had already begun to think about how easy it would be to push on to Ilorin. Only thirty miles more and he would be on the northern frontier. He was fortified with Jacob. Emma had taken the trip well. She might prefer to set up house, but housekeeping was not their calling. Of course he would see to her welfare. But they were within reach of his true destination. He was being candid about a trade school. He could get it started, sketch out the plan. But a native agent could develop it. Henry's calling was to clear the path. Smart as Emma was, she could not be expected to understand the imperative posed by the Mohamedans. He was pressed by time. So much of his life behind him. The Kingdom of God yet to be won.

The next morning, he studied his fingernails and later his hairline in the mirror. He powdered his feet. He thought the toenail was already better. It was the drier climate. Certainly they *should* move north, after the next dry season. Ogbomoso was a way station.

· 21 ·

Revelations

"I PLAN A safari into town tomorrow," Emma said, she and Henry with bowls of morning coffee.

"Ask Jacob to go with you. I'm meeting with a local chief tomorrow," Henry said.

"I'll ask Duro," she said, sorry her husband had not offered to come with her.

As different as Yoruba land was from Georgia, it was still possible to anticipate an outing if you had the energy after coping with the heat. Emma would not see church spires or admire the city gardens, but once in Ijaye's open-air market she had found European china. Anyway, walking was her bent. Her great-aunt Helen had been a walker until she took a stroll on her ninety-sixth birthday and never came back. That was a story her father told. As a boy, he had been sent to look for her and when he found her, she was faceup, next to the goldfish pond at the center of a boxwood grove. Her hat was still on, just a little askew.

That evening Duro came in limping. He had twisted an ankle in the countryside turning up yams. That left Jacob to accompany Emma on her safari. The next morning, Abike and Wole were waiting with him in the outer compound. They all stood at her approach, and she was surprised again by Jacob's height and the smile hovering in his eyes and along his cheekbones that did not suggest obedience. She thought the golden key to the African mind was in that smile.

"I haven't given much thought to our direction," she said.

"We can begin," he said.

She drew on her gloves.

As soon as they passed through the gate and stepped into the street, a band of children appeared out of nowhere, gathering around her as if she were a great odd bird. It was hardly a new experience, but she was disappointed that Wole and Abike simply stepped aside for the throng, unaware of how they betrayed her.

"Whew," Emma said to no one. The houses were as predictable as day: uniformly mud, one story, thatched roofs. She smelled bean cakes frying in palm oil. Here and there stood a palm or pawpaw tree or great shading hardwood. Roosters and goats dawdled; a black-and-white pig tripped past. The lane was clean and open. Some boys sauntered by, pretending not to look at her. Then an old farmer passed so close she could smell the earth on his hoe, but he took no notice of her, as though he had no mental picture she might fit, and therefore she did not exist. When they had traversed the equivalent of three city blocks, a tall woman stepped into the road with the clear intention of intercepting them. Her calves were straight and lean and she seemed of some indefinite and eternal age like a character in Virgil. Emma felt her heart beat in her temples as the woman made a little speech. She used the word *funfun*. A number of the woman's neighbors stood silently in the shade. "What did she say?"

"She says your skin has been rubbed off and is white like raw cotton," Abike said.

Emma was again seized with the sense of discord she had felt when first in the country and her color was called out, not for its loveliness but its absurdity. It made her angry with Abike to be reminded. "Jacob, ask if we may visit," she said.

Jacob addressed the woman, who had put a hand to her cheek as if all skin might now be in jeopardy. In a moment, he turned back to Emma. "She invites you to her house," he said.

"Tell her first, while we are here in the street, that my skin has not been rubbed off. God has made us different for the glory of His creation." She reached for Abike's hand and gave it a good squeeze.

When Jacob translated, the woman went into another speech, her voice moving about on the scale and landing on such unexpected notes that it put Emma in mind of a xylophone.

"What is she saying? Have you vexed her? Tell her I am Mrs. Bowman." A goat came close to her skirts and made ready to do something unbecoming, and Emma shooed it away.

"Mistress Bowman," the woman said, waving Emma toward her.

They followed her through a small room, out the other side, and down a narrow yard where a pawpaw tree hung heavy with oranging fruit. As they walked, children joined them, all in a line. The group stepped through another passageway and out the other side into a large yard and finally to the room the woman had in mind for her visitor. Emma was delighted. This was just as she imagined. She was entering a new stage in her development as a missionary. God was with her and had provided this woman for her first real evangelism in Ogbomoso.

The room had a window of all things, shuttered with a gatelike contraption but now propped open. Their hostess captured a stool out of the corner and offered it to her guest.

"*Joko*," she said.

Emma gathered her skirts and aimed her hind side for the low seat. Once settled, she looked up to see sky. "Your window is fine." She spoke slowly in her best Yoruba, hoping to communicate her admiration.

The lady was arranging herself with a pretty green scarf. Then she took her own seat, a stool so worn the wood was ashen. With clear authority, she told Wole and Abike to take seats on a mat and left

Jacob to decide his own fate. He stood leaning against the wall. When a native beer was offered, Emma tried to resist. But the hostess insisted and then filled her gourd twice. It must have been fresh because the taste was finer than usual. As Emma let her legs float out in front of her, she thought of Jesus taking wine with ordinary people as he ministered. After a moment, she beckoned Wole and then pushed him forward in the fine new shirt she had sewn. The woman took the boy's hands and swung his arms out and back with hers, like girls might do in play. She said something longish and delicate, and the boy nodded in agreement. Jacob translated because Emma didn't catch it all.

"She says one's true nature is like smoke; one cannot hide it in the folds of one's garment."

Emma might have found the woman's proverb a challenge if she hadn't been so relaxed with the beer. Instead she was open to its wisdom—open like the window. "Who is she?"

"She is the mother of the town," Jacob said, "not simply *iya* but *Iyalode*, woman governor. Women with trouble come to her."

"How wonderful," Emma said. She did not recall that Ijaye had included a female governor, but right here she had stumbled across the most important woman in Ogbomoso, well, apart from the pagan priestess. The Iyalode could help her reach other women through a sewing circle. Teach trade, Henry said, and the church will follow.

The woman nodded her head back and forth as if she were, through some sixth sense, in possession of Emma's own thinking. A child's head appeared at the window but quickly disappeared.

"The Iyalode wishes to know if you have a title," Jacob said.

"Not exactly." She wanted to try her Yoruba again, but this sentence could be spoken only in English. "I have a college degree that took several years of study." She peered at Jacob, wondering how he would translate. It took him a while.

"She asks if only women go to college," he said.

This was almost as fine an idea as a women's government. "No, not at all," she said, thinking she might explain women's and men's colleges. But Henry did not have a college degree, and it wasn't such a fine idea to explain that. "My husband is an ordained minister, an *aluffa* of the true God," she said. Unfortunately the Iyalode seemed not as impressed with this as college. Emma thought she must press on in the direction of the gospel, even if just briefly.

"The one God," Emma said, keeping it simple and using her own Yoruba, "sent His son to live with us and open the road to eternal life. His name is *Jesu Kristi*. He brings hope to the poor and all who suffer. My husband and I have come to Ogbomoso to share this true faith."

The Iyalode adjusted her headdress. She talked back to Jacob.

"She wants to know why this God-on-earth was preferring the poor."

"Because the poor are most in need of God's mercy."

Again the woman went through Jacob.

"She says big men also need God; who will come to them?"

This question had not been put to Emma in Africa. She thought of most everyone as poor. "Of course, if the rich man is willing to give up everything to follow Jesus, then the way is open for him."

The dialogue continued to move through Jacob, and Emma was glad to have him. He was a better interpreter than Duro.

"She says the rich man has a responsibility to keep his wealth so that he can distribute it to his wives and children and other members of the town in need."

This was vexing. Emma thought the woman might prove a challenge. She flexed her fingers in her gloves. "As long as the man's primary allegiance is to Jesus and loving God and if he lives a good life, giving freely of his wealth, he can enter the church and be saved," she said, thinking, *That should do it.*

"The Iyalode wishes to know what else is in your head," Jacob said.

"I know mathematics." Emma put him in a stare, meaning to convey that the talk was a little drawn out. "I've studied poets, gurus, astronomy, zoology, physics, and Latin," she said. "I can show her a picture of her own country." This possibility bloomed in her mind like a white morning glory. She could promise to bring it on a future visit. Her back was starting to hurt from sitting so low, and her dress felt snug in the middle. The Iyalode stood, without any apparent effort. Wonderful. They could leave.

"She says you can show her," Jacob said.

"Yes, when we return." Emma had nothing to get hold of, to lift herself. Jacob held his hand out. She looked at it hard and grasped it, feeling her hand small in his. When she was up, standing before him, she was startled to see how clearly handsome he was. For a moment she forgot what they were doing.

"Now," he said. "She says you can show her now."

"Now?" Emma stammered, feeling all tossed up. The Iyalode was out of the room, talking this way and that to children who had converged at the door. Emma struggled with her skirts and adjusted her hat. She drew in a breath. "Very well," she said. "I'll need a good stick."

Out they filed into the yard. Jacob sent a boy to fetch a drawing stick. Everyone else took seats on the veranda. Shortly, the boy was back, his chest puffed out as he passed the stick to Emma. "Where to begin," she said, and took her gloves off. Her hands were already freckling; her mother would be horrified. "Yes, your country, of course." She started with the vast curve of West Africa, remembering it from her father's globe. Blue blue blue. Down she went to southern Africa and the Cape of Good Hope, up the eastern coast to the horn of Ethiopia, up toward Egypt. Her Africa was a little irregular but she kept going, straight across North Africa, smoothing it out as she went. What princes and sheiks and mighty Moors did she topple with her driving Herculean stick-pen, shaving their kingdoms back? Briefly she glanced at Jacob and then on she went, the last lap, all around and back to her beginning place. West Africa was a bit too large, really, about twice its size in relation to the rest. "Now," she said, straightening herself, "we are here," and she made an *X* on the Yoruba country. "Ogbomoso."

The Iyalode waved her hand over the continent and Emma understood her question.

"This is your larger country. Africa. Surrounded all by water, *odi*. It's called ocean, *okun*."

The woman stared at the dirt. She wrung one of her ears out with the tip end of her little finger, as if the image had done something to her hearing. She moved to stand in the middle of the continent, out of the ocean.

"Too small," she said. The children laughed—perhaps, Emma thought, at her.

"It's quite large indeed," Emma said, "so large it would take you a year to walk across it. This is a rendering." Quickly she sketched a human figure in the dirt, a woman with a skirt and a basket on her head. "Now. What is this?" The Iyalode pointed to herself. "Exactly. And yet she is very small, while you are large, *titobi*. She pulled herself up to indicate large.

The woman looked doubtful, cupping her chin in her palm, a worried expression on her brow. Suddenly she erupted, her hand pointing to the map as if to scold it. "Where is your own country?" That would be harder, Emma thought. How to draw North America? She looked again to Jacob, but he was gazing off as if preoccupied. *Gird up*, she thought to herself, using a form of speech he had frequently spoken to the porters on their journey. She did her best, but the rendering of her own continent looked something like the udder of a cow. *Africa is clearly more decorous from a certain point of view*, she thought. She made an X where she estimated Georgia to be, just above Florida. Then she drew a line across the portion of the Iyalode's yard that had become the Atlantic Ocean. "It takes sixteen market weeks to get from

my home to the coast of your country. Be sure she understands, Jacob."
She wanted to bring the man's attention back and for the Iyalode to
know how hard she had worked to get here. "Then it takes several
days' journey overland to arrive in Ogbomoso. In good weather." She
stood back, took off her hat, wiped her brow with the gloves she
had stuck into her belt, and replaced the hat. Her spurt of energy was
gone.

Jacob passed on this lesson and the Iyalode continued to study,
with some disapprobation, Emma thought. The woman moved across
the ocean to stand inside North America. She walked the line back to
Africa, disturbing the illustration with her footprints. She scratched
her head beneath her headdress. Its upward slant reminded Emma of
Mittie Ann from back home and the resemblance brought a torrent
of memory—Uncle Eli standing at the back door that morning, his
feet still whole, the little girl who wrote *JESUS* on a bit of bark. There
was a horrible complication in the drawing, and it made Emma terribly hot. The Iyalode had walked the route of the slave trade, and it
was Emma's own route. How had she failed to see this before? *Something blue, a quilt, Uncle Eli's stars.* Now the woman looked into the
sky, not even sheltering her eyes against the sun. Then she held her
hands, palms down, before her, arms straight, and swept the air. Jacob
relayed: "She asks how you saw this vision unless you have been in
the sky?"

Emma had her drawing instrument to the ground now, like a
walking stick to steady herself. Her head felt dangerously hot. The
Iyalode was too demanding. Let her try to understand Copernicus.
Emma took in a breath and let out a puff of air. "Tell Iyalode men
travel in boats around the globe, around the world, and use tools
to measure the land. The earth is round"—she showed with her
hands—"like an orange. People have sailed, in large canoes, all the
way around her big country"—she pointed to Africa and saw Uncle

Eli's maimed foot. Quickly she pulled her eyes back, and the stick too. She adjusted her hat. "Around her country and across the ocean to my country and back." Jacob explained at leisure and Emma boiled in the sun. Finally, she could continue. "They have even sailed all the way around the earth." About the time sweat started running from her scalp down into her dress, it dawned on her that it took significant abstract thinking for the woman to have realized that the best place to anchor a drawing table for sketching out the earth would be the heavens.

"She says she will think some more," Jacob said.

"Yes, I heard her," Emma said, grateful for her own endurance. What a trial the lady was, over there shaking her head, looking out at the horizon.

"One more question mah," Jacob said, this time with his smile.

"What?" She tried to be impolite.

"She wants to know why have you come so far to this place and left your mother?"

Emma looked at the map she had sketched, but it seemed the earth had slanted funny and the brown dirt was slipping away beneath her. With the Iyalode's walking about the map, the area of Georgia looked like a burst pumpkin. When Emma raised her eyes, the sun nearly blinded her and she remembered for a moment swinging out under the big oak in her front yard when she was a girl, how she would let her head go back to watch the sun falling upside down through the trees. Then when she got off the swing, the right-way world looked upside down.

She put her arm out and the Iyalode caught her at her elbow. What a relief to be led to a mat under a tree. Emma took her hat off and fanned herself. Her stomach was certainly in turmoil. She looked to see if anyone had noticed her weakness. Abike and the Iyalode's girls were comparing hair styles. Wole took turns with the children jumping from the piazza into the yard. Jacob pulled out a lobe of kola nut and was intent on his ceremony. The Iyalode's long legs stretched before her on the mat. She began another speech, using the xylophone sounds, and Emma didn't try any longer.

"What is she saying, Jacob?"

"She says the world began in her country. Therefore your ancestors traveled to America from this place and now you have returned home. She says you managed to leave your birth mother because your ancestral mother resides here. Otherwise you could not have come. She says you will need your mother soon."

Emma caught the Iyalode's meaning right away: The woman meant she was in a family way. She imagined that Jacob too understood, and the idea of that knowledge in his head made her feel out of time. All at once birds sounded. Someone was chopping wood. The loveliness of a huge, perfectly made pot sitting in the shade with a flat stone as a lid confused her. The Iyalode's eyes turned flat and smoky. Across the yard, Emma saw an ugly lizard. In a hidden compartment of her mind—like the hidden place in the writing box—she had known her condition. "My," she said, looking toward the sun, "how the time has passed."

In order not to repeat the stand-up with Jacob, she put her hands flat on the mat, bent forward, and pressed back onto her feet, and then she came up vertebra by vertebra until she was standing, testing with every move the condition of her stomach and her head.

"We part as friends," she said, extending her hand to the woman. "I hope you will call on me soon." A breeze came up the hill, cooling Emma's neck. Jacob said, "Come," and while he meant Wole, she followed.

That evening, Emma jotted some notes, almost all questions: *Why does it seem I will betray Sarah by having another child? Does God guide our every move or does He allow others to bring the daily miracle? I can't simply have happened upon the Iyalode. Did Jacob know? Was he guiding me there?*

"I might be six weeks along," she said, lying alongside Henry before snuffing the bedside candle. "I wasn't sure until today." He didn't respond right away. Quick as the devil came that awful thought: *He's not well; he doesn't wish it; he wants to move again.* She raised herself to look at him. His lips were slightly parted.

"Are you happy?" he said, pulling himself up to meet her.

"I can't say."

"You dwell on Sarah," he said.

"I don't want to lose her," Emma said. She paused, running her hand over the sheet. "I have sometimes thought I was losing you."

He pulled her close and smoothed her hair.

"You cannot lose Sarah. She is eternal." Emma's heart tipped like water spilling out of a tumbler. They came together in that close way, upon the edge and over.

A week later, Emma woke in the night, the space beside her empty. Henry assured her he never left the compound; it was just that sometimes his leg cramped or he couldn't sleep and he needed to walk about. While it was still dark but after the rooster's crow, she dreamed and woke with the sense that she had left something unattended.

When she dressed and came into the courtyard, she saw the sun breaking over the low roof of her dwelling, light shifting through the leaves of her tree, a dragonfly hovering over a water pot, a lizard at its base. The morning was cool and she went back into the bedroom for one of Henry's old sweaters, worn to thinness but perfect for such an African morning. She welcomed the velvety air and rang her bell for tea. *It's only normal I should be tired*, she reassured herself, *with the move and constant commotion, and this.* Just to think how much she had learned and accomplished, and suffered, in sixteen African months. She patted her stomach.

Duro brought the teapot on a tray along with her favorite china cup. Though she was sure Jacob knew, they had not yet said anything to the household.

Henry came through the parlor door, carrying his coffee.

"I missed you," she said. "When did you get up?"

"Not much before dawn," he said. "You were snoring." She thought he eyed her playfully.

"I never snore," she said.

"You do now."

"What's your plan for the day?" she said. Henry had preached in town, taking up his post with the blind man, who had a choice location at a crossroads, beneath an expansive tree. By Henry's report, he often drew more than a hundred listeners at a time. She didn't doubt him. But her husband spent equal time riding to the farms with Jacob and conversing with villagers. He had reported on a nearby hill he meant to explore, *Oke' lerin*, meaning "mountain of elephants."

"I thought to work on my Hausa," he said, meaning the language of the north. "I found a gentleman who knows the grammar."

"We haven't finished the Yoruba book," she said, startled that he would speak of something so far off when their needs were right in front of his nose. Couldn't they do one thing at a time? Focus on one language.

"Of course," he said, evading her comment. "You're forgetting to wear your hat." He retrieved it for her. "I'll check the horse and be back for breakfast."

Emma was just beginning to feel at ease. For several mornings now, she had taken Wole and Abike to the Africa room, the one she had spotted on her initial exploration, with the thatched roof and wooden benches. She knew children would come if she showed herself, and they had. Twice more she had traveled into town, calling at the Iyalode's, taking some sewing with her, and demonstrating for a group of women how to make a buttonhole. It would be so good when African women had buttons to keep their clothes shut. A particularly eager woman named Sade got the knack of everything right away. She was quite short, probably not five feet tall, with scarifications on her shoulders.

"Abike," she called. "Abike!"

The girl came into the courtyard through the passageway Henry had just exited. Her head was uncovered and she had a green feather stuck in her hair.

"What are you doing? Where were you?" She was suddenly impatient. The day was getting on. She should be at work. Besides, there were doubtless all sorts of strangers milling about just on the other side of the compound wall, gazing at the girl.

"I was assisting Jacob mah. He has told me to sweep his yard and make fire."

Emma took care as she stepped down from the veranda. She pulled the feather from Abike's hair and the girl ducked. A wave of heat came over Emma and she tore savagely at the sweater she had put on. As she did, it caught on a hook in her dress and snagged. The pulled string was almost a foot long, and the sweater all bunched where the damage was done. "Call Jacob immediately," she said, feeling she had been caught in dereliction of duty.

The man half ran into the courtyard. She was pleased at his alarm. "What do you mean making a slave of my servant? How do you explain yourself?" she said.

"Please mah." He caught his breath, cocking his hip and resting a hand on one side. "She offered to sweep after she had finished here," he said.

"She tells me you demanded that she sweep and build a fire."

"No mah." He seemed to be laughing at her.

Jacob had enough of the Englishman in him to keep Emma thoroughly confused. He was a black man who didn't seem to need her help, who considered whether he would accept their offer of employment. Though clearly it should be so, it bothered her that he had greater claim on Wole than she did. "You are not in charge here. This girl is not yours!" Emma said, feeling her chest tighten. "As soon as my husband returns we'll sort this out."

"Sort what out?" Henry said, back from the stable.

"This servant of yours is commanding my handmaid. He's had her sweeping this morning and making his personal fire."

"He's not my servant," Henry said.

"He's had Abike in front of his room, sweeping his yard and tending his fire." She meant to make her point.

"What's this, Jacob? What do you say?"

"Sorry sah. The girl . . . it was a mistake. My own mistake." Emma saw the flutter in Jacob's jaw—as if *he* were offended—and it made her even angrier. Henry was being taken in by his manner. And she had thought Jacob was acting as an instrument of the divine!

"I don't see much damage," her husband said. "In future, Jacob, be sure to check with Mrs. Bowman. She's in charge of the house staff."

Instead of a sewing lesson and a bright hour in the school, Emma's morning was ruined. She did not call Abike. There was no sign of Wole. Henry and Jacob went to preach and she was left with nothing. She committed her thoughts into her diary: *Husband's servant worrisome; morning lost. Expect better tomorrow.* Returning the journal to her writing box, she remembered Uncle Eli, who had looked out for her, whose hands were so familiar she could see them now, and she felt worse for what she had written. She pulled the book back out and recommenced. *What troubles me that I should be so harsh? How can I be a witness if I cannot be kindlier in my own household?*

After dinner Henry set to work on his vocabulary. He had jerry-rigged a work space by placing a plane of wood over two boxes in a corner of the piazza, and here he spent two hours before going out to preach in the afternoon. Emma took a nap in the bedroom. She woke feeling drugged and discontent, the way a foreigner does after sleeping in the day in a hot country and with little true refreshment or companionship. She poured water into her wash bowl and dipped her head into it. She combed her hair out and sat in the rocker on the veranda. She waited for her hair to dry and for Henry to emerge, but he never came from the shaded corner. When she went to investigate, she discovered he had finished his work and gone out.

She went in search of Duro. He was waiting at the kitchen. She sensed he had something to say and hoped it was not about her flare-up in the morning.

"What is it?" she said.

"An idiot has come," he said, raising both hands to his head and rubbing his short hair, then running one hand straight down his face as if wringing out some distress. "When you were resting and the master has gone. One of those snake charmers. He is very bad. I cannot enjoy myself when he is coming."

"Did he pass through the gate?"

"He called to me from the wall." He pointed.

"What did he say?"

"He says you have brought something here. 'The *oyinbo* woman is bringing trouble. She has something she doesn't know. It wants to go down.' That is what he is saying."

Emma experienced an encouraging lift of understanding. How grateful she was for her cook, who spoke to her plainly. "But you see, don't you? We have brought the light of Jesus, the gospel. He's against our religion because he's fearful for his own way of life. He depends on people's superstitions and doesn't wish to be discovered for a fraud. You know all of those rain dancers dance in the rainy season when it's going to rain anyway. I don't know how they get away with it. I'm sorry he troubled you." She was happy to be talking it out.

"I was fearful mah. The man is too dangerous. I am fearful for you."

"Thank you for your care, Duro," she said. But still the cook seemed concerned. "Is there something else you haven't told me?"

"He wanted to give me a charm."

"Yes?"

"Ah, mama." Duro shook his head, using that close African address. "A native medicine."

Emma was surprised her cook was so distraught. These things were common but harmless. It would take some while to rid Africa of its pagan ways.

22

Alphabet

JACOB SAT ON the piazza in front of his room, sharpening a saw. He had turned to the work after Mrs. Bowman's outburst. Since their visit with the Iyalode, he had thought the woman was learning. She appeared to respect him. Now this morning she tried to turn him into a boy. She was too proud. He calmed himself through the task, waiting for Tunji, a friend from the caravan and *omo* Ogbomoso, born in Ogbomoso. Tunji was one of the porters who had run with him in search of Wole. That night they had sat up by the fire. Jacob had told how he discovered the child on his return to Yoruba land. Telling that story had required telling of his own slavery, and he was grateful the next day when the man did not reject him. The mark of slavery was viewed as a personal flaw by Jacob's countrymen, or, worse yet, a contagion.

He worked the file against the beveled edge, turning it between the teeth until he captured a shiny edge. Wole lay on his stomach nearby, his legs, from the knees up, swaying apart and back together. He was copying letters onto a chalkboard from a set of alphabet cards.

On a routine job carrying loads for British agents between Ijaye and Ibadan, Jacob came upon his small relation. The caravan had stopped in a village close to his former home. Someone had spoken his father's sister's name. He inquired, thinking it still possible someone

A Different Sun   *189*

from the family may have survived. When he described his auntie's long neck and the way her voice carried higher and higher into the trees as she talked, an old woman declared that such a woman had escaped into the town, wearing only a scarf, and round-bellied. She had died in the next dry season but left a son, who was cared for by a grandmother of the town. There was no mistake; the boy was of his lineage.

Jacob lived in the village with Wole for a season before taking him to Ijaye. He told the boy stories of the family. The child seemed to hear everything as a drama. "Do I look like Baba?" he would say in his Yoruba, meaning Jacob's father, or, "Who has had my head?" *Whose character is like my own?* The stories brought the past back to Jacob so intensely he sometimes felt he would disappear. The boy, however, seemed content, as if he lived at one remove from the world of ordinary people and Jacob understood why it was a commonplace to believe the son is the father returned.

One day in the market he heard of the opportunity with Rev. Bowman. But then the child disappeared on the road. It was enough to finish him. Once he had the boy back, he didn't care if the reverend sacked him, but the missionary was too happy with Wole's safety to suck anger.

He looked down to see that Wole had managed *H* but was stuck on *J*. "Why don't you rest?" Jacob said, half joking. Wole shook his head again and lowered it. "Let me show you," Jacob said, squatting. "It is the beginning of my own English name. Begin at the top, like so, come down, and pitch left, like the base of a tree. Then put a flat roof on top. Eh?" The tip of Wole's tongue stuck out in concentration. Jacob looked at the back of the boy's head. He cupped it with his palm and shook but not hard enough to rattle the child's brains.

Back at his seat, Jacob turned the saw over and worked the other side. When he was through, he rubbed it with an oil cloth. He caught sight of his reflection in the blade, and he thought of Mrs. Bowman.

It was a shame she was so disquieting because Rev. Bowman was a good *oyinbo*. He knew how to work and did not require someone else to haul every small box. Already they had hunted, explored, and preached together. Pastor liked to know everything. What can this plant do? How can you fix this food? How is this wood used? He sat on the ground in the village. It was true he had lost his temper on the journey. All men lose their tempers. The responsibilities of being a man were great, whatever the country. No. It was the wife. He saw now she was a trap that could spring. It was not good for his master. And what of her thin frame? Would she be able to carry the child? It would be bad for the pastor to lose his offspring.

Was it the wife that troubled him, the master? Or something else? Jacob was unable to ascertain the matter as of yet. The man had some struggle in his head. Sometimes, even, he would turn directly from speech to silence. He came out in the midst of the night and walked about in the compound. He might stop, turn around, and walk the other way, as if he had dropped something. He squatted and felt the ground, and Jacob wondered if it was a form of American prayer. When he knew the man better, he would inquire.

In the day, the reverend was very-very exacting. With everything, he would not wish to be off by a quarter inch. Even so, he treated him well, almost like a white brother.

The sun stood higher in the sky and lit the blade of the saw. Jacob remembered the silver bracelets his mother wore when he was young. He had fastened in his brain an image of her as she looked when he was very small, lying with his head in her lap: her round throat, nostrils open, eyelashes, the fringe of headdress above him.

Wole's legs swayed. Jacob was glad his small relation had his protection. Nothing was worse in slavery than to have his body inspected. A stone of anger sat in the front of his brain, remembering a white man's palm on his chest, against his thigh. He watched Mrs. Bowman closely with Wole, but with him, she was kind as a mother. Jacob tried to forgive her for her foolishness. Once he observed her hair fall around her neck, and her gesture of putting it up made him wonder who she might be if she had been born in Africa. He swung his arms overhead and stretched. The child turned onto his side.

"I don't know this one," he said, pointing to the Q card. "How do you say it?"

"You don't know Q because we don't have it," Jacob answered. "It is a strange fruit. I will tell you how to eat it. First take K and put it in your mouth, then U; then chew them together: K-U."

"K-U," Wole tried.

"Say it faster," Jacob said.

Wole spoke something that sounded like a lame bird: "K-yu, k-yu."

"Go on and write it; it will root in your brain," Jacob said.

The affray with Mrs. Bowman had brought too much into his head. As soon as he sat again, his mind traveled to the day he returned to his country, searching for his village. He had been told it was gone, but he would not believe. He fitted himself with a machete and a knife, as if going into battle. He sought for hours in thick brush and woods, at last finding the familiar granite boulder. When the village was not where he thought to see it, he decided it must be on the other side. He had just remembered incorrectly. Still, he felt hollow. Then the village was also not on the other side. He located the iroko tree where vendors once sold food to travelers. He found the river where his mother had washed him as a boy and the lagoon where he and his friends dove from overhanging trees. A foreign town had sprung up around it. Going back to the place of his lost village, no evidence at all but memory, he at last stumbled across an old wall in the grass. He sat down and wept and turned onto his side, onto the earth, and wept, and reached out and pulled up clumps of grass and dug into the earth and tore his fingernails and dug into the earth again and clamped his fists around the dirt and smeared it onto his face and into his mouth and wept. The earth had broken.

Someone knocked his shoulder.

"What are you dreaming of, the girl, eh?" It was his friend Tunji.

"Why are you pushing me?" Jacob snapped. The memory was in his mouth, the taste of dirt.

"No trouble now. You were sleeping with your eyes open. Again. You are becoming like the white missionary."

"Crazy man. Sit down before I beat you."

Jacob relaxed, seeing his friend with his yellow dog. Tunji carried *fufu* dipped in pepper soup and wrapped in a banana leaf.

"I've come to deliver you from the white woman's food."

Jacob rested his elbows on his knees and leaned into the *fufu*. Some of the hot soup ran down his hands, but he caught the drops with his tongue. The dog waited in case he missed.

How did his friend know his thinking on Abike? It was difficult in any case. Missionaries may fire servants if they suspect attraction between them. "Which girl?" he said.

"Which girl?" Tunji was still standing, and he bent over and laughed as he repeated Jacob's question. "You na crazy man," he said. "Abike, *na so*?" He placed his hands on his chest and indicated mounds.

Jacob looked at Wole, but the boy was too involved in his letters to be watching Tunji.

Jacob tried to keep a straight face. "The food is fine. *A dupe.*" Suddenly he wondered if Tunji had hopes for Abike. The man must have read his mind.

"My eye reaches for another girl. She's farther along," he said. One of Tunji's teeth was set at an angle and the effect was to make him so-so handsome to the ladies. He walked in a casual strut. All of the women on the caravan, even the old ones, wanted to wait on him.

"My friend," Jacob said, changing the subject. "Have you decided whether to come to worship with us?"

"What day is it?" Tunji said.

"Imagine every market week plus two days," Jacob said.

"How can I remember that?"

"I will call for you one day. Come to the service, then just count off to seven and come again."

Wole stood. "I am finished," he said, as if he had built a kingdom.

"Finished what, small man?" Tunji said.

"The alphabet."

"Ah. You're becoming an *oyinbo*. Even now, your color is fading. Any time pass now and you will become a ghost. Jacob, have you seen your brother? I don't see him. Where is he?" Tunji waved his arms, pretending the boy was invisible.

Jacob saw the boy lock his knees until his legs were almost bowed backward. "See me this time! I am not *oyinbo*!" he demanded, holding out his arms to prove it to himself.

"Give the boy some credit," Jacob said to his friend. And to Wole: "Latch on to my back." He leaned over and the boy latched on. When they passed under the compound trees, Wole reached into the low branches and grabbed, bringing down a golden spray of leaves.

Jacob caught sight of Mrs. Bowman watching them from the house. She appeared lost. Suddenly he wished to go to her, to ask what she might need. The feeling made his head burn.

23

Dry Season

Recently we visited the night market, where women sell
into the wee hours, their babies sleeping beside them. A thousand
oil lamps on small wooden tables, quaint displays of green and
red vegetables, the low hum of voices.
[A written line blacked out.]
The lack of women friends is a severe hardship. No one to talk to
but one's husband [something crossed out]. My face is darker in the
mirror. I may never be able to go home. What would my family say?
Henry has found a friend in Jacob. I think they trust one another.
The rains will come and we can plant a garden. It must
be I worry about losing this one too.

—EMMA, THE RED DIARY, OGBOMOSO, OCTOBER 1854

A HALF DOZEN BROWN lizards claimed the post just over Emma's head. "Shoo," she said, waving. They blinked their eyes. A wisp of dogwood flittered through her mind. *Our Father who art in heaven.* What was it?

Her belly was just swelling and she kept her corset loose. It was the beginning of her second dry season, her second baby, her second school. The number of students varied, but by October she had four regular pupils besides Abike and Wole. When she showed the oldest boy a primer and explained that the writing was his own language, he pressed his hands on the page as he might examine the leather of a drum, to see if it was tight enough to release good sound.

She encouraged the children to teach her Yoruba words. In exchange, she gave them an English one and then they wrote both on the blackboard. Many of their words were new to Emma; they might contribute to Henry's vocabulary. One boy taught her *deho*: hunting for a cricket by digging out its hole. He acted the word with such zest that *digging* seemed a poor equivalent. Emma asked the word for *blue* and was told "color of sky." "No, blue," she had said, showing the color in their own clothes. This time she was given "color of water."

In her days, Emma felt almost secure, only to discover in moments of solitude that something frightening and unknown lingered beneath the surface of her life. Or perhaps the feeling was more akin to a free fall; nothing substantial held her up. She was not helped when they received news that the new Baptist missionary had died in Accra and was buried at sea.

"Poor man," Henry said.

"Yes," Emma said, imagining the tiny bark of the man's casket, the cold water enveloping it, there and gone. She clasped Henry's arm against her chest.

Since the confrontation with Jacob, she tried to avoid him except in Henry's company. She did not believe an apology was due, though she felt regret and hoped a natural remedy might be accomplished. There might come a time when she would need him.

Two weeks later, Henry and Duro made a large fire for roasting guinea fowl. Henry had bagged them on his way back from a neighboring village. After Duro had cleaned the birds, Henry dredged them in salt and a little flour, his shirt sleeves rolled up as he worked, and she took pleasure in watching him. His forearms were one of his best features, taut and purposeful, a bit hairy but not wildly so. She admired the way he secured the fowl in a dress of sacking, tight and true as a bolster on a divan. The birds were now hidden in the ashes, where he had put them to roast along with several coco yams. Henry's ways were charming when they were alone. His use of a hillbilly colloquialism or his penchant for washing his face squatting at a bucket out of doors became again the attractive elements of the daring man she had met in Georgia, and she welcomed every moment of such feeling. It seemed to her that a marriage needed rekindling, just like a fire, or it would lose its power.

Evening came on and the moon with it. By eight o'clock, a soft wind blew in the compound where they were still sitting around the fire, she in her hammock chair, Henry on the ground. He had some piece of writing and the tin lantern, and they were quiet. She thought about Georgia, where, in the afternoons, light was slanting across yards and fields, the shadows of pines stretched out long as roads. There, in the mornings, her father might be having some acres turned to lie fallow; in another field, root vegetables would be fattening. Standing, he would look at the land, holding the bridle slack, the horse, damp nose to the ground, searching out the last of the clover.

Her husband kept working. She felt the smallest impatience, something the size of a walnut. At last, he spoke. "Jacob tells me a diviner sees Wole being a book boy."

"What did you say to that?"

"I reminded him diviners don't light our path. But I figure a *babalawo* must be right on occasion; otherwise he would lose his station."

She brooded. Her impatience with Henry's inattention to her was now about as large as a bucket. Just as the impatience was nearing elephant size, she heard a most rankling sound, thin and determined, and her first thought was of the guinea fowl they had eaten, risen charred from the fire to perform a lamentation. Henry's pen jumped across the page. "What in tarnation?" he said. The sound came again.

"Jacob's banjo," she said. "We haven't heard that since we arrived."

Her husband gathered his writing and the lantern. It sprinkled light. "I hope he's not trying to woo a woman with that song," he said.

Emma lifted her head with a start as her mind went to Abike. She found the girl with Duro. "Let me help you to bed," she said, feeling suddenly alert.

After her time with Henry, she was still wakeful. "We'll have to tell them soon," she said. "My dresses are getting tight; I'll need to let them out again."

"Yes, soon," he said, and turned over to sleep.

On the Sabbath, Henry shared their news with Duro and Jacob. Emma told her handmaid. Emma felt awkward Monday morning when she wore one of her looser dresses, but by afternoon, the idea of a new baby seemed woven into their communal life. Even Jacob saluted her, and she felt the natural remedy had come.

She was sitting in the Africa room with Abike, threading a needle, when the Mohamedans arrived on horseback. The men looked very fine indeed. Their faces were oval and dark, their movement fluid as smoke. Henry wished her attendance and she was happy to oblige. The silver tray came out and the china teacups. They gathered on colorful mats. Emma knew a smattering of their language, Henry a fair amount, and they, being traders, knew some Yoruba. One was Fulani, the other two Hausa, from the north, former enemies but all cozy now through mutual interest in trade. They were headed for Ilorin, the Mohamedan citadel Emma thought of as a siren calling her husband. But today she was too full of life to be worried about Henry's wanderlust. They would be in Ogbomoso for some time; Henry had spoken of a church.

The men showed her beautiful objects, including an ivory tusk carved out to create a multitude of elephants, walking single file, head to tail, the work so dainty it looked like lace. Emma dared not ask the price. As a gift, they left an ornately patterned leather stool. It was a pleasant evening. She only rebuked herself a little for thinking, at one point, that the men were a bit arrogant to show her such fine things that were beyond her means.

The dry season leapt forward. Henry laid the mattress near the door, where they might catch a breeze. In the day, every bit of shade brimmed with those retreating from the heat: men, women, children, goats, chickens, squirrels, lizards, birds. Just when you wanted water, rivers shrank; creeks vanished. Turtles pressed into muck. Leaves withered and the shady spaces shrank. The sun proved itself daily, coming and going, chariot of fire, the Yoruba god Shango. Yet Emma discovered a new will and a different thirst. She made herself a loose African dress that would not bind her waist or her wrists, and everyone admired it, even her husband. She went to the Iyalode's and worked with the women, especially Sade, her petite student and champion buttonhole maker. Back home, she dipped Henry's tin cup into the cooling water pot, drank lustily, and saved the last bit to pour over her head, even dousing her dress. Emma felt she was getting very close to something that had been worrying her for a long time, something more troubling even than Sarah, something fiercer than Henry or her father, something as frightening as where you would be if you had never been born. Perhaps she was finally breaking through to a true experience of God. She had tried so hard to have it.

Just as she was on the cusp of this awakening, she and Henry were invited to the Baale's compound for a festival day. Emma resented it. She did not relish the thought of buzzing insects and warm drinks and grilled meat—who knew *what*. Nor did she welcome an opportunity to observe the king's wives dance for him. She already had her sweet domestic view of the women, gained when she called at the eldest wife's house. She did not wish to upset it if they should dance half naked. She sidled over in her mind and caught a glimpse of that question. She had touched it more than once, but not recently. *Was Henry ever stirred by the notion of more than one wife?* It was a frightening thought, but in moments of fear and longing she had caught herself pulling on it as one might press a wound to gauge the extremity of feeling and find an edge.

"*Must* I attend?" she said to her husband. "It will be taxing to sit so long in the heat."

"We're living in the man's house," he said. "The priests will be there. They have given permission for us to attend and would take our absence as an affront."

Emma went to her husband and took his thick brown hair in her hands. She kissed his mouth hard. "I hope I don't die," she said. "It would serve you right."

Emma wore the muslin dress from Ijaye and a green ribbon at her neck. Henry was waiting for her in the compound, talking to Caesar, explaining that they would be riding to the festival. There would be other horses, drums, and shouting. The horse should not be afraid. Henry assisted her in mounting, then handed her their gift to the king, a goblet purchased in England, now nestled in a native basket. He swung up behind her. A dozen men dressed in white skirts arrived to lead them. Briefly Emma considered Abike and Jacob. Was it appropriate for them to be left together, possibly alone? Well, it was too late to worry about it now.

The streets were thronged with people. They found the Baale established on a chair at the front of his house. He wore a long white skirt, no blouse but a huge necklace of red coral around his neck, and a most beautiful beaded crown, not so tall as some Emma had seen but intricately done in blue, brown, and yellow. Atop the crown's cap, four crescent buttresses rose skyward, and right there where they joined sat that ever-present bird. There were drummers off to the side, dressed in fine *agbadas*, some working with the talking drum that was supposed to send messages hither to yon. The interspersed beats entered Emma, and she felt the vibration inside her.

A royal servant stepped forward to offer the salutation. "The Baale salutes the *oyinbo* and his wife. He is happy you have come. You are welcome." The king did not look at them directly but moved his head in agreement. Emma thought it an odd way of doing things.

"Hold your hat so it doesn't fall," Henry said. "Then bow your head when you present the goblet." He gave her arm a squeeze, and she was reminded of their knowledge of one another, deepened because they lived in a country where they were foreigners to everyone but themselves. Emma wasn't sure if she should hand the glass to the king or his attendant. The Baale was exercising a horsetail whisk, whether as a fan or to keep off flies she wasn't sure. Just as she made a motion toward the servant, the king opened his hands and she offered it to him. He turned it over, ran his hand along the smooth sides, and shook his head in agreement.

"Thank you. It is fine. You are welcome." He looked into Emma's eyes, and she thought his face registered grave responsibility and a momentary joy. The servant pointed in the direction of two European-style chairs. Thank the good Lord. They were arranged in the shade of a tree and there was enough space around them that she and Henry might breathe. From her seat, Emma took stock of the mounds of yam and cassava laid out on mats. The drumming started back up and reached a crescendo. Everyone looked toward a large passageway. It might, Emma surmised, lead to the king's private courtyard. Sure enough, his eldest wife, Ronke, was making her appearance, her long neck ringed with gold. She pushed the air out in front of her and then brought up her backside, as if the air offered points of leverage. Seeing the woman's chest covered, Emma thanked the Lord again. A second wife appeared. She made a circle of her arms in front of her, gently raising and lowering them, as she moved to the drumming. A third wife lowered her hands and face, turned herself in half circles, and made progress over the ground by scooting back on her legs rather than forward. And so on until all the wives were dancing, no two alike. But they wore identical dresses with beads sewn on a fringe that swayed as they moved along. Emma joined the clapping. The women processed to the king. Now he stood and danced briefly with the wives, lightly shaking out the whisk. There was lots of clapping and he returned to his chair. The drummers began to sing. Emma could not catch the words, but Henry gave her the gist of it. First the Baale was praised for his purity, honor, and courage. He had killed a number of elephants and even as a young boy he was a great warrior, fighting off the infidel Fulani who had been rebuffed at Ogbomoso. Finally he was praised for his generosity. At last the drums and the singers had told enough stories. *Oh good*, Emma thought, *we're drawing to a close*. But other men must dance. Drums must talk again. Children must perform gymnastics. Palm wine needed drinking. Emma's head listed to one side. She was so sleepy. At last they reached the grand finale, what everyone had come for: distributions of yams and cassava to the head woman of each compound. Emma was worn out. Certainly the afternoon had deteriorated: men laughing with their mouths full, children relieving themselves in public. She found herself repelled by the women's large flat feet and the king sliding down in his chair. She couldn't imagine why she had earlier thought he reflected the seriousness worthy of a monarch. Flies swarmed everywhere.

"We'll salute the king and take our leave," Henry said.

"Thank you," Emma said. She reached for Henry's arm. The king straightened a bit as they approached.

"Ah. Baba Bowman. I hope you have enjoyed your visit," he said.

"You are a magnanimous king," Henry said.

"We are ready for you to stay in Ogbomoso." This was all ceremonial, Emma knew. She wished the Baale would stop it.

"We remain as God wills," Henry said.

The king looked off somewhere. "In our own thinking," he said, "God directs the people through the king." As he spoke he lifted his hands to the heavens and then tapped his chest.

Emma saw Henry's blue eyes go funny. "We believe God speaks directly to His disciples," Henry said. "Good day, sir," he finished, and bowed only slightly. Emma stumbled backward, unsure of what had just happened. Some of the attending chiefs started a twitter, and the king laughed deeply out of his belly. Emma caught sight of a man looking on them with what seemed absolute contempt, a priest perhaps.

She was surprised when Henry didn't turn Caesar into the compound but headed out the city gate. A brief shower came up and they rode right into it. Emma could smell the earth. *My husband is as disgusted as I was*, she thought, *and needed a breath of fresh air.* They came to a large flat rock, and the horse's hooves sounded prettily on it. Henry pulled Caesar up and dismounted, took his hat off, and ran his hand through his hair.

"Did you hear him?" he said.

"What do you mean?" She had thought Henry would say something sympathetic toward her. She put her hand on her newly round belly.

"The Baale announcing in public that I'm his prisoner!"

"Did he say that?"

"He claimed divine right to direct my movement."

"That was more or less the case in Ijaye," she said.

"He announced it to the town. If I submit, I might as well agree that the Baale is more powerful than the Christian God."

"He was making traditional conversation," she said. Why did Henry continue so prideful? Couldn't he come in love toward her pain, sharing the heart and mind of Christ against the heathenism of this country? She needed him.

"I'll leave any time I'm ready," Henry said. He pulled out his flask and drank fiercely from it, then wandered for a bit on the rock before coming back to mount the horse behind her. In Emma flowed the tide of sorrow women feel when husbands tout their power but expose only weakness.

· 24 ·

Souvenir

Henry brought Emma sliced bananas on a plate. She took it to mean he was sorry for losing his temper after the Baale's birthday. She and Duro prepared omelets, using onions and tomatoes from the market. Emma didn't know how tomatoes could grow in the dry season, but they did. While the children helped Duro with morning chores, she finished off one of her patchwork pillows. She held it at arm's length for a final study. A square of native silk in the center and around that swatches from an old print dress. The work was good. She might save it for Anna Hathaway. Before going out for her school day, she checked on Henry. She found him in the parlor studying his maps of West and North Africa. He had marked out the line of stations. At the moment, his eyes appeared to hover over Ilorin, and her husband seemed hardly to notice her presence. He had often shown her how, from Ilorin, he could reach Zaria, then Kano; beyond Kano, the vast Saharan trade route opened up: Agades, Ghat, Murzuk, and finally Tripoli and the Mediterranean.

"Why are you studying that map?" she said, knowing full well why. She felt dropped from a cliff; look how he had just lulled her into thinking he would be kind and fair. Her anger grew like a storm.

"Why shouldn't I study it?" Henry said. "It's the country we live in. There's not another man out here thinking on how to develop the mission. Who else is going to do it?"

"But we aren't going anywhere soon," she said, determined to halt him. Her mind was a muscle of argument: the baby, its needs, her needs, Henry's own need for recuperation, their marriage! She would not speak to him if he was going to plan their destruction so willfully. She left the room, her head buzzing with fear. She wished for her mother or Catherine, someone who would bring a bit of fruitcake and a large dose of sympathy. She longed even for Henry but a different Henry, the one who had said so tenderly, "Hold your hat so it doesn't fall off."

For days she and her husband were like wandering pilgrims who have lost each other in the mist and will only by some fantastic happenstance find each other again. They did not pray together. She was hurt and withdrawn; he acted as if she were indulging a mood and he would not help her out of it. *Our work is not so trying as are our relations*, Emma wrote one evening. *A gift given and retracted. These hardships might lead to despair. Where is our remedy?* She was afraid to express herself more directly, lest she cover pages of her journal with complaint against Henry. She turned her affections to Wole and Abike. The boy came often wishing to look into her "oracle." She could not get him to stop calling the writing box by that name, just as she had not yet talked him out of the blue beads around his waist. She had shown him how to hold the prism to his eye, to see a spectrum of light.

"Is it God?" he said.

"A reflection of God," she said, somehow believing he would understand. She had great faith in his brilliance.

At last a minor crisis offered respite to Emma's marriage. On the last day of October, Duro reported that death was chasing his mother. He came to them wearing his native *agbada*, asking for leave to visit her. He looked quite distinguished in the traditional man's dress.

"Her right leg is swelling," he said.

When Henry asked how long this had been the case, the man thought briefly before answering.

"Several months."

"And not the left leg?"

"Not so bad," he said.

Emma thought of the woman she had seen in Ijaye who suffered the swelling disease. It seemed too hard that poor Duro must find his mother in that condition.

"Let me discuss it with my wife," Henry said.

The phrase *my wife* sent a sprout of happiness into Emma's heart. She was immediately refreshed. They left the courtyard and moved to the parlor. "The mother isn't far," Henry said. "I doubt she's seriously ill. A true swelling disease would have carried her off. She wants her son to visit. But who can cook for us?"

"I've seen a woman from the caravan," Emma said. "We ate some of her food on the trek. It wasn't bad."

"That won't do. She'd be run off. A man wants the job."

"But surely Abike could learn. She already works for us," Emma said.

"What about Jacob?" Henry said. "You can teach him."

The memory of their confrontation surfaced in Emma's mind No, she thought, he would be too much of a challenge. But before she could object, Henry went out of the room, found Duro, and brought him back, along with the medicine kit. She stood as they entered.

"Mrs. Bowman and I have talked; you may have leave of four market weeks. Take these bandages. Soak them in cool water and loosely bind your mother's legs." He took in a breath. "You must tell your mother again about the Lord and Savior Jesus Christ, our only hope for everlasting life."

"Yes sah. Thank you sah," Duro said.

Emma looked at her cook, his brow creased. She took his hands.

"We will pray for you and your mother and your safe return. I will miss you."

"Yes mah." He tipped his head down and then looked back into her face.

Emma watched him leave through the passageway. "I hope he's safe on the road," she said. "But why go to so much trouble if you think the woman is not even ill?"

"It's possible she is. And if she is, you can be sure they'll seek a native remedy. What I gave him won't cure her, but it won't hurt. She'll enjoy her son's attention. We can't repeat the story of salvation often enough. I sometimes wonder about Duro."

"Why do you say so?"

"I found a bolus of native witchery stored in the kitchen. He had put it back in one of his clay pots, expecting, I'm sure, we wouldn't find it."

"Oh," she said, vaguely remembering the cook's report of an idiot who wished to leave him a charm. Yet she was sure of Duro's faithfulness. "I'll speak to him when he returns," she said. "Let's work for an hour on the vocabulary." So with her husband, the tension was eased, and she didn't think to ask him why he was looking in the kitchen among the pots.

The next day, Emma tried to consider some relation of her life that might prepare her to train Jacob as her cook. The last thing she wanted was to let herself get vexed. But it was hard to find a parallel. If Jacob was Henry's assistant, he was also his only friend here. He was a brother in Christ. Yet he often performed as a servant. She gave up and prayed for wisdom.

They began with the finer points of simple tasks. "Eggs," she said, "are not set upon the fire to cook indefinitely in an open pot. They are only brought to boiling and then moved to a stone with a dish laid over top until they cool." She demonstrated by cooking one for an hour and another in the proper way, and then they compared the texture. Jacob described the overcooked egg as having come from a very old chicken, and she felt a bit tipsy in her delight with him. Each morning she reminded herself that she stood in a relation of respectful authority over the man, but his cleverness made it difficult to keep aloof. By the end of the week, he had worked up a wonderful chowder of peas and local greens. By the end of the second week, she was certain Jacob could be a friend to her. If, for example, Henry was ever away and they were in the night market, and she felt she might stumble in the dark—in such a case, she might reach out for this man to steady herself.

Emma was showing him how to peel tomatoes so that he did not lose half of the fruit in the preparation when she nearly sliced off the end of her thumb. At first she thought it wasn't so bad. A bloody fringe appeared in a semicircle, and she looked at it with curiosity before the burn hit. She pressed the injured hand with the other, the lid of skin popped open like a flap on a tent, and blood gushed from the wound. She grabbed a towel to stanch it. "Henry," she cried.

"He is out," Jacob said.

"What will I do?" Emma waved her hands up and down. When she let go for a moment, the bleeding seemed to ease, but then it started again, oozing between her fingers and over her wedding band.

"I will fetch a bandage," Jacob said. "Sit down."

"Quickly," she said, beginning to rock forward and back in her seat. Then she stopped rocking and stared flatly at the ground, until she saw white dots and closed her eyes.

"Give me your hand," Jacob said.

"Oh," she murmured, and opened her eyes, looking up to him.

"Give me your hand," he said again. He forced her fingers open and apart and pushed her hand into the water pot they had set out for stewing tomatoes. The pain subsided for a second and returned, throbbing. Emma tried to pull back but found her hand might as well have been set in stone for the power with which Jacob claimed it. He held her thus with one hand while loosening the bandage with the other. Looking up at him, she had the briefest vision of being his captive. When he decided the thumb had soaked long enough, he raised her hand above her head. She bit her lip. His power was a demand, and with every press of his hand, her blood surged. He brought the thumb to eye level, positioned the slip of skin just so, and pressed the end of the bandage on the wound. Emma felt a thread of pleasure coil around the throb of pain. She observed as Jacob made the first turn of the bandage. He continued weaving around the thumb. Emma's back arched. A tremendous energy filled the space between them, as if the entire world had been condensed into this moment, and all people and places with it. Surely Jacob felt it as well, this condensed field, the currents of power. "Come," he said, still holding her bandaged hand. She stood, searching out his face, but she could not tell his thought. She leaned into his shoulder as he led her to a chair on the interior piazza and pressed her to sitting. "Wait," he said. He returned with a cup and Henry's whiskey and poured her a drink. "I will go for Pastor," he said.

"No!" she said. "Don't leave." She began to weep.

"I will find him," he said. In a bit, Emma looked up to see light filtering through the trees. The colors of the world gained greater brightness, as if a film had been drawn away to show their deepest hue. What had happened? It must have been the shock of her wound. But the slightest thought of Jacob and the feeling came back, a dense flame, a flamelike secret. She sought to resist it. Too impossible. An African man. Then she invited the feeling back.

She was dozing when Henry woke her. "Emma," he said. He squatted in front of her in that position he sometimes took, inspecting the bandaged thumb. "Jacob did a fine job," he said. Then he kissed the wounded hand. "Take it easy for the rest of the day." He went to wash up.

Emma began to rehearse what had happened, picturing herself sitting as Jacob pulled hard on her arm. He had pressed her sleeve up to her elbow. She thought of the man's tunic, broad and fair against his brown arms. Henry came back through the courtyard on his way to the kitchen, and she was flooded with remorse that he was too late.

In the late afternoon she woke to voices and wandered through the passageway. Henry was out in the compound, playing with a group of children, Wole included. Her husband ran about this way and that, letting them catch him. As soon as he was tagged and they all gathered round, he would take off again, zigzagging. The point was to let the *oyinbo* escape and then hunt him down. Each time he was caught, Henry threw his arms up in pretend alarm as though his life were now over, and this created an almost uncontainable joy among the children, who leapt straight in the air. Abike was watching too. She had one arm nestled behind her, across her lower back, and latched on to her other arm at the elbow so that her chest swayed out. Emma's heart seemed almost sore. For a long time she had nurtured such a romantic vision of her husband, playful and free. But now she felt sad for him.

It was almost dark, rich blue clouds, a rind of light beneath. Emma let her eyes rest among the walkers on the road. As she wandered back into the courtyard, a swarm of yellow weaver birds lifted from the odan tree. Henry came and kissed her bandaged thumb again. His ruffled-up hair was sweet like a memory. "Jacob and I made a corn pudding," he said. "The man is handy in the kitchen."

"He must have a natural gift," Emma said.

IN HER DREAM, Henry's clothes lie crumpled in the back of a wagon. She and Jacob are in the storeroom; his arm is around her neck to stop the bleeding of her finger; her back is to his chest. Her arms fly open. She wakes in a cry.

"What?" Henry says.

She turns over, sits up, and pulls her legs into her chest.

· · ·

THE FOLLOWING DAY, Jacob was back at the kitchen.

"Good morning mah," he said, his eyes focused on the eggs he was peeling.

"Good morning, Jacob," she said. She watched him in profile, but he did not look at her. "Thank you for your help yesterday."

"Yes mah," he said, still not turning to her.

Any moment, she thought, he would say something more, but he did not, and his self-control made him more vital and more danger-ous. She filled her diary with a page about her husband. She must get Henry into her book: his arms, the flare of his nose, his broad fore-head, the fineness of his neck as he concentrated over her. Not that she wrote any of that. She wrote about his preaching, the vocabulary, folks in the yard calling on him to offer a prayer, the swell in the num-ber of people attending church.

If she had a woman to talk with about the dream, such a friend would assure her: a trick of the heat, lingering effects of the malarial fever, her delicate condition. But she had no one.

One morning in late November, Wole came carrying a package. It was an English cake in the most beautiful tin sent from Rev. Moore in Ijaye. And right behind Wole was Duro. Emma's heart jumped. She had almost forgotten her first cook in the magnetism of Jacob. His mother had survived—indeed she had survived so well she sent him back with two gourds of palm oil.

"*E kaaro* mah," Duro said.

"Welcome," she said, truly glad for his return, but sobered too.

Gradually, the old schedule returned. Henry was often out and Jacob with him, and Emma ate alone under the odan tree. She looked at the scar on her thumb as a kind of souvenir. Perhaps her experience with Jacob was meant to wake her to some knowledge of herself, even g God. She could not make herself repent. Only as she recalled how the anniversary of Sarah's birth had come and gone and she had hardly paused to remember it, had not called Henry to her side to remember the child in mutual love and sorrow, did she feel regret. She rededicated herself to her Savior and prayed over her impure thoughts.

Pulling herself back to her responsibilities, she spoke to Duro. "Mr. Bowman tells me he found some sort of native medicine in the kitchen. In one of your pots. Why do you have it?"

The man's chest bent inward. "It is *oogun* mah, the medicine left by the idiot, against evil force."

"We will have to let you go if you practice native charms."

"Please mah. It is very powerful. It cannot be thrown away." The cook made a swatting motion with his hand. "It can even move against a good something, if the owner is not careful."

"But there is no power."

"Yes mah."

"You must agree to get rid of it."

"Yes mah."

"We will pray together—for your faith."

That evening she and Henry ate supper in the courtyard. One fine quality of the dry season was the diminishment of insects in the twilight hours. Emma told her husband how she had spoken with Duro. "I think he truly understood," she said. Henry didn't seem to hear her. "Henry," she said. "Henry!" When he looked up, he seemed lost, as if he were perceiving another world, not the one they were in.

"Are you well?" she said, dismayed.

"Of course," he said. "I just had the oddest sensation—you know the kind—when you feel something has already happened."

In the night, she woke frightened, remembering how Henry had been lost when they were in Ijaye. She nudged his arm, and he pulled her close.

The next day she saw Duro go out of the compound, and she thought: *He's taking that medicine to bury somewhere.* And then she knew, as if it were something she had been knowing all her life, like the dominance of the number four, that the charm had been for Duro's protection, perhaps even against her. Just as Uncle Eli's arrangements that she had taken for stars were surely against her father. And though she didn't believe any of it, she shivered in the heat.

25

Living Stones

J ACOB FELT HER looking at him from the courtyard through the parlor doors.

He knew her eyes now. They were brown like his, almost as dark. Her hand had been like a bird in his hands, fluttering, afraid, white.

What was she, this pastor's wife?

Jacob had a world in his head, and it depended on the *oyinbo* man.

He was glad when he and the reverend went into town, inviting people for church. The man spoke with him about the meaning of scripture. He even asked Jacob's opinion about the parable of the vineyard in which everyone is paid the same regardless of how long he has labored. His heart warmed in their conversation. So he was concerned when Pastor spoke of Ilorin. It was no good to move again. Abike's mother would not wish her to travel so far. Then what would he do? He was saving for the bride price. Without even having planned it, having spoken with no one about it, he had begun to think of Abike as a mother for his children.

ONE SUNDAY IN December, the earth so dry the ground had split, a large crowd arrived for services. Jacob was encouraged.

First, the missionary read scripture. *"Come, and let yourselves be built, as living stones, into a spiritual temple."* Then he talked on it. "The sacrifice required by the true and living God is nothing short of your life. God does not require your fish. Give that to your children. Neither does He require your drink. Save that for yourselves. Such sacrifices laid at the feet of the Shango idol merely rot."

Instead of living stones, Jacob saw turtles—turtles in droves, brown and green, old turtles and young, clamoring one over the other in chaos. Pastor was taking direct aim at the Yoruba pantheon, and few divinities were more favored than Shango, divinity of thunder and lightning.

"Ah!" a man erupted from the back, throwing the sleeves of his *agbada* over his shoulders.

Jacob waited for more of an outcry, but the people seemed intrigued by a white man speaking about their deities in their own language. It was like watching a lizard fly.

"The true God has come to us through His son, Jesus, because God loves us and wishes that we will not die but live with Him eternally—*titi lailai*—if only we believe." Pastor dug into his pockets and pulled out a stone. "This is your life now," he said. With the other hand, he held out a green branch. "This is your eternal life in Jesus." Pastor rested, closed his Bible, and wiped his forehead. It was a good place to stop, Jacob thought. But the missionary started again.

"Your *orishas* cannot speak, nor can they give you everlasting life." Pastor waved the living branch. "But when you come to Jesus, the Christian God speaks to you directly."

The man who had protested earlier stood up. "Shango speaks loudly," he declared. "First the lightning, and then he clears his throat! He speaks well-well-o." A number of men laughed and clapped. Jacob could have anticipated this response.

"Lightning is merely a natural phenomenon," Pastor said. "God may use it to chasten those who forget Him." He paused as if he were remembering some personal experience with fire. "Only God directs the winds and rains. And He will not be appeased with scraps from our tables. God demands more, like a king!" Now he seemed to have hit upon a point. "The king of Ogbomoso is most powerful, no?" Agreement from all. "More powerful than the warrior, the chief, even the *babalawo*."

Jacob would have stopped with the impression of the strong king and not brought in the high priest. Still the people agreed.

"Yes. Yes," came the reply.

"And will the king accept mere gifts of food from his warriors? By no means! He requires the warrior's absolute devotion! So much more is it with the living God!"

Another man sprang up: "The king will also take food for his belly!" Now the crowd rose up in a swell. Jacob bent his head to hide a grin. The townspeople who had shown up didn't dislike the *oyinbo*. Their idea of things was to debate and see who could tell the best story. A few of the congregation, doubtless, hoped Rev. Bowman might work as a charm against the more ravenous race of Europeans who were interrupting their trade and demanding tariffs. Some might see the point he was making. It was true that God was the origin of all things. But they also saw their kinsman's point; the king had to eat—and so did the *orishas*.

After the service, Rev. Bowman said he would not eat for two days, as a demonstration of spiritual sacrifice. He invited Jacob to join him. Again Jacob felt confirmed in their friendship. This *oyinbo* did not call him *brother* and then treat him as a slave. The reverend explained his thinking. "The people understand one God. The *orishas* are merely a mask to cover the darkness. To their credit, they conceive the darkness. But they have no idea how to find the light." Jacob thought briefly of Pastor at night, bent to the ground, feeling the earth. Was there some light in the dark that Pastor sought? Had he found it there?

"It's up to you," the reverend was saying.

"I will join you," Jacob said, but wondered that the missionary did not know that the Yoruba often fasted for their divinities: fasted for rain, for harvest, for battle. He saw the turtles again, but now they were dispersing, some leaping into the river, some even mating. The Pastor departed, and Jacob pressed his fingers against his temples. The man's essence was restless. Mrs. Bowman knew this as well. He had seen her look from her husband to himself, Jacob, then back at the husband. Her eyes spoke what she did not say.

Tunji called in the evening after Wole had fallen asleep, carrying food as usual. He poked fun at the reverend, who had been bettered in his word game. "Watch where your tongue walks," Jacob warned, even as he smiled at him. "It may pick up sand but never find meat." To answer, Tunji offered up a gourd of cassava with sauce. "Sorry, brother." Jacob tried not to look at the gift. "I am fasting."

"Ha! You won't last. Anyway, this food is happy to meet my belly." Tunji fell into his dinner.

Later, when his master did not appear in the outer courtyard and the moon was waning and Tunji had lain down on a mat, forgetting to go home, Jacob picked up his banjo and found a tune in it he hadn't heard before. It came from the small place on the back of Abike's neck.

26

A Letter

EMMA HELD HER tongue over her husband's fasting, but it wasn't easy. His health was never far from her mind, and not eating seemed an invitation to weakening. Furthermore, an *oyinbo*'s denying himself nourishment did not seem a route to the African mind. Then Jacob joined him, and she was faced with thinking on the two of them: Jacob quite capable of going two days without food; Henry, already too thin, much more vulnerable to some sort of attack. The comparison did little to unknot her tangled feelings. On the second day, Henry traded old horseshoes for a length of wood, to create a trough for Caesar, and she watched the men in the work of carving out the log. Her husband seemed to be holding up well. She was relieved enough to imagine that her infatuation with Jacob was passing.

In her school, Emma meant to make books of fables, but they were short on paper so she taught through memorization instead, though she worried that Wole learned too quickly. By the time she had the books, he would know the stories by heart and would not read but recite. It had been the same with word cards. He just knew them. Over and over he said, "I know that one mah. I know it." She thought it quite possible she had found a boy genius in Africa.

Two weeks later, she woke early to see the moon still bright on the horizon. It filled her with well-being, as a pristine egg swaddled in her palm had always made her feel whole. She felt everything linked: the heavens, this African town, Henry's sermon on life, her own body's life, their household—Jacob, Duro, Abike, Wole. God had led her to the Iyalode, and she had begun her women's work.

She found Henry at his table, occupied in copying Yoruba words into manuscript. It had become his custom first thing in the morning. She stood near him, energized by her vision. She bent to kiss his nicked ear. She ruffled his hair. "We were meant to come here," she said, gazing into the courtyard to see a chicken with its biddies. Henry said nothing but continued at his work. Emma often liked him for his masculine reserve, and she rested her hand on his shoulder. She wandered over to a chair that had been left on the piazza and took advantage of it. She had a piece of mending in her apron pocket, which she pulled out now. She threaded her needle and continued her morning reverie. "Look how well you are. The people are so eager." The morning smelled like water in the grass. She glanced at Henry. Wasn't he going to say anything? "When do you expect to build a church?" she said. It took him no time to respond to this.

"I don't think we'll be here long enough to build," he said, stopping to wet his index finger. "The next missionary, perhaps." He sorted through some notes.

She set her mending aside. "Why do you say that? There is no one else."

"Didn't I tell you"—at last he looked up at her—"we've heard from the board. Two new missionaries, along with a Negro agent; they're due to arrive in May. One can stay in Ijaye with Moore, and one can be stationed here with the agent. We can move soon after the baby."

"No," she said. "You told me nothing of it." In her dreaming on Jacob, she had missed some vital sign from Henry.

"I thought I had."

"Were there other letters?"

"Yes. One from your mother, I believe."

"I don't believe you. I don't believe you haven't told me." Her shoulders felt suddenly brittle. "How could you not tell me these things?"

"I set the letter right there on the table by the parlor door. I thought you'd see it." He looked at her as though now she should be pleased; certainly he looked pleased.

Emma found the letter just as Henry had said, only it was half hidden under a book. She ripped it open and a seed packet fluttered to the floor. She picked it up and went straight to the bedroom to stow it in the trunk. Her eyes rested a moment in the darkened space until she understood she was looking for Henry's rifle. It wasn't there. She cut back across the courtyard to Henry.

"You have deceived me," she said. The words echoed in her strangely. "Your actions led me to understand we would stay; I've set my mind to the work here." Her husband's head was down over his papers, as though she were speaking of a dress pattern or some such trifle and he hoped to escape the details. "We're so well along."

"You're in my light," he said, continuing his study.

"I thought," she said, "you seemed quite energetic in your preaching here. I counted sixty people last Sunday. You've played with the children as though they were your very family." It tore her to recall that beautiful scene, and this man would uproot it now and throw it to the fire!

Finally Henry looked at her, and she believed she hated him as fully and roundly as ever she had known a feeling.

"One of the Hausa men invited me on to Ilorin," he said. "I didn't say anything because there seemed little possibility. But with new missionaries, the way is open. Someone else will take Ogbomoso." He looked back over the table as if he were surveying a field from some height and trying to imagine where to start clearing.

"A way has opened here," she countered. "My student Sade will be a true believer. But she needs us to guide and support her. Duro will not travel as far as Ilorin. Jacob may not either. I can't go there alone."

"I've seen little evidence of true faith in anyone as yet," he said. He looked directly into her face. "What do you mean alone?"

She felt a flurry in her chest. "I believe the signs suggest we should stay here."

"You sound like a pagan, speaking of signs. This is a crossroads bulging with refugees. I made this mission and I'm the head of it. I'll do as I see fit."

"I thought you were fond of the place. The Baale wishes us to stay." She knew exactly how she was using her anger in raising the specter of their benefactor.

"We'll not decide the route of the gospel based on the wishes of an African king."

"But we will. If the king of Ilorin decides against you," she said, fiercely. She drummed her fingers on the table.

"Will you stop that everlasting tapping. It's like a Chinese torture."

Emma grabbed Henry's arm and shook it. "Will you think about us?"

"Let go of me," he said. He ran his fingers through his hair, then ran his hands down the sides of his face, and at last picked up his pen. His gaze turned from her. He began to write something, but he pushed the nib too hard and tore the paper. When he looked up, it was to ponder the courtyard. "Well, that will need copying," he said and stood, hitting against the table and upsetting slips of paper that fluttered to the floor. He walked over them and stepped down from the piazza. Emma could see his figure retreating, how he aimed himself toward the passageway and then into it as if to save any unnecessary step. In a little bit she heard Caesar's hooves and knew he had ridden out.

She sat for a good while and felt her hot misery. She saw her husband being led not by the gospel but by some baser need. He spoke of humility but jousted for power with these native kings. Certainly it was fine for her to sister the load, work with the women, but to him it was so much embroidery. She wondered if she had married a man who was spiritually less worthy than she had thought he was. It was one thing to be stricken with fever, quite another to use one's energies for vanity. He kept her in the dark on purpose, contemplating things of utmost importance to their work. She put her injured thumb to her lips. An image of Jacob's walking away rose in her mind, and she was suddenly enraged with him for distracting her. When Abike found her, Emma was still brooding.

During the school hour, she let her passion flow into her teaching, and she thought it was the best class she had ever led. Abike was developing a beautiful voice, a lovely soprano. Emma wished she had a piano in Ogbomoso. At midday, she took her repast in the parlor where it was cool, and once or twice she raised her head to listen for the sound of Henry's horse, not because she was through with her anger but because she nursed it and looked forward to expressing it. They could not keep riding into the unknown world.

As afternoon shadows grew, she began creating a story in which she could see just how far Henry had ridden and so could imagine him on his way back. She would still be angry when he returned; in fact, she looked forward to keeping her anger for a week at least. But he would be here and she would not have to carry the responsibility of the entire compound. She had only to survive the next two or three hours. For a moment, she dozed in her chair and then woke with a start. Everything was still and Emma felt on the edge of an unfathomable void, the world without shape or reason, the hot day an eternal suspension. A terror gripped her, so frightening it seemed hellish. She wished to scream; someone must come to break this awful spell. In that moment, she remembered her mother's letter left in the parlor.

Who knew what might be in it. It was one of only a handful she had received in a year and a half. Emma scanned it quickly—Catherine's new house, a revival in the church, nothing about her father being reconciled with God. And at the very end, almost an afterthought. *Old Uncle Eli finally died. We made him a nice grave in the Negro cemetery. The seed is from his garden.*

Emma twisted the letter and pressed it against her chest. At first she was calm, almost reassured, as if she had been transported home. Then she thought of the old man's hands that last time, lying gently on the quilt, all of the beauty that had come out of them. She closed her eyes and tears flooded her face. She was a small raft on a great ocean, nowhere a mooring. Her shoulders rose and fell. Poor Uncle Eli. She conjured the old man, his open smile for her, the wonderful look of surprise that came to his face when she was a girl, how special he made her feel.

Someone touched her shoulder. Little Wole. She caught him into her arms and sobbed. She rocked back and forth with him, recalling in her mind whole scenes of Uncle Eli, his whittling, finding her at the stream, saving her from the elephant, tending the garden, and always his turning to her. *It's the white bird come to visit.* But not again, not ever. "I have never been in the world without him," she said aloud. Wole looked into her face. Suddenly Emma remembered the letter opener. *You find a place.* Her torment doubled. She hugged the boy back to her.

"Mah?" he said into her shoulder.

She broke the embrace but still held his hands. "I lost a friend," she said.

"Jesus?" he said.

"No, not Jesus," she said.

Into evening, Wole stayed with her. Abike brought tea. Jacob came to ask if she needed his help. She looked at him sadly. *Mend me*, she wanted to say. "An old friend died," she said instead. "My mother wrote to me."

"Ah mah, *e pele o*," Abike said, "I am sorry."

No one in the house spoke of Henry. Beneath the odan tree, Emma committed two sentences into her journal. *Husband too much desirous of the north. Uncle Eli passed.* Out of the last wispy clouds, she pulled to her mind the wild rhododendron of Georgia.

Finally it was dusk and Duro brought the lantern. Soon he returned with her evening meal. She ate most of it, for the baby. The cook came back to collect her dishes. "Where is Abike?" she said.

"She is with me in the kitchen," he said.

"Send her to bed."

Emma watched her handmaid enter her room. She saw the curtain close and soon after, Abike's candle was shut, as the girl liked to say. Duro returned to ask if she wished him to sit as a night watchman by her door, but she said no. She took the lantern and went to bed, but when she entered the room, the terror of the afternoon hit her again, the absolute cold absence. She steadied the lantern on the bedside table and opened Henry's medicine kit. She let her eyes rest on the contents, waiting for her vision to adjust. There was the small decanter of wine. She took it out and poured half a cup. In a moment, she found the slender amber bottle of laudanum. It clinked against the others. The sound seemed monstrous. Like a thief, she turned her back to the curtained door of the room and hid the bottle as she tried to open it. The stopper had been set in odd-angled and it was stuck. She was afraid of breaking the vessel if she forced the stopper. Why in the world had it been pressed so forcefully and wrongly? She rubbed her damp palms against her skirts and tried again, and this time it gave. She thought six drops would put her to sleep. She stirred the tincture, set the cup on the table next to the lantern, applied the stopper back to the bottle, replaced it in the kit, and set the kit back on the trunk. Her ears seemed to be ringing. She lifted the cup and drank it in one gulp and set the glass down. In a bit she couldn't tell if her skirts belonged to her dress or her nightgown. It didn't seem to matter. She made herself think harder about the light, being sure to snuff it, and then waiting to be sure she could see nothing, not even her hands, before turning herself into the bed.

27

Fire

CATHERINE WAS CALLING. "Where are you, Emma?" She was hiding under the bed; that was where she was. Likely her sister knew, but the game made her pretend not to know. Catherine must look all through the house, circling the table in Papa's library, tiptoeing into the dining room, looking behind the neat stuffed chairs of the sewing room, climbing the stair, opening Mama's wardrobe, and finally their own rooms. Emma smelled ash in the floor boards.

"Sister?" Catherine was getting closer. This was the part that so thrilled Emma she could hardly keep still. How would her sister find her? Kneeling to tug her slipper? Emma pulled her legs up under her skirt. Oh! Catherine was leaping on the bed. The great furniture groaned as if it might break. Emma was scrambling to get out. *Hurry. Hurry!*

Someone picked her up. She wasn't under the bed at all.

She had dreamed! Henry was home. How swift he was, but why? At the doorway, he pressed her head to lower it and they tumbled onto the piazza. Her feet felt the cool clay.

"Come," he said, pulling her fast, and they were into the courtyard. It was not Henry but Jacob. Such an odd cast of light and voices above them. She wrenched her hand away, bringing it to her throat; she must find her shawl. Turning, she saw men on the roof, yellow flames. They heaved against the fire with branches, pulling out wads of thatch where they could. The fire had caught in a corner of the house they had not occupied.

"Where is my husband?" she cried.

"He is not returned."

"Wole and Abike?" Emma's voice seemed hot.

"There." He pointed to the piazza behind them. Abike had her arms around the boy.

Emma pulled her hair close to her face. Out of the corner of her eye she saw the fire leap and a man tumble from the roof. The charred thatch broke his fall, and he limped toward them. "How long has it been going?" she said, her hands crossed over her chest.

"Only now," Jacob said. He snapped his fingers to show how brief a time.

"Were you up?"

"Yes," he said.

"Where did these men come from?"

"They saw the flame from the other side."

She had mistaken someone's call for Catherine's voice in the dream. Her head felt wobbly and large, and she remembered the laudanum.

"How did it start?"

"A spark from a near fire," the fallen man said, using his arms to show a bit of flame going up to lodge higher.

"Is that what you think?" She was looking to Jacob.

"It could be," he said.

"My writing box!" she said, veering back to her room.

"No mah, wait." Jacob held her arm. She pulled, but he would not let go.

The fire was out, but the men watched it a good while to be sure. Near dawn they began to leave. Ashes had fallen on Henry's vocabulary work in the corner of the piazza, but nothing of theirs was lost. Still, the look of their work—covered now in soot—depressed Emma deeply. "We should try to sleep," she said to Jacob. Wole had his thumb in his mouth, a habit she had never seen him indulge. "I don't mind if someone brings mats from my room. I feel safer out here than under that roof."

She settled under the odan with Abike, though when she closed her eyes the yellow fire still leapt, like a burning bird.

When Emma woke, she judged it to be midmorning. The girl's mat was rolled and propped against the tree. A dank sooty smell filled the air, and Emma saw the ugly black section of burned roof. When she walked into her room, it was just as she had left it except that the bed was made, the floor swept, and a pitcher of water waited for her on the washstand. Her writing box sat sturdy and neat beside the bed. She pulled the curtain and peeled off every piece of clothing, tied up loose ends of hair, and soaped herself. Halfway through her toilet, she felt a darkness in her center. Henry. The force of his absence hit her full on. She stared at her white thighs, her breasts, full and dipping, her abdomen like a moon.

In her underclothes, she held the box on her lap and hugged it to her. She fingered the scallop, then opened the lid and took out the carving. She ran it over the planes of her face. "Can you bring someone back to me?" she said.

Emma came out to find a crowd in the outer compound. She remembered the people at the church service, how they said, "Shango speaks. First with lightning." *Or fire*, she thought. Everything seemed hazy and unreal. Now all she wanted was Henry's return. She wove her way over to Jacob.

"Good morning," she said, one hand on her midsection.

"Good morning mah," he said.

He seemed subdued, and she imagined he disliked Henry's absence. It wasn't a good thing to explain when there was no explaining. "Why are they here?" she said.

"To clean and repair. The king has sent them."

"Is it possible we are the cause of the fire?"

"Yes."

"Someone could be against us."

Jacob lowered his head and ran his hand back and forth across his neck. For a moment she thought he was going to tell her that they had to leave. He would not catch her eye even when he spoke.

"By rebuilding, the king expresses his wish for the *oyinbo* to stay. These people will mend everything."

He will not answer directly, she thought.

Jacob swept his arm out and across the space in front of him to indicate the Baale's largeness and ownership. "If someone has lit the fire, he will not try again."

Emma's hand drifted toward his, but she stopped herself. How she longed for Henry to take care of her.

28

Escape

Henry detested Emma's pressing on him. She knew it and did it anyway; that was what made it so blasted infuriating. When had she become the head of the marriage and the mission or even the parlor? When they had met, he thought how different she was from her mother; she could come to Africa and stir her tea with a twig, eat *fufu* and sauce. But now he saw the common thread running through the fabric. She paid fierce attention to pillows and was forever scolding him for scattering the bedclothes when he sat to pull on his boots.

There she came this morning talking of settling in Ogbomoso, speaking of God's signs. She played the king card—*but you will do as the king says*—and grabbed him. He feared he might hit her. He was more afraid after the scene, knowing how close he was. She could have fallen, her head split like that young man who fell from the tree, or the baby could have miscarried. He saddled Caesar and took right off. No word to Jacob nor anyone. He passed fields where farmers fired brush. Smoke was dense and he enjoyed drawing it in, the smell fundamental and damaging. "Jesus forgive me; I'm taking a day off," he said. Under the forest canopy, he urged Caesar forward. In the way he had been doing for years, he flattened a hand against his abdomen. Only the usual tenderness.

He rode up the hill at a trot. Caesar's clip-clopping raised his spirits. Ahead, two basins of fruit were set near the path. The sellers, he surmised, were resting in shade, out of view. Close by were the handmade amulets—*aale* they called them—that would make a thief think twice. The one used here was fashioned from a kako seed pod with a palm frond turned around it: *The thief will be turned in on himself.* Henry stopped, and sure enough a woman came straight out of the woods. She waited on him to buy *akara* and three bananas, hardly as big as his finger. He rode on, passing fragments of an old wall. An anthill encroached upon it so that the structure looked in the shade almost like a cathedral with an extended nave. Henry touched his scabbard, the rifle in it. He felt an ancient tide. Greenery ten times the volume of Georgia smilax sagged from the trees. Turning downhill, he maneuvered around a rock splashed colorful with lichen and moss. Here the dry season met its limit. An updraft brought a sudden cool from his left. A creek. The horse picked up his feet, expectant. Caesar was a tad knock-kneed and his barrel swung low, which was how it came to be that Henry could afford him. But so far the animal had proven competent.

Henry ate his lunch, boots off, sitting at the creek, his feet in the water with Caesar's, who stood and drank and then stood, head to breeze, his mane lightly lifting. Into Henry's reverie stepped a lone man bearing firewood. The man did not turn his head but called out the customary *E kaasan*, good afternoon. Henry replied the same, thinking the man must get into town right often as he was unsurprised to find an *oyinbo* in his forest. Henry mused on the past weeks. "I expect to have no abiding place," he had said to Jacob one day after hours of preaching, "but to go from place to place, breaking up the ground, sowing for others to reap." His natural thrill and his spiritual punishment seemed one and the same—wanderlust and exile. It was often hard for him to tell which was which. "Ah!" Jacob had said, sounding sympathetic, though Henry was not sure whom the sympathy was for.

It was true what Emma said; they had only begun in Ogbomoso. People were attentive, but they weren't serious enough. They liked the story of Jesus, but they wanted to lay it alongside their own stories. "You cannot take several paths," he said over and over, "and arrive at your destination." "There are many paths for one man's feet," they said, "one for market, one for palm tree tapping, one for farm." "Not to arrive at God," he countered. "You arrive at God only through Christ Jesus." They shook their heads in apparent understanding, but what they really meant was, *We agree with you and with ourselves.* That was how it was with the Yoruba. They wanted it both ways. What Henry loved about the Mohamedan mind was its exclusivity, the devotion to one way. If only he could turn it the right way.

Henry swatted at the air in front of his face. Often it seemed a wandering army marched down from the far field of his vision. Troops wound in flimsy columns, their lines wobbling. For a moment the army would disappear, but then it reappeared, coming down over his eyeball, serpentine but constant, dots of black and white. It was a phantom; there was no army. He supposed his eyes were ruined from the African sun.

Finished with lunch, he knelt at the creek, threw water on his face, and wiped back his hair. Without thinking, he reached for an unusual stone, sparkling in the stream, and plucked it for Emma. She studied such gifts as if they were fragments of heaven. But he remembered his annoyance and shot the stone downstream. It skipped four times before sinking.

He moved to higher ground. No sound as heat gathered. His thought moved to Ilorin. He had visited once on his first tour and was tantalized by caravans coming in from the desert, where they journeyed to some Saharan crossroads and traded with men from northern Africa. Ilorin was wedded in his imagination with date palms and blue pools of water. If these considerations were immaterial to the gospel, Henry brought ballast to the vision through his conjecture that the northern people were superior and through their wealth influenced the kings' courts. If the Mohamedans were brought to Jesus, all of Africa could be won. What a triumph for the One who loved him and gave him a second chance. Emma knew his calling. And hadn't he made large concessions to her, giving her freedom to develop her interests? Of course he would look out for the child. What more did she want?

Much more, apparently. Right this morning: He was doing as he said he would, working on the vocabulary. They both knew how important the book was. His name would be at the center of all discussions of Africa. Every note he finished put them closer to the goal. And there she came telling him about God's signs. It made him feel whipped when she took such tones. Let her have a night alone to eat dinner on china and silver, enjoy herself.

Late in the day he bivouacked on a rocky shelf at the crest of a hill. He wanted to exercise the rifle and looked forward to what he might get. But he found nothing big enough to shoot at, only ground squirrel, and he claimed two with a slingshot. Not bad, he said to himself. He still wanted to practice with the firearm and found target in the large fruit of a tree. He took several shots, hoping some villager might come to see who was trespassing. It pleased him to be interrogated by local men, to discourse with them on hunting and battle lore, country and cattle. And then he would take up God talk, which was an easy thing in Africa. Every man was a theologian. But no one showed up.

He sharpened his clasp knife on a granite stone to make a clean cut, then slit the squirrels' bellies stem to stern before peeling back the skin. Then gutting. Whittling the green-sap branch. He took his time. He felt easy. His mind was clear as a Texas sky. When he pierced the pink whorled bodies longwise on the sticks, he prayed. He prayed for the meat, for the brown sweet crackle of the skin over the fire, the tender bits near the bone, the haunches, the heart. He prayed for God's direction and for the brethren at the mission board in Richmond who supported his work. He prayed that people in Georgia might open their hearts and their purses to support the mission. He prayed for his unborn child.

He found slips of paper in his pocket and read them by the firelight, as a person reads a love letter memorized for years and still in hope.

Baba	*Father*
Baba agba	*Senior father*
Baale	*Head of a town*
Baba Olodumare	*Father God, God the Father, God the Baba*

"Baba Olodumare," he prayed in Yoruba—but to his own God. "We're short on money. I need some help." He prayed it more truly than most prayers, as he might ask his own father. He had evaded Emma's recent questions about finances. "I've set funds aside." It was true, but not as much as he implied. In his day-by-day life, it irritated him no end how he must think on such trivia as money and physical need.

Henry didn't have paper to roll a cigarette, but he had a plug of tobacco, which he bit off for a chew. He took a drink of whiskey and felt the area of his spleen. For once, it was not a bit tender. With the courage of a well man, he pulled a small notebook out of his haversack, turned to the first unmarked page, and wrote across the top: *Possible Causes for Spleen and Liver Disease.* Beneath the heading he allowed a line for each cause he had considered, with extra space beneath it, thinking he might come back and make further notation.

African fever
Chronic ague—the malaria
General strain, poor diet
Stagnant air
Poison?
Personal strife
God's own hand, for chastisement and to teach humility

He had run out of thought when some animal called, and he took it to be a night heron. It seemed time to turn in. He closed the notebook.

Henry broke camp early. What came to him in his devotional was *Forgive your brother*. He thought the sentiment might extend to wives, and he was sorry he had parted with the pretty stone in the creek. He thought of Emma's arms in moonlight. She was his anchor, even if she did act as though things were due her. He was eager to be home but had to take care with Caesar descending the hill. At one point he seemed to get turned around, and he missed the creek where he had seen the man the day before. From the canteen, he shared what water he had with the horse, and when he broke out of the forest into a cassava farm, he was closer by town than he had thought.

And then he came home to the remains of fire. He had run to find Emma and embraced her, and she had relaxed into his arms. But then she had stiffened as if remembering a grudge, and when Duro brought dinner, she seemed to turn chilly. She began to treat him as a royal stranger. He had been prepared to ask forgiveness, but her unyielding made it impossible.

He thanked Jacob for rescuing his family. "One day, I will repay you."

"No sah. I was only doing my job. But if you can sit down, still yourself"—he pressed the air down—"it will be better."

"Still myself? I'll do what I can."

"Yes sah."

A day or two later, he saw Emma making her bath and experienced a deep remorse. But when he sought to touch her, she rebuffed him. If she was going to be stubborn, he might as well make a quick trip to Ilorin. It might be his only opportunity before the rains and the baby.

29

Ilorin

EMMA SAT ON the piazza, counting stitches as she sewed—stopping at intervals to run a hand over her abdomen. The day was hot and the smell of ash still hung in the air. She had cared only for Henry's return until he showed up, and then she was consumed again in anger—that he should leave her unprotected, that he should leave at all, that in his leaving, he also left open her heart. The household had not celebrated Christmas. Now her husband approached. She set her sewing aside and he laid eleven guinea eggs in her lap, one by one. They were beautifully small, dark brown, and neatly speckled.

"I've hired a night watchman," he said. "He comes with the king's recommendation; he has a rifle. I'll be back in five days."

She had prayed God's forgiveness for the hardness in her heart, but when Henry and Jacob turned away, she let herself cherish it, knowing she sinned even as she did so. His sin was greater. She thought she noticed Abike leaning toward the two men as they left, as a flower bends toward light, and took it as a sign of her own feeling. She called her to come sit. "They won't be gone long," she said. To herself, *I have Duro, the Iyalode, I have other resources and friends.*

The next morning, she took up her writing box. She had hardly opened it since the fire. With the desk unfolded on her lap, she opened the red journal and dipped her pen. But she could not decide on what to record. Too often her diary reported on Henry. What would she say about herself? She saw Uncle Eli's gift and thought on him, how he had worked even when times were hard, harder than any she had known. With his spirit in mind, she jotted a sentence. *In God's time, all things are possible.* The words seemed empty. She looked out the parlor door to the compound gate. The king's guard. At least she was safe. She dipped her pen in the inkwell.

How will I live amidst turmoil? She studied her sentence. Her left thumb still tingled where it was cut. Did that mean it was still healing or never would? In pregnancy she had no blood flow. That was a great relief. Her eyes went back to her page.

Turmoil: inner and outer states of unrest.

With her scarred thumb she pressed the lever to release the secret compartment of her box. No secrets there. They were inside her. *Jacob*, she thought. And wrote, *finish shirt for Henry.* She fancied sewing a shirt for Jacob. She would be required to measure him. *Spend more time in morning devotional*, she wrote. She put the scarred finger to her tongue. The baby kicked. She put her hand there and closed her eyes. Had the day turned even hotter? She was tired and rested her head against the chair. She woke in a chill, feeling it would take hours to open her mouth and call Abike. Duro found her and helped her to bed. When she woke again Abike was bearing blankets into the room. By that evening, she was so ill she could not lift her head. Intermittently in her illness, Emma woke and hugged her belly. "Stay with me," she said, "stay," turning to sleep again.

EMMA KNEW IT was afternoon by the way the sun fell across the bed. She lifted her right hand, and its movement was wondrous and complex. She made a bowl out of her palm and set it on her tummy. "Keep humming," she said. Her thirst was enormous. Now she could hear the regular sounds of people in the street, the din of voices, music, drums. The orb of the sun slipped down like a huge mango into the upper portion of the low door. Only then did she remember the bell on the table beside the bed. She expected Abike, but Henry came.

"Hello," he said.

"You're back," she said. He looked beautiful to her. "Water, please," she said.

He brought to her not the clay pot but a pitcher, and a glass. They sat awhile.

"I have badly wronged you," he said finally. "It was not my intention. That doesn't matter. I don't know what got into me. Sometimes I fear for what I might do. But I was wrong to leave again when you are so close." He turned her palm over and traced the lines in it. "Can you forgive me?"

She waited a moment to begin. "I must believe we can do better," she said, a little righteously she hoped. They continued to sit. The mango sun was gone now, though the light at the horizon still threw up shafts of light.

"You know I love you, Emma. I guess you do. But I don't suppose you would have married me if you'd known how things would be, how difficult I mean."

She wished to affirm what he said. He might emphasize even more how difficult he was.

"You were right, in fact," he said. "The emir was inclined to let me come, but his council turned him against me. I was refused."

She felt the slightest sorrow for him. Ilorin had been his dream. But she could not help feeling the elation of victory.

"I'm at rest on it," he said. He bent and placed his hands on her belly and kissed that center of life. She could still be crushed by the sight of his hands.

"I brought you something," he said. It was a lovely oblong of pink rock, studded with mica, about the size of his thumb.

· 30 ·

The Promised Land

How stupid and faithless, Henry thought, to go off again half-cocked. In how many ways would he hazard Emma's life and the child's? He loved Emma, was deeply fond of her. Her strength was what kept him upright. He would likely die without her. Then he got angry that he was in such a bind. The mission board might give him more help. After all, his assignment included exploration. He couldn't do that sitting on a piazza. True, Ilorin could wait. But he hadn't wanted the Baale to imagine his power over him. He also didn't want to think on the limits of their economy. When would he learn? All of these impediments were God's hand, God leading him, God chastising him. Why couldn't he look at the Baale and see God in him, instead of a Comanche warrior? But enough of fighting with himself. He needed land, and there was only one way to get it: ask. Let the man crow over his failure in Ilorin. Get it done with.

When he arrived at the palace, the king was loquacious. He required Henry to come and see the tortoise he had recently gained. *The animal is fifty years if it's a day*, Henry thought. It had pressed out a cool bed under a shrub, and the king pulled back the low branches for a better look. The turtle raised its head and if the man didn't go and pet it like a dog. The animal lurched when his owner offered a large green leaf and the Baale let out a hearty laugh. They watched until the tortoise swallowed, pulled his head back, and bedded even farther under the bush.

"How have you been, my friend?" the Baale said.

"Quite well, thank you. I hope you are well."

"How is your beautiful wife?" the sovereign said.

Henry had never heard his wife so praised. Maybe the man's view of Emma would work to his advantage. "She was ill, but she's much better," he said. The next part was always difficult. "And how are your wives?"

"They are all well, only the youngest one continues unhappy until the day she obtains a hair comb such as your wife's." The king chuckled again. "Women are our joy and our ruin. Is it not?"

Henry tried to agree without seeming too enthusiastic and briefly considered how he might talk Emma out of a hair comb. One thing at a time. "I've come on a serious matter," he said.

"Yes, I can tell," the Baale said.

"I might as well be direct. I had thought on moving to Ilorin."

The king made a noise through his teeth.

"I felt God was leading me in that direction. But the emir turned me down."

"Yes. I have heard."

"I figured you might have." Henry thought he wouldn't mind a drink of native punch. "If you give me some land to build here, I'll start a trade school for your young men. We'll bring books. I'll build a church."

"What of your love of Ilorin?"

"There is work to be done here. My wife expects a child. I'll be much indebted to you." Henry was beyond glad that Emma was not present to hear the next bit. "I see now that God means for me to remain here. Your town is peaceful. The children in my wife's school have brains to catch knowledge. You have a number of fine artisans." Henry looked back at the tortoise.

"Since you favor the north, I will give you land near the Ilorin Gate," the Baale said.

The Ilorin Gate, Henry mused, the one leading out of Ogbomoso to the northern city. He's not going to let me forget how I miscalculated, preferring another town to his own.

"You can look to the place where you are not going," the king said, appearing grave.

Henry thought his leg might give. That line of soldiers started coming down his eyeball.

"In time," the king continued, "you may see that Ogbomoso is the promised land." Henry turned and looked the man straight in the face.

The Baale paused before smiling, and then he laughed in a high, soft way, as if he amazed himself. "You were the one who told me the story of Moses. Do you think only children remember stories?"

Walking back to his temporary abode, Henry ruminated on Moses. The prophet had never entered the promised land. What else had the man endured that had not been recorded in scripture? How did he doubt? Did his legs tremble like Henry's and his eyes give way to queer visions? In the distance, a white egret swept over a brown field, looking for water. Henry didn't have much time. Layers of brick had to be laid and allowed to dry before more could be added. Heavy rains could begin in late March. He would start tomorrow. But he would not tell Emma. She might be too pleased. Or he might wish to surprise her later. Let him be stolid and let her wait.

31

Tea

*I sometimes wonder if I write letters for myself as I have so
little assurance you receive them. Wouldn't I love to bring you
here for an afternoon to see my life! So much I take joy in but no one to
clap and say, "Well done, Emma." So often a setback and no one to
say, "Sit here, Emma, let me assure you of all the good you have
already done. Let me tell you of the good yet to come."*

—EMMA IN AN UNSENT LETTER TO HER MOTHER,
OGBOMOSO, JANUARY 1855

WITH ABIKE, EMMA called regularly on the Iyalode. By now she
and the woman governor could hold a fine conversation. If
they got to an impasse, the girl helped translate. One evening, Emma
chanced to mention to Jacob the pleasure she found in her friendship
with the townswoman. She expected he would be pleased, seeing how
he had been so instrumental in their first acquaintance.

"The Iya trades in native medicine," he said.

"All the more reason I should continue to see her," Emma said,
confounded that he was not glad to learn of her progress.

"She will not hear the gospel," Jacob said. He seemed almost
insolent.

"Why do you say that?"

"She is very wealthy. She will not give up her life."

"We were not sent here to do easy things but difficult ones," she said, annoyed at his implied challenge to her.

The next time she and Abike sought the Iyalode, they passed a hairdresser's shop. Abike pulled on Emma's arm. "Please mah," she said. "I wish to have my hair plaited."

Emma had noticed that the girl's hair did not look so neat as when she first joined them. "Of course," she said. "I can go alone to the Iyalode's." She made arrangements with the shopkeeper and headed on her way, glad for the opportunity to prove herself. She meant to press into her the message of Jesus. Her friend was in her yard, sitting on a large red mat, organizing goods on trays.

"My girls will take it to the market for sale," the Iyalode said.

Emma observed the lovely assembly: groundnuts in bits of calabash, fresh *akara* on green leaves, red peppers rising into small pyramids. "What is that?" she said, pointing to a tray she couldn't make out.

"Chicken," the Iyalode said.

Emma could see now and caught the stench. Very dead small chickens, still fully feathered but clearly inedible. "No one will want those," she said.

"They will buy it for medicine," the woman said. She seemed impatient and took a moment to stand, open her wrapper, and retie it. Emma caught a glimpse of cowry strings tied around her middle. She was lost in thought when the Iyalode commented on her new dress.

"My friend in Ibadan sent the fabric," Emma said.

The Iyalode frowned. "The Ibadan should know that he who digs a pit for others must invariably fall into it," she said.

Emma could not guess why the Iyalode was against Ibadan. Its reputation was no worse than any other town as far as she could tell. Except Ogbomoso, of which she had become quite fond through her resistance to Ilorin. The Iyalode offered refreshments, and Emma insisted that she let her contribute tea. "If you will only boil some water on your fire," she said, and drew from her basket two teacups and tea leaves in a tin. The woman was willing. While they waited for the water, the Iyalode stretched out her legs and Emma, on her stool, let her legs relax under her dress.

"How is it coming?" the Iyalode said.

"What is that?" Emma said. "Oh yes, the baby. Well-well. Thank you."

The tea was successful, though the Iyalode commented that a little sugar was always nice.

"We have decided to stay in your town," Emma said, changing the subject.

"Ah. It is good," her friend said.

"It depended on my husband's judgment. At first he wanted to go to Ilorin." Emma felt fortified, making a kindlier statement about her husband than she might have a week ago. She was wending her way into conversation about their mission, the mission of Christ.

"Ah!" the Iyalode said, as if Emma had just said her husband wished for them to live among thieves. "Even," she continued, "if your husband moves on, you will continue here." She patted the ground. Emma had gleaned that the Iyalode had a husband somewhere but they didn't live together; it was often the native practice.

She said to the Iyalode, "That would not be possible. Where my husband goes, I must follow."

"What of the sewing class?" the Iyalode said, placing a hand of claim on Emma's arm.

"Of course I should miss—"

The Iyalode interrupted her. "Sade has been beaten."

"What do you mean?" Emma said.

"The husband," the Iyalode said, as if that explained everything.

"Her husband beat her?"

"Yes mah, for coming to the sewing class and your husband's meeting." The Iyalode nodded her head in agreement with herself.

"That's terrible. Why didn't you tell me sooner? Where is she?"

"Mah!" the Iyalode said. "Even now, you were prepared to leave her."

"No! I was not prepared. We are staying."

"You were prepared to leave with your husband."

Emma could see she would not win. "But why was she beaten?"

"The husband does not like her to offend the town gods."

"I must go find help," Emma said, "right now. Where is she?"

"She is in her compound," the Iyalode said. "Everything is settled. I have done it."

"How is it settled?"

"I have spoken with the chief; he has gone to Baale. I have told them Sade must come to the class. She can visit your meeting. Baale has agreed. The husband—" She dusted her hands. "He is required to buy Sade two goats."

Emma left her friend's house in a state of consternation. The woman had dominated the conversation entirely, and she had had no chance to speak of Jesus. Instead, she had to learn that the Iyalode had interceded for Sade, a woman Emma meant to be leading to the light of the gospel. Jacob probably knew all about it. He certainly knew about the Iyalode's side business in native medicine. At the hairdresser's, she found Abike's plaits only half finished. A woman with anklets walked by, the silvery sound like a forgotten promise. What was the gospel? Sometimes it seemed to elude her, which was very strange. Jesus loves us and died for us. But how was Emma to show this message?

"I'll send someone for you," she said to Abike, wondering if she ought to be trusted even with this one life. What had her actions shown the girl about God's love? Then she thought of how she would find Jacob in the compound, and she moved in his direction.

32

Paying the Hairdresser

Jacob LIKED THE way he felt, lifting the ax, the wood splitting perfectly, the motion of it, the rending sound when he knew he had hit the log perfectly, the living smell of wood, the assurance of his arms. He reflected on the journey to Ilorin with Pastor. The whole time he had hoped for his sponsor's failure because he did not wish to move or to be cast out again to wander. The journey was not difficult, but it caused heaviness inside until he could hardly mount the horse the reverend had hired for his use. He coaxed himself to reach for Jesus, God's very son, slaughtered like a goat, but risen into new life, present by his side, closer than a brother. By the time they reached Ilorin, a boulder had lodged where his stomach should be. He had heard one English woman speak of homesickness and wondered if he had caught it. Then when Pastor was denied by the emir, he felt immediately better. His stomach became his own again. His hands opened to take food. Every mile they passed in returning to Ogbomoso, his legs were lighter.

Stacking the wood also provided joy. Lodging the pieces one upon the other so that they formed a pyramid.

At some point he began to imagine Mrs. Bowman and Abike returning as he worked. The sun stood at midafternoon. He was surprised by their delay. He ran an arm across his brow and as he did, Mrs. Bowman appeared at the compound gate. She stood like a deer observing a hunter, exposed, hoping not to be seen.

He had wakened one night and the first image in his mind was Pastor's wife, her eyes when he pressed her thumb. She had entered him with her eyes. Now she stepped toward him sideways as if she protected something, her center, her heart. In a moment she seemed to be running, her hat in her hands. She stood before him, holding her stomach. Where was the girl?

"Jacob," she said. A smile came into her face. Her chest rose and fell. The night he had pulled her from the fire, she had been warm in his arms, her body smelling of salt and medicinal herbs.

"Yes mah."

She paused as if she had forgotten her thought. She looked toward the kitchen, took out a handkerchief and wiped her brow. At last she brought her eyes to his, but the smile was gone. He felt his arms would fly up to grasp her if she did not speak of Abike.

"What mah?" When before had Pastor's wife not been able to speak?

"Abike," she said, as if it were a word whose meaning was lost to her. "Her hair. Plaited. Go fetch her presently."

She pulled three cowry strings from her basket but held them against her chest. He pressed his eyes against hers until she handed him the strings. What was she saying this time, without words?

He washed in a grass booth built against the stable. He poured water over his head. Why was he unsettled? For a moment he thought he might weep. He elbowed the stable wall so that the force of his own arm ran back through him.

Abike was just there at the hairdresser's shop, beneath the tree, chatting with some other girls. Seeing him, she stood and stepped back, as if she needed an invitation. It was as if they had not been together all of these weeks, the way she acted shy and unknown. She held on to the scarf she had been wearing, now untied. He felt proprietary paying for her hair and was immensely grateful for the errand.

"Come," he said, and the girl advanced, holding the scarf, which she kept running through her hands. He loved the way she walked, her posture delicate but determined, the motion of her hips. They strolled slowly. By his greater height he could look down upon the becoming weave on her head. The hairdresser had made several parts from Abike's forehead across her crown and down to the back of her neck. These rows were separated into squares and a plait turned within each square so that they made a neat curl out, the last plaits at her neck like feathers against her skin.

"Thank you for collecting me," Abike said when they were near the compound. He thought her voice more lovely in their seclusion.

"You are welcome."

They entered the compound and separated like two seeds sprung from a pod. Jacob thought how he would be required to send a delegation to the girl's family with the proposal. How would he stand a chance? His joy was suddenly checked and he wished to run after Abike, make her promise him, though he had never spoken with her about marriage at all. Even the look of *yes* in her face would defend him against Mrs. Bowman's eyes.

He wondered how an American arranged for a wife. Could he ask Pastor?

In the night by his fire, Jacob turned an okra pod in his hand. His friend Tunji, ever ready with food, had brought a basket full from the market. "Where can it be from, in the dry season?" Jacob had said. "From heaven," Tunji had said. Turning the fruit, Jacob considered Wole's head—what would the Americans say? Wole's soul. He considered Abike. Could she already know about his slave years? Perhaps she only pitied him. His past would surely be a stumbling block for the mother, unless he found enough money. The girl would not be able to go about like a European woman, making up her own mind, if that was what they did.

As the fire died, he lit a lamp and entered the room where the boy slept. The room had been made with a mud bench built against the entire length of one wall. Even in the heat, it was cooling to lie on his side, his back to the room's wall, his side against the bench. He would put such a structure in his own home.

At one end of the bench, Jacob had his altar. Here was his Bible, given to him in Sierra Leone. His name was written in it. Here also a remnant of the wall from his village. Also, a picture of Jesus the size of his hand. He kept a fresh kola nut in a bowl before the picture. Jacob made his prayers here. The dark years of servitude fell away. In his mind, he burned their residue to nothing. He dwelled on green things. The palm tree, the feather he had given Abike, green river grass beneath the water's surface.

He placed the candle and the okra pod at the altar and his thought became prayer. He prayed for the girl. Then he prayed for Rev. Bowman. These *oyinbo* people wore too much sickness. The fever found their body. Then it throttled their heads, making them crazy on and off. He would be sorry for the reverend to be like that. The man must stay well and make a good house. He would help him. Then he could build his own house. Ha! A former slave owning a house. His need blossomed within him as if need and the fulfilment of it were the same thing. In God, perhaps they were.

In the morning, Jacob made an excuse to call in the courtyard. He tried to catch Abike's eye and gain some idea of her thinking. But she was already sewing, her head bent over and the headdress covering her plaits. If only she would raise her head and look at him, her face might confirm something for him. Instead it was Mrs. Bowman's face reaching for him.

· 33 ·

Turnings

A RELIGION OF shade would win converts, Emma thought, her vision listing toward the blue haze beneath the tree. It was late
afternoon. She sat in the courtyard, waiting out the heat with Henry.
In a bit, Duro brought a lamp and they dined on a simple meal of
hominy. After dinner, Henry smoked. And then as the night settled
around them, her husband recited Ecclesiastes 3, *To everything there is
a season*. When Emma finally went to the room to sleep, she counted
to a thousand. At last, she felt the creak and sway of the mattress as
Henry settled in. Later she woke and Henry was out of bed again. The
moon was up, casting a gray light. Some awkward form filled the
corner of the room. But it was only a chair covered with her shawl.
"What makes me frightened?" she said aloud. She lit a candle, then
grew impatient. Henry must be out in the compound. She pulled on
her boots but not the dressing gown; it was too hot. The candle lit the
corridor. Out in the compound, she found cooler air. *We should be
sleeping here*, she thought. The curtain of Jacob's room glowed. Surely
Henry was not there, but she moved toward it anyway. Tapping on
the outer wall, she heard Wole answer and drew the curtain just a bit.
The boy had been looking at a book. The native oil lamp was his.
Jacob lay on his back asleep with an arm over his head. His neck
was tilted up, his throat exposed and large in the soft glow. How va-

grant and solid he was, as a Greek god might be at rest. She forced her eyes away.

"Yes mah?" Wole said. She remembered her gown and stepped back from the door. Just as she did, Jacob's voice erupted.

"Yes, master?"

"It's Mrs. Bowman," she said. She imagined him rousing, pulling his cloth about him, coming toward her. In a moment, he pressed the curtain aside but did not step out.

"Yes mah."

"Mr. Bowman," she said. "Do you know where he is?" She slipped back again, meaning to pull him out into the night.

But he stayed where he was, his look odd, as if she were fully naked. She stepped back again, meaning to be less exposed. But of course she held the candle. The light moved with her. Dimly she knew she had taken this chance on purpose, moving about in her nightdress.

"The compound," Jacob said.

"What compound?" She cinched her gown in front of her, aware of her extended belly against the cotton fabric.

"The Baale has given land to Pastor. Near the Ilorin Gate."

Emma felt hot in her head. For the briefest moment, she thought of Henry with an African woman. "What is he doing there?"

"He is looking at the moonlight falling. Where your new house will be laid. We have already begun." And when she didn't answer, he said, "He is making a gift to you."

His gaze seemed to press like the flat of his hand against her.

"Don't tell the reverend I spoke with you," she said, and turned, trembling for the risks she took, her impure heart. Had she been mistaken? She had thought Jacob shared at least an affection for her, a secret running beneath their lives like an underground spring.

The next day, Emma called off her class, and Duro took her to the new site while Jacob and Henry were preaching in town. It was a fine place, near the northern gate of the city. The first low round of the perimeter wall was already up, eighteen inches thick. She had seen the process before—the balls of mud, one laid next to the other and patted into shape, followed by trimming away any excess and then plumbing with every round to check the straightness. Henry must be letting this layer dry before the next was laid. Her feelings turned strongly in favor of her husband.

Henry told her three days later, after dinner. "I'm building an Ogbomoso house," he said. "The Baale gave me land." He had washed his hair that morning and looked refreshed, his back and shoulders straight and purposeful.

"How marvelous," she said. "Thank you." And then, wanting to be sure he understood that she meant *he* was marvelous, she added, "You cannot fail."

"The site needs further clearing," he said, his eyes momentarily at odds, as if he were embarrassed by his generosity. "I'd like for you to mark the trees you wish to keep."

She threw her arms around his neck, feeling the babe in her womb in their embrace. They went over the layout together and she kept touching his wrist, tight and strong.

"I'm using the same plan as in Ijaye," Henry said, "with a few improvements, more windows for better air flow. We'll have a room in the house for the girl and build living quarters for the others in the back. I've planned a kitchen garden." Emma thought of the seed packet in her mother's letter as he showed her the little area. "We'll use a hedgerow in front to make a courtyard."

"I'd like to keep an Africa room," she said. "We'll plant trees for an arbor."

"I don't see why not," he said.

"Can we afford all of this?" she said.

"The Baale is letting me trade wood from the property for the labor. Jacob and I will do a great deal of it ourselves. It means less preaching. I figure we have another six weeks before the rains."

In the mornings, Duro carried her hammock chair and Wole toted the writing box as they trekked to the new compound. Emma held school in the shade, and after school she wrote letters or made small sketches in her journal. Palm trees were a favorite item in her drawing. She thought she had also captured in one sketch the very essence of a Yoruba goat. One morning it seemed they were in for a shower, but the clouds dispersed and light fell beautifully through the trees.

"Look mah," Wole said. "God has come."

She contemplated her pupil. He remembered from the day with the prism, when he had asked if the light in it was God. "God is the light in our hearts," she said.

The boy didn't seem ready to give up the light he could see. Yet it seemed a propitious moment.

"Your blue beads, Wole," Emma said. "I wonder if you would like to give them to me so the light of Jesus can come into your heart?" He seemed perplexed and ready to pull away from her. "I can put them in the writing box," she said, knowing it might be too much for him to throw them away. He wasn't an adult, after all, but a child.

He turned sideways and sucked his lower lip into his mouth. His hands went to his head and he seemed to be in deep consideration of himself.

"Yes mah," he said.

"I will have to cut them. But I will tie them again."

"Yes," he said.

Emma's joy was enormous. Wasn't this her life?

Back at the compound, she and Wole followed through on her design. When she opened her writing box again, to place the beads there, she was reminded of Uncle Eli, and it seemed she had finished exactly half of something.

The house walls went up, layer by layer. Once dry, a mud plaster would be applied. Roofing with thatch would come last. Meanwhile, the men dug more clay for the kitchen and for a second house,

the one for Jacob, Wole, and Duro. Women hauled water in cala-
bashes from a nearby creek. Emma could hardly believe it the day she
took her stockings off and exposed her feet to the daylight so that
she might join the other women in a clay pit, treading mortar.

"Be careful mah," Jacob said. His concern was as delightful as
a wand of cool air.

When they broke for food, she turned from Duro's boiled eggs
to the women's bean cakes and bananas. At night she saw how her
arms and legs grew stronger. She wore her loose dresses with only a
soft belt beneath her chest and over her stomach. By her calculations,
her progress was at seven months.

Henry worked with the best of the men. His skin was darker than
ever, and Emma thought how brilliantly his design shone as the rooms
went in. The day they laid in the plank floors, he did a little jig and
the baby in her seemed for all the world to clap.

One evening Henry examined her biceps as she changed into her
nightgown.

"Your arms are as strong as Abike's."

She hardly knew what to say. "Yes. I'm working steadily."

He pulled her close, taking her face in his hands, and pulled out
the pins that held her hair.

· 34 ·

Caesar

ENRY BENT TO check the worthiness of the house wall at its base. Finding not a break anywhere, he stood and something cracked, like a branch. He looked up. Then he heard the horse cry, though the sound was more like a whale being slaughtered, a sound bad enough to clean a whole village of ghosts. He turned to see that Caesar had backed into a hole near the clay pit. No doubt he had broken his leg. To a one, the laborers ran to the other side of the property while the horse kept up the awful mewing. One woman lost a basin of water and it splattered orange mud onto Emma's white dress. "Heavens!" his wife said.

Caesar tried to right himself, scrabbling with the other legs, throwing his sad head over and over to the right, but there was no good in it. Henry kept his eye on the animal. He heard Emma gathering Abike and the boy. "Where are you, Jacob?" he said.

"Here sah."

"You know where I keep the rifle. Go get it."

Henry had seen an injured horse drag itself over a man and lame him too. Nevertheless, ownership of such an animal meant you had to be ready to kill it if the time came. Right now he had to get the rope off the saddle. Caesar ceased his struggle, watching Henry come up. The poor horse had shifted to the one good hind leg, the bloodied one hanging odd-angled. He showed his yellow teeth and tried to snap, but Henry thought it wasn't meant for him. It was for the pain. He winced to see how the animal's eyes were wild, but there was no fire for them, nothing to draw on. Henry lifted the rope from the saddle horn. He wanted to keep Caesar still and tried slipping the noose over his head. But the horse didn't want any part of it. Henry sensed the animal had found the barest ledge, the place with the least pain, and he wanted to stay there. "I'm mighty sorry," he said, running his hand down the horse's neck.

He watched Emma lead Wole away with the girl, Duro following with his wife's chair.

Jacob came at a run and the poor horse tried to pull back, then whinnied and cried.

"Have you checked it?"

"It is ready."

Henry put the muzzle to the horse's head, just behind the eye, and pulled. The sound was cannonlike in his ears as the animal fell. When he looked at the sky, he saw a large gray cloud tipped in yellow.

"Ask some men to take care of it," he said to Jacob.

"They will want to make chop."

"I can't help them. Just take care of it."

"Yes sah."

It was hard business. Caesar had been ragged, but Henry had grown to like him. The animal had been as good as he could be.

Henry walked to the back of the yard and retched. It seemed the day had grown suddenly cool. He listened for something. The crack when he had heard it sure enough seemed to come from above. Now he smelled fire and started in some direction that might be its source.

"Where are you going, master?" Jacob said.

"Don't call me that. I'm a mere steward. I'm going where the road goes, following the will of God."

"I will come."

"As you like." The road was red dirt, the sides sloping away to make gullies. "Gaining heaven won't be so hard for you," Henry said. "You never did what I did, killing Indians and Mexicans, taking pleasures when I ought to have been praying for my soul. You're the one who was wronged."

"But I have also sinned."

Henry almost laughed. He clutched at the air in front of him. Jacob caught his arm.

"Sorry sah. It is only the horse. I will find you another one. Come." Jacob led them to the blind man's mat.

This is good, Henry thought. *I can breathe now.*

They told the man what had happened.

"Ah," the man said. "It was the horse's time. All animals have a set life." He bit a piece of kola nut and handed it to Henry. "You have helped the horse. You must not concern yourself." His head bobbed a little as he talked.

Henry wanted to ask if it wasn't bad luck—shooting a lamed horse in the yard of your new house—but it would seem heathen to do so.

"Thank you, sir," he said.

When Henry got back to the new compound, he felt sure he'd see a bloody outline in the ground, but there was no such thing and he thanked the good Lord for Jacob and his management. It did worry him to think the hired men might be eating the horse the next day in whatever stew their women brought, but then he considered that in such a way the animal might be useful to him one last time and if it gave them strength, so be it.

That night in the courtyard, after Emma was asleep, he tried to pray. "Let me empty my brain of my own thought that I might be filled only with your desire," he said aloud. But as soon as he said it, he was filled with his own thought: other directions he might move if not Ilorin; Saro, for example, or Offa. Now how was he going to buy a new horse? He tried not to see the Niger River but it was there even so, winding in grand muddy ochers, green stalky reeds alongshore. How hard to diminish his thought when it was so large and purposeful. And then he was back to the poor dead horse and the shattered bone.

Epistle

Feb. 20, 1855
Ijaye

Dear Mother,

Joyous news! The little boy, Wole, who lives with us and is my best pupil, has come to know Jesus. All the time he has been in our care he has worn the blue beads of paganism around his waist and we allowed him to keep them, for the poor child had lost his mother and his village. Only our assistant, his one relation, remained to him. But when I asked him last week if he would like to take the beads off and invite Jesus into his heart, he agreed. You cannot imagine what happiness I feel in this small life, brought to the threshold of salvation.

I pray you will share my news with the church, urging them to send money to the mission board to support our work. And wherever you go, ask any of like mind to do the same, that we may carry on in the light of the gospel.

Just this week, we had a setback in our economy. My husband is building a house, which we must have for we are living in a borrowed one. It is quite modest but good enough and will help us prosper

physically so that we might do the work of the Lord. Yet in the midst
of building, our horse stepped into a hole and broke a leg. The poor
animal had to be shot. It was quite shocking to all of us. The dear boy
I just told you of was there, and the young girl who is my handmaid.
I swept them up and we removed ourselves to our present house, but
we still heard the gun. Both children trembled and wept, though I
sought to comfort them and in the end we were all weeping.

Pray for my dear husband. He works without ceasing.

Emma was uncertain how much more she could commit to the
page. She believed if she were in her mother's presence, she might say
to her things she never had before. But letters could be waylaid,
opened, and read.

It will cost us twenty dollars at least to replace the horse, longer to
recover from the sorrow. In Africa, we feel so deeply what joys we
find, and deeply as well, anything lost. I know you hold us in your
hearts, as we do you.

And finally, dear mother, if you have not done so already, I ask
you to place a proper stone at Uncle Eli's grave, that I might visit him
when I return home. As soon as we can, we will start a garden with
the seed you sent.

Remember me to Papa.

With great affection,
Your Emma

She felt better for writing as much as she had. There were things
that would never be written, nor spoken. Emma sat on the trunk to
pull on her boots, and then she opened it almost without thought
until she understood she was looking to see that the rifle was returned
to its place, but again it wasn't there.

· 36 ·

After an Onslaught

Jacob found a place in the creek where a log had fallen, creating a secluded sandbar. He and Wole went there on Saturdays to bathe and wash their clothes and the boy played. They were returning to the compound when he observed Pastor headed his way.

"Word has come Rev. Moore is ill. I must travel to Ijaye," he said.

"I am ready," Jacob said.

"No. I've got a horse and two men from the king to go with me. I'm trusting you to stay here and oversee the building. Roofing needs to be done. You'll look after my wife."

Nothing puzzles God, Jacob thought. Here was the reverend, giving him supervision over building and leaving his wife again, the deerlike wife with the dark eyes.

They walked back to the compound. "We've been over the plans. Tell the workers you will pay them in four days. That way you establish authority. After the first payment, tell them the same amount will follow four days hence. Mrs. Bowman has the funds."

Monday the workers were surprised the *oyinbo* was absent, but they went to work without delay, and the second day the same. They labored in a current of kind conversation until the last hour when a man began a ballad about a poor tailor who lost his wife to a palm wine tapper. When they finished the final round of bricklaying, the men laid off and rested in the shade. Wives showed up, made fires, and cooked their husbands' dinners, and Jacob longed for the same for himself.

Midmorning of the third day a flat-faced man with bloodshot eyes wanted to bargain. "I return to my farm tomorrow," he said. "Pay me now."

"You will be paid tomorrow. You must work until then to collect," Jacob said.

"Pay me this evening for three days. I go to my farm."

"It cannot be done," Jacob said. He imagined the strings of cowries in their cool piles, how they were laid out like necklaces for separate women.

"You are not the *oyinbo*. I do not take instruction from you." The man spat. "When the *oyinbo* returns I will come for my pay."

Jacob stood in the sun, watching the man's back as he walked away. He glanced at the other workers. They were erecting the bamboo frame for the roof. No one laughed at him. In a moment, he was on the roof working with them.

Mrs. Bowman arrived under a large black umbrella, Abike and Wole with her. Twice she walked around the house, Jacob watching the umbrella pass, seeing her ungloved hand emerge from beneath it to stroke the exterior wall, hearing her voice come up to him.

"To think it's part my own work," she said, as if the mud she had pressed with her feet had crept into her blood, as if all of her life she had been waiting to build an African house. She was softer now with her round center and it seemed she praised him, if indirectly, and some part of him leaned toward the dark disk of umbrella below him.

By the time she left with Abike and Wole, the women were binding thatch into bundles. They handed these to men perched on the roof's frame who bound them to crossbeams, starting at the lowest point of the roof. They had almost completed the first round when a windstorm rose. At first it sounded like rain. Jacob looked toward *Oke' lerin*

hill to see a yellow cloud, a wing of driving sand. Trees bent and the
air cracked. The sound picked up like a waterfall. Men slid from the
roof. Women lowered their heads and tried to hold the fronds. But
they were torn from their hands. One frond hit a man in the thigh,
and the fellow limped away as if he'd been shot. Cloth laid out to dry
took flight like huge blue birds falling into the sky. The sand became
a thousand tiny knives. Jacob took shelter within the walls of Pastor's
new house, sitting in a corner, his face down.

When the storm subsided, he came out to see fronds snapped and
scattered like a fallen tribe after an onslaught. People emerged from
their houses, shaking sand from their wrappers and their hair. A
stunned silence reigned. Jacob sat with his back against the front of
the house. After a bit, some of the workers came back. They tidied the
yard, making a pile of the broken thatch. Looking for a moment at
the incomplete house before returning to the mistress for her to tell
him what to do next, her deep eyes on him, feeling the sting of humiliation, not that he had failed —he could not have bent the wind
back—but feeling nonetheless that now she would tell him what to do,
wishing it were otherwise, that he were telling her how he had finished
the top rung of thatching, considering how satisfactory was the making of houses with thatch laid in rounds like the bricks, wondering if
they could make up the time so Pastor would not be impatient, hoping they could even if he had to follow Mrs. Bowman's instructions,
imagining Abike listening as he was told what to do when he had
known what to do and did not need the *oyinbo* woman's advice, but
still he would have to take it, thinking on his master's displeasure
when he returned if the roof was not complete, how Rev. Bowman
would demand an explanation, how he would have to hurry like a dog
being run over by a horse to tell the story, all the while feeling still he
had failed after the man—his sponsor, his friend—told him he had
proven himself, Jacob was stung by a memory of being beaten as a boy.
He had been in charge of a younger child, also a slave, who had be-

come ill and died on the road. There was nothing Jacob could have done. Yet the boy's owner had come and beaten him, lashing his legs and breaking the skin into red ribbons.

"Can you find more thatch?" Pastor's wife said when he found her. She ran her fingers over a white airy cloth. She called it lace.

"Yes."

"Duro tells me many roofs were lost to the storm. Will it cost more?" She held her hand at her brow against the sun so her eyes were in shadow.

"It may be."

"What do you think we must do?" She lifted her head so he could see her eyes. They did not press against him. They seemed almost green and translucent.

"I will find it," he said. Jacob felt the ground firm up. But even roaming out of town he collected only enough thatch to lay one more round. He commissioned men to go farther out and cut fresh fronds and paid them out of his own pocket. It might be three days before they had enough. The mistress seemed oddly at ease, as if the storm had shaken all the sternness out of her. She told of how she had been in the courtyard when the wind came. "I ran to put my box in the trunk and we scurried to collect Pastor's papers. I kept saying, 'Don't worry about the order; just stow everything in the trunk.' We were all in the bedroom. Duro and Abike pushed the wardrobe in front of the door. It was so dark we could hardly see. Duro stood by the wardrobe and the children sat with me on the trunk, and it sounded like a train!" It seemed to amuse her, the storm and her success, and Jacob blazed in a mix of anger and envy when all he wished was to get a job done.

They spent evenings sorting notes and papers. Mrs. Bowman lit the lamp and the two of them sat at the parlor table. Wole lay nearby with a book on his mat. Abike sat close with her sewing, or she just sat until she began to doze in her chair, and then she went to her room and his eyes followed her. But Mrs. Bowman seemed not to tire. She was completely happy.

"Now let's work on this batch," she said, pulling out a handful of stray note cards. A moment later, she pulled up a sleeve, indicating the inside of her wrist. "Right there," she said, "an ant has bitten me. Well, it's not so bad." She hit the pink spot. It shattered him, the way she showed him the inside of her arm, the way she drew up her sleeve. She was defiant, and the act transformed her. This power in her seemed self-derived, and his anger gave way to admiration. If she could own herself, he could too.

Part Four

THE GOLDEN KEY

37

Oddities

B Y THE TIME Henry arrived in Ijaye, men from Moore's congregation had carried the reverend to Abeokuta to be nursed at the Anglican mission. Henry spent two days in the town, letting the horse rest, doing some repairs on his old house. The fellow he had hired to look after it was proving reliable enough, but no one cared for a house as well as the man who made it. He joined a group of traders for the return journey. Now that it was the dry season and the roads were firm, they might be required to camp only once. The Oba River could now be forded by foot. They spent a night near a drying creek, more like a swampy pit. In the evening, he felt a sting at his wrist and slapped at the mosquito. It left a bloody smear.

Henry rode first to the new house. He would only look to see the progress and greet Jacob. He wouldn't even dismount before going to check on Emma. But he found the roof framing exposed as a skeleton except for the lower rounds and no one on the premises. Everything was extremely neat. For a moment, Henry wondered if the rapture had come and he had been left behind. Not even a leaf stirred, but he heard a susurration. He bellowed against it. "What has the blasted man done? The job was laid out!"

Had something happened?

He turned the borrowed horse, switched its rump, and made

straight to the compound. In the same instant, he saw Emma at the
kitchen—she appeared perfectly fine—and he saw Jacob, off to the
left, propped against a tree, leisurely reading a book. It seemed he recognized something. They had been together in a way he had not comprehended before; some exchange had been made. He was outside
their knowledge. They had thought him a boy, stupid. He dismounted
and aimed himself at Jacob, who seemed to him now filled with a terrible sluggishness. "What are you doing here when my house stands
naked in the compound? He pointed back in the direction he had
come. "Why aren't you doing as I told you? Where are the workers?
Have I spent six months teaching you and when I go off, trusting
you, I come back to find you taking your rest?"

The man rose and looked beyond him. He shook his head and
set the book down calmly, as if it were a photograph of a sweetheart
he had taken to study before his execution. And then he ran off, lop-
ing down the hill, straight through the Africa room, and out of the
compound.

Henry learned the story of the windstorm from Emma. Immediately he felt deep remorse for assuming the worst about Jacob, who was
a loyal friend and a good worker. Then he resented feeling guilty. He
had been called away and traveled unnecessarily and found nothing
but damage and financial setback when he returned. He felt a thumb-
sized wizard enter his head and go about knocking over every good
thing he had ever done. He fumed. And then the specter of his bony
death rose before him and hung like a dark shroud, heavy and weight-
less. He was chilled, as if some old crime had come up and embraced
him. He needed a whiskey, just enough to calm his nerves.

In the morning, he saw Jacob back at his fire. He watched the boy
lace his hands through his brother's arm. When he approached the
pair, the boy looked at him in a manner close to scorn. *What a cad
I've been*, Henry thought. *Even Abike must consider me half-crazed*. But
he could not find the humility to throw himself on Jacob's mercy. He

apologized indirectly by asking for help. "Mrs. Bowman tells me you expect new thatch today. Can we get some women to help us lay it?" Jacob agreed, though it seemed with smothered rage. *I'll deal with his mood later*, Henry counseled himself, *and Emma's too.* Since his outburst she had held herself aloof from him, as a college girl might tend to a country bumpkin. She probably had that very concept in her head. Well, she would need him soon enough. A chicken dared to cross his path and he kicked at it, but the bird was faster than his boot.

He and Jacob worked twelve-hour days, completing the roof, hanging doors, carrying out last details of house building. In the evenings, Emma would not share his lamplight. Jacob ignored him. With one kind word, he might repair the damage, but nothing in his life had taught him to back down. One afternoon he took off his boots to wash his feet and thought: *I should wash Jacob's feet.* He contemplated the notion for a moment, and the beauty of the gesture nearly brought him to tears. Then his feeling made him agitated. He put his boots back on and went to the new house and worked by lamplight. There was a house to finish, and it had to be done now. He thought he was happier working alone. Indeed, he considered that such a state of mind as his was necessary for all great accomplishment. Michelangelo did not worry about children as he painted. Leonardo da Vinci did not make up to his wife in the midst of inventing. Columbus did not sail for the New World wondering if his crew was disappointed with his temper. Moses did not consult his servants on the exodus. Whether Moses took a bit of laudanum to calm his nerves, Henry could not say.

One evening the moon came full, offering pale light, and Henry went to the parlor to collect his journal. He wished to describe a granite boulder he had examined between Ijaye and Ogbomoso. Emma's letter opener lay on the table, seeming to catch light from the doorway, and it drew his gaze. He was a man who studied oddities, but he had never seen wood so fetched by moonlight. He picked the thing up and it felt warm, which was odder still. Direct sun might create such an effect but not moonlight. He passed his hand over it, and the glow seemed to brighten. It spooked him. All this time, he had observed Africans worshipping queer carvings and he had never seen a one that made an impression on him. He was seized with the notion that this one had taken on power. His chest felt hollow. "What kind of wood is this?" he wondered aloud. He called to Emma, forgetting his anger. "Look here," he said, pointing to the implement. They gazed at it for a moment. "This pagan relic has no place in a Christian home," he said, picking it up. Emma laid a hand on him.

"Where are you going with that?"

"I'm throwing it out."

"You'll do no such thing. That carving is mine. You may be the husband, but you are not the owner—" She paused. "You do not own that."

He handed it to her and retreated onto the piazza. His hand shook all night and he never got to describing the boulder.

38

A Matter of Trees

For Emma, those evenings with Jacob—sorting the Yoruba notes, Wole and Abike in the room, Duro sitting at the door, constant as Jesus—were a moment of Eden in which the human family is perfect. How odd that it required her husband's absence to make it so. She was late in her seventh month, almost two years married, twenty-two months in Africa. Wisps of lavender veins showed up in the pale skin of her breasts. They seemed to sing like happy birds every morning as she dressed, pressing her light clothing against them. The feeling was delicious all through her. She kept Henry at a distance, but she could not stay angry. There were too many sources of joy. She wrote them out, humming to herself.

Wole came today with the most lively drawing of Caesar. In the image, he had set himself, not Henry, on the horse. He wanted me to keep his treasure in my box and of course I obliged him. I surprised myself yesterday, toting a bucket of water. It seemed quite easy. I seem stronger in every way and not the least anxious about my time. I should write to the board recommending that any woman bound for Africa build up her strength before coming: in riding, walking, lifting, rifling. I wonder what the good reverends would think.

When Emma woke the first morning in the new house, shutters open, sunlight spilling across the bed, she felt she was in a storybook. She stretched herself as she walked out through the bedroom door, thrilled by its height. Though she knew the place already, she took a stroll in the yard, running her hand in a circle about her large middle. Wole came to join her, taking her hand. There was the encompassing wall with a lovely portico at the front of the compound where she envisioned a climbing morning glory. In the distance she could see the Ilorin Gate, the northern portal of the town. In the other direction, southward, was the borrowed compound they had just left, and yet half a mile farther on was the Baale's palace. Emma and the boy walked around to the backyard, toward the kitchen with the extra room where Duro, Jacob, and the child were sleeping until their house could be built. "Have you had breakfast?" she said.

"Yes mah," the boy answered.

At the back of the property stood a thatched shed. She peered into it. Leftover wood and unused brick and the hammock. The privy stood nearby. Some honeysuckle there, she deliberated.

During lulls in unpacking, Emma made sketches for a garden. The rains would come and she had Uncle Eli's seed: cucumber, radish, onion, squash, zinnia—and pole bean seed from the Hathaways. Once in her sketching, she thought she heard the old man's voice: *You find a place.* His face came to her with great clarity. "I've found one," she said.

The Iyalode came to call, bringing English tea as a housewarming gift. Emma was amazed at the woman's capacities. At night she slipped into bed against Henry, lying on her side, resting her hand in that hollow beneath his ribs.

One Wednesday evening a group gathered at the edge of the new compound, and Henry spoke on Lazarus. "*Eyin ore mi,*" he said, "my friends. Until we know the Savior, we are all dead, shut up in tombs. But when we open our hearts—" Here he opened his jacket front as if opening a gate. "When we open our hearts and Jesus comes in, he awakens us into new life. You will know it because you will cry with joy."

Emma watched passersby, several of whom came and sat with them as they sang. She thought hungrily about the chicken stew Duro was preparing for the evening meal. Her eyes lingered on Jacob. The next thing she knew, two vultures flew into the branches of a nearby baobab. They perched wretchedly among the copper-colored leaves, their squawking raw and ugly.

Later a report came that a great strangeness had occurred: A melee of cattle had crushed a girl in the borough where the *oyinbo* had erected his house. The strangeness lay in the cattle's stampede. Cattle from the north did not act so. It was hard enough to make them move when you beat them. Two days later, the district chief arrived at the house. He and Henry sat on the piazza. Emma observed them through the window.

"I am sorry to hear about the girl," Henry said. "How old was she? Please tell the mother—" Emma observed him testing his midsection. He seemed at pains.

"A sacrifice must be made to the *orisha* of the tree," the chief said. He pointed, Emma thought, toward the baobab. "You have offended it since you held your meeting here. The leaf is falling. An omen was placed by the vulture."

Henry looked up as if he had forgotten the chief and was occupied in another train of thought. "The tree?" he said.

"Yes," the chief said.

"The living God has not done damage to the baobab," Henry said. "The leaves fall because we have had no rain, though I wish we would."

"The mother will also require some payment," the chief went on.

"I would like to speak with the mother," Henry said. He seemed to be finding himself again. "She may prefer a God who does not crush little girls to make a point. There is no payment sufficient for a child—"

Again Henry stopped. He looked away and when he turned back his face was wet.

The chief's cap was like a smashed turret of a castle. "Your words are distressing to us," he said.

Distressing. That was how Emma took his Yoruba, and she wondered that he could not see that her husband was distressed. Then she wondered about Jesus. Had His death been necessary in order for God to make a point? Wasn't that what she had believed? It didn't seem a clear and shining idea at the moment.

"I'LL CALL ON the Baale," Henry said later, stern again, as if it had embarrassed him to cry. "It's his intention for us to settle and work here. One chief won't stand in our way."

Drums sounded in the distance.

"I'm afraid," Emma said.

"There's no reason," he said.

"Yet I am," she said.

"Have you ever been frightened in a dark room?"

Jacob came to the parlor door. Emma gazed at him, beyond Henry, where Henry could not see him. "Yes," she said.

"If someone brought a lantern and showed you that nothing was there, were you still afraid?"

Yes, she thought. "I suppose not," she said, her eyes in flight between the two men.

How exacting this country was, how hard to proceed, how difficult to be a woman, to find peace.

39

Keep Running

H ENRY CLEANED HIS boots and rubbed them with lard. He was
behind on the vocabulary. There wasn't yet so much as an Africa
room for regular preaching on the Sabbath. His wife expanded by
the day but not their funds. His servant was still at arm's length. He
woke in the new house one night to hear voices coming from outside the window. It froze him.

"You've put a lot of weight on her shoulders."

"Why do you speak as if I intended it?"

"Intentional or not, she has too much to carry."

"She seems to be bearing up well. Her body gains strength while
mine diminishes. You'd think the baby she's carrying was feeding
from me."

"You sound awfully self-pitying."

"Look at her and look at me. She shines like a girl in love."

Henry thought to reach for Emma but hated to wake her. Besides,
what would he say? "Do you hear those voices on the piazza?" He
pulled up the cover.

"You can't hide from yourself. It plagues you, the lack of converts. The people you think of as yours were baptized by someone else:
Jacob, Duro, even Abike. You feel yourself to be a eunuch."

"You come around when I'm weak. You're nothing more than a forked-tongue devil, tempting me to nervousness."

That was himself outside.

"You were spooked by that old man's carving."

"I like a mystery."

"Tell yourself what you wish. It's you who torment yourself. You're the one who impales himself on the sword, who keeps picking at yesterday's wounds. Maybe you can trace your errors back to the day of creation. Maybe you're Adam. The whole story is about you. All I said was your wife bears too much weight. Why is it, by the way, you keep running, from her and everyone else?"

"Silence, will you! I'm not running but following God's will." Were the voices in his head?

"If you're so fine and dandy, why do you keep a personal supply of laudanum stashed as a boy keeps his pictures of girls?"

"There's no crime in medical treatment; my wife, as you say, has enough to worry on."

"It's your own thought I'm speaking. And why do you hide the rifle?"

"You are not my true thought. Beginnings have to be made. I had hoped for more by now, but even the Yoruba know that our time is not God's time. If I give myself as an instrument, God cannot fail, though I may not see the harvest. I came to lay the foundation. What's the firearm got to do with it?"

Henry thought maybe he was dreaming and tried to press out of the vapors, but it was too hard and he could make no headway.

"Soon you will talk about hacking away at stone for a foundation, as if it were your job to build a church out of the very rock of the earth. You expose your vanity in your choice of images. You have always thought Emma lucky to be courted by you. You've always loved your own beauty. But you'll be out of cowries soon, and then how handsome will you be? You had better swallow your pride and ask for a loan from Hathaway. Emma needs flour, not yam."

"I have other ways of making do. I can sell the saddle."

"Who do you think you're talking to? I see around that, and so does your servant Jacob, by the way. The Hausa can make saddles aplenty. You've not got much of a store in that particular item. The help you need is within reach. You get it like other men when they have to. Ask a friend. Humble yourself. But you don't believe you've achieved anything unless you suffer. You behold your past as a cathedral of sin and carry it on your back every day. If you're so serious about paying up, whip yourself into shape. Draw the sting to the surface. Do it so you can attend to your wife and the people who depend on you."

"Your language is poetic, but I stopped listening to you a while back. Leave me alone so I can sleep."

40

Tax Collector

THE CHILD WAS kicking so much that Emma at last rose from bed. Soon she slipped out the back door, stirred up the kitchen fire, and made tea. Back in the parlor, she sat in their one comfortable chair, observing the world emerge into day. The bedroom she and Henry slept in was to her left; an extra room lay to the right. No one had said so, but she imagined it the child's room. One of the improvements Henry had made over the Ijaye house was a hallway leading from the parlor to the back piazza. To the right off the hall was Henry's study and to the left a room for Abike and a nice-sized pantry. The layout provided a wonderful breeze all through the house from the front door and parlor windows down the hallway and into the yard. There were two other rooms, accessible only from the piazza. These were for guests as the mission grew, though already Emma anticipated a visit from the Hathaways and Rev. Moore.

Duro came in from the back door. She knew him by his walk. "The tax collector is here," he said.

"I didn't know they collected taxes door to door," she said, turning.

"For the baobab tree mah," he said.

She called Henry. He came from the bedroom looking disordered, as if he had done battle in his sleep.

"I thought you were going to the Baale," Emma said, "to settle all of this."

"When have I had time to go to the Baale to report a tree losing its annual leafage?" he said, running his hands through his hair. To Duro he said, "Where is the man?"

"At the front of the compound."

"Very well, I'll speak to him."

Emma got up and buttoned Henry's shirt. She swept her hands over his chest to iron out the wrinkles. He was too thin. She must see that he ate more heartily. "Now," she said, "that's better." She kissed his cheek.

"What does he want?" she said when he came back.

"They're asking for a goat for the tree and twelve kola nuts. The mother appears to need not only a carving of her daughter's likeness but a new piazza on her house. In her grief, she has seen yours and desires her own. Or more likely, her husband has." His eyes had their slightly odd look.

"What will we do?"

"Preach and build the church," he said.

She said nothing, and for once it appeared her silence got through to him.

"I'll do as I said. I'll call on the Baale tomorrow. Get this thing sorted out."

Charcoal-colored clouds hung on the hills all day. Thunder rolled in the distance. A wind came up and grew, and the clouds fell in upon the town like a huge conglomeration of dark snow. Mist flew into the open windows, dampening Emma's face. She lit a candle though it was midafternoon. Henry came in and they sat through the din of the storm. "We must plant a garden," she said, raising her voice against the rain. "We can be harvesting squash by May." She nearly shouted it and they both laughed. After the rain, the light was pink and toads appeared everywhere. Emma pulled her garden design from the writing box and left it on the dining table.

By the time she was dressed in the morning, Henry was starting the job.

"I thought you were going to the Baale," she said.

"I thought you wanted a garden." He turned back to his work, whistling.

One more day, what difference can it make, she thought, and pulled her canvas chair onto the piazza to watch. Jacob had made stakes out of discarded lumber. Henry had string to mark the plots. They were collaborating on measurement, referring now and again to her plan. Jacob took the paper into his hand and insisted on something. Henry appeared to agree. They set in the stakes, tied the string to the first, pulled it taut, circled the next stake, and so on until the entire garden appeared in outline, an L shape. Jacob and Henry dug a shallow trench about the whole to show the design. Then they disassembled the string that they might dig up the soil. Wole pulled out the stakes and stacked them next to Emma. The men made good progress but the sun came out, creating that steamy hot of the tropics Emma found near intolerable. She patted Wole's hand and concentrated on yellow squash, the curved neck of it, the lovely sleep implied in the fruit's form. Surely some restitution had been made through their work—larger than Henry and Jacob, larger than their personal lives, something immense that had to do with the crossed stars of Georgia and West Africa.

In the night, she felt a tug and woke up. She turned to Henry.

"What is it?" she said.

"My chest feels like broken glass," he said. "I'm freezing."

HENRY FELT EMMA unbutton his sleeping smock and remove it, and she was terribly slow. He was grateful when she pressed him back down into the mattress. He turned and pulled into himself, and he felt the weight of blankets. When he woke it seemed morning. He leaned over the bed and was nauseated over a bucket and felt a minor joy when it was over. He thought he heard someone come into the room and take out the bucket. A smell of sulfur wafted in from somewhere. Then he started shaking, something inside him loose and sharp.

He slept and it seemed someone snuggled up in front of him and held his hands close, and he thought it was Emma but then it seemed someone alien and he feared. Later someone sat on the end of the bed, on his feet, and again he thought it was Emma. But then he considered, *No, it is someone else.* At last he woke. His head was hot but he could not tell what the rest of him felt. The shutters were closed and he didn't know the time. He needed to use the chamber pot and he called Emma. She helped him and that was over. He wanted to tell her about his sensations, but she said, "It's the fever, rest." She placed a cloth on his head and took away the blankets and he was too tired to resist.

He slept and woke sweating. A candle was lit in the room and he saw a gecko on the wall and envied the animal its cool fluid life. He wanted to turn over, to relieve his spleen, but it was too difficult. He plowed against his helplessness but only became more exhausted. "Jesus," he cried, but there was no remedy. Someone came into the room, but the sound was far away like an echo from a distant valley. Water was on his lips and he was suddenly furious with thirst and gulped. *More*, he wanted to say. He tried very hard to open his eyes, to get out of his head, but he could not and he sank in sadness at his distress. Time and again, he fought to press through to waking. He saw a crack in the earth and he didn't want to be alone with it and he said to himself, *Just turn around*, and it seemed easy now. He was better. He was completely well. The prairie was clear and green. He heard a gunshot.

He woke and opened his eyes. *What are they doing now*, he won-

dered. It was day. The shutters were open. The dead girl, the one stam-
peded by the cows, stood in the middle of the room. He raised himself
onto an elbow. How had she gotten past his wife, past Jacob? It confused him that he knew her, since he had never seen her living or dead.
But she seemed pleased to have found him. Her hair was fuller than
he expected, and he remembered that hair continues to grow after
death. She bent to curtsy, keeping her black eyes on him. He saw the
edge of the wounds where the animals' hooves had pierced her, but
the stuffings seemed neatly put back as if a mother had picked up the
pieces and gently refigured her insides. Her lips were burgundy and
her smile grew.

"What are you doing here? What do you want?" His voice broke
out like a knife through a membrane. Finally he was free. He felt a
great relief. He would call for help. But the girl opened her mouth.
Maggots fell out. She slipped her right hand into the upper portion of
her chest as if she were holding her heart in place. "Get out of my
house. Get out of my room, witch." He put a hand to his heart.

"Master." It was Jacob, standing right there at the window, looking
in on him.

"Tell her to leave before I shoot her."

"Who, master?"

"The girl," he said, and he pointed at her but the man didn't see.
That was how tricky she was.

WHAT DOES THE *master see in his eyes? What has he said?* Jacob felt
something had hit him from behind. He had to reach out for the window ledge to catch himself. There was the wife whose eyes were now a
bottomless lake, the rest of her face blank, standing in the doorway.

The Country of Her Mind

S HE SAW FROM the doorway Jacob observing Henry, who had wakened in delusion. *Oh God of heaven, see Your poor servant, my dear husband. Oh God, see Your poor servant, my dear husband. God.*

Her eyes met Jacob's and searched them and said *quiet*. Henry turned to her.

"You want some water," she said. She poured it for him, and when he was finished she made him lie down and put her hand to his forehead and rubbed his temples until he slept.

"You have to be strong," she whispered to herself, leaving the room, and she slapped her cheeks twice on each side. Her dresses were out as far as she could let them. Just beyond the doorway, she almost ran into Jacob.

"What can be done mah?"

She leaned forward and her stomach touched him and she let herself rest a moment in that touch. *One two three four.* She pulled herself back.

"Where is the rifle?" she said. "We must hide it. We'll stow it in the rafters of one of the extra rooms."

He hesitated.

"Get it," she said.

That night she prepared to sleep in the rocking chair next to Henry. *Even now*, she thought, *I must seek and expect God*. At dawn she found her writing box, lit a lamp, and committed an entry to the page.

I fear but how can I fear? All this living. Do I not know how to die? But it is not my death. I could step through that gate as if passing into a room. That is a lie. I love life too much. My own life. I fear the spectacle of death. Henry's. Being left. Ogbomoso, March 1855.

I will mark through that later, she thought.

It stormed again. In the morning when she went out she saw that a gully had formed in the front yard, a swath of detritus: chicken feathers and sow gunk and wadded leaves stained with palm oil and fruit shavings, all manner of foulness. The smell was just beginning to ripen.

Henry stirred only to turn and sleep.

Emma had no way to know if Moore had returned to Ijaye. She must get word to the Hathaways. Someone must come to them. Alone she could not manage the baby and her husband and the palaver with the chief over the dead girl; one of those, maybe, but not all. If the rains weren't too bad, a runner could get to Ibadan and Rev. Hathaway might be in Ogbomoso by the end of the week.

How unfortunate that Henry had not gotten to the Baale to work out an agreement with the chief. Now what would she do? Go to the king and report on her husband's illness? A Yoruba sovereign wanted a white man to bring good luck, not go crazy in his backyard. Her mind ran wild. If Henry died, she would be husbandless. What would keep a powerful chief from entering her house or the Baale from throwing her out of town? She could be made to do anything. If it were only herself, she could take her own life, but not with the baby.

. . .

SHE OBSERVED JACOB sending Abike and Wole to the market with Duro. She watched him set up his work near her back door as she had asked, a new pulpit for Henry's church. She went back and forth from the back door to the bedroom, checking on her husband. He was feverish but not in chills. At midday, she slipped outside and took a seat on the piazza. A man with a monkey passed by on the road. Drums sounded. For several minutes she said nothing.

"Mr. Bowman is ill," she said finally, as if addressing the trees.

"Yes mah," Jacob said, resting in his work but not looking at her.

"My husband is ill in a different way," she went on, gazing at the trees, her speech sounding in her ears like a part she was rehearsing in a play. "I don't know what way, really. He told me in America that sometimes before"—she waved her hand—"when he was here the first time, he sometimes had nervous seizures." She looked now at Jacob, and he was watching her. She thought he frowned and wondered if he didn't understand what a seizure was. "He sometimes had spells when he could not control his limbs. The fever would cause him to go out of his head." There, she'd said it. She wanted to repeat the part about the fever. "The fever made him go out of his head. Temporarily. He might thrash about on the bed until he fell from it and woke up bruised."

"Ah," Jacob said. "I am sorry."

A wave of compassion swept over her.

"Perhaps Duro has already told you."

"Small-small," he said.

She was surprised to feel her pride wounded—the staff talked of them. "Lesser men have left the mission rather than endure such agony," she said in her husband's defense. Two women had stopped on the path running alongside the house. "Would you mind coming closer? This is a private matter."

Jacob stood beside her, and she was reminded of the first time they met and she had felt this force in his presence. Now she and Henry were in his hands. She looked back to the trees. "He appears to see things that aren't there." That was it, the thing she needed to say. Jacob already knew. Immediately she was fearful. "It's the illness, not his true nature." She sought Jacob's face. He was looking steadfastly at her.

"Pastor is ill," he said, as if committing something to memory. "He is not at fault."

It sounded wooden. She wanted more from him. And then she wanted Henry to rise up and provide her with what she needed so she would not be here, tumbling into this man's eyes. She pulled herself up, meaning to make her face unconquerable. She proffered a letter. "Find the most reliable runner you can," she said. "I'm asking Rev. Hathaway to come to us." She imagined the epistle as a slender white string that must stretch over a vast distance. She felt Jacob claim the letter.

"Will you help me?" She had to look at him.

"How can I help you?" he said.

She could not tell if he was asking what he could do or telling her there was nothing he could do.

"We will erect a temporary church. Build a pulpit." This thought came out of her like the red scarf a magician might pull from his mouth. "But go slowly. Tell the workers Rev. Bowman is tired from building the house and has an *oyinbo* fever. Tell them we are expecting Rev. Hathaway from Ibadan, tell them"—it was a lie and Jacob would know it—"tell them Pastor has a deadline for the Yoruba book. They should be pleased with that."

The man hesitated and Emma believed she had gone too far, should not have spoken about the Yoruba book, should have stuck with the fever. Why had she let herself go on?

"Can we trust Duro?" she said.

"Yes," he said. "But it is better if he does not find the reverend speaking."

"Speaking to no one."

"Yes mah."

So this was what she had: the elegant man beside her, a cook whose eyes must be spared her husband's hallucinations, a girl, and a boy. She put her hand to her mouth and tapped her lips.

"Very well, tell Duro I am also sick but not so severely. Pastor prefers you to deliver food. It will hurt his feelings, but it can't be helped. Tell Wole he mustn't come by because he may catch the illness. Ask Abike to look after him."

By the following afternoon Emma felt so tight she thought she would scream. Henry remained stuporous, moving only to relieve himself, and she helped him because she would not allow anyone else to see him in such need.

"You look clever," he said once, and it seemed malicious. It stabbed her heart. Then he slept again. Twice she had gone to the pantry and counted the cowries. There were enough perhaps if Henry was well and could travel or if they heard soon from the board or if someone from Ijaye or Ibadan came up with gifts of food.

On the third day Henry's fever broke and Emma gave him a bed bath. The cool, rough cloth seemed to revive him.

"It must have been too much sun," he said. "I saw it happen to a man in Texas, knocked clear out from the heat."

"Are you sure?" Emma said. She had not thought of such an ordinary cause and felt a tide of relief. She helped Henry into sitting and fed him a cup of mutton broth. She had neglected herself, but now she took her own bath and rewove her hair. Soon she was tidying up. She was about to tell Henry about the pulpit Jacob was building when she saw he was about to doze off. "You're truly better," she said, almost a question.

"I'll be up before you know it," he said, turning to sleep.

The afternoon was quiet. From the back door she observed several nice planes of mahogany, but she didn't see any of the household. In a moment she saw Jacob emerge from the kitchen. He wore a native tunic over loose trousers, and the tunic fluttered in the wind. She was captured by how he had grown slenderer, yet broader in the shoulders. There was such a natural manliness in the flow of his movement, as if his being in the world were completely in accord with the world, his head tilted slightly upward, his pace set according to the very pulse of the universe. She opened the door and stepped onto the piazza. As he came close, she saw his face was marked by concern.

She stepped from the piazza into the yard, feeling herself drawn. "Rev. Bowman has wakened," she said when they met. "He's much better."

Jacob put his hands to his face, then released them. "Praise God," he said. He tilted his head farther back and when he lowered it, there was the look of his hidden smile. She thought there might be something in his eyes for her, and she wasn't sure what to do next.

"Wouldn't you like to come into the house—I have water cooling in the pantry." Stepping through the door into the hallway, she hesitated, letting her eyes adjust. She had not perceived his coming and turned to be sure. He was right upon her. She felt her mouth open slightly as they met, her abdomen against him, her hands on his arms to brace herself. Her eyes caught the gleam of his collarbone. The man's nearness pulled every longing of her life into a living mass. She felt an exquisite stream of ardor and laid her forehead against his shoulder, aware of the rough cloth of his shirt. His hand came to rest on her abdomen. She abandoned herself to the shelter of him, believing in his sagacity and power, the pressure of his hand there. His smell was like green stalks burning. She was a flame in his strength. Leaning into him so, she sought the coves where his arms lay against his sides. She breathed and expelled her breath, feeling his pulse, the lightest touch of his other hand cupping her head. It seemed all of her life had been coming to this moment—his arm a root of her life.

He stepped back, breaking from her.

"Excuse," he said. When he turned sideways he seemed to disappear. But she saw him at the door, his solid neck, the flutter of his shirt, the white blind of sun.

"Please," she said into the empty space.

He had laid his hand there; the pressure was unmistakable. But he was beyond her.

Emma sat for a long time in the parlor, watching shadows lengthen.

On one of their journeys Henry had told a story. How he had seen a woman's head impaled on a post. Adultery, he had said. At the time the story didn't seem for her. It seemed Henry spoke it to God as if thrusting up toward heaven some evidence of the world he occupied, its fickleness. He had seemed sad. The woman still wore gold earrings, he had said. No one took them off. "Why?" she had said. "Fear of contamination, I suppose, as if sin is an illness." And then he had said, "I suppose it is." And she had said nothing, unable to formulate any reasonable picture of this story. Her husband observing a head on a pole. "I tried to have it taken down and buried," he said again, as if speaking to God, as if he needed forgiveness for what he had seen and not been able to help, had been no help against. She had never really believed the story. It seemed now very close but also foreign. Maybe it was a story from Texas. She couldn't remember.

At some point she began to cry.

Then she felt only a dull misery. What were she and Henry here for? What had she hoped to do? They were ill or they were at odds or she was dreaming madly of a native. More aware of Jacob than the baby, she ran her hand up and down her abdomen. Her mood shifted again. Wouldn't the man's gesture mean something different here, an affirmation of her womanly self? As in her world a man would lift a woman's face to kiss her mouth? She moved into this thought. How the Yoruba imagined the white bird, a woman's capacity to create life. It was like that, wasn't it? He had felt the same as she, linked in their essence. Only he feared for her. He was noble. She went to check on her husband. At once, the hard light of midday robbed her of her dream. She had no certainty of Jacob's feelings. It seemed tragic to her that he could not love her.

In late afternoon she stepped out to the kitchen.

Duro looked up. "Welcome, mama," he said, using that sweet African address. He was bringing a chair. "I will make you a tea," he said. *He knows nothing*, she thought, and was slightly comforted.

"Thank you," she said, remembering to report on the state of her health. "I'm feeling much better." Her gaze moved over the yard and down to the front of the compound. In a moment, she sighed deeply, and quietly she began to weep again.

"Sorry mah," Duro said.

"I'm fine," she said, looking up. "I'm happy my husband is much improved."

"Ah," he said. "We are grateful."

"Where are Abike and Wole?"

"They have gone with Sade to the Iyalode's compound."

When the two returned half an hour later, Emma gave each a hug, feeling as she did her bruised heart. At dusk, she saw Jacob come around the far side of the house. He must have seen her by the kitchen because he went to the back door of the house and entered without knocking, and she knew he was going to check on Henry.

Inside she found him sitting on a mat in the bedroom and her husband still asleep. Her hair had fallen in the upheavals of her afternoon, and only now did she think of it.

"Has he spoken?" she said.

"No," he said, not, "No mah."

"It was overexposure to the sun," she said. "I suppose it's another *oyinbo* illness, but not so frightening as we thought." She tried repinning her bun, but it didn't want to stay put. Jacob got up, rolled the mat and rested it against the wall, and left.

For no reason at all Emma opened the wardrobe and looked at her husband's clothes, his white shirts with the high collars, suspenders and belts, the coat he had worn in their marriage ceremony. She could not stop herself from leaning into his things. The cool sturdy cuffs reminded her of his past strength and how she had loved him.

Emma sat on the bed beside her husband. Then she lay down and curled into herself like an infant, her hand across her mouth to hold her groaning. Oh, she had wanted Jacob to hold her, to pull her in, had wanted his breath on her face, all of that muscled greatness of his desiring her. Let her give in to that smile, his brow above her strong and demanding.

She dozed, and when she woke a sheet of fear swept her back. Her misery came back fourfold. She stood again, moving heavily in the dark toward the rocking chair. "Criminal," she spewed in a loud whisper at herself, "a base sinner." She was sundered to think on the baby and herself full of tortured longing. What a poor witness she was, a horror, and she had thought herself worthy, special, an instrument of God. She laughed in self-loathing. She almost wished Henry dead. She would fling herself on Jacob. Oh! She had thought herself a white bird, had seen herself in Africa gloved and fine, living clean and beautiful. Now look at the country of her mind.

The next day Henry asked for corn cakes, and she served him in bed.

"Your eyes are swollen. Have you been troubled?" he said.

"Yes," she said.

"I hope there have been no more tricks with witches dressed like girls," he said. Emma felt a chill up her spine. Why couldn't he lay it aside? He said it was the sun. That could account for the delusion. *Because he thinks he actually saw something.*

"Do you remember in Ijaye?" he said.

No please no.

"An old witch came to frighten Rev. Moore."

He was right about the old woman, her skin grayed with chalk, she bearing some large instrument with the most egregiously carved bird biting a snake.

"We haven't had any visitors, husband," she said. He must stop pitching onward this way. She could not bear it. "You dreamed."

"With my eyes open?" He hit at the bedcovers. "I have to admit she frightened me."

"Who frightened you?"

"Whoever came in here dressed like the crushed girl. Ask Jacob. He saw it."

"There was no girl," she said.

Disappointment came into Henry's eyes. They sat some time, the sun sending crosses of light into the room.

"I need to trim my nails," he said finally. "Could you bring my pocketknife? I looked for it earlier."

She had not suspected he had been up, searching things out. For a moment she forgot her wretchedness. "Your clasp knife," she said.

"Yes," he said.

"Where was it last?" she dissembled.

"In my pocket," he said.

"Washed," she said. "It would have been taken out when we washed. I'll bring scissors."

"Soon we'll get back to the garden," he said when she returned.

"Henry, you've been very ill."

"I suppose so," he said, looking downcast.

She helped him with his nails and slipped the scissors back into her pocket. Wole's letter was there. She had forgotten. "Look," she said, "The boy has written to you."

She pulled her skirts around, the whoosh of them somehow reviving her.

Henry unfolded the page and she looked on.

Pastor, it read. *You are welcome. The thatch is hold. New chicken come. This day the Lord Is Made. Jesu Christi Amen. Wole Ladejo.*

Henry closed the letter and laid it on his lap, his hand on it. He opened it and read it again. "We have not failed," he said, looking out the window.

HENRY ASKED FOR his papers. She brought a selection. "For an hour and you must rest."

"Four thousand five hundred," he said when she returned.

"What?"

"Words. We have four thousand five hundred words for the Yoruba vocabulary."

Henry kept asking for his papers. She brought them and would find him later, arms at his sides, slouched in the bed, pages smeared across the sheet.

"I can't find it."

"What are you looking for?"

"I can't remember. I am unwell and no help to you nor anyone, least of all God. I believe my personality is diseased."

Don't say that. No no. You must be well. You must care for me. Show me your nobility. Bring me back into loving you. Forgive me my trespasses. "What do you mean? You've been ill with overwork in the heat. If you could wake in England, the cool weather alone would cure you. Here it takes time."

"My fevers are at least half my own doing, don't you think?" He stopped and rubbed his fingers. "There never was a witch."

"No, husband."

"I'm back to my visions, great monsters rushing upon me."

She sidestepped. "How do you feel today?"

"Aggravated," he said, then softened it. "But better."

"What can I bring you?"

"A month of cheerfulness," he said, and smiled and touched his earlobe, the one with the nick. It seemed a sign he would not give up on himself. A little wave came into Emma, of hope that she might yet love him.

She had to speak with Jacob, but he maneuvered at every turn to avoid her. The depths of Henry's illness had put them in a new world. They had to make everything up now; every step was a crossroads.

Forgive me. She folded the slip and carried it to Duro. "Give this to Jacob when you see him," she said. "It's something I need him to do."

It had been six days and still no word from Hathaway. Emma wondered if she should send another letter, but she needed first to hear from Jacob.

The next morning she found half a head of cowry strings pushed into a basket and forgotten—how had she missed it in the move? The discovery eased her mind. God always provided enough. She put on a clean dress. She and Henry dined on chicken and he went back to bed. As she helped Duro with the dishes, he told her the local chief would call again after the next market day.

"My husband is just recovering," she said.

"Master is well by now," he said, and she remembered he did not know how ill Henry had been.

"He's on the mend, but we must be patient," she said. And did not say: *I must get a man here to represent my husband.* She meant a white man, another missionary. She would even take a Catholic. What was the date? Failing to keep her journal, she hardly knew. March 20, 1855, the first day of spring in some other world—where she had married two years ago.

"Can you remind me when the next market day is?"

"By Thursday," he said.

This was Tuesday. Duro was telling her the chief wanted to call on Friday.

She had to wait for Jacob to return from town. When she saw him in the yard, she flew straight out the door. "The chief wants to call again," she said, her eyes looking just to the right of his face.

"Duro has told me. One of his men hails from a village where children died after the explorer Richard Lander passed through several years back. The problem lies with him. He is inciting the others over the girl who was killed." He said all of this in a kindly detached way, as if she were a slow learner.

"I wish there were something we could do for the mother," Emma said.

"The husband will not allow you to come."

"You mean unless we do what he wants."

"Yes."

For the first time, Emma didn't think she saw that hidden smile in Jacob's face. *Bring it back*, she wanted to say. "What will we do?" she said, meaning everything.

"Let me think," he said. He moved past her and away.

I will never read him, she thought.

She rubbed her freckled hands. She ought to turn to Henry, tell him about the chief, ask his opinion. But he would pull himself up, ignoring his fragile state. If she cautioned him, he would only push harder. She almost wished the chief had called when Henry was ill. It might have kindled sympathy.

In the morning her writing box was oddly placed on the dining table. She opened it cautiously, thinking somehow a snake might be curled in it. On top of her journal lay a mite of packing paper. She lifted the note.

We call on the Baale.

Jacob. He had come in while she was occupied elsewhere and opened her box. She closed her hands lightly around the note like she might hold a butterfly. She walked about the house, tapping her chin with her fingers. It would be necessary to keep Henry in bed. Otherwise he would insist on going himself. What if she slipped just a few drops of laudanum in his morning tea? She would have to use a lot of sugar to hide the taste. It wasn't as though she would be harming him.

She put her hair up in the way Henry liked, using her favorite combs and more than she had need of. They were three inches wide and four inches long with a pattern of waves across the top. She prepared Henry's breakfast herself.

"How can I be so sleepy?" Henry said, finishing his meal. "I've slept for days. You look beautiful this morning, Emma. Have you done something differently? Your cheeks are flushed. It must be the life of the infant flowing through you. Why have I ever lost my temper when I am blessed with such a wife?"

He had never spoken to her in such flowery language, and Emma felt the sting of it. But she had no choice.

"Don't be sad," Henry said, his eyes beginning to drift. "Try to hope. Things will change. God's Providence begins in our calamities but ends in restoration." He pushed his chair back. "If you'll excuse me for a few minutes, I'll take a brief rest. I shouldn't have eaten so well."

When he slept, she slipped out the back door.

"What of master?" Jacob said when she met him in the yard.

"He's resting."

She took off. In a moment, Jacob stepped in front of her. They came to the Laka River where they used to draw water, fullish with new rain. Planks had been laid across where it narrowed. Children splashed and called *oyinbo*. Emma had never taken this route, not having been to the palace since the move. They passed some women at their indigo pots. Here was a section of town where tanners and blacksmiths operated their businesses. They had to cross several more ditches, walking on slender planks.

"Please. Be careful," Jacob said, and she felt bright in his concern for her. Though when she looked at him, she had the sense he had built a wall around himself.

At the palace, Emma was offered a leather stool of tolerable height. Seated, she checked her hair. The Baale entered the room and she stood. He waved her back down. Suddenly she felt sure she was over-stepping some boundary, coming without Henry. A small girl, just toddling, passed by the king's open door. Emma pulled herself to the tallest sitting she could manage. "Your royal highness," she said. "*E kaaro*—good morning. I hope your family is well." The man waved his fan again. She took in a deep breath. "My husband, your friend, is momentarily ill," she said, "but he sends greetings." It was somewhat true. In general, her husband wished the king well.

"You are welcome," the Baale said. "You are looking very well. I am sorry for your reverend husband's illness. I have heard."

Oh, she thought, recalling how nothing here was secret. "Please," she said. "I have brought gifts." She pulled the combs from her hair so that it fell down her back in a long braid. "They are for your wives. My husband tells me they might like them."

"Ah," the Baale said. "Ah, ah!" He sent a boy across the room to collect them. "Thank you," he said, leaning from his waist and clap-ping his hands in front of his legs as if she had given him a pet, some thing that might respond to encouragement. "It is good." He looked to Jacob as if he would understand what women liked.

She took another deep breath, for strength, one she would take before a burst of running. "I have come to ask for your understand-ing." She felt oddly free with her hair down.

The king was still smiling, his eyes moving from Emma to his toes, which he flexed back and forth in some royal morning exercise.

"Not long ago my husband held services on our new compound." Emma waited for him to look back at her. "Many of your people came to worship and sing. They are very curious to learn more about God."

"The people like to pray," the king said.

"Yes, well," she said, not sure he took her point. "Later we were told that a young girl was trod to death by long-horned cattle near the place where we worshipped. One of your chiefs accuses our prayer service of causing this sad event. He claims we dishonored the baobab tree. Your Majesty, we have cashew trees around the house. Furthermore, my husband tells me your cattle do not behave in this manner unless they are sick. If they are sick, the herd should be destroyed. But the chief has set his mind on taxing us. We can make a gift of love to the mother of the child, but we cannot offer sacrifices to a tree."

She looked at Jacob. His jaw was set. She thought perhaps she had sounded too unbending in her message to the king.

The Baale coughed to clear his throat. He pressed his legs out in front of him and brought his hands into his lap. Emma felt her heart beating in her ears.

"I have heard of the problem," he said. "The chief tells me his ancestor is disturbing him over Pastor's meeting. You tell me your husband is ill. Therefore," he said, raising his hands and looking at them as if they represented the people he spoke of, "therefore, two men are unhappy."

Emma let out a puff of air. This wasn't so bad.

Now the king seemed to use his tongue to check on the status of a tooth. "The cattle has passed on to Ibadan by now," he said, waving his hand. "It cannot trouble us." He laughed gently, as if he were humored that a rival town might be receiving ill cows.

"I see," she said. "But the chief."

"Invite the chief for a feast on your compound. It will be enough." The king motioned to a lad, who brought a kola nut. The king rolled it in his palm, the deep red nut. He smelled it. Then he took a bite.

Jacob seemed to motion to her, as if the interview were complete. Wasn't there something else? Yes. She remembered. "But the family of the girl. They demand recompense. The husband wants a new piazza."

"The owner of the cattle has already paid. The husband will not trouble you. Give something to the mother. What do you say? A gift of love?"

Emma had her hand at her breastbone. "What would be acceptable?" She looked at Jacob.

"Ah," the king said. "You are a mother. You can know."

The king ushered the lad in her direction. The boy stood at her side and she leveraged herself up using his shoulders. A breeze came through from the palace door. The toddling girl passed by again, falling and picking herself up. Emma glanced once again at her combs. "Thank you," she said, patting the boy's shoulder. "Thank you," she said toward the Baale, bowing her head slightly.

Jacob led them home. Emma's hair loosened in the breeze, and her hat flew off. Jacob retrieved it, and she felt cleansed and hopeful in the minor gesture of kindness.

In the bedroom, Henry woke and asked the time.

"Late afternoon," Emma said.

"Why haven't you gotten me up?" He pulled himself to sitting, and she thought he looked better restored. She moved to sit next to him. Her fingers traveled across his forehead.

"I thought you needed to rest," she said. "While I was in town, I stopped by the Baale's palace. He knew of the trouble. You were exactly right. He is on our side. The girl's father has already been paid by the owner of the cattle. The king believes it will ameliorate the chief if we invite him to a meal."

"I should have met with the Baale," Henry said. He pulled at the bedsheet as if it hobbled him. She smoothed the sheet and leaned over so her abdomen was against his lap and kissed his ear.

"They had no more complaints about the tree or the girl?" Henry said.

"No," she said.

From the window they could see Jacob and his friend Tunji raising a bamboo frame for the church.

"The work here must be done by Africans," Henry said. "We are like that frame put up for scaffolding. But we will be torn down once the brick is laid while they will remain."

When she walks out the front door and down the lane, carrying her teapot to the woman whose daughter was killed, Emma does not imagine being torn down. She wants something of herself—the wave of her hair, the impress of her hand, words she writes into a wall—to be in this place forever.

FRIDAY CAME. EMMA had made a sweet potato pie, which the chief found powerful enough to shout over. The most surprising moment occurred when the native executive asked Henry if they could salute his ancestor. Henry had looked up as if it were the very question he had hoped for. "You can salute my mother. Her name is Lila Bowman. I've missed her a great deal." So the chief and all his men with him saluted Lila. It was Emma who wept, not Henry.

Though she intended to take control of herself, first thing Saturday morning, Emma went to her writing box. It seemed the light of the new house had brought to it the look of rosewood. Its sheen like his skin. Whose skin?

Open. The interior a heart. A heart with four rooms.

Press Here. A hand.

A page.

Write. Breathe.

A word, an utterance of being. Ineffable.

Her private thing as complex as life. The same word truth or untruth.

Depending. Depending on everything.

The note she hoped for lay gently upon her red journal.

Another runner has been sent to bring Hathaway. Jacob

The letters were neatly formed, more vertical than forward-leaning, a kind of artistic printing. Jacob had undertaken to act of his own accord, and he had signed his name. Emma placed the note back in the box, as if it were a living creature that might escape.

When she finished her toilet, she found Henry outside with Duro, drinking coffee. She went back inside and wrote a response.

Give word when you hear from Ibadan.

She did not sign it. What name would she use? Emma, Mrs. Bowman? She closed the lid.

When she reached the yard again, Henry was talking with Jacob about topsoil for the garden. He was squatted at the fire, sunlight through the trees falling on his hands. "Jacob has found a wagon and horse. We've only got one shovel," he said to Emma. "My assistant has claimed it. Don't worry about me. We'll be back with a load of topsoil before the sun peaks." He was still so handsome, and it hurt Emma's heart that her feelings did not match his intention of pleasing her.

The men left, and in her morning with Abike she was suddenly seized with how the girl needed a corset.

The next note she claimed more eagerly than the last. She was in two lives, the one propelling the other.

I will assure you when I hear. No signature. Was that good or bad?

Bamboo and thatch arrived and a garden fence went up faster than anything Emma had seen in Africa. She looked at Henry with his tossed-up hair and his blue eyes and she prayed. *Let me be true.* In her most interior mind she hoped she would not be required to choose between what was true and what she felt she needed.

Saturday morning they put in seed for squash, radishes, and zinnias. After the planting, they all prayed over the garden. Emma kept her eyes half opened and saw that Wole's were shut tight. Then she saw Jacob looking at Abike, and she felt stricken.

"You look as if God has left," Henry said after the long *Amen.* "Tomorrow is the Sabbath. The children are bringing palm branches to services as a sign of peace and hope." He looked calm and she thought to herself, *I should be reassured but I am not.* That night she wrote another note and put it in the box. There was no need for it but she couldn't stop.

When do you expect to hear?

A large crowd attended the service under the compound trees. Jacob sat in front of Emma wearing a golden jacket. He had constructed a cross of green bamboo and planted it in the dirt next to Henry's pulpit, and now he leaned forward, listening. Emma recognized the farmer who had helped with the fencing and a girl who had attended her school for two days before disappearing. She saw the familiar face of a deaf woman who worked at the indigo pots. Sade was there with her bead-covered gourds and shook them when they sang. Rather than using her buttonhole-making skills for buttons, she had put her art to use as a form of embroidery, little holes cut into the neck of her garment stitched all around, her brown skin showing through these tiny windows. It was most becoming, though Emma knew it would not be becoming on her. The Iyalode appeared with two of her girls. The woman looked grand as a peacock. Emma saw them all as her people and felt full and brimming. Rev. Hathaway might arrive any time, but it seemed to her that his coming would no longer be a rescue for her but a respite for Henry. What she wanted now was to be let go. She imagined herself alone in Africa with this full and buoyant congregation, the women swaying, the men too, moving so beautifully in their cloth. This world could carry her, and she could be in it with her child. She would go where she wanted and say what she was led to say. The children started forward carrying palm branches to the foot of the cross, and some of them laid wreaths of red flowers from the African tulip tree that grew in the central market. This was the peace that passeth understanding.

She woke in the night. Her feet slipped across the floor. In the parlor, she lit a candle. She pulled out her journal.

I have begun to dream in Yoruba.

· 42 ·

Jacob's View

THE WOMAN COMES and stands on the piazza. Routinely, she pushes up her sleeves. She waves at the lizards, trying to get them to move. Her hat is large and round and it casts her face in shadow, but still Jacob knows her eyes. She walks in the shade. Wole goes to her, first skipping, then slowing to a walk, then dashing. She leans to receive him. He talks into her ear. She pulls a book from some pocket of her dress. They point and exclaim. He watches them. She has a great capacity to forget everything but what she is doing. He suspects it is an American quality. In a bit, the woman and Wole put the book aside and stand. They are going to take a walk. They do so naturally, out the front yard and into the street. They walk toward the Ilorin Gate. The way is shaded in trees. Other children come to greet them. The woman used to pick up the toddlers, but now she is too large. She stops to speak with them. They pat her dress. Wole turns on his heels. He waits for her until he is impatient, and then he tugs at her hand and they go on. She used to carry an umbrella, but now she forgets it. That is just the sort of thing she does. She forgets.

She had rested against him once, an accident. She did it again on purpose but also in her forgetting, turning into him, her head against his chest, her breath deepening. He thought she might be ill. But she moved her hands in against him and pressed herself into him and sought him. That was not illness. The smell of her hair was in his nostrils, an earth smell, like water and grass. He had been aroused. He wanted to punish her. Press her head against the wall, her dark eyes wide in wonder and fear. It was he who remembered. No, he had said. That was not what he said. Excuse, he had said. She had looked as if she had been found by the hunter and in her animal mind she wondered for her life.

What sort of name was Emma?

When the correspondence began, she seemed grateful, and he regretted ever wishing her ill. Her hair fell around her face and he saw how young and unpracticed she was. If she were an African he might love her and nothing would be puzzling, though she would still be a deer. He knew now why Pastor had chosen her.

His worry for Pastor was great. He missed their outings, the camaraderie, everything he learned from the man. He also missed teaching. Pastor never ran out of questions. In his childhood, Jacob had missed his own father, who had taken a younger wife and moved away from his mother, into a new house on the compound. Jacob wanted to return to those nights when the reverend walked about the compound communing with himself and the wife awoke in the morning and tended to Wole and did not let her eyes wander so much. All of those small motions were one large motion which was the turning of a wheel which was the day which was his life, the life he was making.

Abike was a melody. She would know how to be a traditional wife and a new one, reading and writing. She could help him get ahead. But he needed Pastor, a salary, a house. He needed an anchor.

Sometimes he felt grief overtaking him, battering his chest, and in those times it seemed he would never find home again.

He called on the Iyalode, not about Abike, about Pastor's wife.

"No native charm," he said. "Just help her through."

The woman clucked her tongue. "What of the husband?" she said.

"He has sometimes been ill," he said, thinking how the man must improve.

The Iyalode clapped her hands. "The woman is doing well," she finished, as if to imply that Mrs. Bowman would not need a charm.

Then she arrived at Sunday service and he worried she would relay to Mrs. Bowman the purpose of his recent visit, but she only came to show off her wealth. In the meantime, Mrs. Bowman had turned Abike into a new shape. It was very surprising and he could not make up his mind about the effect.

Tunji showed up with his dog and an extra leaf of *fufu*, red with palm oil.

"You have a new trick," he said to Jacob when they had finished eating.

"What is that?"

"Looking out of your eyes in two directions, like your master."

"What are you saying?" Jacob said.

"One is going to Abike, the other to your master's wife."

43

Heal Thyself

Henry thought he could remember now: the morning when he slept and Emma went into town and called on the Baale. His mouth had tasted of laudanum when he woke later in the day, but at the time he had suspected nothing as he took it often. Later, seeing how his wife eyed him and observing her new independence, it occurred to him that Emma might have put something in his food to get him out from underfoot. It was an African man's way of thinking, *and for good reason*, he considered. But the medicine kit offered no evidence.

He looked for Emma's journal in the writing box, thinking she might have made a record—she was sometimes that silly, writing down her crimes—but before he could get to the red volume, he found a series of notes. His wife was writing to his assistant behind his back. Her impudence burned him. Jacob was *his* man. She had Duro and Abike and the boy, three to one on her side. Why couldn't she let him have something? Later he looked for the rifle and it was missing. Emma was still holding school. He went outside the compound to buy native food from a nearby stall. In Africa, it was an insult to your wife to eat from the market, and that was exactly what he meant.

Later he looked up to see Emma at the door to his study.

"What were you doing, hiding the gun?" he said. "Did you think

I would shoot myself? And I know about your correspondence with Jacob. You can stop that foolishness, tempting him to duplicity. I guess you think it's warranted. You consider I haven't been much of a husband lately. Do you believe I'm bettered by a wife who over-reaches me with the staff?"

He thought she looked a bit afraid now, and that was better.

"I have always honored your name," she said, fiddling with her collar. "You have been in a poor state of mind of late."

He could not argue with that point. "There is more than my name you might honor," he said.

She came forward and unbuttoned the top of her dress. She took his hand and placed it there. He felt her warmth. "My heart hurts," she said. She turned and walked away, her skirts like a fallen cloud, her throat still exposed, her hair down her back.

Henry found pretext for sending the household out, every last one of them.

He must regain himself. A young wife in Africa. What did he expect? She was a girl practically, susceptible to every whim of her own as well as the atmosphere of her surroundings. He had heard of a woman, a British official's wife, who had let herself go native, abandoning an ill husband for an African man and worshipping a river goddess.

He had a church to start, reports to write, a book to finish.

Henry gathered what he needed in the bedroom. Bloodletting was quieter than whipping. Whatever ill went into the body had to come out—or it would go, as it already had, to his head. Afterward, he would eat well and pray.

He washed the clasp knife in one bowl and set it on top of a napkin on a bedside table. Then he threaded a needle and knotted it and put it with the knife and beside that a glass of whiskey. He took off his trousers and sat on a chair nearest the window. He washed his left leg and then looked out the window for a time. A boy across the way had found a large seed pod and was using it as a weapon against an invisible enemy. Henry's upper chest had the cool tight feeling of birds flying against a glass dome, and the lower part of his belly was thick, swamped pressure. He observed his spleen, protruding from his rib cage. He pushed it, and it stayed back for a moment but reasserted itself. He tried it twice again with the same result. He felt with his fingers along the inside of his mouth and touched the sore there, a blister, some sort of eruption.

He had not put on his shoes, and the floor was pleasant under his feet. He looked out the window again. In his mind he wandered up a hill in the distance. He thought on the green-turning world, roots reaching for water, leaf for light, the most minute life form. "God gives the desolate a home to dwell in; He leads out the prisoners to prosperity; but the rebellious dwell in a parched land." He spoke the verse to himself, thinking how the rains had begun but still no letters from home, no payment from the board. His wife would deliver any day and he had little means to support them. "You have to let go your demand," he said to himself. "Have faith." But it was hard to stifle his calculations. Again the house had cost too much. Yet what choice had he had? To keep Emma in a mud room to bear the child? And what if the infant died from the damp and chill? His wife and the mission would be ruined. No. The new house was a necessity. But so were food and transport, payment for Jacob and the others. If Moore were in Ijaye, he might appeal to him. But he would not lean toward the Hathaways, who were, to him, like figures in a painting in a museum, always looking down on him. Well, he might yet be required to kneel that low. He ran his fingers through his hair and prayed that God would help his rebellious nature and bring him to His divine will. All of his worry availed him nothing. Even his toenail was worse. He would release his temper with the blood.

Then he thought he might do better if he sat on the floor. There was a prominent vein on the inside of his left calf. He brought it up in a squeeze of skin and set the second bowl beneath the leg, held the knife, and looked up through the window. Then he dropped his gaze quickly, set his sights, and cut. The achievement was not great enough, and he went back over the shallow slit. It pained like fire, bringing blood in a bright spurt. The burn gained sharpness like a stab, and he rocked onto his side, trying to keep the wound above the basin. His eyes met the angle of the wall abutting the floor, and it pleased him how tight and sound it was. He remembered that he must locate the rifle, but he would not lower himself to asking his wife as to its whereabouts. Or Jacob. The cut throbbed and he found himself counting like Emma. At fifty counts, he managed to push himself up. He figured he had a liter and that seemed about right. If he let too much he could kill himself. Henry grabbed the napkin to stanch the wound. The cloth soaked through and he reached for one of Emma's ornamental pillows. He held it to the cut and sat. After a bit, he took the whiskey, pouring half on the wound and leaving the rest to drink when he was through. The cut bubbled and burned again and he pressed the skin together, edges out. He tried a stitch with a quick jab and the sting was not too bad. He came back and took another. The second stitch was worse, like a hard, primitive ache. He put the knife between his teeth and bit down and took the other four straight, without stopping. He knotted off the end, cut the thread with the knife, and lay back onto the floor. Before he wanted to, he lifted himself up, rinsed the knife and then his hands again, and then he rinsed his chest and sopped up the floor with Emma's pillow. He had made a bandage from three handkerchiefs knotted together and he fitted it tight against his calf. He got back to the chair and drank the last of the whiskey. Then he slipped the needle into a groove in the windowsill. He wiped and closed the knife, poured the contents of both bowls into a slop jar, and pulled on his trousers. When he went out back, the sun felt hot and good on his head. The wound was tight but not too painful, and he thought it was nice work. Walking crosswise over the yard, he emptied the slop jar in the privy and threw the pillow after it. He washed the cup and bowls and jar and left them out to dry.

Waiting for his household to return, he felt drowsy and lay on a mat on the back piazza. In his dream, he rode a horse on a rise above a river and he knew he was nearing a falls, huge and magnificent. Descending, he felt the temperature cool and suddenly he saw he was not wearing a coat or even his boots, and his trousers were torn. But he knew Jacob would be at the falls waiting for him; he would have the boots. In another moment, he thought of Emma and her hair and how he would stroke it as he told her of the discovery. He would make a sketch of the falls and it would go into another book he would write, this one about his African adventures. But then he remembered he could not approach the falls on horseback. He had to get into a canoe. Jacob would have the canoe. He came into an open plain and rumbling seemed to shake the earth. In the distance Henry saw men. As his horse approached them, he recognized Jacob and called to him, but his assistant would not look up. He was talking with another white man. They were eating together and laughing. Henry called again, but Jacob refused to look in his direction. *Any moment*, he thought, *Jacob will hear me and jump up in joy and lead me to the canoe and the other man will vanish*. But when Jacob looked up, he took no notice of Henry and rather turned back to the other white man. Finally, they looked in Henry's direction.

"We know you are here, but we are not allowed to talk with you," Jacob said.

When Henry looked up he saw his horse was going over the falls, the poor animal's legs up and over and then nothing. When he looked upon his own body, his trousers were entirely gone and his private parts wept like candle wax between his legs.

44

Portuguese Coin

HENRY'S ACCUSATIONS DISCOURAGED Emma. The way he spoke of her writing box, Jacob's lines to her. She felt he had drawn her clothes away and shown her naked. She moved the box to a corner of the parlor where she often sat in the afternoon. It might have happened because of Wole's washing her things months earlier or the long time in this country, heat and moisture, but it had come to be the case that bits of paper could be hidden in the seam beneath the secret drawer and drawn out with a needle. Bits Emma had written and later cut from her diary she sometimes kept there, though she often brought these out and tucked them into the pockets of palm trees formed where fronds were cut, or she shredded them first then tossed them over the back fence for birds to build into nests. Now she chose to slide Jacob's notes into this space. She closed the box and placed her Testament on top against anyone who would open it. For days she herself did not open it. But her process of reclaiming the box affected her like a wrapping of cloth. She felt centered again in the urgency of their lives.

"We must consult one another in talk," she said to Jacob.

"He is not coming. He is gone to Lagos."

"You mean Hathaway?"

"Yes mah."

Hathaway was not coming. It was useless, but she went through the list. "And his wife?"

"She is with him. Gone."

"Any news of Moore?"

"He remains ill in Abeokuta."

"Letters?"

"Nothing."

Emma let her eyes wander the yard. "We will rely on each other," she said, "and on God."

She meandered back into the parlor and sat at the dining table. Henry had brought Jacob's bamboo cross into the sitting room. Aside from that, Uncle Eli's carving on her special shelf was, as yet, the room's sole ornamentation. Emma thought the letter opener looked happy, set on the straight side against the board and the arched side up, the man's head facing downward and the little bird atop the head turned the other way, the bird's beak pointed heavenward. She clasped it in her hand, reminded of the old man and his affection, and she saw again his look of welcome, almost like an anointing. She placed the treasure in her apron pocket and went out to meet Sade and the children for school.

Later, out of kindness toward his manhood she appealed to Henry, but her mind was made up. "What do you think of selling some items we don't need?" she said, "to tide us over, for our work."

He looked out the window, his brow furrowed, before finding the words he wanted. "I'm sorry you have to do it," he said. At least he recognized her suffering, and then she was sorry that in all of their wanderings and mutual struggle they had not come closer to knowing each other. She was suddenly visited by a memory, some months after Sarah's death. She had been ill when her bleeding started and Henry had washed her there, so delicate and kind. And they never spoke of it because the act itself was the speech. But so much had happened since.

EMMA ALREADY HAD several baskets filled with biscuit and tea tins and wooden spools and mismatched buttons when she called for Abike's help. "We mean to sell these items to support our work," she said. "I'm surprised we even moved all of this. There are dishes we never use." She pushed her hair back and tried to restore its order. But with fewer combs, it kept falling. "Go get the dress you've outgrown," she said.

At dinner, she offered one of her dresses for sale. "The one I wore for our portrait," she said to her husband. "I will never wear it here, and I have a better travel dress besides."

"But will someone buy it?" he said.

She felt her sacrifice had not been acknowledged.

"I believe so." She poured tea into her cup using a tin kettle and spilled some. He might offer something he did not wish to part with: his new saddle, for example, or one of the colorful Fulani blankets from Ilorin. She looked out the parlor window. Heat swells hovered over the ground. A storm likely. The baby kicked and she found her determination again. "What of yours?" she said. Henry fidgeted; he was touching his side but pretending not to.

"We might as well put up the saddle," he said finally. "I won't buy another horse in this territory." She knew it pained him, and she felt sorry and glad and laid her hand on his.

"Thank you," she said.

Before anyone could get to the market to sell, the Iyalode called. Emma saw her coming up the lane. She hadn't seen the woman since she showed up to services in her powerfully built costume of purple and orange, but this was not a good time. It would be awkward to explain the sale items all piled up in the parlor. Emma rushed out to greet her and they sat on the piazza. Duro brought out the tea tray, tea already poured. He offered one of the china cups to the Iyalode, who spied the sugar bowl and asked for it.

"Have you had sweet tea before?" Emma said, "*O dun?* Sweet?" She had precious little sugar left.

"Not at all. Even so, if you drink with sweet, I will do it," the woman said. With the first sip, the Iyalode lengthened her legs out before her. "This tea will make me strong," she remarked. "It is very potent."

"Miracles never cease," Emma said.

"What is that?"

"I only meant that I'm surprised you like the tea. Most Africans don't like sweets."

"I am not like most people," the Iyalode said, pulling out a fan and beginning to circulate the air. "I thought I would find your baby by now."

"Not yet," Emma said, patting her belly, happy to be sitting in a chair.

"What is the name to be?"

"We don't know until it comes."

"You are carrying a girl. You can decide the name."

"Thank you. I will tell my husband. But I doubt he will believe you."

"Yes. Men want sons. But you are carrying a daughter."

"No. He will be happy with a girl."

"It doesn't matter anyway what he wants," she said. And then she seemed ready for another topic. "The young women in the town want to know, if they join the *oyinbo* church, will their hair straighten?"

"Of course not. They are Africans."

"I have told them," she said.

"The church is not about the body. The church is about the spirit," Emma said.

"Yes. But women consider the body, is it not?" The Iyalode was like a branching tree with her questions and comments. "I have heard that your husband is ill. Is it true?"

"He has suffered the *oyinbo* fever," Emma said.

Of a sudden, the Iyalode set her teacup down. "Who has been to see you?" she said.

"Why, what's wrong?"

"Some strong spirit has passed by," she said. "Ah!"

Emma suspected the Iyalode was creating a diversion. She had never met a woman who delighted more in maneuvering. "Are you ill?" she said. "Do you need medicine?"

"No mah. It is not myself. Something is troubled for your compound. It needs to rest." She looked over her shoulder as if in fear of a ghost.

Emma turned to study Duro across the way, to see if he had noticed anything. But he seemed perfectly stable, and she thought again that her visitor was drawing attention to herself.

"Perhaps you would like to see the garden we have begun," Emma said, breezily as she could. She still had Uncle Eli's carving in her apron pocket and she touched it now, surprised that it felt woolly. It must be lint. If she could get the Iyalode standing, perhaps the woman would soon leave.

Leaning over the fence, Emma spied the first tender shoots of green breaking the soil. "Oh look! Look! The zinnias are up," she called back to the Iyalode, who was taking her time.

"Will you make a soup?" the woman said, still looking about the yard as if it could not be trusted.

"No," Emma said, "it makes a flower."

"Ah," the woman said, seeming unimpressed. She had turned her attention to her purse. Emma watched as she pulled out a gold coin.

"You have a dress to sell," the Iyalode said, the Portuguese coin in her palm.

"Yes. How did you know?"

"I will like to buy it," her guest said.

Emma started for the house. When she returned, the woman relieved her of the heavy garment, somehow tying it into a bundle that she gave to her handmaiden, who carried it on her head. Passing out of the compound, the Iyalode stopped and shook her hands toward Emma's yard as if to disclaim something. The taffeta dress glowed in the sunlight like a small blue moon.

The next day, the Iyalode sent her handmaiden back to the compound on instruction that she was to help Abike sell the Bowmans' items in the market. Emma did not argue or even try to imagine how the woman knew her business. Jacob took the saddle, and the two girls together turned out to be skilled traders. With what they made at the market and the Iyalode's Portuguese coin, they now had enough money to maintain them for another four months at least.

Emma felt keenly the hardship of finding herself beneath the Iyalode, who was wealthier in her world than Emma was in hers. She cried when she was alone, and being alone her sorrow was greater. When she roused herself, she considered that her heart was not pure. Didn't she believe that the meek inherited the earth? Hadn't she wished for a world in which white people did not always lord over Negroes? Vanity. She had hardly read the scripture for days. Who was she to talk of giving everything? But then she felt the child move and was reminded that she must protect them. Surely she was required to look after things with Henry weakened. When she lay down to rest, she felt a discomfort—Uncle Eli's carving in her pocket. She took it out and laid it under her palm on the bed.

45

Lost Pilgrim

*We know of the great Yoruba kingdom of Oyo. In many ways these
people had achieved an advanced civilization. Their language is
complex and lyrical; their religion affords every concept necessary for
moral reasoning. Their skills in trade cannot be surpassed. What one
wonders is why they have not built finer cities. A woman can exit her
house looking like a queen. Why does the house look like a hovel?*

—HENRY, PERSONAL PAPERS

Henry laid his pen aside. He was seriously weakened by the latest
illness. Occasionally he found himself overly vexed with Emma,
the way she had taken liberties, going to the Baale without him. More
than once he had considered how he might, should the good Lord show
up for conversation, ask Him to take her back to Georgia.

Let me try a walk around the yard, he thought. *I can rest on the piazza if need be.*

Within the week, he and Jacob were taking evening strolls on the
lane in front of their compound. He looked up to see his wife waiting for them as they returned. She seemed to hesitate, as if she had
perceived some problem in welcoming them. He thought it was his
problem, not hers: He was not apprehending or could not apprehend
the intention of movement; his body and mind were not yet recon-
firmed in belonging to the same man.

The next morning there were a thousand yellow flowers blooming in the field behind the house, like morning glories. Henry picked a bucket full and brought them to Emma. Many were wilted but perked up when she put them in water. After breakfast, he thought to take a ramble on his own, before the heat set in. Rains had brought the trees into full leaf, and he didn't see the women who had set up their cooking and selling at the church site until he stumbled over them. Nearby, a man was sleeping at the roots of an old tree, or he was resting because every few seconds, his hand rose and slapped his face—to free it of flies. Henry remembered watching out the window as the Iyalode claimed his wife's dress like a captive animal and set it on her girl's head. When had things gotten so out of his control?

"What in heaven's name are you doing?" he said to the women before him. "Get up, all of you. Be up! This is not your place. This is God's place." He meant to be stern but not mean.

The sleeping man slapped his ear and opened an eye. Henry walked over and needled his legs with a stick. That brought some attention, and the man sat up and began to rub his face. But he made no effort to stand, and Henry suddenly felt he might have misapprehended his own whereabouts. He looked around. But he was exactly right. Here was the scaffolding Jacob had begun. "I say! Get up. Find another place. This is ground for the church of God."

"Please sah," the man said. "I am waiting for food."

"Waiting for food! Wait somewhere else. This is not a market."

"For long time I sit here," the man said. The women kept turning their cakes or fish or whatever it was they were preparing.

"You poor lost pilgrim," Henry said. One of the women was leaning straight over a tray. She had stacked it high with *akara*, and he could see she had in mind to set it just where he meant for the altar to stand. Watching her move with her casual swaying walk, he burst into flame. "You," he said, and pointed to her, "making profit on holy ground." He flew to her, grabbed her tray, and swung the contents out across the ground.

The squatters picked up what they could and ran into the road. Henry took off his coat, the one he had brought with him to Africa five years ago. He held it from the base and gave it a good yank. It tore like a piece of paper. He yanked again and the garment was sundered in two, all but the collar. He pulled a third time and the collar ripped apart. He could hear the threads give way and saw the ragged edges of the fabric. When he pulled at his shirt, buttons flew like tiny birds.

"Why not sell the clothes from my back," he said, and under his breath, "*niggers*." He almost laughed. They didn't even know that word. Who was he talking to? He found his handkerchief and wiped his face. He was a man who kept to maps, who charted cities, who considered the angle of a building set on a landscape. Could he call to these witnesses and say: "Don't you see, I am already looking out the window of my church and into the firmament?" No. The silence around him seemed to grow like smoke, and he thought he smelled gunpowder. He didn't know how to go forward, and he could not retreat. The women stared. He saw that others had come out of houses, even children. He must seem to them repulsive, a lost soul.

He stormed back to the house, claimed Jacob's cross, and slammed back out, twisting his leg as he stepped down from the piazza. At the church site, the crowd was still gathered. A little girl was favoring a rough wooden doll she pretended to bathe in an empty bowl. He held the cross aloft.

"Jesus died for you poor sinners," he called. "You may find bread today, but what will save you when the Lord of heaven returns with all His hosts and you have not repented?" Now he was in better control.

The little girl tied her doll onto her back with a strip of cloth.

"What is it you wish?" someone finally said, though Henry did not believe it was one of the folks before him who spoke. It was someone from another landscape and another time.

If I could walk out into the farms and fields, he thought, *I might be whole.* He started for the Ilorin Gate, limping, still bearing the cross.

At one point, he turned and looked behind and saw his house, but it appeared to be miles away. What foolishness. A garden. What are zinnias for Africa? He turned again, but the path in front of him had lost its particularity. It could be any path. It could be Oklahoma, Georgia, or Texas. It was the same path he had taken after his mother died. He had lost his hat somewhere and the yellow sun pounded his head until his hair felt hot enough to burn his hand when he touched it. The cut place on his leg still smarted.

Henry suddenly recalled the date, his forty-first birthday, and not even his wife remembered. He felt icy cold. His body seemed to walk away from his mind so that he watched himself but was not himself.

"There's nothing I want but relief," he said, and shooed the children who had followed him. He sat outside the town's wall with the cross propped beside him and looked out toward the great city he would never reach. He sat for hours, until sunset, and then he walked back to his house. The little start of a bamboo church seemed to mock him. He skirted the site. When he entered the house, his wife was sitting in the parlor in her huge way. She had wept. Her hands wrenched a handkerchief.

"Have I ruined us?" he said.

Her eyes seemed to grow, and she pulled in a cry rather than letting one out. The sound was of an animal in pain.

· 46 ·

In the Shed

WHEN SHE CAME out of her dressing closet, her husband was no longer in bed. Emma found Abike sitting on the piazza.

"Have you seen Rev. Bowman?"

"He has gone to the shed mah." Her tone sounded flat, but Emma could not worry about the girl's feelings now.

Be careful you don't trip and hurt the baby, she told herself.

In the shed she found her husband clutching the horsewhip.

When his eyes met hers, they seemed the color of the sea.

"Emma, you must leave me alone. It worked before. It drove out the devil when nothing else would. I cannot go over that precipice again. I may not come back."

"Where did you find that thing? I thought it was gone," she said.

"Duro had it in his kitchen, among his pots."

She remembered how Henry had spoken of finding the bolus of medicine; he had looked for the whip earlier then. How horrible that her husband had gone snooping about like a thief. "No," she said, "you must not do this. I will not allow it." She meant everything: destroy their station, destroy himself, Jacob, Wole. "You must not do it. It did *not* work."

"Have you heard the voices in my head?"

She said nothing.

"I didn't think so," he said. "Jacob will help me."

"No. You cannot ask a native man to whip you. It's the most dreadful notion I've ever heard."

"Yesterday, I nearly hit a woman. It was sickness coming on to madness. How many unholy visions do you wish me to suffer? A shock to the system may drive them out. Otherwise I fear I'll do something worse."

"Pray to God."

"Do you think I have not already prayed?"

"Our Lord never ordained beating as a means of healing."

"Our Lord was crucified."

"What will it mean to the babe in my womb if you do this? It's not right. You cannot." She raised her hands to frame her face. She thought her head might split.

There was the soft rhythm of someone approaching. It was Jacob at the shed door. "Duro is serving breakfast," he said, his face dark toward ruin.

Henry leaned against a sawhorse. "Emma, leave us."

"No. You must not."

"Leave us or I will continue with you here."

At the house, she called Duro. "Bring Abike. Bring Wole. We must pray for Rev. Bowman and Jacob. Come into the parlor. You have to trust me," she said. "Whatever you hear, whatever happens, God is with us. Remember." Abike was making the hiccupping sound that was her cry. "Stop that, please. Hold my hand." She would not have heard a scream if there had been one because of the walkers on the road and the drums, constant as life itself, and Abike, and the thrumming in her head like hummingbirds' wings.

47

On My Father's Plantation

EMMA COULD SEE that the single lash hadn't even broken skin. But Henry had collapsed and fallen against the sawhorse. He seemed oddly vigilant as she bent to him. "Splint it and bind my chest and make a trundle before you move me," he said. "I might have broken a rib in the fall."

Jacob's jaw kept flexing, and there was a sheen of tears in his eyes. Certainly he would have struck Henry only at his insistence.

Once they got him to the house and into bed, Henry fell asleep. In the afternoon, he jerked in his sleep and a look of intensity came to his face. Emma thought surely he would wake, but he did not. She pressed his hair out of his face and washed his forehead. Later she found the sewn cut on his leg. "My dear poor husband," she said. All that she had dreamed of, all she had suffered; what would happen now? Her back ached. She could not care for anything: dinner, her schoolchildren, her hair. How ridiculous she had been, imagining herself strong without her husband and in this remote place where no one could rescue her. If she were in Lagos, she could board a ship or someone could come to her. But here—how long through the forest, rivers, feuding villages, angry kings, beasts of prey, before she came to someone who could help her. The route to the stars seemed clearer than the route to Georgia. She was shut off. *God, God. Help me*, she prayed.

In the night, Henry thundered awake. "How dare you!" he cried.

Emma pressed away from him, felt how near she was to falling from the bed, then turned, holding her belly, and slid down to the floor. For a moment, she crouched, then crawled on her hands and knees toward the doorway. Moonlight cast Henry's figure up against the wall, and she shrank from it.

"Husband!" she called. "You dreamed. I am here."

"It was a painful dream," he said, and sank down.

At daybreak, she left the room, hoping her husband had exhausted himself. At the back door she called for Jacob. "Take Wole and cut green palm fronds and stand them in the soil—around the church site—as a sign of peace." She rubbed her forehead. "That's good, don't you think?"

"Yes," he said. He looked not to have slept in days. "How is Pastor?"

"He woke with nightmares," she said.

"Ah," he said.

"I need you to move the trunk into the parlor. The baby clothes are in it. Leave the rifle where it is. When the time comes . . ."

Later Jacob called at the back door. He reminded her of the story of the good Samaritan.

"And what has that got to do with my husband, pray?"

"The one who nursed the Jew on the road was not of his nation."

He meant, she supposed, a *babalawo*, a witch doctor. "What can a native doctor possibly do for us? He practices rubbish, throwing bones and beads." She remembered Uncle Eli's bundles.

"One man here has some science."

"Something besides dead chickens?"

"He spent time in Abeokuta, conversing with Europeans. He has used quinine; one missionary hired him for cupping."

"That's very interesting. But we are not in the swamps. My husband doubts that quinine works here. I think he already tried bleeding."

"He has used an herb with a European to pull him back to life," he said.

"You mean to keep him from madness?"

They came to no agreement. *Husband very ill*, Emma wrote in the red journal. He seemed in a stupor, and she spent another horrible night, waiting for Henry to erupt again. But blessedly he slept. In the morning it rained. Taking tea on the piazza, Emma watched Wole catch toads and release them. Once he asked for the prism. "It won't work in the rain," she said, and he looked at her, perplexed.

"Who will help when the baby comes?" she said when Jacob called her for dinner.

"The Iyalode," he said.

"What if there is trouble?"

"She can do it."

"If you have to decide," she said, "save the baby."

He didn't seem to take long enough to agree.

Once Henry called her "mother," and Emma didn't know if he meant his mother or herself, the child's mother. She prayed at his bedside, on her knees: *My Lord, have mercy.* If only she could lay her head on her husband's chest while he stroked her hair and told her he would take care of her. "I'm so fond of you, Emma." She would move to Ilorin. She would go anywhere.

At the window she sang the nursery rhyme she had sung so long ago.

The maid was in the garden,
Hanging out the clothes . . .

She longed for a lake, a shore against which she could push and by pushing reach the other side. She wondered if the thought was an intimation of death and if so, whose? Then she could not decide whether to lie down with Henry. If she did, could she pull him back? It seemed they had known everything together.

. . .

THE FOLLOWING MORNING was sultry. Emma prepared a bed bath for her husband.

"I've seen you," he said when she pulled up a chair. His eyes were still closed, and he chuckled.

"I didn't know you were awake," she said, pulling back. "Are you better?"

"Crack my head, lady, you tell me," he said, his eyes suddenly open.

She shrank from him.

"I have nothing to tell," she said, "excepting that you have been ill. You made Jacob whip you. You believed it would better you. It has not. It has driven you to greater delusion. Now hear me."

"Send Jacob," he said, "or Abraham."

A shadow passed over her husband's face.

Whom did he mean—Abraham? "Yes," she said. She moved as swiftly as she could through the house. From the piazza, she called for Jacob. When he didn't come, she walked into the yard. There was Wole. "Dear child," she said, "where is your brother?" He pointed. There he was, coming up the lane.

Jacob reached the room before she did. Emma entered to find Henry standing on the bed, holding on to his hair. "Rascal," he said. "Rascals all. They've caught me out here in the night; one of them is going to scalp me."

Emma moved to him.

"I'll shoot," he said, convulsed, and fell onto the bed.

"We have to tie him down," she said. "He'll harm himself. We must give him laudanum and tie him and get help from the Babalawo." They used strips of burlap. She dared not look at Jacob as they did it.

"Now we must tell Duro because he will need to watch over my husband, to spell us," she said.

In the evening, Emma lit native oil lamps and placed them in the windowsill. She sang the song of sixpence again, and between stanzas she counted the number of times she had lied or been untrue to Henry. The number kept shifting because some things seemed so necessary and others so innocent and others not innocent at all, as when she told him she had been true. Her husband scarcely moved except in his breathing, almost as if some part of him were secretly relieved at being held down. Near dawn, she rehearsed a future drama in which, at some dinner or get-together with the Hathaways, she would tell about her fright, her decision to visit the Babalawo, the native doctor's prescription, how Henry had revived and how they had laughed together over it and explained to their household staff that the search for African remedies might be a means for spreading the gospel. Relieved, she slept for two hours, only to be started awake when the baby moved. She had dreamed of the hammock ride, but the carriers had left her at a stream bank and walked off into the woods. She saw snakes in the water, hundreds of them. Then she saw the king and the archway into his compound, but she was getting swallowed up in the crowd. *I have to have help. I am nearly there*, she thought.

Oh God, where is Thy mercy?

She looked at the house of her belly. "Stay," she said to the infant at her door.

They left Duro in charge. The man was very grave. Sade was given firm instructions to take charge of the children outdoors. Emma carried her satin purse with the Portuguese coin. As she put on her gloves, she directed Wole and Abike to prepare for the other children who would come for school. "The two of you will lead a lesson," she said. "Take the chalk and board and practice the alphabet. You may use the *Yoruba ABC*. Take turns reading the stories." She had never before let them use the primers without her.

The native doctor's house was closer than the king's, eastward along a series of shady lanes. Under different circumstances, it would have been a pleasant walk, even in Emma's condition. Today, she counted it as a small blessing that she was not sweating through her clothes.

She and Jacob could not rouse anyone at the Babalawo's compound. "What shall we do? We've come all this way. But I don't like to leave Rev. Bowman very long with Duro," she said.

"Let us call one more time." Jacob clapped his hands again. Finally a boy appeared. He opened the gate, turned, and they followed, passing through a gatehouse. Emma had to lift her skirts and step up into the dark space, and then she stepped down into the courtyard. It was the cleanest and prettiest courtyard she had seen in this part of the country. Several trees shaded the interior, and she saw that mats were set here and there. The boy zigzagged around them. When they reached the far side of the yard, they entered another gatehouse. Again Emma stepped up and down, and then, to her amazement, she walked out into a large wooded grove. A man was standing there like a lieutenant.

"Wait," he said to Jacob in Yoruba.

"He's with me," she said in her own Yoruba.

"He waits," the man said. Emma halted, but the boy was moving ahead and in a moment she stumbled after him. They walked a way on a path, beneath low, verdant trees. Just as she was stepping over a large root, she glanced to her right, catching a glimpse of a door that seemed to open onto another courtyard. When she looked back, she didn't see the boy.

"*O ku irole*—is anyone here?" she said, but heard only her echo as reply. "Well, he must have gone that way," she said aloud. It seemed very important to hear someone's speech. The baby moved, and Emma's skin rippled furiously. She nearly fell into the next gatehouse. Someone seemed to sigh in the dark, and she quickened her step. Here was a smaller courtyard, filled with large earthenware pots covered with palm fronds. *Someone is watching me*, she thought. A green-and-yellow grasshopper jumped at her feet. Suddenly she felt so fatigued she thought she might faint if she didn't sit down. She was less afraid now than provoked. *Well, this has been a waste of time*, she considered. *I'm not sitting in here where I can be watched like a bug.* She started back for the doorway she had passed through but could not remember which one it was. *I'll try the one right in front of me*, she reasoned. As she approached, she saw that something was painted all across the wall, one image over and over, like four split cocoa pods in a square. It seemed familiar, and she pulled off her gloves to touch the mud wall. Red camwood paint came off onto her fingertips. She mashed her hands against the wall until both palms were red with dust. She followed the pattern with her fingertips to discover what she was see-ing, but she couldn't quite tell. The more she felt along the wall, the more she sensed life moving in the brick. Something seemed to leap from it into her. She shuddered and stepped back, seeking to brace herself. A brown lizard scuttled by and as she looked at her skirts, it seemed that the fabric was shedding petals; they fell to the ground like flowers before a coronation. She looked up at the sun. It was red as blood.

When she came to, she was lying in the courtyard with her head on a mat. A turtledove bobbed by. She coughed; the dove flew up to the painted wall, hovered for a moment with its mate, and they flew away. She had dreamed something but she couldn't remember what. It was almost on her tongue. She sat up and a damp cloth slipped from her head.

"Jacob?" she said. "Jacob!"

"Yes. I am here." He was just behind her, squatted on the ground. She must have fainted and he found her.

"Who was with us?" she said.

"The boy brought the cloth," he said.

"We have to get home." He helped her up, and then she stumbled and nearly fell, and he caught her arm and she leaned into him all the way to the compound.

When they reached the house, she swung open the back door, care-less of its slamming, and walked directly to the trunk. The smell of starched cotton seemed otherworldly as she pulled out the blue shoul-der cloth from Tela, given just as they were leaving Ijaye in the down-pour. It was the same pattern as the painting she had seen on the Babalawo's wall, the same as the diviner's board she had seen in the market once near the indigo pots. It was the same design as the faint blue pattern on Uncle Eli's quilt. She was startled to realize she had seen it elsewhere—in the cornice molding of the fireplace in her fam-ily's Georgia parlor! Four petals or pods. And between each petal a drop like a dogwood berry, the whole design set in a square as if it meant the four corners of the world, or the universe.

When she looked at it she heard Uncle Eli, "You find a good place." *One two three four remember.* She could see Mittie Ann churning but-ter, her pitched-up scarf. Emma examined Tela's cloth as a person might study a page from a book written in a language she did not know until a word here or there seems discernible so that suddenly a light is cast on the page and the reader knows its intent. A shiver ran down her back.

Uncle Eli was Yoruba.

Immediately, she wanted to tell Henry. *The old slave was Yoruba! The man I knew always. He wasn't just from Africa. He was from here, this very place. This is the old man's land we came to!* She recalled his best memory: a large brown yard full of brothers and sisters and moth-ers. How astonishing that she had come so close to him. Everything would be all right if she could tell Henry. She would tell him like writing words on his skin, as they did long before, before dying, before shame. Henry wouldn't scoff at her. He would say, "Of course; God works in mysterious ways." Such a miraculous moment would make her life worthwhile.

Jacob was silhouetted in the doorway. His shirt fluttered at the tail and she felt a breeze. Rain. She thought of the children and the ABC books. A crack of thunder brought them running in. She seized the cloth to her chest, remembering Henry. They must not see him. "Stop!" she said. Jacob strode into the room and took the books from Abike. Emma was surprised to see a dimple in the girl's cheek. She had never noticed.

"Wait outside in the kitchen," Jacob told the handmaid.

Wole came and squatted beside Emma, chalk all over his forearms, white streaks across his forehead.

"A boy like you," she said to him, still clutching the cloth, thinking of long-ago Uncle Eli. What might Uncle Eli's true name have been?

"Mah?" Wole said.

"A boy like you should become someone big," she said. "A boy with big brains like yours. Should become something."

She dusted his forehead.

Over and over, Emma checked Henry's breathing. He was only mildly warm. She checked the burlap strips across his chest to see that they were tight enough but not painfully so. She and Jacob had circled his wrists and bound them together over his chest, and it worried her that he would not be able to attend to some personal need if he should wake in distress.

She ate dinner alone in the parlor. She thought it quite possible she might die in the night. The baby would be born and she would die. Someone must know her miracle of Uncle Eli, how he was Yoruba.

Jacob came to ask how she wished to rest for the night.

"Would you come in?" she said. "I want to tell you something." The air was cool and she pulled her shawl around her shoulders. Sitting at the table, she found herself trembling with expectation. She had a story, fragile and immense. Later, she knew, she would record what had happened today. It would go into her writing box. *I discovered a most unusual coincidence.* Not coincidence. *Today I discovered that God ordained I should come to Uncle Eli's very home. He laid the path.* No. That would sound like the old slave laid the path. *God laid the path.* But before she wrote it, she must tell it, and in telling this particular man, she would be linked with him in an unbreakable, sacred bond.

She took a breath. "There was a man on my father's plantation," she said, "an African slave. He took care of me when I was very small. You see this pattern, here"—she held up the cloth she had recently pulled from the trunk—"I saw it this afternoon in the Babalawo's compound, but I saw it long ago, this very pattern, in cloth and wood in my American home. It came from the old slave's hand. He must have been from your country. He must have been Yoruba."

Jacob looked at her with his smile and turned something in his hands, a stick, a twig he'd picked up. His head was cocked to one side; she sensed that somehow he had long seen from a beginning and into a future she had just now glimpsed.

"You never told me your father has owned slaves," he said.

It startled her. It wasn't what she imagined he would say. "No, I never told you." Slavery wasn't what she meant to communicate. She wanted to tell the story of the design she had seen and Uncle Eli. She wanted to ask him to think with her. What clues might tell them where the old man had come from, how close by?

"Ah," he said. "Why haven't you told me?"

"I thought it would make things difficult, between us. The old man, Uncle Eli, was cut, his foot was maimed, on purpose. My father ordered it as a punishment."

"Ah," he said, low, as though *she* had been guilty.

She was toppled. Such an ecstasy of knowing and she had no one who understood how powerfully she had been affected, how she had divined this deep connection in her life that must, after all, be the key to her life. It was like some grand design in a magnificent stained-glass window in a German cathedral, hidden for centuries, but waiting to be discerned by a person who had readied herself to receive it.

And then it was not like that at all. She felt the deep scandal of her life that she had not told because it was a scandal: *My father owned slaves; he crippled them.* She was her father's daughter, the daughter of this scandal.

Jacob stood and very carefully pushed the chair up to the table and left her.

She touched Henry's forehead, and the creases across it seemed to deepen. A line of drool escaped his half-opened lips and formed a pink spot on the sheet. She wet her handkerchief in the wash bowl and dabbed at Henry's lips and cleaned the spot. Her stomach was enormous. Her back ached. When she sat, she wished to let her legs splay apart. In her makeshift bed in the parlor she could find no comfort.

In the morning Jacob called at the back door. He looked bereaved but she did not believe it was on her behalf. "Have you eaten?" she said.

"Small," he said.

"You must eat," she said.

"I will try," he said.

"After you've eaten, go and get the Babalawo. There must be something we can do."

JACOB ENTERED THE parlor first and the Babalawo after him. Emma hurried through the Yoruba greetings, then offered the native doctor a seat, but he had brought a mat and sat on the floor. She felt awkward looking down at him.

"*Oko mi nsare,*" she said. "My husband is ill."

"*Mo mo,*" he said.

"How do you know?"

"You came to my compound. Now you have sent for me. Is it not?"

She felt reluctant again. But she had to press on; otherwise, in an hour she would be exactly where she was this morning: no plan, no idea, no relief, a husband bound to his bed.

"My husband," she said, "falls into deep sleep from which he awakens to alarm. His fever is not great. Yet I am concerned for his life."

Already she was relieved to say it, just like that. "I can offer you this." Emma pulled the Portuguese coin from her purse and put it on the table between them. The Babalawo studied it and put it between his teeth and then set it on his mat. He pulled out a bag. She knew it was his oracle. "I don't want that," she said.

"All the same," he said. "I can speak without it." He pulled on his little goatee. "I have watched your husband in the marketplace. He speaks well-well about your *orisha*. Jesus must be a peaceable god. But your husband is too hot. His skin is now white, now red like fire. He is tempestuous."

Emma was shocked by the man's frankness. She thought he had worked up his answer in advance—using such a word as *tempestuous* in Yoruba. But his depiction of Henry was as likely a one as she would have given herself.

"Your description is not entirely wrong," she said.

"Someone may wonder if your own husband believes in his own Jesus," the man said.

"My husband's faith is absolute," Emma said. "He has only lost his temper when fever was overtaking him. You are wrong to cast aspersions on him."

The man moved to rise, bringing his bony knees back toward his chest.

"Wait," she said. "You've given me nothing. You must tell us something that we can do to help my husband. He has sometimes spoken of useful herbs. I don't know what. Something to restore his balance."

"Ah," he said. "Your husband has gone into a journey. He has traveled a long time. Is it not? Have patience."

Emma wished she were alone with Jacob, to ask what he thought. She imagined the Babalawo had heard about Henry's explorations, his trip to Ilorin. He knew nothing about her husband's early life or his calling or any of the doubts and fears that plagued him. He was just making things up from the little he did know. Then she wondered if the Iyalode had gone into town and gossiped about Henry.

"We've *been* waiting. Your riddles cannot help me."

The man opened a beaded satchel and pulled out some dried leaves. "This bitter leaf, pawpaw leaf, mango bark. Boil in water. Give to your husband. It will cool him. Also I give you quinine. Beyond medicine, your husband must help himself." She watched as the native doctor reached back into his bag and pulled out three tablets in a bit of dirty paper.

The man began to pack up, and at first Emma thought he spoke to someone else.

"You have overtaken him," the Babalawo said.

"Do you speak to me?" she said.

"Yes mah. You have overtaken your husband. A woman such as yourself"—he pointed to her middle—"is very powerful. He is not so powerful."

"We don't have that belief," she said. "The child belongs to both of us."

"There is something else you wish to know," he said. The Babalawo had stopped his packing and looked at her, his eyes hazy and full, as if he had become old.

Emma felt a slip in time, lightning fast, as if she had seen her whole life.

"Yes," she said, rushing. "The pattern I saw on the wall in your compound, four petals in a square. I've seen it elsewhere, even in my home in America. An old African man used to carve it in wood. His name was Uncle Eli. I don't know how to say *uncle* in Yoruba. How do you say it, Jacob?"

"*Uncle* is brother of the father or mother," Jacob said.

"Tell him that," Emma said. "Tell him Uncle Eli's daughter stitched the pattern into a cover. Ask him what it means."

Jacob translated.

The Babalawo turned his hands flat up against the air as if there were a wall. "It is not a meaning," he said. "It shows completeness. Four. Whole. It is the base number for Ifa divination."

The light shifted and Emma got a better look at the medicine man, his mouth half opened, his graying hair, long, lanky limbs covered in dust, the poor, awkward cloth of his shirt. *Strange*, she thought; *he is poor as a beggar.*

He moved his head to look up at her. "Your uncle," he said, "your mother's brother?"

"You misconstrue. He wasn't my uncle. He was my father's"—she stumbled—"slave; we only called him Uncle Eli because he was old and we had known him."

"Why do you say the man is your mother's brother and now you deny it? Is it possible in your religion to deny your own family?"

"It was a term of endearment; he was not my actual family."

"Ah!" he said, and turned his head to look behind him. "Mah, something troubles this place; it is feeding your husband's illness." He rose from his mat, but not before nipping up the Portuguese coin. In a moment, he was gone.

"Do you think my husband is dying?" she said, turning to Jacob.

He had the mysterious smile she loved, and he looked away out the window. "My life depends on Pastor," he said, turning back to look on her. "I pray not."

The baby kicked again, and she felt her water break. The child was not going to wait. She looked hard into his eyes. "The baby is coming."

48

In Africa as It Is in Heaven

"Bring Abike's mattress and a tarpaulin to cover it," Emma said, speaking to her cook.

"Yes mah," Duro said. "Have no fear."

In moments, the birthing bed was laid in one of the rooms that opened onto the piazza. Duro went to boil water, and Jacob left for the Iyalode. Emma saw him take to a run, his shirt flying behind him, and remembered that day on the road when Wole was lost. Abike slipped into the room. "I need two sheets," she said, "all the pillows you can find, and a gown." The girl didn't move. "Yes, you must go into the master's bedroom for the gown. Mr. Bowman is asleep. Nothing will happen to you. Go straight to the wardrobe."

"Why is master tied?" Abike said when she returned.

"For his safety," Emma said.

"I don't like it," Abike said.

"Listen here," Emma said. "You're mature enough now for me to rely on you. Look after Wole. Please get the bell."

Emma was not yet in urgency. She only felt a kind of warm glow, a hastening and engorging, almost a joy. She took off everything but her cotton undershirt. Then she pulled the gown over her head. She held the windowsill and began to squat, her knees full-angled apart, belly lowering between them. Finally she managed to roll back onto the birthing bed. When she settled, she saw two geckos near the ceiling. They remained just as they were when Abike knocked on the door and entered. "Go for Sade," Emma said. "The Iyalode may be slow. Hurry!"

She hugged a pillow and watched the ceiling. She thought she smelled potatoes frying, but of course not. She wished for berries in sugar water.

"You're coming," she said to her belly, "out of a house and into a house. Don't be afraid." She thought of the fragile plants in the garden, redolent with life. Her hands were on her center. Her knees fell open. Out the window she could see the top of a hill and a sliver of day moon. She wondered if anyone else in the town saw it, or if not, who did see it in some other part of the globe. A bird winged by and a broad cloud passed; Emma thought she might sleep.

Then a cramp in her abdomen pulled her to sitting. "How far," she said to herself. Somewhere a sheep brayed. She rang the bell furiously. Her hair was knotted up, but it was already falling around her neck and a sweat broke over her. She rang again and subsided back onto the mattress.

"Abike," she said, as soon as she heard her funny step.

"Yes mah."

"I need a drink."

She rocked with the next one, backward and forward, her hands on her knees.

"Find Rev. Bowman's medicine kit and bring it," she said.

They laid out a white cloth and scissors and a wooden spoon. She felt sick and turned to her side and heaved.

"We need a basin," she said to the girl.

The next pain made her think of a huge crab clawing at her insides. Her back ached as if it would split. She groaned, deep and hard. "Where is the Iyalode?" she said. Her hair was slick against her face. "Abike, cut my hair."

"No mah."

"Yes." Emma reached for the scissors, but Abike seized them.

A ripping pain turned her inside out. Emma tried to swim; it seemed the only way to get out of her body, pulling and pulling into the air.

At last, Sade appeared, squatting before Emma, her hands on Emma's spread knees.

"I have to push. Help me," she said.

"Not yet mah. Not yet," the woman said, throwing one hand out in front of Emma's face over and over as a way of emphasizing her *No.*

"Where is the Iyalode?"

"Soon mah. She will be here soon." Another pain roared up Emma's back.

"Now," she screamed.

"No mah. Hold."

When it passed, she lay down and tried to turn over. She thought she would die if it came again.

"I thought you were my friend," Emma said when she saw the Iyalode. "Where were you? I'm going to die."

"What are you saying? Am I here?" The woman looked around the room as if to confirm her bearings.

"I hope I will die. Jesus forgive me."

"Mistress Bowman. Wake up. I command you. The baby is coming. You must help us."

As soon as Emma lifted her shoulders, Sade called. "Here is the head. I am telling you mah, push." It burned there and her bones seemed to split.

"Again!"

She cried until she could no longer hear herself, until she heard the baby. It was a girl. She knew before she saw her. The little flesh was shocking red, slippery, long bodied, fat cheeked. The Iyalode wiped the child's head. Faint blond hair. "Now where did that hair come from?" Emma said. "We shan't cut your hair. No we shan't."

In the night, thunder came and then it rained a storm. The Iyalode and Sade took turns in the room and Emma woke to nurse and the baby she kept with her, cradled in the nest of her arms, and she talked with her often. "You star, you beat of the world, you mango girl, lily rose, tadpole, name of mine, Madeline."

The next morning, she wrote in the red journal: *April 15, 1865. Baby girl, healthy. Henry yet ill.*

As soon as she had dressed, she asked Abike to call Jacob. "My husband?" she said.

"He has not changed. The king has sent two heads of cowries for the baby."

"But my husband is not worse," she said. It seemed ages ago she had cared about money or gifts or dresses.

"No mah. Not worse."

Good," she said, with something like victory in her mouth, though she thought she would cry. Couldn't Jacob be a brother to her? Then she thought Henry must wake up. He must know about Madeline for the birth to be real.

"Have you been giving him medicine?"

"Some mah."

"We must keep trying," she said. "I'm taking the child to see him, her father," she said. "Now."

In the yard, wispy fog still hovered below the trees. She saw Wole at the kitchen. "Come say hello," she said, and he came to her, touching the child's hand. "I mean it; say hello."

"*Ago*," he said, sounding it out, *ah go*.

"Say 'Hello, Madeline.'"

"*Ago* Madeline."

The baby held his finger. Wole looked at Emma with something like hope. "Is it your baby?" he said.

"Yes," she said.

"It is not so ugly," he said.

Henry lay on his back, his breathing like short winds through his nostrils. Jacob or Duro had bolstered his elbows so that his hands rested comfortably on his chest. They were still handsome. "Come home," she said to him.

In a while, she took the baby and placed her in the crook of Henry's arm and sat herself on the edge of the bed. "Papa. Madeline," she said. A deeper crease came into Henry's forehead. He was cool though his hair was wet, and he had a look of concentration on his face as if he were tracking progress or remembering a long recitation and was afraid he would forget his place in it.

Later in the day, women of all sorts came to pay their respects to the baby. Sade brought a huge pot of yam. None of the women appeared surprised that the father was not in attendance, seeming in their manner to convey that men do other things; women are for children.

In the afternoon, Emma carried Madeline in a basket and went to pray at the church site. The palm fronds were still there, bent by the rains. Two doves bobbed their heads and walked sideways as she entered. Emma sat on a bench near a little white flag where the cornerstone would be laid—when Henry was better, the next dry season.

Our Father who art in heaven, hallowed be Thy name; Thy kingdom come, Thy sweetness done—Madeline scrunched her nose and yawned—*in Africa as it is in heaven. Give us this day our daily remember and forgive us our trespasses as we rekindle those who love us. And lead us not into pride but deliver us from sorrow. For Thine is the kingdom and the birdsong and the blue day, forever. Amen.* The baby snuggled on her belly, monked in light cotton. Emma prayed again. *Henry Henry Henry God God God Henry I beg you. God forgive us. Have mercy have mercy. He loves you. Love.*

Love endureth all things. I have endured. Bring me something. I beg.

Minutes passed.

Emma examined Madeline's feet, rounded at the bottom—still unwalked on the earth. The little blond hairs of her head blew up at the slightest wind. She seemed more complacent than Sarah, who was ever demanding to nurse. This child woke to look around with her big blue eyes. "Where dost thy temper come from?" Emma said. She wondered if Henry had been a boy of curly blond hair.

In the afternoon she sat on the front piazza. A cart passed down the road, a rare sight. Wole ran to watch it, and Emma saw how tall he had grown, his legs so long and brown. She held Madeline tight and rocked her in her arms, singing a song about *lavender's blue, dilly dilly*. She glimpsed a white egret flying to the top of a young palm, the tree bright with life. "I know who you will be," she whispered into the child's face. "You will be a brilliant artist."

Duro came running out the front door.

"What?" Emma said.

She heard a scuffle. In one curving motion, she stood, handed the child to her cook, and moved into the house.

From the bedroom door she saw Henry still reclined, Jacob leaning over him. They looked almost like father and son, the son, Jacob, bent over the ailing father, Henry.

Then she saw that Henry was no longer bound. He had Jacob by the wrist and in the other hand he held the open clasp knife. His hair was wild, his lips moving in silent speech as if he held audience with ghosts. She remembered his sinewy strength. It had always surprised her because he was not a large man, but she knew if he was enraged, he could be fierce.

Her movement away from the door seemed to take forever, as if she had turned into a dense liquid. But her thinking was swift. She prayed the rifle was in the rafters where she and Jacob had stowed it. On tiptoe, she reached to claim it, but it was gone. In her anger, she shoved against the only piece of furniture in the room, a bookcase

Henry had set into the wall. To her amazement, it gave. There must be space behind it. In a fury, she pulled the shelf toward her. Close against one side of the hidden closet was the rifle. In reaching for it she remembered everything: how Henry had shown her. *This is the ball. Ram it in. The percussion cap.* But the gun was already, horribly, loaded.

She strode toward the bedroom, the heavy firearm half hidden in her skirts, pausing briefly outside the door.

"Someone here has betrayed me," Henry said. She crept close enough to see. The knife seemed serpentine, the way her husband waved it in the air. She wondered if it would break his spell if she shot out the open window. She gripped the rifle, bringing it out from her skirts, remembering, eons ago, what Henry had taught her. *Line up the bead with your target.*

"Look here," she said, stepping into the door frame, the rifle half lifted.

The two men turned to her. "Stop that," she said.

Henry grinned, as if he could see her secret places, as if he walked in a country where all evil was unveiled. She kept her eyes on him.

"Are you loyal to me?" Henry said, his eyes fixed on her.

Emma breathed deeply. "I have birthed our child," she said, wishing she could look to Jacob, but she could not. She must keep her eyes on Henry.

"That's not an answer."

She had done a fair amount of lying, of telling half-truths, of fooling herself. She could not fool God. What was true? What was true enough? Her arms were tired and she brought the firearm to rest on her hip, meaning still to look prepared.

"Yes," she said. "I am."

"And bound me to the bed."

"For your own good," she said.

"I don't think so," Henry said, tightening his grip on Jacob's wrist.

"Let go of him," she said, raising the rifle. "Let go of him now."

Her head wove and spun though her vision was steady. She thought of Henry's nicked ear and in her frenzy aimed at a pillow instead.

"You would not," he said. "You poor girl."

Her gorge rose and she thought she might back down. Henry would come to reason. He would not, surely, in any state, hurt Jacob. And he would not hurt her in such a way. It was impossible. But her mind veered to a story Henry told her once, late in the night, of killing an Indian boy with a knife. *In a flash*, he had said, *before I knew what I had done. I wished many a time I had killed myself instead.*

I'm saving us, she thought.

Henry became very still. His eyes were disastrously blue.

"You let him go," she said again, "or I will." She brought her cheek to the cool wood of the stock, closed her left eye, and took her aim.

Never pull back the hammer unless you're ready to shoot. She pulled back the hammer. The sound was cold.

Henry seemed to shift. She sensed he had released something. All at once, Jacob stood in her sights. What was he doing? Without moving, eyes full open, she turned her look to him and saw his breathing under his tunic, his collarbone, the slope of his shoulders. He pushed her arm so the rifle pointed at the wall.

"Give it to me," Jacob said.

She lowered the weapon and her eyes were suddenly flooded with light. She staggered back against the wall. She heard Jacob leave, and she sank to the floor. In a moment, she heard a brittle thud and knew Henry had dropped the knife. She imagined Wole. What if she had hurt someone, anyone? How would she have explained? She remained curled into herself a good while, remembering Henry's face, his thin shoulders, his still-beautiful hands. "I would never harm you," she said to everyone she had ever known, "any of you."

At last Madeline cried. She pushed herself up and saw Henry turned away from her, the sad burlap rope poured out around him like

broken netting. "I'm so sorry," she said. He said nothing and she tip-
toed to his side. He seemed again asleep. She picked up the knife.

"How is Pastor?" Jacob said when she carried Madeline outside.

"He is resting. We must give him the quinine and the Babalawo's
medicine, but not the laudanum. It makes him wild when he comes
out."

"Yes," he said.

"Why was my husband untied?"

"He was in pain."

"You untied him?"

"Yes."

*Let all of my crimes be counted. I will not leave my husband to be
cared for by someone else. We will die with him if we have to,* Emma
thought. She asked Duro and Abike to move her things and the baby's
cradle back to the bedroom where Henry lay. Her husband opened his
eyes occasionally. Once he said, "It burns." The moon rose early.
Henry was calm and she moved her pillows to sleep with him and the
baby between. When she nursed Madeline, moonlight fell upon her
naked breasts.

Two days later, the bedroom door was open and Uncle Eli's carving
lay on the threshold, pale yellow and gleaming like polished bone. She
had taken to carrying it in her pocket most days. How had it slipped
out? But then she understood as well as she had ever known anything:
Uncle Eli's carving meant to be just where it was—at the entrance to
this room. Something powerful stirred in the air.

She lifted Madeline and placed her in the shoulder hammock
Henry had made for Sarah, and she watched the letter opener the
whole time. "God," she said, as she lifted her skirts to step over it and
out of the room. She looked back at her sleeping husband once and
then moved through the house to the back door, her shoulders bent
around the child. On the piazza, she had to squint against the sudden

light. No one was about, so she walked in circles with the baby in the
yard. She thought about the carving inside and her ailing husband.
She was sheared in two, part of her flying back to her father's farm and
Uncle Eli's toes and Mittie Ann's naked head and her mother in
prayer, the other part flying over Africa, surveying Henry as he pressed
his spleen and Sarah's hair over her cheek in death and Jacob's smile
and Wole's brilliant head. Two worlds, one world too many. Finally
she thought she must go back to Henry. "I'm leaving the door open,"
she said aloud, and propped it with a stool. She took a breath, held
Madeline tight to her chest, and moved into the parlor. It was lovely
and quiet as a chapel. She snuggled the child safely against the back
of the good chair.

Standing at their bedroom door, she stared hard at Henry and saw
the slight rise and fall of his shoulder as he breathed. She let out a deep
sigh. The yellow carving lay quiet as a house lizard on the threshold.
She leaned to pick it up, blood rushing to her head, and she stopped
in her motion, not knowing what she could trust in her mind.

She would wait. The chair she chose allowed her to look down the
hall and out the door to the backyard and through the bedroom door
to the bed and Henry. It was midday, the quiet hour, and she heard
only the shift and tremble of the house rafters under the hot sun. It
calmed her, such a familiar sound. "God is with us," she said. "God
with us. God is."

"Yes, ma'am," she thought she heard, a comfort, another voice. Her
shoulders relaxed.

Just like that she felt him. "It's you, Uncle Eli."

He could have been standing behind his cabin looking out at the
hills, his hands at his sides, the worn trousers, the calm bearing of
him. Only he was here, in the room, watching her and in an attitude
of sprightliness, as if he meant to tease her as he had long ago, as if
any minute he might say, *Was a snake just now where you sitting*, and
watch with glee while she sprang up. She almost laughed.

"You shouldn't sneak up on me," she said and felt herself smile, like she was waiting for the biggest piece of lemon cake. The sweetness of it almost knocked her over and she thought, *This is how angels come.*

And then she was rushed with guilt and purpose. There was something she was supposed to do. What was it? She almost leapt from the chair, claiming the slip of wood for her hand. Power shot through her like the flame of God. *Breathe myself into it. Find a place.*

She pushed the letter opener into her pocket, scooped up the child, and got to the back door just as Abike and Wole were coming into the yard. The child started to cry, and Emma patted her back and walked with her until she quieted. Then Wole wanted to hold Madeline, and Emma had him sit on the piazza and make a cradle of his legs and she placed the baby there and the boy took the baby's hands and brought them together as he sang a song in Yoruba he seemed to invent on the spot. "Abike, please watch Madeline," she said, and the girl came over and sat beside Wole, her arm draped over his shoulder.

She lit a candle in the parlor. "What do you want me to do?" she said. But no answer came from God or Uncle Eli or anyone. Emma thought on the great stories of the Bible: Mary visited by the angel, the shepherds watching their fields by night, experience beyond reckoning.

"How do you release a spirit?" she said to Jacob, across from him at the dining table.

"I don't understand."

"If someone of your country has died, how will the people prepare for burial?"

"Ah," he said. "Pastor?" His chest heaved.

"No!" she said. "No, no. He is as he was. I mean one of your people."

"Ah," he said.

"I'm sorry I frightened you," she said, and waited for him.

"A diviner may be called." He paused for breath. "The body is cleansed and the house as well. Then the women are mourning while the men feast. Lamentation may go on for a long time until the spirit is sent on its way."

"But what about the body?"

"It can be wrapped in cloth and a grave made in the yard. Sometimes the roof is removed from the room where the person died."

Emma thought of the wads of burning thatch torn from the king's house the night of the fire and how the rooms had lain desolate and black the next day.

"I believe I have an obligation," she said, pulling Uncle Eli's carving from her pocket. The letter opener had been between them like a butter dish or a lantern for months now. There was nothing new to point to. "What can you tell me about this?"

"It is peculiar mah. You have brought it from Ijaye, I believe."

"I brought it from America."

"Ah!" he said. "Someone in America has made it?"

"The old slave I told you about."

"Is it true?" he said, as though she must be confused, and he reached for the slip of wood, turning it over and even smelling it.

"What is it for?" she said.

"Ah," he said. "It resembles the staff of some divinity. But this one is thin, made for the *oyinbo* to open letters."

"Perhaps he needed it to be useful to me," she said, and studied Jacob's face. "But I think the carving is of himself."

He didn't blink. "It can happen that way. A powerful townsman may carry a walking stick with carving like this, to show his head, blessed by the women. He will want to be buried with it."

"The old women who turn into crows."

"Any powerful woman."

Emma seesawed on the brink of two worlds, her chest cool but her head hot. "Well, whatever it is, Uncle Eli meant for me to carry it here, to bury it, as if his soul were in it."

"If this is the case, you are holding the man's effigy," Jacob said. "It is very serious."

Emma studied Jacob's face. "Do you believe that? Or do you mock me? You'll betray me because you're angry with me."

"Why do you say so?"

"Say what?"

"I am angry."

"Aren't you, for my father's slaves, for my own father?" For a moment she saw Jacob shackled, and her head buzzed.

Jacob tucked his chin. "It is better to close the mouth," he said.

"I've got a newborn infant and a husband teetering somewhere on the edge of the world. We've had the Babalawo in, which is right upside down, missionaries appealing to witch doctors. I almost shot my husband. You and I have been"—she hesitated—"in close proximity. This is the time to open the mouth, Jacob."

"Ah," he said, and turned to look out the back door as if he might escape. Then he turned to face her. "Mah. You are proud. You speak of God as if you are the only child. Ah!"

He'd better have something to say to soften it, she thought.

"Go on," she said.

"You talk of suffering, but you have not been pierced," he said.

She was afire. "I have suffered a good deal," she said, furious, her face hot hot hot. "I buried a child! I gave a child for this country. Do you hear me?" She thrust the flat of her hand forward and hit his arm.

He put his hand on hers and would not release it, and he spoke slowly. "I have lost a village mah. Can you comprehend? I have been a slave. I am sorry for you but even with your loss, you have not been pierced. You believe you are better than I am, than all of us. We are children to you. Ah! You keep the truth from me. You never tell me of your house in America. Slavery in your yard. You pretend in secret. You think I will not learn."

"That's not true," she said. He must take it back. She loved him. She loved Africa.

He released her hand.

She looked out the window, her eyes blurred with tears.

Jacob broke the silence. "Would you approach a white man as you came to me? What do you think it will cost me?"

"I didn't think of that."

He made a sound like a person makes who is hit.

"Forgive me," she said.

He looked at her and what was in his eyes was his country.

"The carving may have afflicted your husband because you have not taken care of it."

"I'm trying to do what's right," she said.

"It has taken you a long time."

"I didn't understand."

"Because you do not listen."

"I've learned your language," she whispered.

"But you could not hear an old man's plea. Isn't it so in your religion, to bear another's burden?"

"What do you mean my religion? You mean *our* religion."

"But we are talking of you. Why can't God use you to relieve an old person? Because he is black? Why is it difficult to believe Pastor is ill for a black man's pain?"

"But there must have been more. We can't have come here just to relieve an old slave."

"What of me?" he said.

"You," she said. "You?" And thought: *I would have come for you.* And yet she had meant to come for multitudes. The husk of her life— reason and calculation and the ferocity of her own will and even her demanding faith, all that had armored her since college—fell away. If she had entered the kingdom of God, it took a shattering.

"I have been in agony for your husband," Jacob said. "He is my support. Do you not see with your eyes? Do you not see my feet where I stand?"

"I AM TRUSTING you," she said to Jacob when she was ready. "But I will do it myself, in memory of Uncle Eli, and I will read the Bible. And you must pray for Rev. Bowman."

"Yes," he said, "I will pray for you."

"Tell me what to do," she said.

In any other place at any other time under any other circumstance, with Henry well or in sight of another white person or within the sanctity of a brick church or not nursing a child or without Jacob's knowledge of her family's past, Emma would not have stepped across the threshold into the spiritual world of Africa. But none of those things was, and she did.

She remembered the camwood-painted wall in the Babalawo's compound, the energy moving into her. "This is himself," she said. "He prepared. It was what he could do. He made it and gave it to me. This is the least I can do." The broad world of Africa filled her mind, warm and living, and stamped, like Jacob, with a memory of iron. She had tasted it as a girl, cooked air, and she tasted it now. She thought of the day she had seen Uncle Eli as a buffalo. He had called her the white bird. And then she considered how Henry had tried to throw the carving away, and she half wondered what powers Uncle Eli exercised even now. The idea wafted about the room like a downy feather kept aloft by wind.

She did what she could think of to follow Jacob's instructions. The ceremony required little: her Testament, the carving, a bowl of water, the last bit of cinnamon she owned, and Tela's beautiful blue cloth close by. "He prayed; he gave it to me to carry. He knew all of my life I would do it; he sent me," she said. Madeline lay in her cradle, her big eyes seeming to watch her mother. Emma sprinkled cinnamon into the water and dipped her fingers into the bowl, then flicked her fingers in the four corners of the room as a cleansing. A few drops hit the baby, who looked perplexed and turned her head. Emma laid the carving entire into the bowl and opened her sacred text. But she knew the words she wanted without depending on the page. *Do not let your heart be troubled. In my Father's house are many rooms; if it were not so, I would have told you.* Now Uncle Eli would find a room with God. "You find a good place," he had said, and meant, *for me.* Emma cried in the glory of the hard miracle that the lame man will leap and the poor enter first. "Jesus help us," she whispered. Then she folded the carving into the cloth and just as she closed it tight with string, she knew. *This is the African key, the golden key to eternal life. What's so wrong with joining the ancestors,* she thought. *How different are they from saints and angels? If Jesus walks and talks with us, why not our own beautiful departed?* No wonder Jacob smiled.

She looked out the window, saw the garden pushing up green and warm, and heard a goat bray; their clothes dried on the line; she heard her daughter cry.

Emma picked Madeline up along with the bundled remnant of Uncle Eli's life. She went into the yard and there was Jacob. He waited near the young sapling she had let stand when the land was cleared because that corner of the lot was otherwise barren and she thought it would grow, reach for the sun, and offer them shade.

"Here," he said.

She watched as he dug. He went three feet at least. Then he stopped. He squatted and she handed him the bundle.

After he piled the dirt over Uncle Eli's effigy, Jacob packed it down, tapped it, and caressed it with his hands. She had never seen anything more loving, and it touched her deeply.

"Lay a stone there," she said. "A large one."

"I will do it," he said. "The old man is my father."

She knew how he meant it—in the African way of belonging to

the family. It went deeper than calling the old man "Uncle"—the practice of her country. It meant *we are one.*

The egret she had seen about the house flew north toward the Ilorin Gate so that Emma felt the moment was offering itself to God.

"Jacob," she said. "I was wrong to"—she breathed in and out—"approach you as I did. It was an accident, but I didn't stop it." She looked at her hands and then she looked at him, in the shade of the tree.

"Why have you done it?" he said.

"Because I am inclined to you. Because I needed help." She took a pin out of her hair and replaced it. "I felt drawn to you. Do you see?"

"Yes," he said. "But, even so, you cannot do it."

"But you have also felt something for me."

"Yes," he said. "You are like a deer."

"A deer?" Her heart expanded and then it contracted. *He sees me but he cannot come near me.*

"We cannot be close," she said.

"No."

"But if I went away you would miss me."

"Ah," he said, looking down. "It is true."

"Yes," she said, watching his profile, hearing the drums in town. The day was brilliant, the air clear and breezy. She remembered how Uncle Eli had befriended her against all likelihood. She saw the path they were to follow.

"If you would be my friend," she said.

"I am willing," he said, and looked at her.

She felt humbled, already nostalgic for him.

"One more thing," Emma said, "please take the rifle and bury it in the bush."

IN AN ODD WAY, it was a beneficence that a festival day came. The town's attention was elsewhere, in stilt walking and masquerades and women's dancing and throwing food into the river as a sacrifice. Emma had been given a revelation from God. But she also had a husband lingering toward death or madness. *I must live today in the sufficiency of God,* she told herself, *only the normal things and a bath.* So she held devotionals with the household, kept her school, cut pawpaw for dinner, played with Wole and the baby in the shade of the compound trees, and in the late afternoon asked Duro to bring water. She washed her hair. Combing it out, she let it dangle in front of the baby, whose clear blue eyes followed the curls. Emma thought it likely the little girl would be a beauty, with Henry's chiseled features, not her round ones. In the early evening she instructed Duro to bring lanterns to the piazza. "We'll eat outdoors," she said. Later she called everyone together in the dark and they sang hymns. Jacob played an African melody she recognized.

In the morning, she changed Madeline's diaper on the piazza and pumped the child up and down in her arms. Emma was stiff from little exercise and her mind felt cold and blank. There must be some relief. After breakfast she walked into the bedroom out of habit. Henry had pulled himself to half sitting. "My Lord!" she said, just as her mother might. She squeezed the child tight to her breast. It seemed she had chanced to find her husband in a field after a war, his hair long, face whiskered, shirt crumpled, and himself dazed and wintered-looking in spite of the tropical heat.

"Look at you," she said. "Henry."

Still he did not speak, and she thought: If he *were* in a field, he would turn and take another way, believing he had gone wrong. "Dear you," she said. "It's me."

She took a step toward him, and it seemed to loosen his voice.

"The birds," he said, "woke me. Or someone singing." For the first time in some while, his voice was normal and his eyes reflected recognition and something close to joy when he saw her arms full of the baby.

"You're here, with us. You're home." Her throat was full and she started to cry. "We have a daughter," she said, pressing at the tears with the flat of her hand. She sat in the chair by the window and drew Madeline out of her bundling cloth.

"I got lost," Henry said. She said nothing while he looked at his hands, and she thought he cried without tears. When he was through, she put the child in his arms and she sat next to him and caressed his hair.

"You must have done something to save me," he said, still looking at Madeline.

"Yes," she said, and did not say: *I opened a door for an old man.* Surely it was the mixture of quinine and the Babalawo's medicine that had worked some miracle. And the spirit of God brooding over them.

49

Jesus, the African

Jacob leaned toward Abike, and he could see now her eyes were for him. He spoke with Tunji about his hopes.

He read to Wole, who was missing his school.

He had considered packing them all, including Duro, and leaving. He might have if it had not been for the master's baby. Or if it would not have hurt Wole to be uprooted again. Or if it would not seem to Abike a disloyalty, enough to make her wonder if he would turn his back on her if she were ever ill. Or if the gospel had not been the first religion he knew that believed even slaves could come to God, believed their children mattered, believed them worthy of an ancestor and gave them Jesus. Or if it were not for the woman who exposed her heart.

"Tunji," he said. "I need you in the church."

"Ah," the man said, engrossed in the labor of peeling an orange. "I am your friend. But I won't allow any *oyinbo* to drown me for Jesus' sake."

"Jesus is not so far from us," Jacob said.

"What do you mean?"

"He is not so far from our country. You know he has lived in Africa as a boy. He is closer to us than to America."

"Is he an *oyinbo*?"

"He is not an *oyinbo*." Jacob looked around for some color that might explain. "He is the color of earth," he concluded.

50

Small Miracles

O NCE, WHEN HE called the newborn Sarah, Emma thought Henry was slipping. But it was only a momentary lapse, a confusion of love.

There were nights of little sleep with Madeline crying, and days of caring for Henry, who wasn't sure the rib had healed; so he was moved about the house and onto the piazza using a pallet. But there was also the garden growing. Well-wishers stopped by with gifts for the baby and the mother. Sade called often in the afternoon and sat mending and singing under the trees.

When Henry finally walked outside one afternoon, Emma saw how pale he had become. For the second time the old blind man came to call. Henry asked Emma to bring Madeline. They laid her on the mat and let the old man touch her.

"The hair is not right," the fellow said.

Emma hadn't seen Henry laugh so for a long time, and when he held his side, she thought it was not from sickness but wellness.

As far as she could tell, Henry did not remember threatening Jacob or remember her threatening him with the rifle. Sometimes she wondered if it had been a dream.

Henry sat in the yard to preach, and his color came back. Nowadays in his preaching, Henry dwelled on children: Jesus calling the children, humble yourself like a child. He lingered with the men as if he had finally put his head under an African umbrella. At night Emma lay with him, the babe in the cradle. They were together in that sweet, ferocious way, and it seemed to Emma like her own cradle. Everything written and beyond writing between them like pages in a book. The courage and loneliness of Henry's face she had always loved. He seemed to her an entire civilization. Now she began to love her husband's survival. His voice had changed, as if some great struggle had burned out of him and left a blue lake.

Emma remembered their one trip out into the hills around the town, taken in their early Ogbomoso months when they still lived at the old compound. They had put Wole and Abike on Caesar. Emma had walked with Jacob and Henry. Duro knew the path to an outcrop of rock pocked with large basins that held pools of water. Midway up, Emma had felt fatigued and hot. She had urged the others to go ahead. She would sit beneath a tree and rest before catching up with them. But Henry said no. She had tried again. *Go ahead with the picnic things. Wole can stay with me. No,* Henry had said. *The rest can go and I will stay.* When at last she and Henry reached the summit and looked out across the hill, they saw the white flag of the tablecloth tied high in a limb. Below them the land spread out green—except for Ogbomoso, brown and ochre, dotted with groves of trees. Most of the pools were shallow enough for Wole to step through. All but the amethyst blue pool, which Duro said was too deep to measure.

"Does it ever dry up?" Emma said.

And Duro said, "No. As God is eternal."

To Emma's surprise the Iyalode didn't leave. She was there like a mounting stone firm in the yard. Every day a child brought her food and she kept her mat stowed under a tree near the kitchen. She made her own fire and didn't interfere with Duro. She seemed busy, but Emma couldn't tell that she really worked at anything except retying her wrapper and combing up her hair and fanning her legs.

"What is she doing?" Emma finally said to Jacob.

"She has established herself as your mother. She will not leave for a month."

"My mother? Is there anything that comes with that, anything she wants?" Emma had about come around to Jacob's view of the Iyalode as a keen businesswoman, though she felt great affection for her.

"She may wish to give the child a Yoruba name."

Emma smiled at him, open and full, because of what they knew together and what, she thought, they had agreed never to know of one another. "My goodness," she said.

Small miracles returned: water in a bucket, an evening smell of roasting corn, wildflowers in a vase. Emma taught the children hopscotch. The Iyalode christened Madeline *Enitan*, meaning "embodiment of a story." Emma gazed at the woman and then at her child. One was a mystery to her, the other her own mystery.

"Thank you," she said.

The rainy season bore itself forward into June. Henry grew stronger and worked on the vocabulary. He kept Madeline's cradle in motion with his naked toe on the rocker. One afternoon he came in with three seedlings in a wood tray.

"What are those?" she said.

"Lemon trees," he said. "I started them with seed from Ijaye. They've been growing behind the shed while I was ill. I suppose it wouldn't be too great a sin to call this a good omen." He grinned largely and she went to him with all of her stories of love and disaster, but love gaining.

51

Touching God

HENRY WATCHED JACOB direct the building of the temporary church. The idea was to put up scaffolding, a three-foot wall, and a roof for a temporary sanctuary and come back later to fill in, when there was more time and more money. In late afternoons, the two of them circled the perimeter of the compound, Henry using a Yoruba walking stick. One evening they visited the closest market. They began walking regularly to the Ilorin Gate. Sometimes they walked in silence, and Henry once or twice thought he heard the sounds of a harmonium in the air. Probably bells from an *orisha* grove.

Once or twice he wondered at the vividness of a dream in which his wife was threatening him with the rifle. He couldn't remember if he had had the vision before or after his recovery. He tried to remember why she wanted to shoot him. He could almost remember but not quite, and, the more he tried to remember the more the dream eluded him. Certainly there was no cause for him to think so of her. She was immensely gentle and kind, as if her heart had met its meaning. He was fairly certain he could remember asking Jacob to whip him.

"I have sought to be true to my calling, to keep the Redeemer before me as my standard," Henry said one afternoon, returning with his assistant from the blind man's mat. The day was overcast and almost cool, the palm trees lush in their crowns. Henry inhaled deeply. "Asking you to flog me was a sin."

A child ran past with a tray of bright red peppers balanced on her head.

Henry stopped. He had to look into Jacob's face. The man appeared a little shaken, as if some nerve had been touched. "I wasn't sure if I dreamed it or if it was real, but now looking at you, I see it was real enough. I'm mighty sorry."

"Ah," Jacob said. "Now you are well I am happy. Life is difficult; no man can say otherwise." In a moment, he spoke again. "The sun is always here, even when we sleep." They walked on. "There is one thing I am asking," he continued. "I will like to marry."

Henry looked at his assistant. Of course, why had he not thought as much? "I'm happy for you," he said.

"I will need your patronage."

"Yes," Henry said. "Whatever I can do." They were out the Ilorin Gate, moving along a path. Henry stopped again. "You'll need a house," he said.

AT LAST, THEY had news that Moore had returned, recuperated, to Ijaye. A few days later, they received mail and supplies, the first staples in months: coffee, sugar, flour, paper, hymnbooks, two payments from the board, newspapers from Savannah and Richmond, and two letters for Emma from home.

Henry watched his wife tear open the first one. In a moment she called out. "Look here, look here. Mittie Ann and Carl finally had a baby. I don't believe it. Look here. A baby girl." He thought she looked happier than on their wedding day. Over and over, she kept saying it:

"Mittie Ann and Carl had a baby." She kept saying it as if someone had risen from the dead, as if she were Mary Magdalene sent into town to announce the Savior's resurrection.

ONE AFTERNOON, HENRY and Jacob cut their walk short. He saw Emma watching as they approached the house. *Poor woman*, he thought, *she will always worry about me*. In the parlor, he spoke with her privately.

"Jacob and I have been deliberating on an issue of gravity," he said. "I wish to know your opinion." Emma was rocking, holding Madeline before her; the child had begun to focus on faces and spasmodically attempted to find her mouth with her fist.

"Yes, husband." Emma looked older, but she was more alive than ever.

"Jacob has put away the equivalent of forty dollars; he has even purchased some goats and arranged for land. He's quite frugal, as you know, never wasting his money as others do on drink or gross indulgences but tithing to the church as regularly as we." He stopped to draw his breath. Emma was smiling at him as if she were the cause of the man's good character or bore some relation to him that made the praise shine on her as well. It was hard to know how she would respond. He might as well go ahead. "He wishes to marry Abike," he said. "Of course the mother will have to agree." And when Emma said nothing, only seemed to sit up straighter, he added, "I was thinking we might make a gift to him, considering all he has done for us. We are as close to family as any he's got. He wants our blessing."

His wife's look changed significantly; a furrow came into her brow and she stopped rocking the baby, put Madeline into the carry basket, and went to the window to look out. He wondered briefly if she knew some cause why the two should not marry. There had been time enough in his illness for him not to know a great many things. "What are you thinking?" he said.

She turned, and he saw she had him in her sights though there were tears in her eyes.

"I've come to know something," she said.

"Yes?" he said.

"I've come to know that I am less advanced in charity than I had thought."

"Wife, you are too hard on yourself," he said, running his fingers through his hair, feeling peculiar in regard to her confession. "Think of all you have borne."

"You don't understand," she said. "I had thought I followed God, that I loved Africa. Yet I am surprised when Africans are more rewarded than we are. Even our own people. I find it hard when they prove better than I am, when they have their own happiness. I have a long way to go, don't you think, to share the heart of Christ." She paused as if remembering something.

He had not known she had the courage of such candor. "Look what you have learned, then," he said, feeling more contrite toward her now than he had ever before when she was haughty and certain. "It's enough to be born for. I wonder what I missed when I was sleeping." He tried to smile a bit, and now she looked elegant and brave but also a little sad.

"Abike will make a wonderful wife," she said at last. "Jacob betrays more tenderness than most men, black or white. It may be a hindrance to him some day." Henry thought she might have been talking to him about a lack of tenderness and to herself about how its absence had strengthened her.

"You approve?"

"It is you who approve, and I assent," Emma said, picking up the baby again.

They sat for a moment, their pearl settled to her mother's breast.

Henry touched his ear. *I am not so wicked or they would not be here*, he thought. *Jesus, do not let my head become my antagonist again*, he prayed, a supplication he had learned from a man in Ijaye. Emma gazed out the window.

"Your church will be beautiful, Henry," his wife said. "The sun on the thatch."

· 52 ·

Moving in Light

EVEN MEN OF God who are not godly experience miracles.
The Sabbath came like butterfly wings, light and airy. Henry
preached before his flock in the partially built church.

"*Bi'le aiye ba wu e koo gbe, dede ni, sugbon bio ba si fe gbe lodo olo-
run, dede na ni pelu,*" he said. "If you prefer to live in this world, then
you are welcome, but if you prefer to live above in heaven, then you
are equally welcome." The congregation voiced an approving hum.
Maybe the horse is in heaven, Henry thought. He felt that morning
neither old nor young but rather as if he were floating in some region
in which there was no age. He moved his legs without effort, or, more
to the point, it did not seem he who moved them. In like way, he
opened his mouth but some other power spoke.

The road to God is the only true road.

He could not tell if others felt as he did, but *he* believed and that
in itself was a miracle, a transcendence, the words so close to him, they
were his breathing. Acts 17, beginning with verse 24.

*The God who created the world and everything in it, and who is Lord
of heaven and earth, does not live in shrines made by men.*

Henry thought it odd that he had never heard the poetry in the
verse, the balance of the phrases. He considered for a moment God's
desire to be *in* the world, indwelling, and he was mildly comforted as

he had been in certain stages of illness when the pain was not great but his energy was entirely suppressed and he was aware that life was passing and could not be held. At the moment Henry knew that all of his illnesses were caused by grandiosity even if they were also predicated by the sting of an insect or a drink of foul water. It seemed likely he would suffer more, but it didn't matter anymore. God was in him.

It is not because He lacks anything that He accepts service at men's hands, for He is Himself the universal giver of life and breath and all else.

When a wind came from behind and slipped up the back of his jacket, he thought he might be lifted sideways into the air.

He created every race of men of one stock to inhabit the whole earth's surface.

Did Jacob stand up then, or had he been standing through the entire service? Maybe he was dreaming. Henry smiled to think he might be required to wake and preach the sermon again.

He fixed the epochs in their history and the limits of their territory.

For one beat of time, he felt a skirmish in his chest; he thought of a maimed thing, and an idea of struggle entered faintly into his consciousness before it was carried away.

They were to seek God, and it might be, to touch and find Him.

How odd the idea of touching God seemed, though one might imagine touching Jesus as the disciples had. What a rapturous possibility. A thrill ran through him and he paused. What had Jesus' hands looked like? Were they flat and rough or were the fingers tapered? That was what the verse meant, of course, Jesus. Unless it meant something like his sensation this morning of moving in light, without fear or effort. That could be touching God.

Though indeed He is not far from each one of us, for in Him we live and move, in Him we exist; as some of your own poets have said, "We are also His offspring."

He meant to expound, but the scripture seemed sufficient. Hours had passed, or no time at all had passed. He led a final prayer and then spoke in a detached and intimate manner with the men while his wife greeted women and children. The men's hands were like supple bark, and they clasped his hands between their own. Henry could not tell whether they agreed with him, but they were kind.

If he dreamed the sermon, he did not remember waking. Perhaps the vision, if it was one, was a trace of heaven.

Part Five

REMEMBER ME

Hold the Light

The first thing I knew for certain—as certain as my backbone—was
the break in human beings, our bondage to error. Cast out of
Eden, we harm one another. But we retain a memory of God.
What is the resurrection but the possibility of return?

—EMMA, LETTER FRAGMENT NEVER SENT

EMMA TURNED THE page in her journal for the new month, *July*
1855. Two years in this country. *We have harvested our first squash,*
she wrote. *Madeline can turn herself over. Wole claims her as a sister.* At
intervals, Emma paged through the red diary from its inception. One
afternoon while Henry was out strolling with the baby, she washed
her hair and left it down to dry. Her spirit seemed to expand in her
aloneness, and her feelings moved in every direction. "My heart is
still an open book," she said aloud to herself. She had drawn a veil over
her time with Jacob, over Henry's illness, the rifle, her desire to be free.
But some days it was a thin veil. Now, her hair still damp, she picked
up the journal and walked into the yard. She sat in the shade. Rather
than open her diary, she pressed it to her chest. The simple act opened
something in her, a secret well, a spring. She remembered how Henry
had come to her young in his age, almost a boy in his claim of her, and
she thought how she had been young and tender and aflame and she
considered how they clung to each other in the night and in the day
and how they must always be so, matched hands meeting and folding,

how all hardship was a means to love, all darkness an avenue to day. She wept with relief that the spring was still there.

One night she woke from a dream in which she was flying.

Two weeks later, the Hathaways at last came for a visit. Anna had been ill for weeks and her husband had taken her to Lagos, where they had boarded ship for England. But the freighter was held up in Dakar and in the time they were there, Anna recovered. They had returned to Ibadan. Now they brought news that a new Baptist minister had arrived in Ijaye.

"And we didn't even know a new missionary was on the way," Henry said. "I wonder where he's from? What state?"

Emma pondered the workings of the divine, how her miracle with Uncle Eli had depended on Anna's illness, the Hathaways' absence, even, perhaps Henry's illness. How infinite and complex was the mind of God. In the light of such profound insight, she had to work up her enthusiasm for the impractical pink silk dress her friend had brought as a gift.

Sitting down to dinner, she felt how awkward not to include Abike and Jacob, Wole and Duro, and she called them to come to the table. It took a long time with Duro, who had never dined with an *oyinbo*.

"Please sit beside Rev. Bowman," Emma said.

"No mah," he said.

"Please," she said. "Bring out the *fufu* and soup."

She ate with her fingers and let Madeline suck on them after each bite.

"The child is an African," Duro said, and everyone laughed.

They planned Sade's baptism in August at the Laka River, near the borrowed compound where they had spent their first Ogbomoso months. On a Sabbath morning they walked up the hill, past the old compound. Emma remembered it as a dark place and was surprised when she saw how light and pretty it was on the hill, filled now with the Baale's brother's family whose journey to the ancestral home had left the place open for them. *They don't even know we were there*, she thought, feeling oddly as though she might evaporate. She missed a beat in her step, and Wole pushed her along.

Near the river, the palms were deep green. The land sloped gently and the grass came up to Emma's shoulders. But there was a natural path made through the regular passing of feet to the edge of the water. She saw the river was deeper now with the rains but even so hardly a river, more a fine stream. Emma had stitched a lace bonnet for Sade, but the woman wore her own scarf until the moment she was called by Henry into the water. She was enormously serious, making her way, saying "ah-ah" over and over as she stepped into the water up to her waist. Henry caught her hand and she clung to her wrap, and when she came up out of the spring she waved her arms like a person winning a race. "Jesus has paid for me," she cried. "Praise my God!"

It was a beautiful moment, but Henry's face was a little screwed up and Emma knew there was pain in his side.

That night he rocked Madeline in the cradle, whispering a story about a little girl climbing the pawpaw tree. Later the two of them sat in the parlor. Neither took up a task, for the day seemed complete in itself. Emma was in the bedroom pulling her dress over her head— half on, half off—when Henry said, "I think we ought to go home for a brief furlough, maybe six months." Emma pulled her dress back down.

"Why? You're better. Everything is so lovely." She could hear her voice rising as she spoke.

"We both know I need a rest," he said. "We'll go home for the winter in Georgia and miss the dry season here. I'll do nothing but sit by the house fire, eating ham and grits. We'll see the baby through her first year. The vocabulary is on hand; we can deliver it together. With Rev. Moore in Ijaye, the new missionary can come up to Ogbomoso. Hathaway told me of a freighter leaving Lagos in early September. It goes up to Monrovia, then straight to Savannah. When we return, we'll resettle here. I promise."

Something reared up in Emma like a horse. *Why, no,* she wanted to say, *this will not do. I have waded through the swamp and am on dry land. I have endured forty days in the wilderness and manna has come from heaven. I was blind and now I see. No!* She felt her interior beating as a moth would against silk, trying to get to the light. She realized her mouth was open and she closed it, looking at Henry.

He left the room. Madeline was fretful for once. Emma tried to soothe her. "Of course you don't want to go. You'll stay here with me." She dozed and woke to the image of Henry in the river, the pain on his face. She wandered to the bedside table. Her husband had begun a letter to the mission board. *I shall think about this country by day and dream of it at night,* he had written, the letters scrolled out. He loved this country just as she did, then. It would always call him. For too long she had battered against his ideas and it had not helped. Then she thought of their other daughter, Sarah, buried. If they left as Henry suggested, just briefly, they would avoid the season of that dear child's death.

The next day, Emma glanced out the window to see Henry with Jacob studying the church. Her husband looked fine to her, his hands resting on his hips, his elbows out. He was the person to whom she had confessed her spiritual limitation. *I am not as advanced in charity as I had thought.* And he had found in her confession something to praise. He was her secret drawer.

"When did you first consider going home?" she said that evening.

"I was thinking it before I was so ill. With the baby coming. I thought we ought to go as soon as the child was old enough. For a season. To keep us safe."

Emma felt a gentle shift in the current of her will. Wouldn't it be lovely to arrive on her front porch with Madeline in her arms. Henry's plan to go home and recuperate was not his usual pressing. It was re-leasing. Already she was on her way to imagining their next return to Ogbomoso.

In the night, Henry wound her hair with his fingers. He stroked her forehead. His features were fuller now that he was gaining strength, and in the dim light of the moon she traced his eyebrows. He was smoke and rain, as familiar and permanent as her face in the mirror.

The September evening before their departure, the air was unusu-ally cool. Emma awakened some time in the night, pulled on her shawl, lit a lantern, and stepped out the back door onto the piazza. From there, she could see compound fires burning low across the town's hills. Jacob lifted the curtain of his room and stepped out. He still gave the slight ritual bow.

"I think you don't need to do that now," Emma said.

"Is everything fine?"

"Yes. Everything is fine. I woke up and couldn't go back to sleep." He sat on a bench near her.

"I'm going to miss this place—even for a few months," she said.

"My heart is heavy," he said.

"Yes. Mine too. But we must praise God for such ties as bind us in faith and cause us to"—she faltered—"to love one another."

He put his hand to the back of his neck, his head lowered. Then he looked up and stretched his legs out in front of him.

"I have learned from you," he said.

"What's that?" she said.

"You cannot be defeated," he said.

She felt a flower open in her chest and she laughed.

"Nor can you," she said.

They sat for some minutes.

"I can build up the fire," he said.

"Yes," she said.

They sat close to the flame. She prodded it with a stick. "You will have a good wife," she said. "The new reverend will soon come up from Ijaye. You and Duro have employment. I know how important that is for your life. I have not learned nothing." She smiled with her head lowered at her double negative, how she had learned to speak sometimes like Duro. "You have little Wole." She watched as he lifted his arms, linked his fingers, and placed them behind his head, and her heart leaned toward him for his goodness. "We will be back in just six months," she said. "After we have had time to mend, and spread the news about the mission. My husband has promised we will stay here. We'll make a whole village." She turned to him with a smile on her face, but he seemed engrossed. Emma felt that all she had said was wrong. It wasn't sufficient. "You've been a friend to my husband."

"Please, as we are living, you and your husband will return," he said.

"Yes," she said.

The next morning, Emma said good-bye to Duro. "Thank you," she said, extending her hand. "You kept me alive. Stay well in God."

"Ah," he said. "I am pained."

She kissed him on both cheeks.

She hugged each child in her school. She was leaving the books for Jacob to teach until the new missionary arrived. The Iyalode took Emma into the wing of her arm and said too many things for Emma to capture. All through the good-byes, Emma felt a pear lodged in her throat. Any moment she would weep a river. Sade started singing her own version of "We're Marching to Zion," continuing even as Emma kissed her cheek, turned, and entered the hammock. The seat across from her was now fitted with a baby carriage for Madeline. Standing beside Duro, Abike wore a native dress, looking like a girl back from a sojourn. "Oh," Emma said. She had forgotten to say good-bye to her handmaid. She stepped back down from the hammock. "I have left a wedding gift for you," she said. "Jacob is holding it." She kissed her hands. "Travel to see your mother. I'll be back soon."

"If you make a book," Abike said, "place me in it."

"How could I not?" Emma said.

Just as she was ascending again into the hammock, Emma felt certain they were forgetting something. "My writing box?" she called to Henry.

"We have it, wife," he said. "Everything."

Wole and Jacob went with them for two days, as far as the Oba River. The journey was perfectly calm. The ferrymen were there just as they had been a year ago. The one who had pushed Emma across recognized her.

"*Iya*," he called. "I am here to carry you." And he swam over with his raft, making certain he didn't miss his chance.

Henry and Emma talked a good while about who should carry the baby.

Finally the ferryman made a suggestion. "Put her for your back, *iya*," he said. They pulled cloth from a basket and tied the child tight.

"Snug as a clam," Henry said.

There was Wole still. She hadn't paid enough attention to him since the baby came. Fishing in her writing box, she pulled out the prism. It looked like sapphire, color of heaven. Emma surveyed her surroundings: the palms and the sandy soil and the river grass and a red flower flown high in a tree. She looked at the boy. "This is the light for you to hold until I come back," she said. Just as she placed it in his palm, she thought, *I may never see any of this again*, and she was shot through with wonder and loss. "Remember me," she said, determined to catch the boy's eye.

"Yes mah," he said, looking back at her, nodding his head in seriousness, his brilliant bold head.

She looked to Jacob. There was something more she wished to say to him. But before she knew what was happening, Henry and the ferryman were steering her into the water.

HISTORICAL NOTE

A DIFFERENT SUN is inspired by the writings of Lurana Davis Bowen and Thomas Jefferson Bowen, the first Southern Baptist missionaries to Africa. My mother gave me a copy of Lurana's diary when I was working on my memoir, *Gods of Noonday*. I was tantalized by its suggestive brevity. My own parents were missionaries. I knew how large and complex our lives were. But in this young woman's diary I found sentences so compressed, they seemed nearly to explode.

Feelings deeply wounded, for example. No story, no explanation, no context.

Others—

After a watchful, sleepless night we find our babe no better, but rather worse.
A neighborly present refused and sent back.
One slips away to pay an old grudge.

I first imagined a work of creative nonfiction in which I would seek to expand Lurana's story, using all the historical evidence I could find, as well as my own experience. I found instead that fiction was the best medium for conveying not Lurana's story per se but my own vision of what might have happened when a young, well-to-do woman from

Georgia fell in love with a former Texas cavalryman and traveled to
Yorubaland. What motivated her? What did she long for? What were
her limitations? How did her marriage evolve under the duress brought
on by illness and profound loss? And perhaps most critical: Who aided
her? Who were her West African tutors? For this part of the story, I
am indebted to my own mother, Anne Thomas Neil, who has told
story after story over the years of how her most critical instruction
during her first years on the mission field came from Nigerian men
and women who befriended her, some of them domestic workers in
our home, some of them church workers and colleagues.

For access to the Bowen's writings, I am indebted to Cecil Rober-
son, who archived "The Bowen Papers" for future generations of re-
searchers and readers. I am grateful to Cliff Lewis for his 1991
compilation of Bowen letters: *Ah, Africa: The Letters of Lurena Davis
and Thomas J. Bowen*. I am grateful for the reissue of Thomas Jefferson
Bowen's own *Adventures and Missionary Labours in Several Countries
in the Interior of Africa from 1849 to 1856* (Second edition, Intro. E. A.
Ayandele. London: Frank Cass & Co. Ltd., 1968).

In a very few passages in the novel, I have borrowed sentences and
phrases from the Bowens' papers—for the unparalleled power of their
words. *No one knows where the stone fell*, for example. Another: *I shall
think of this country by day and dream of it by night*. Again: *We do not
grieve as those who have no hope, and yet we cannot help but grieve*.

In addition to the Bowens's writings, I was inspired by *Seventeen
Years in the Yoruba Country: Memorials of Anna Hinderer*.

Other books and sources critical to my writing include, but are not
limited to:

Ade-Ajayi, J. F. *A Patriot to the Core: Bishop Ajayi Crowther*. Ibadan:
Spectrum Books, 2001.
Bryant, Jonathan M. *How Curious a Land: Conflict and Change in Greene
County, Georgia 1850–1885*. Chapel Hill, UNC Press, 1996.

Bailey, Anne C. *African Voices of the Atlantic Slave Trade*. Boston: Beacon Press, 2005.

Burks, Edgar H. *Planting the Redeemer's Standard: A Life of Thomas J. Bowen, First Baptist Missionary to Nigeria*. Columbus, Ga.: Brentwood Christian Press, 1994.

Clarke, W. H. *Travels & Explorations in Yorubaland (1854–1858)*. Ed. J. A. Atanda. Ibadan: Ibadan University Press, 1972.

Falola, Toyin. *Yoruba Gurus: Indigenous Production of Knowledge in Africa*. Trenton, N.J.: African World Press, 1999.

Hillman, Mamie Lee. *Green County Georgia: Black American Series*. Charleston: Arcadia Publishing, 2004.

MacKethan, Lucinda H., ed. *Recollections of a Southern Daughter: A Memoir by Cornelia Jones Pond*. Athens: Univ. of Georgia Press, 1998.

Olajubu, Oyeronke. *Women in the Yoruba Religious Sphere*. Albany: State Univ. of New York Press, 2003.

Peel, J. D. Y. *Religious Encounter and the Making of the Yoruba*. Bloomington: Indiana University Press, 2003.

Pinnock, S. G. *The Romance of Missions in Nigeria*. Richmond: Foreign Mission Board, Southern Baptist Convention, 1917.

The History of First Baptist Church, Oke'lerin, Ogbomoso (1855–1999). Church Historical Committee. Ibadan: Baptist Press, 1999.

A DIFFERENT SUN

DISCUSSION QUESTIONS

1. "In her mind, Emma had ascended to a place of significance in the family. She was the smarter daughter and the chosen one." How does Emma perceive herself as different from her sister, Catherine? Why does she sense she was meant to do something different? Have you ever felt "called" to take a different path than those around you? How did it feel?

2. Explain how Emma describes Africa. What kind of language does she use and what comparisons does she make? How is Africa a character in the novel?

3. Have you ever been a stranger in a foreign place? How did you cope with being different than everyone around you? How did you adapt or grow over time?

4. Why does Emma cherish her writing box and journal? What does writing symbolize to her?

5. Describe Emma's relationship with Uncle Eli. Why is Uncle Eli being Yoruba so significant to Emma's journey?

6. What is Emma's first impression of Jacob? Do you believe Emma's feelings for Jacob were unfaithful to Henry? How does she compare the two men, especially when Henry becomes ill with delusions?

7. Henry and Emma's struggle with their marriage is a main conflict in the story. How is her marriage different from what Emma expects? Do you think Emma falls out of love with Henry? Why or why not?

8. How do both Jacob and Henry let their troubled pasts define them? How do they try to overcome them? Do either of them succeed?

9. Although the novel is written in third person from Emma's point of view, many chapters take on the viewpoint of Jacob or Henry. How do their stories give you more insight into Emma's own journey?

10. Emma writes in her journal, "It may be that we follow God only by losing our way." Describe the challenges Emma faces as a missionary in Africa. How do each of these test her faith in God? When does she question her faith the most?

11. How is the role of women in society similar between Georgia and Africa? How is it different? Describe Emma's relationship with each of these characters: Mittie Ann, the African king's wives, Tela, the Iyalode?

12. What are some of the successes of Henry and Emma's mission?

13. Emma often talks about her "two worlds." Which one does she belong to? In what ways does Emma reconcile the slave-holding south where she grew up, and the African culture she sees as a missionary? Does she ever feel guilty? Is she ever ashamed of her white skin?

14. Emma admits to her husband near the end of the novel, "I am not as advanced in charity as I had thought" (317). She sees this as a spiritual limitation. How do you think Emma grows as a person throughout her story, if at all?

15. How would Emma's story be different today? What same struggles would she encounter? What would be easier about being a missionary in modern times? How would her role as a woman and reverend's wife change?

16. At the end of the novel, Emma and Henry begin their journey home to America, but plan on returning to Africa. What do you think the future holds for them? If you were the author of the story, how would you write the sequel?